A HAUNTING HERITAGE

AN AFRICAN SAGA IN AMERICA A NOVEL BY

ALASAN MANSARAY

A HAUNTING HERITAGE

AN AFRICAN SAGA IN AMERICA

A NOVEL

by

Alasan Mansaray

SAHARA PUBLISHING
DALLAS, TEXAS

This is a work of fiction, partially derived from the legacies of griots. Names, characters, places and incidents are either the product of the author's imagination or are used fictitiously. Any resemblance to actual situations, locales or persons living or dead, is entirely coincidental, and is highly regretted.

This book will be available at special quantity discounts for sales promotions, premiums or fund raising. Book excerpts can also be created to fit specific needs.

Request for permission to use excerpts or make copies of any part of this book should be directed to:
    The Publisher
    Sahara Publishing
    4151 Beltline Road, Suite 124-188
    Dallas, TX 75244

Cover design by Adiwanna Heads

Publisher's Cataloging-in-Publication Data

Mansaray, Alasan.
    A haunting heritage : an African saga in America : by Alasan Mansaray.
    p. cm.
    ISBN 0-9639497-5-6

    1. Africans—Immigrants—Non-immigrants—United States—Fiction 2. Africans—Afro-Americans—Relations—History—Fiction. 3. Africans—Mandinka Customs. 4. African spiritualism—Natural Bone Healing—Invocation of Jinns. I. Title

    PS3563.A573H39 1995   95-92063
    813'.54—dc20   Preassigned LCCN

This book is dedicated to my mother, Hadja Aminata Waritay, my father, late Alhaji Idrissa Mansaray, and with love to my wife, Fredica, and our children, Aminata and Idrisa.

A portion of the sale of each book will be donated to a relief effort for victims of the no-end-in-sight guerrilla war that has been raging in Sierra Leone since March, 1991. A war that has resulted in the death of over 200,000 people, the outbreak of cholera and the dislocation of countless civilians in two-thirds of the country, including the author's family.

"A crusader is a spokesman of the inarticulate, a friend of the forgotten men and women of society, a champion of the oppressed and a maker of history." Dr. Nnamdi Azikiwe, former Nigerian President, the Owelle of Onitsha.

CHAPTER ONE

As British Airways flight BA229 zoomed into the American skies, on board among its many passengers was Yaya, the African. As the pilot announced on the intercom of the aircraft the weather conditions of New York and the estimated landing time at the John F. Kennedy Airport, Yaya smiled to himself and reached for the knot on his tie. He was at the pinnacle of joy. Finally, he was able to visit America, the cornerstone of his aspirations.

"Wow! I made it. I'm practically in the U.S. now," he muttered proudly at this significant milestone. "Well, hello America, you melting pot, here comes Yaya, the dreamer and the haunted. I hope you have more room."

"Did you say something?" The man cramped at his side in the tight sitting confinement of the aircraft asked curiously.

"Not really," retorted Yaya, implying whimsically that what he said was in personal conversation with himself.

In his eagerness to blend in America and with an open mind, the 25-year-old, 6'3" tall Mandinka black African was dressed in a brown striped business suit, instead of a flowing *buba,* his ethnic gown. And knowing now that his arrival was near, he pulled unconsciously at the collars of his white oxford dress shirt and straightened his pink silk tie, lost between excitement and fear of the uncertain.

"Attention all passengers!" a female voice on the intercom announced over the dull hum of the airplane's engines, with echoes cutting above the muffled chatter of passengers in the cabin.

"If you are not a U.S. Citizen or a Resident Alien of the United States of America, the U.S. Immigration and Naturalization Service requires that you fill out INS form I-94, the entry document for all non-immigrants.

"Also, please remember, all passengers would be required to fill out U. S. Customs Declaration Form 6059B. I will be bringing the forms to you now. Please, when through, keep your forms with you. You will need to present them to U.S. Border and Immigration officers upon landing."

A few minutes later, a petite blond stewardess came down the aisle of the aircraft. Like one who loved every minute of her job, she was exuberant, smiling and chatting cheerfully with passengers as she briskly but meticulously passed out the forms.

Many passengers were now shifting in their seats and sighing in anticipation of an end to their journey. They inspected the forms like anxious students about to take an exam. Some carefully read the documents, a few were contemplating, while others began scribbling in earnest.

Being a non-immigrant visiting the U.S., Yaya had both forms. As he deliberated on them, the middle-aged man with dark slippery hair who was sitting next to him—whose English was even poorer than Yaya's—and who had persistently bothered Yaya all along the journey, patted him on the shoulder.

"Hey Joe, you have to be berry careful with am those forms when you fillam them."

As if to compound Yaya's anxiety and frustration, he added, "Fillam them berry carefully and fillam all parts. Make am no scratches on them, because they are go to put am like that upon the computer. Yes, examply like am carbon copy."

Yaya laughed to himself, because he was as amazed as he was inwardly agitated, and not only from the foul doze of garlic that hung at his nose from the man's breath; he wished his talkative travel mate made sense. That might have somehow made this trip easier. But since this plane left London, his flight connecting point, Yaya had been quick to note that his seat companion, who probably was non-American like him, somewhat, seemed to immensely enjoy babbling nonsense. And he had done an excellent job at grating on the African's nerves.

Yet, with Yaya's sense of cultural restraint and civility, he endured and decided to be polite and to honor the man. He raised his head from the form he was reading and looked at the man searchingly and humorously, and nodded as he said, "Sure, thank you, sir."

The man laughed mightily, gaping such that even a lousy pitcher could have thrown a baseball straight to the back of his mouth. His big gray eyes danced buoyantly. He rubbed his beardless chin, and patted his dark slippery hair. He clearly was proud of himself, like some self-centered ego maniac that blooms to total amazement at any wink.

Now, obviously encouraged by Yaya's response, the man turned and faced the passenger sitting directly behind him. He repeated the same thing he had told Yaya to a young man dressed in a faded blue jeans suit that had patches and bleach marks all over.

By a bored expression on the young man's face, it was apparent he was grossly indifferent to the sermon, and was probably wishing that the verbal intruder—took a hike to Mars!

"Ha-ha! Heh-heh!" the man boisterously laughed as he turned in his seat. And then he raised one hand to his face and gleefully clinched his thumb against his index finger in a few quick strokes, and slanted his head, gazing senselessly at Yaya. The silly stare only made the African more uneasy.

What a nuisance! Yaya thought. He wanted to challenge the mister say-anything's comment about the meaning of: "...they are go to put am like that upon the computer. Yes, examply like am carbon copy." *Indeed! What utter nonsense!*

Computers were not common where Yaya came from, but he had read of them, and knew better. He knew that usually when one puts data as input via a keyboard, a card deck or some tape device in a computer, you can process that data and produce results. The results can be stored in the computer, on auxiliary storage, be printed on paper, or transmitted via telephone lines as electronic mail.

But for goodness sake, Yaya reflected, could this man be saying that when they arrive in America, somebody would put their forms, scratches and all, exactly in the computer?

Classic misinformation! Yaya concluded to himself.

Somehow, this broken-English speaking man, who was more olive-skinned than white, immediately reminded Yaya of Pa Kunfa, a man in his village. Pa Kunfa was a stark illiterate who could not decipher the letters of the alphabet even if they were written the size of an elephant. Yet Pa Kunfa was always to be seen with a newspaper, sometimes turned upside down, pretentiously reading and explaining the news of the day to a group of his similarly illiterate town's people.

Evidently, this man at his side, Yaya thought, must be Pa Kunfa's sort; the type that are always making up and volunteering information they do not know.

Yaya, his mind heavy with more serious things, resumed filling out his forms. His immediate worry now was this trip. Then things should take an upward swing for him in America. Yet on this trip, Yaya knew he was like an unguarded blind man who ventures away from his sanctuary, leaping and risking mishap. Only that in his case, he knew what that mishap could be and thought only chance could avert it.

The burning question was, upon landing at JFK, would immigration agents permit him to enter the country? Would they?

The B-1 visa in his passport clearly stated that a visa does not automatically guarantee entry into the U.S. "Then what does?" Yaya pondered. Throughout this trip, the fabled high-handedness of U. S. Immigration officers, like a horrifying nightmare, frightened and appalled him, increasingly, leaving him totally bewildered.

Yaya restlessly wondered, why give some people visas and have them spend what to them is a fortune on airline tickets from Africa to America only to have them refused entry upon landing? As bizarre and chilling as that spectacle seemed to him, he remained tensely aware that it was no fairy tale, not with U.S. Immigration agents any way. They had done it before, and they would do it again and again.

And now Yaya considered himself a prime candidate and fair game for their infamous: "entry denied" and "repatriation in order" *double blows*; with those heartaching and dooming prospects highly bewitching him.

Indeed, wasn't it possible that they could totally deny him even a glimpse of the country, and worse still, have him sent like a piece of luggage, on the next available plane back to his place of origin? But would they do that to him? The question of chance in such a crucial matter was what bothered Yaya.

Do those immigration people know what is at stake for some people on such trips? Do they know what such treatment means to an African? He wondered if every foreigner, with a valid visa who came to America, simply counted his luck to enter the country? Or if indeed all people were equally liable to be treated that way, whether African or not?

"But, it can't be," Yaya rationalized, "maybe that's meant only for us Africans." His anxiety was at its peak.

But why can't they try to understand the African situation? Is it due to the abject poverty in Africa? Or the distorted image born by chronic misinformation and misunderstanding which the Western world harbors about Africa? Or is it just a treatment to a people regarded as the world's step children? If so, what about all the money spent on the ticket and the visa, and the efforts to prepare for the trip, or the sacrifices made by a family to make the trip possible—not to mention the dashed hopes!

Truly, for Yaya, nothing could be more devastating than falling victim to such dilemma. He had much at stake on this trip, knowing what he had just been through—*which was sacred and a secret!*

But suppose he was any other African, and got treated so shabbily? Yaya sighed, reflecting that besides the financial losses, there is the feeling of complete failure, and the degradation of such rejection to think about. And worse, the sometimes emotional disturbance, the stigma and the pointed fingers that a disgrace like that puts on one in an African society.

Silently he prayed that such a sad experience should pass over him, and stay away. He dreadfully lamented how experiences like those have shattered the lives of many people he knew.

CHAPTER TWO

There was Munda Lamboi, for instance, later called Munda-*Fatorkeh,* which means in Yaya's native Mandinka, Munda-the-insane man. It is folklore in Manika Kunda, Yaya's country, that in 1970 when the country became independent, Munda who had won a prize for a poem that he wrote on *National Self-Determination,* read it at the handing over ceremony from the British. He was in his final year in high school then, and had great academic potential but was of acutely indigent background.

Yet, because Munda was always first in his class—a straight 'A' student—a Peace Corps volunteer who had taught him in high school, and was impressed by Munda's outstanding scholastic performance, had promised the boy that he would help him come to America for further studies, if he had no opportunity to continue his education beyond high school.

True to his words, one year after the volunteer left for the U.S., he wrote and asked Munda about his academic status. If there was no opportunity for Munda at home, the volunteer suggested that he joined him in the U.S. However, the ex-Peace Corps worker made it clear that the invitation was not a guarantee of scholarship or even schooling but that it might open up such chances for Munda. The condition was that Munda should buy his ticket for the trip. When he arrived, the volunteer promised to provide temporary accommodation and to help him find affordable schooling, a scholarship or a job so he could pay his own expenses.

Although by implication the agreement hinged on uncertainties, for Munda, the prospect of going to America was in itself an opportunity. It was the most he could really ask for. Munda believed that as long as he could make it to America, like all immigrants who had gone over there through the ages and made a successful life for themselves, he too would make it. Deciding not to let the best chance he had ever gotten in life slip through his fingers, he promptly wrote to the volunteer stating how excited he was for the offer and expressing everlasting gratitude.

How he would pay his way to the U.S. in his destitute condition didn't occur to Munda. But in his letter he assured the Peace Corps friend that he would be ready for the trip in a mere seven months.

What? To go to America? The land of all opportunities? Away from the drudgery and hopelessness of his village life?

Munda resolved to do all he could and leave no stone unturned to make the trip possible. With such hope he decided he would not rot anymore in that village, which offered nothing but subsistence farming and little hope for the aspiring mind.

Despite his father's initial skepticism, Munda convinced the old man that it was the chance of a lifetime. A chance that came only in dreams to many of his ranks in the country. But his was real. So he needed all the help his father could give him to buy an airline ticket from Sobala, the capital city of Manika Kunda to New York, the hometown of his American friend, the Peace Corps volunteer.

Pa Lamboi, Munda's father, was poor, barely surviving on a meager salary as a night *watchman* on the storefront of an Indian immigrant's merchandise store in the village. The old man's salary saved for a whole year would not be enough to buy Munda, his only son, a ticket to the U.S. However, he promised to do his best.

With that goal in view, together father and son faced the task of fulfilling a son's dream; a task for which the only assets they had were faith, health, and physical strength.

The farming season had just started in their village. With most people in the village being farmers and everybody farming at the same time, there was always a need for an extra hand. Munda and his father, announcing their mission, thus passed word to all the farmers in the village that they were willing to work for pay.

The farmers reacted favorably as they engaged Munda and his father, one farm after another and one process after another. The old man and his son toiled from dawn to dusk through the entire farming season, cutting barren forests for rice farms, burning others, clearing the burnt debris in others, ploughing rice and corn seeds in some, and still weeding others, until the start of harvest time for rice, the staple food. By this time, the seven months—which Munda had hoped and told the Peace Corps friend that he needed to be ready —were steadily creeping up on him. There was barely one month left!

Munda was restless as time for his departure neared, day after day. He was also physically exhausted from the intense labor on the farms, as was his father, who had additional duties on his night *watchman* job at the storefront. The pressure and the hard work soon started to take their toll on the old man. He was getting thinner and thinner, and even though he never touched alcohol, his eyes stayed dim and bloodshot almost constantly.

There was rumor in the village that the old man was senselessly harming himself, and fear that the boy was killing his father by setting him on an impossible course. Munda dismissed the charges as part of the reckless and negative thinking common among their people, and the very malaise that had kept them behind with no progress.

Pa Lamboi on the other hand, a man of great will and resolve, bore it all with silent dignity. His mind was clear and set.

"My son, this is a choice I've made," he told Munda. "You are my own blood. I made a promise to you. I will see you through, even if that is the last thing I do in my life."

There were times when even Munda would grieve helplessly at the situation into which he had put his father, but he kept on. He had his eyes on the big prize; the gateway that his going to America would open for him. He would say to his father:

"Daddy, I know what you are going through. You are a great and rare father. I am aware of the pains and sacrifices you are making for me. I'm sure I will make you proud of me one day. Please don't give up!"

The old man, of course, never gave up. From the proceeds of their combined labor on the farms and the old man's salary saved religiously for six months, plus some help from relatives, they raised two-thirds of the money required for the ticket. But then Munda and his father were stuck, and yet the months had already dwindled into weeks. Just three weeks remained. Word about their mission had gotten around, provoking desperation for Pa Lamboi and his son, knowing the inevitable shame that lurked around, should they fail.

Some cynics in the village were already starting to laugh. They said Munda and his father were like the proverbial leopard who brought shame and belittlement upon himself by boasting that he would eat all of a hefty bush-rat, but failed to devour the head, which earned him the title, *big-mouth and liar,* among other animals.

In fact, some people were saying that Munda and his father had failed the Peace Corps volunteer by not coming up, till then, with the ticket. And there was speculation that the white man had probably already changed his mind, because white people live by principles and hate folks who don't keep to their word.

Even amidst all that negative talk, the old man was determined to let his son go. As a last resort, he decided to pawn his house for the balance of the money required. A Fulani petty-trader, who operated in the village like a little Shylock, loaned them the money which was to be paid back with one hundred percent interest in one year.

The price was high but the joy was great as Munda finalized his travel arrangements. One week to his departure, the Consular Officer at the U.S. Embassy in Sobala granted him a B-1 visa, which was a visiting visa. Getting the visa itself was an easy process for Munda. There was practically no hassle, nothing like the usual problems that other people encounter when they go for the 'almighty' visa to visit the United States. All Munda had to do was present his passport and a subsequent letter from the ex-Peace Corps worker reaffirming his invitation to him for a visit to America.

At the visa interview, Munda looked at the Consular Officer straight in the eyes and proudly stated that the American who invited him to the U.S. was his teacher and mentor, when he was in the country.

"I like Americans, they are very good people," he said, good-naturedly. "And almost all those I have met here have been nice to me. That is why I want to visit and see America myself and meet more Americans."

The Consular Officer smiled, contemplated briefly, and leafed through the passport. He glanced at a few pages and without any further questions, he reached for his stamp pad and stamped the passport, and scribbled a few lines on the page he had stamped.

"Enjoy your visit to the U.S.," the *enviable* American Consular Officer said, *almost pleasantly,* as he handed back to Munda the passport.

"Thank you, sir," a grateful Munda gasped, grinning to his wisdom teeth. "You see, I said so, you Americans are all nice. Thank you. Bye-bye."

He rushed out of the room, hastily flipping through the pages of his passport to see where the visa was stamped.

"Behold, so this is the almighty visa!" he muttered excitedly as he stepped out of the building into Sobala's bright tropical sunshine.

Cars screeched, horns blared, and pedestrians screamed at Munda who had jumped on Fula Road, the street outside the Embassy, with his eyes glued to the engraving in his passport. Amidst angry shouts of, "Are you crazy?" and "Do you want to die?" he made it across the street, only to promptly resume reading, fascinated by the stamped visa.

It read: *"The United States of America, Non-immigrant Visa issued at Sobala, Manika Kunda. Classification B -1, entry for one. "* This was followed by the date of issue, Munda's name, the period of validity of the visa and the signature of the Consular officer. The visa itself was valid for only ninety days. But that not withstanding, it was sheer joy to Munda.

Having got the visa, Munda left Sobala that very afternoon for Pewala, his village. It was now indeed time to say good-bye to all his folks. He arrived at Pewala shortly after the elders had rounded the children indoors from their prankish pastimes in the moonshine and had themselves folded their mats and gone into their houses to rest for the night.

By the time he got to his compound, even though the moon was shining and the stars were bright in a clear milky African sky, there was not a soul in sight. Not even a single human voice could be heard anywhere. As usual, the night life in the village was left to the unseen, and goats and sheep, and the dogs that roamed.

Munda's home was empty, as expected. His father had gone to work at the storefront. Immediately he stepped in, he dropped his bag by the door of his room, took out his passport and went to his deceased mother's picture hanging on the wall in the living room. Opening his passport to where his visa was stamped, Munda raised it towards the picture, and solemnly looked at the blank eyes of the deceased woman's portrait. He spoke like he was talking to a live person.

"Mama, I am ready to go. My trip is finalized, I got my visa today. I am going to America, after all. I will remember you, and I will remember Daddy too. While I am gone, I want you to pray and watch over me, and watch over Daddy also. We are always praying for you, so that God's blessings may pour on you. Please let me go see Daddy now and tell him the good news too."

Pa Lamboi had just finished his first round on the job; his usual routine of checking the windows and the vicinity of the store to ensure that no intruder was trespassing. Satisfied that the place was safe and sealed, he went to his little make-shift tent, constructed from broken cardboard boxes, which sat before the main entrance of the shop. He was just settling for a nap, when instinctively, he raised his head up towards the street and saw Munda coming. Even from the distance he could see Munda beaming with joy. Pa Lamboi immediately knew all went well in Sobala, in his son's quest for that thing they call, "visa."

"Daddy, I got it! They gave it to me! This is the visa!" Munda joyfully said, as he handed his father the passport opened to the page the visa was stamped.

From the flickers of a kerosene lamp in his tent, the old man marveled at the engraving which actually made no sense to him, but happily, he said, "Praise be to God, my son."

16

A HAUNTING HERITAGE : AN AFRICAN SAGA IN AMERICA

The news that Munda had obtained his visa for America and his ticket was ready bypassed the casual routine of the voice of the town crier at dawn, and took the legs of the morning breeze. In one sweep, it was all around his village. In spite of the initial skepticism of some detractors who had deemed it all impossible from the start, the news was greeted with excitement all over the village. Suddenly, everything to do with Munda's trip became everybody's business; a characteristic skepticism of the people of Pewala, who will doubt anything until it's proven successful.

Munda's success instantly got translated into a success for the village. It became a communal occasion that called for jubilation and ceremonies. What? One of their own, a son of the soil going to the white man's land? It was an occasion to crown! Libation had to be poured to the ancestors of the land. Mandarwah, the great grandfather, founder of the village, even long gone as he was to his grave, must be exalted for the blessings he has poured on his grandson who now goes across the seas to the strange land of the white man; the great masters of mystery and witchcraft, who designed the radio, the aircraft and traveled to the moon.

Pewala was a land of the Mendes, a minority ethnic group in Manika Kunda. Average size people, mostly between five feet and six feet tall. Unlike many other ethnic groups in Manika Kunda, the Mendes admired the white man's knowledge and knew it was the future. The white man is wonderful, they maintained. So with Munda leaving for the white man's land, it was assumed that, certainly, he would be just as wonderful as the white man. All he had to do was learn their secrets and return home to be one of the leaders of the country; even as Doctor Ñkodor S. Saccoh, the Prime Minister of the country.

Almost a decade ago, Dr. Saccoh had gone to England, studied for seven years as a medical doctor, returned home, practiced medicine for a few years and joined politics where eventually he became the Prime Minister. In the eyes of some of the village people, Munda was already a little Dr. Saccoh—a success story! Somebody to be proud of and definitely a future savior of the people and the land. As customary, the whole village had to bid him farewell.

The Paramount Chief of Mulu'eh chieftain, who resided in Pewala, in consultation with the elders in his court and Munda's father, agreed to perform the farewell rites on the last Saturday before the boy's departure. That was to be four days from the night Munda arrived back with the visa.

When the day came, the people of Pewala stood tall. They were at their best, supportive, cooperative and in a festive mood. The spirit prevailing here was all cultural and indigenous. Every adult member of the village seemed present at Pa Lamboi's compound. Moreover, they all seemed to have brought some food or drink to share as their contributions to the ceremony.

There was more than enough for everybody to eat and drink. It was a field day for teenage wanderers like Yaya from the neighboring chieftain of Bonbala, and for the freeloaders of the neighboring village, Neckehbla, who in the true spirit of African neighborliness invited themselves to the occasion, as they heard the beats of the drum that was used to invoke the spirits and ancestors of the land.

"Silence, the Chief is ready," was echoed through the crowd as the Paramount Chief moved into a circle of elders in the center of the compound. Immediately, the silence that is customary in the land when the Chief is about to speak ensued.

In his gesture of speech, the Chief cleared his throat, gathered his gown and started: "My people, I greet you all. I must say I am happy to see all of you here today. This is the type of gathering, we know well, that we all wish for. It is also a gathering of a sort that we are all thankful for. And it gladdens my heart to say that we have been blessed. As our people say, a blessing to one of us is a blessing to us all. Many thanks to the Almighty God for this kindness. Many more thanks to our ancestors, to whom we owe this great opportunity. As it is customary, I shall now submit, invoke, gratify and glorify the spirits of those same ancestors, whose guidance endow us all and whose blessings have bestowed such honor upon us."

The Chief then poured libation by subsequent droppings of a specially-brewed spirit, potent and undiluted, on the ground in the center of Pa Lamboi's compound. He declared as he poured the libation, that it was on behalf of himself, the people of Pewala and the Lamboi family.

Traditionally, as the political, social and religious head of the village, the Paramount Chief constituted the link between the living and the dead. And while on other occasions he would assign the responsibility of communicating with the spiritual world to others that were more dedicated in that field, the occasion in progress was a ceremonial matter, no miracles were needed. It was a rite to give thanks and express joy, one of the Chief's benevolent functions.

When the libation was poured, Mandarwah and his kinsfolk in the ancestral world were invoked. The spirit of Munda's deceased mother was invited and those of Pa Lamboi's parents in the spirit world were also called upon. They were all given a drop of undiluted spirit and thanked for the generous blessings they had poured upon the village, as evidenced by Munda's opportunity, which was perceived as a gift not only to the Lamboi family but to the village in general.

After the Chief's opening prayer offered along with the libation, a relay of prayers ensued from the elders, for the village, the land and Munda's trip. The Chief concluded the rites by thanking God and invoking the blessings of both the living and the dead, asking them to be merry and to rejoice in soul and in spirit. As was customary for him when one of his subjects must go out of his realm of jurisdiction; he handed Munda over to the ancestors, asking them for their guidance in the boy's journey to the unknown land, across the oceans, in the world of the white spirits and the masters of this material world. On that note, the festivities started.

The village drummers started pounding their instruments with passion, as maiden dancers jumped to the beats in short raffia skirts and with pointed breasts, naked and provocative, like the smile on their faces. Their unclad feet tapped in rhythm with the drums as they swayed in harmony and differently within a cheering semi-circle of onlookers.

The atmosphere was colorfully cultural. Some women similarly dressed, in matching bright cotton prints, head-ties and full gowns, down to their ankles, were singing and shaking the *segbulay*—a beaded net over an oblong—shaped gourd used as shake-shakes. The *segbulay* made a *sheeh-sheeh-sheeh* sound. This they shook and danced to, as they moved within the crowd.

The *segbulay* women happened to be entertaining but sometimes demanding, as the Prince of Wales found out during his visit the previous year—June 1,1969—which was the year before Independence and, amidst cries for it everywhere in Manika Kunda. Now, they gingerly steered 19-year-old Munda in front of their little bouncing group, and sang a special song, *From Me To You In The White Man's Land*. This was composed for Munda's departure; it went as follows:

This is my message, *sheeh-sheeh-sheeh;* this is my song, *sheeh-sheeh-sheeh.*
From me to you, *sheeh-sheeh-sheeh;* my one time stranger, *sheeh-sheeh-sheeh.*
My stranger, the white man, *sheeh-sheeh-sheeh;* in the white man's land, *sheeh-sheeh-sheeh.*
You who brought your ways, *sheeh-sheeh-sheeh;* to the black man's land, *sheeh-sheeh-sheeh.*

Our people were whole, *sheeh-sheeh-sheeh;* and the land was wholesome, *sheeh-sheeh-sheeh.*
Our Kings were the law, *sheeh-sheeh-sheeh;* and they ruled the land, *sheeh-sheeh-sheeh.*
They fought our battles, *sheeh-sheeh-sheeh;* and we followed their rules, *sheeh-sheeh-sheeh.*
Then the white man came, *sheeh-sheeh-sheeh;* and things changed, *sheeh-sheeh-sheeh.*

We had no money, *sheeh-sheeh-sheeh;* and needed no money, *sheeh-sheeh-sheeh.*
We gave from the heart, *sheeh-sheeh-sheeh;* and met our needs, *sheeh-sheeh-sheeh.*
And the land was pure, *sheeh-sheeh-sheeh;* so we cured ourselves, *sheeh-sheeh-sheeh.*
Then the white man came, *sheeh-sheeh-sheeh;* and things changed, *sheeh-sheeh-sheeh.*

Now our men wear chains, *sheeh-sheeh-sheeh;* and our women wear pants, *sheeh-sheeh-sheeh.*
They go to bars, *sheeh-sheeh-sheeh;* deserting the fireside, *sheeh-sheeh-sheeh.*
So now no more link; *sheeh-sheeh-sheeh;* with all the past, *sheeh-sheeh-sheeh.*
Because the white man came, *sheeh-sheeh-sheeh;* and things changed, *sheeh-sheeh-sheeh.*

Now we have disease, *sheeh-sheeh-sheeh;* but have no doctors, *sheeh-sheeh-sheeh.*
Now we have schools, *sheeh-sheeh-sheeh;* but have no teachers, *sheeh-sheeh-sheeh.*
Now we have roads, *sheeh--sheeh-sheeh;* but have no vehicles, *sheeh-sheeh-sheeh.*
Because the white man came, *sheeh-sheeh-sheeh;* and things changed, *sheeh-sheeh-sheeh.*

Here comes Munda, *sheeh-sheeh-sheeh;* my stranger the white man, *sheeh-sheeh-sheeh.*
For you showed us how, *sheeh-sheeh-sheeh;* but didn't show us all, *sheeh-sheeh-sheeh.*
You left a void, *sheeh-sheeh-sheeh;* that must now be filled, *sheeh-sheeh-sheeh.*
So here comes Munda, *sheeh-sheeh-sheeh;* my stranger the white man, *sheeh-sheeh-sheeh.*

Please make him a Doctor, *sheeh-sheeh-sheeh.* Please make him a Lawyer, *sheeh-sheeh-sheeh.*
Please make him a Teacher, *sheeh-sheeh-sheeh.* Please make him a Pastor, *sheeh-sheeh-sheeh.*
Please make him a Leader, *sheeh-sheeh-sheeh.* Please make him a Savior, *sheeh-sheeh-sheeh.*
From me to you, *sheeh-sheeh-sheeh;* in the white man's land, *sheeh-sheeh-sheeh.*
From me to you, *sheeh-sheeh-sheeh;* in the white man's land, *sheeh-sheeh-sheeh.*

Showcased in the festivity was also the *Far'lui,* a traditional masquerade in a tattered flowing off-white gown made from native cloth. The *Far'lui* speaks a unique blend of mixed ethnic dialects in his throat, usually interpreted to the people by one of his followers. Unlike other serious Masquerades, the *Far'lui* is jovial and more of a clown.

As always in such gatherings, soon the variety of food prepared invited the attention of the people. There were boiled yams and chicken soup, bean stew and boiled cassava, rice and cassava leaf stew, etc. All the various foods were indigenous, and good and palatable, for those who didn't mind the spicy taste—and most people in that crowd didn't! Soon, almost everybody was eating and drinking.

People dined in groups siting on wooden benches and short tools, and sheepskins spread on the ground. Meanwhile the drums kept beating and the professionals and high-spirited continued dancing and singing. The *Far'lui* was making rounds, chatting, entertaining and bogusly threatening those who dared to hassle him.

By sunset, everybody that wanted to had eaten and drunk to satisfaction; and most of the people present had used the chance to pull Munda aside for a chat, some advice, or to wish him well. Then they started to leave. Everybody was gone by the time the stars asserted themselves with vigor, surrounding the moon which was crawling to the center of the sky, already illuminating the village brilliantly.

Munda and his father had fulfilled a dream. People got home that night in Pewala with memory of the day shelving in their minds. The occasion had touched their hearts and their souls, and linked them to the spiritual world. Even the ancestors by invocation had been stirred. It was now up to Munda and the future.

"Well, Daddy, here we are," Munda said sadly. It was their last evening together.

The old man nodded and said nothing, reflecting on their bitter-sweet success and what that brought—the parting! He knew he had done it all but could not say all. And even now, he must take it with dignity. Munda would leave Pewala the next morning, Sunday, for Sobala, where he would spend a night and leave for America in a big airplane at noon the following Monday. With that sense of finality, what more could he say?

The old man said good night to his son; both of them over-whelmed by mixed emotions, and they quietly retired to their separate rooms, lost in thoughts.

In his little mud room, on a wooden bed, with dried grass for a mattress, Munda laid awake, thinking and tossing. He pondered his concern for his father while he would be gone. He worried about the loan, and the danger of them losing their house—should the worst come—considering the obvious uncertainties inherent in his eminent trip. Like a heavy load, these thoughts weighed heavily on his mind and kept him pondering.

Still turning, well after midnight, Munda eventually resolved that the die was cast and that all that remained was to be positive, by putting hope in the future, and by being ready to do his best in whatever that lay ahead. Then he dozed off.

Like a visitor waiting anxiously to call on you when you return home—the moment Munda slept—he had company.

"Shshshs! Munda, let me speak!" It was his deceased mother

who had died when he was ten years old. She seemed disturbed, standing over him at the foot of his bed.

"My son, I'm an unwilling messenger," she said. "Your paternal ancestors are crossed and cannot permit your trip. For as an only son, they ask, who would perpetuate your lineage in your native land, when you are gone to the white man's world? It is a world that has gotten more from us than it has given back. And your forefathers should know. That's why they wouldn't take a chance on your going. They want you to stay to continue your family line and live in dignity or go and choose otherwise!" With that she vanished.

Munda woke up sharply. He couldn't believe the dream, and yet it seemed more like a revelation. The spirits of his ancestors disapproved of his journey. *Because I'm an only son!*

That got Munda thinking. What about all that he and his father had gone through to make this trip possible? To cancel it now; how would he tell the people? No, the ancestors couldn't mean that! It must be some joke, he consoled himself; then he heard the first cock-crow and noticed his eyes burning.

But okay, I'm an only son. Who said I won't come back? I am not going to make America my home town! No way!

"It is a world that has gotten more from us than it has given back."

Yes, that's why I'm going to get their knowledge and know their secrets and come right back. Really. The ancestors shouldn't stop me. For the die is cast. Munda should go at all cost. Yes, I've to go at all cost. The ancestors should not....

"Knock, knock, knock." The old man was at his son's door at the second cock-crow. "It is time to get up, son. It's dawn. Odofo and his old van will be here soon. You must not miss it if you should leave today, as that is the only vehicle from all this area that goes to Sobala."

"Thanks, Daddy, I will be right up," Munda drowsily said as he gradually woke up to the sound of his father's voice. The urge to roll over and go back to sleep was overpowering but he fought it.

"I have set the fire and your water is warming. Your food too should be warm when you finish bathing."

Munda willed himself out of bed. He opened the door. "Thanks, Daddy." As their eyes met, the old man turned and hastened away. He quickly bathed, ate and stepped out to meet a small group of elders sitting in the verandah, whom he surmised had gathered to see him off. Seeing them, they reminded Munda of the dream and what his ancestors were demanding. He quickly dismissed that thought.

The elders got up and surrounded him as he bowed greeting them.

"I dreamt last night——" one elder started.

"Pa Saffa, please, I'm getting late." Munda interrupted, fearing a replay of the dream.

"Yes, he's getting late." His father supported him.

Pa Saffa with his aged wisdom sealed his lips. He looked at the other elders with whom he had evidently confided, but seeing the determination of Munda and his father, they quietly decided on a conspiracy of silence, and shook hands with Munda, bidding him farewell.

As expected when a sole heir embarks on a strange journey afar, leaving behind an only aging parent, emotions overwhelmed father and son at separation. Like men, they held back on speech so as not to provoke tears. The vital words said at the final moment of parting were in their hearts, minds and with a hug. Thus Munda departed from Sobala, knowing his father's task was done and the bond between them immense.

Glen Perkins, Munda's friend and former teacher who lived in Manhattan, woke up pleased with himself on the day Munda was due in New York. But as he was going into the bathroom to shower, he heard what sounded like a screaming and shouting match. He presumed it to be from the ever-fighting odd couple next door. Glen wondered, why would some people rather settle to live like cats and dogs? That confounded him. He went and showered, and dressed.

However, as he thought of his plans for the day, Glen felt rather than knew that something would go wrong. It was a foreshadowing instinct reminiscent of the day his twin brother perished before enemy fire in Vietnam.

On this day, Glen had taken off from his job specially for Munda's arrival. The distance between where he lived and the John F. Kennedy Airport in New York where he was to pick up Munda was a forty-five minute drive; that depended on, of course, if the notorious New York traffic did not go into a frenzy. And with Munda arriving at 9:45 a.m., just around rush hour traffic, he wanted a two-hour head start.

So at 7:30 a.m. Glen was swallowing coffee and gobbling a sandwich, hastening to take off to receive his guest. He decided he would make an omelet and fry some bacon, or better still have brunch with Munda, somewhere after he picked him up.

The previous day he had stocked his refrigerator with groceries for the extra mouth that was on the way.

A few weeks back he had moved into a two bedroom place for Munda—his liability—until he could get on his feet. To Glen, like being in the Peace Corps, he was doing a service to humanity— *a mind is a terrible thing to waste!*

Satisfied with his efforts so far, promptly at 7:45 a.m. he was all set to go pick up Munda.

Glen stepped out of his apartment and turned to lock the door. But suddenly, even before the door flank touched its hinges, and even before he could put his key in the bolt lock, slugs suddenly slammed into him from behind: *"Paw! Paw! Paw!"*

Glen gaped, jolted by the piercing and chilling pains in his lower back, between his shoulder blades, and below his left shoulder. The keys dropped. He plastered himself against the half-closed door, which gave way. Glen fell with blood oozing out of him everywhere, it seemed. He couldn't have said who had him, as he laid gasping out blood with a desperate look of anguished wonder in his eyes.

The doomed shots, strayed, came from the combatant couple who lived in the apartment across from Glen. The gun-slinging couple, from better to worse, were violently closing the chapters of their marriage and their very lives. It was a sad success for them because they shot life cold out of themselves. As for Glen, it was even more tragic; an innocent man who got caught in a violent spree, and lost his life pointlessly.

At JFK airport, KLM flight KL513 arrived within the same hour that Glen officially was pronounced dead. On board, Munda was ecstatic, with a larger than life perception of the man he was coming to meet. He was all obligations and anticipation. As he disembarked from the plane and set his feet on American soil, Munda felt a sense of joy and exhilaration that almost swept him off his feet. With darting eyes and stumbling steps he was like one possessed. He got turned around in the terminal, but found his way by following other passengers to the check points. Nobody seemed to notice, but from the glint in his eyes and his grins, it was obvious that Munda was the happiest man in that crowd.

"Kpooh!" Munda exclaimed undertone, admiring the magnificence of the airport— as a native Mende would when stunned! *"Kpooh!* This is Glen's country! His fatherland, America! I can't wait—"

"Your turn, sir," Munda was called to attention from his day dreaming by a clean cut but grim looking Caucasian gentleman with thick glasses sitting behind a desk.

"What are you here for, err.. Mmuerda?" The man asked, trying to pronounce Munda's name from the passport he was examining.

Munda's eyes, meanwhile, were fixed on a badge pinned to the Man's shirt. It read U.S. Immigration Officer and it bore the man's name and his picture. Lucky people, Munda reflected, and he turned to the officer.

"I am visiting a friend, sir," he replied.

"How long do you plan to stay?" the immigration officer asked.

"Maybe six months or a year."

"Do you have any money to support yourself for that period?"

"No, sir, Mr. Glen Perkins, my host will be responsible for me."

"In that case, sir," the immigration officer said, "I would like to see Mr. Perkins before I can let you into the country. Do you know how we can reach him?"

"Yes, sir, he is out there waiting for me," Munda declared, pointing to where the other passengers who had been processed were going.

In response, the immigration officer reached for the telephone on his desk, dialed the airport operator and asked to have Glen Perkins paged; that he should meet his guest at the south terminal immigration check point.

While waiting, Munda was told to step aside so other passengers could be processed. An assured Munda politely stepped back, convinced that Glen would show up any minute to take care of the situation. He fantasized the imminent thrill of seeing and reuniting with the man he idolized. That anticipation, mixed with the feeling that he was now indeed in America, made him euphoric.

Already Munda was envisioning the excitement and stir his first letters would cause back home. He imagined how he used to feel to have letters from Glen and other acquaintances in the U.S. For the letters he would send home, he would use the aerogram, because aerograms usually have the U.S.A. stamp already printed on them; in that case, there would be no denying the fact that he, Munda Lamboi, was now *live* and *home* in America. In fact, he would start writing that night, if Glen had any aerogram to spare.

While Munda had been lost in his thoughts, all the other passengers were gone. Suddenly he looked at his watch and realized he had been waiting for over an hour and yet there was no Glen.

Where could Glen be? And why is he not here at the Airport to pick me up?

As he puzzled and tried to find answers to these questions,

the immigration officer beckoned him over to his desk.

"Now mister, where are we? We cannot find the man you said you came to." The INS officer had blatant skepticism in his voice. He was probing Munda with his eyes. "Did you hear me? I said, there's definitely no Glen Perkins waiting for you. You heard him paged on the intercom yourself. It's been an hour since, and so far there's no sign of him anywhere. Are you telling me the truth?"

"Yes, sir."

"In that case, do you have a number where we can reach him, just in case he has mixed up your arrival time and cannot be here at the airport to pick you up?"

Munda gave him Glen's home telephone number.

"Come with me, sir, and bring your luggage so we can clear it through Customs. I'm sorry, but we may have to keep you until we can contact your friend."

Now he was speechless. What if Glen did not show up? Suppose there was no way to contact Glen? Did he have anybody else in the continental U.S. he could call to come to his assistance and assure these immigration people that they would be responsible for him? Anybody who would help him to get out of this bind?

Munda looked in his address and telephone book and came up with numbers for Nyallay Gu'wah, Menzura Er'yepeh and Sidi Béreté, all people from Manika Kunda living in the U.S. Except for Nyallay from Sendembu, he wasn't sure the others knew him. He got those numbers from friends in Sobala as he was leaving. However, he decided to give all three numbers to the immigration officer, if there was no way for Glen to be contacted.

But Munda really was now wondering greatly. He knew it was unlike Glen to behave in such a manner. What could be the problem? Could he have changed his mind about him? If so, why did he not tell him when they spoke on the telephone just the other day when he called from home to tell Glen the details of his flights? In their last telephone conversation, Glen was so reassuring. There was no way he could have changed his mind so suddenly. There must be something wrong. That speculation alone, worried him very much.

Meanwhile, Munda was taken to an upstairs floor, to a big room with partitioned offices and work stations, in a dark glass building within the vicinity of the airport. There was a big round sign on the wall that said, U.S. Immigration and Naturalization Service. He was told to sit on a bench in a small room at the back of the offices. Besides that bench, the room had a Coke machine and three tables, each with four chairs. An orange ashtray filled with burnt-off cigarette filters stood in the center of one of the tables. There were droppings of ashes around the ashtray from quick nicotine puffs by some people who came to smoke cigarette; they came alone and in pairs. When they came, they appeared rushed and said nothing to Munda, and he looked away as they chatted, puffed and dashed out. Behind them, films of smoke lingered, and stale cigarette scent suffocated the room. But Munda didn't mind. He waited.

The INS officer that had gone to call Glen returned. He was walking briskly towards Munda, who was now gazing at him perplexedly.

"I am sorry but we cannot reach your friend. Not at all. Do you have any other numbers we can call?"

Munda gave him the telephone numbers of Nyallay, Menzura and Sidi. He explained that they were all his kinsfolk and that any of them would be willing to serve as guarantor for him. The INS officer paused to reflect on this and left saying he would call them instantly.

Munda crossed his arms, waiting. He sat and stood, and walked to the window and looked outside, where everything looked strange: the people, their dress patterns, their hair types, their eyes and their various shades of the white skin, which was in the majority.

Man, Munda, now, I'm really in a white man's country. A typical African like me. My black skin will be so unique among them. But... maybe, there're other blacks here as dark as me, like some of the African-Americans. They are Africans too, you know, by origin....

Through the glass wall, Munda saw INS officers talking in a group. He started feeling ill at ease, thinking that they were probably discussing his situation. What a bad beginning for him in America, he thought, to be stranded at the airport on his first day in the country.

Munda's kinsman, Sidi, was born in Kurudu, about fifty miles and two Chieftains away from Pewala, Munda's village. He was alone in his one bedroom apartment in Southwest Washington D.C. So far it had been his usual day, straight from work after sweating the first shift—mopping and sweeping from 7 a.m. to 3 p.m. He was getting ready to go to night school, in the next hour, for a five o'clock class. Then the call came from nowhere—dropping the bomb on him!

"Is this Sidi Béreté?"

"Yes?"

"This is Officer Paul Doe, at Immigration, JFK."

"Oh! Immigration? Okay?"

"We have a gentleman here, his name is —let me spell it for you: M-u-n-d-a L-a-m-b-o-i, from Manika Kunda. He arrived at 9:45 this morning and was expecting somebody to pick him up at the airport, but nobody came; so we kept him here. He gave me your number, to call you, to come pick him up."

"Uhh?"

"And please bring your passport, or green card and verification of employment."

"Wait! Hello? Hello?"

"Yes, I'm here."

"I mean, you said, Who?"

"Mmeurnda, hold on!" The officer again spelled Munda's full name.

"No sir, I don't know him."

"What? You don't know him? But he gave me your number. Aren't you from Manika Kunda?"

"Not at all! By no means, sir. Not me. I'm not from anywhere around that area."

"Well! Then I'm sorry."

"Yes sir. I'm sorry too. Wrong person and wrong number."

"Bye."

"Bye-bye, sir." The line disconnected. Sidi blew out a sigh, panted like he just did a 100-yard stretch and held the dead phone to his ear, sweating, eyes bulging and hollow. "Good gracious!" He stamped a foot, and with an open mouth, stared at the receiver briefly before carefully laying it down. "Good God in heaven! Blessed Spirit, what's this?"

Now Sidi was marching, perturbed and panicky. That call from INS was too close a call. His visa had expired, so the last thing he wanted was any such contact with anybody from INS.

"What?" Sidi screamed to himself.

"He gave me your number, to call you, to come pick him up."

No way! Sidi thought. He wouldn't dare drag himself, claiming to rescue anybody at an INS office; and that stood even if his own blood brother was being detained by them; for the same reason that he was currently an illegal alien on the run himself.

From an F-1 visa to running. He had dropped out of school last year and had taken two jobs to get himself together—to buy a car and fix his apartment—and he became an illegal alien by that token.

Now Sidi was back in school, easing in, part-time, which would not get his papers straightened. He was living with that torment, on the run. Then a Munda!

A Munda? The fellow must be kidding. And to give my number to those people too?

Sidi had been cooking before the call, his flattened stomach tired with cries for food, but the cooking stopped instantly, midway. He went pacing. He was frantic that the Munda fellow, whom he could not even quite recall, wanted to get him into trouble.

Okay, let's say I know him. He has come and he is stuck but does he know how I am here? Or does he want to sell me? But maybe, he wants us both in the same boat, back to Africa. So I think!

Pacing, Sidi took a peek in the peek-hole of his front door and paced. Feeling shattered and sagging, he swung his arms forward, facing his front door.

"Yes, I should go to the immigration people, and say hi, I'm Sidi Béreté, an illegal alien, and just give myself up to them, for deportation, with only this shirt on my back. Right Munda?" He looked at the door as if expecting an answer. And then he walked towards his couch.

"Very smart! Really smart! To totally wreck everything I'm struggling for in this country. Indeed, just to be... *a jolly good fellow, a jolly good fellow, and...* an empty foolish fellow!" He sat down, despondent.

Sidi thought of the classes he just registered for, and all that money he just spent on tuition and books, out of his pocket, from his little janitorial job in a hotel. That job which he valued for everything, for being able to keep this little apartment which he called his own, and for seeing himself through school...

And suddenly a Munda?

But supposing Munda was truly a bosom buddy. Didn't Peter deny Jesus to save his head? Sidi felt relieved that he had unhesistantly and blatantly informed the INS officer that he did not know and had never known any Munda Lamboi or whatever that name was. And also, he was happy, he made the man understand that he was not from Africa or from any where around that area. In fact, he canceled school that day.

About one hour later, when Sidi had calmed a little, and after second thoughts, he decided to call some of their better-situated countrymen in the Washington D.C. area to tell them about Munda's dilemma.

The time now was 5:45 p.m., seven hours since Munda's arrival at the airport that morning —finding himself stranded—with no hope in sight!

The INS officer had returned two hours ago to inform him that two of the numbers which he had given were disconnected, and that at one of them, the person he spoke to denied knowing any Munda Lamboi and said he wasn't even from Africa. The officer then went and busied himself at a desk doing some paper work. He was waiting to see if anybody would come fetch Munda before he left at 6 p.m., or he would request deportation for him.

Still, Munda was in the little cubicle in the back, and was now worried like a lost child. Hungry, with dried lips and weary eyes, he felt desolate, all alone and in the dark. His heart was savagely pounding in his chest and a lump had formed in his throat. It was like he was having a bizarre nightmare even with his eyes wide open. In his dilemma, his stomach rumbled as if some rusty motor was being started in it, and his palms were sweating like he just had them over a steaming pot.

The sophistication and grandeur of the airport had paled, and were now a torment, in the face of the depressing mystery that held the non-appearance of Glen.

Munda's apprehension was, what result would this predicament bring? Struggling silently with his increasing internal moans, at 6:30 p.m. he was taken to an immigration cell, pending the emergence of a guarantor, they said. *Or whether to await the finalization of arrangements to have him booked on the next available flight back to his country?*

The detention itself was already proof that Munda had been denied entry and was now prey to repatriation. But so far, that news had not been broken to Munda in exact words.

In a daze, Munda looked around the cell—some old deserted dungeon with paint peeling off the walls—which made him think of an old store house in his elementary school. He looked for cobwebs, but saw none. There was an open toilet sitting sourly in one corner; and four camp beds, with some dark blankets thrown over them anyhow; and a strong stench, which he suspected came from those blankets, hung sourly at his nose.

In this cell, Munda lamented that it was a suffocating sort of solitary confinement, to which he resigned himself. He crouched on the cold cement floor in an opposite corner from the toilet and inadvertently preoccupied himself with a delusion; a morbid struggle to dismiss the whole experience as a bad dream; a dream that he would wake up from any time and be with Glen, his idol.

But wait! He remembered the dream in which his deceased mother appeared two days before he left Manika Kunda.

"My son, I'm an unwilling messenger. Your paternal ancestors are crossed and cannot permit your trip. For as an only son, they ask, who would perpetuate your lineage in your native land when you are gone to the white man's world? ....They want you to stay to continue your family line, and live in dignity, or go and choose otherwise!"

Well, Munda thought, at least the ancestors were right on this one. He came with hope, but evidently he was choosing otherwise; for now he was in jail without his freedom or dignity. Throughout his nineteen years of living in Manika Kunda, he had never even stepped into a police station, not to talk about being put in a cell; yet on his first day in America, he was sitting in solitary confinement and locked up, like some public enemy—number one!

Sitting there, Munda bowed his head until it rested on his knees and laughed an unhappy laugh. *Well America, this is quite a good way to treat strangers! Or is it all a bad dream?* He wondered.

Promptly at 8 o'clock that night, with a thudding sound, a tall, broad-shouldered and humped-back white male came hovering at the door of Munda's cell. The man had on the gloomy green uniform worn by INS deportation officers and acted with a big sense of authority. There was a pistol strapped on one side of his hip and a handcuff hooked on the other.

With a piece of paper and keys in his hands, the officer eyed Munda suspiciously for a second, and flung open the cell.

"Mmundah Lambort?" he stammered reading from the piece of paper.

"Yes sir. Munda Lamboi!" Munda said, rasing his head up from his knees in his squatting position, without moving an inch.

"Here, let's go, mister," the officer said, standing aside against the widely-open door. Munda got up.

"Mister, I will not handcuff you, but don't give me any problem either. If you do like I say, everything will be fine."

"Sure," Munda responded.

He followed as instructed, in step with the officer, without asking a question. He had no handcuffs, but the trained bearing of his escort bore on him like a clamp. He knew he looked like a prisoner now, except that he had no uniform on, and—thank God, he thought—no handcuffs!

With the officer directing, they walked quietly through the crowd in the terminal to Swiss Air Counters where the man stepped ahead to a counter, instructing Munda to move forward at his side, where he could be seen.

Munda suspected that they were going to fly him somewhere, maybe Washington D.C. or some big immigration detention camp, like the types he had read about where they put illegal aliens who come on boats, until they could locate Glen. He thought that was bad in itself. But he knew somebody would come and save him.

The Swiss Air agent, a slim black lady who attended the officer, knew differently and seemed touched by Munda's fate. She kept giving him sympathetic glances as she processed the ticket.

Munda noted her shining coffee complexion. *Perhaps she is an African.* Feeling awful and down in that embarrassing position, he showed an appreciative eye contact, managed a smile inside, and bowed his head.

The agent gave the boarding pass to the officer, with a heavy sigh and a cold hard stare. And then she smiled at Munda, knowingly, shaking her head, as if to say, 'That's how it for us here, brother. Be brave.' Munda nodded a thank you, eyes down, embarrassed.

"You are all ready to go, mister, back to your country, seat SA100 on Swiss Air, departing in ten minutes." The officer with a straight face waved Munda his boarding pass. "Your luggage is already on board and here are your luggage claim tickets."

Munda was standing absolutely still, stunned. He took a long pause, not knowing whether to believe this. The officer officiously moved crowding him.

"Let's go!" He tugged Munda towards the gate that led to the aircraft.

Now Munda believed that, indeed, he was being sent back. That he won't enter into promising America after all. He looked at the almost familiar black woman at the counter, and noticed her sympathetic glare and thought of back home. He has failed. Images of his father broken, bewildered, ruined, their house gone, their money gone, their efforts and hopes in vain; and thoughts of all that hard labor, day-in day-out, on peoples' farms—for nothing!

The great farewell it was. And now the everlasting shame upon him, his father, all around the village, the land... He was finished. This was the end, his destiny. Oh, Munda, why?

His head pounded and flooded like he had razor-like slashes all over inside, with blood pouring and causing havoc. Suddenly, as if mercilessly kicked from behind, Munda fell face down, wishing the ground would eat him.

"What have they done to him?" an old white lady cried in panic.

"Let's go, darling." Her husband pulled her away as she started going towards Munda.

Laying flat on his stomach, Munda faintly heard the voices and imagined an uproar of concern from people around. Do they know him? Does somebody here know him? Quickly, he got up, on all fours, looking wildly around. His eyelids terribly swollen, his eyes red, his mouth emitting a groaning sound, indecipherable. He forced a smile, stooping, heavily panting and wide-eyed, missing all the eyes focused upon him in the lounge, with folks not knowing what to think.

"Yes? Yes? W-h-a-t? W-h-a-t?" he stammered, finally, staggering to stand.

The officer steadied him, only to shove him instantly.

"You are going on this plane, mister, let's go."

Overwhelmed by devastation and drenched in chilling perspiration, Munda went berserk.

"Oh no, it can't be! Leave me alone! Don't push me. You Imperialist! Neocolonialist! Desecrator! Come, Kwame Nkrumah! Come, Sekou Touré! Come, Tafewa Balewa and Sir Milton Margai; and come you, Jomo Kenyatta! Past and present voices of Africa, come! Come and speak! Come! Come! Come! Your son is being demeaned in the white man's land. I refuse! I refuse! No, don't touch me. You slave drivers. People stealers. Diamond stealers. They are stealing me, oh! No! No! I refuse!"

In Munda's outrage, he didn't notice that the officer had been joined by another officer. The two officers forcefully dragged him into the aircraft where he was handcuffed to his seat, a stiff red seat that seemed to have been adapted specifically for that purpose.

"If I were you, mister, I would sit here and not cause any more problems," the muscular officer said. "We will give the captain of this aircraft the key to the handcuff; he will free your hands when he thinks it's safe. So you better behave yourself, and enjoy your trip."

Munda sat quiet, with a fresh wave of unbelief. Yet he knew this was real. As the aircraft took off, he knew his fate was sealed. Nothing could change it now. At 19, he had never cried since his mother died when he was ten, but now he burst into sobbing....

"I am dead! My father is dead! Oh me! Oh Munda!"

Through his tear-coated eyes, as the aircraft flew its might past structures beneath, Munda saw his dreams flying past him, going down like the structures below that he would never touch and never make out.

The shock, the humiliation and the disappointments might have been too much for him, because a loud cracking laugh, followed by a stream of laughter with some reckless abandon, became the tell-tales of his state of mind. It seemed in one blow, both his dreams and sanity were dashed.

Munda never became himself again after that experience. Even when he got home, as anxious as people were to hear his story—there was nobody to tell it!

News about what happened to Munda reached Yaya through an air mail letter from the U.S. The letter was written by Sidi, a first cousin to Yaya, who at that time lived in the District of Columbia, in the nation's capital, Washington, D.C. He was the one whom the immigration officer called when Munda was detained at the airport.

In his letter to Yaya, Sidi had expressed regret that he could not come to Munda's aid promptly as expected, because he was himself then an illegal alien in the country. He said he had tried to rally support from their countrymen in New York and the Washington D.C. area to rescue Munda, but help came too late. He said that Ahmed, a kinsman in Washington D.C. who was a student at Howard University and in good standing with immigration, had volunteered and given up classes that evening to go to New York to sign for Munda as guarantor.

However, when Ahmed arrived at the immigration office at JFK, about 8:30 PM; they sent him to the airport where Munda was being processed for deportation. Ahmed was just in time to witness the erratic scene that Munda was putting up. Ahmed said he tried to talk to one of the officers, but was brushed aside, and told it was too late. So he stood helplessly aside, sad and embarrassed both for himself and Munda.

Sidi and the Manika Kunda community in Washington D.C. learned the details about Munda's expulsion from Ahmed. It was sad news. The whole Manika Kunda community was shocked at the speed and the unbecoming manner with which Munda's issue was handled. Some said his civil liberties were compromised.

In the U.S., the constitution provides for the due process of the law for everybody. This is the norm, the rule of law.

"Was there a due process of the law?" This was the question that some Manika Kundans were asking. Munda certainly was detained, but was he tried before any judge?

As unsatisfactory as the issue seemed to most Manika Kundans that day, who among them wanted to take up an issue with the 'almighty' U.S. Immigration? Quite unlikely that a Manika Kundan would do such a thing! And it was not a matter of fear or ignorance; that would be a misjudgment, for many Manika Kundans in New York and the Washington D.C. area, who heard news about Munda's dilemma, were if not *educated,* quite *intelligent*—way beyond what *The Bell Curve* purports! And, they knew their rights, quite well. But, as striving immigrants, they preferred peace.

Their rationalization to confrontation edged on, letting it go, if no violence was directed at them, and as long as there was no pronounced or concealed threat singling them out.

In Munda's case, with him gone, the damage done was already beyond reparation. And besides, what happened to him was not so unusual at JFK and other American airports anyway. It was always happening to vulnerable Africans of all origins. This was a problem that had been acknowledged in the American press but yet eluded any concerted efforts at correction, by either Congress, pressure groups or a constructive African effort.

CHAPTER THREE

Due in New York any minute, Yaya was quite aware that what happened to Munda could happen to him too. When he had called Sidi just before leaving home in their last telephone conversation, Sidi told him that he had nothing to be afraid of; that all Yaya had to do was be himself and stay calm when talking with U.S. Immigration officers; and that on no account should he panic, as that might create a wrong impression in the minds of the officials who were constantly scrutinizing for potential illegal aliens, and people who come to the U.S. purposely aiming for economic asylum.

Hovering over JFK airport at 9:30 AM eastern time, BA229 was on time, awaiting landing instructions from the Air Traffic controllers. The sign warning passengers to put out all cigarettes and fasten their seat belts had come on. All passengers and service staff on board the plane had been told to get seated for landing. Then the aircraft sloped downwards, giving the passengers a sensation of something being pulled from under them. Finally, there were wheels rumbling on the paved runway, and the engines whining down.

The fatigued passengers, relieved of their tedious journey which seemed to have lasted for eternity, wasted no time pouring out of the aircraft and marching to the immigration check points.

As the incoming throng approached the vigilant officers, there were those to whom this last phase of the trip was a casual matter, one of basic relief and anxiety to get home. These were American citizens and resident aliens. To this group, the immigration routine was no different than queuing at the grocery store and waiting for their turn to check out at the cash register. And there were others, although foreigners, to whom, too, passing through these check points was no big deal. They were confident that nothing was going to stop them at this point. These were citizens of the Western world or preferred countries, new immigrants, people of status, wealth, and influence. But still, there were also a few, mostly from the Third World, who were perhaps more excited than all others at coming to America but not so confident of fair passage. Yaya belonged to this latter group.

With all the stories Yaya had heard about these immigration check points and what he had seen with his own eyes as the aftermath of the ordeal some people encountered with them, he could not help but be nervous. Despite Sidi's lectures about confidence, composure or what not, Yaya uncollaboratively found his knees jerking under him, in rhythm with his silent but fervent prayers—as he stood in line waiting for his turn to be scrutinized.

It crossed Yaya's mind that this was the final call or the *D-day*; the one that required every iota of his will to pull through. Shaking inside like a vanquished flag pole riddled with holes from enemy bullets, he took several deep breaths. He had heard it worked to calm one in a situation of anxiety. But now, for him, it didn't. What next?

Desperate, Yaya recalled a skill that he had learned as a member of the literary and debating society in his high school. The idea was to imagine superiority over your audience by demystifying them, or even ridiculing them mentally, and thinking there was no way they could measure up to you, because you were special, better and good, which was why you were speaking, or the audience would be up at the podium—and not you! Yaya had used this feat before to gain confidence until he became comfortable as a public speaker. He rationalized that if it worked then, it might work now. With that thought, he promptly raised his head up, looked at the officer that was processing the line he stood in and decided to demystify the man with humor.

The officer was partially bald-headed with a receding hairline and a forehead glaring like lighted crystals on a chandelier. As he bowed to write, he gave Yaya a fair profile of his baldness. He thought, if I were close by, I could see my face in that.....

And what a good sounding drum that would be, he mischievously mused, for one to beat some authentic African tune on and let everybody at this airport dance their heart out to it. It would certainly be a nice treat and quite a froggy dance, like those by Peace Corps volunteers at the sound of a wild beating drum at home.

Reflecting that since there were no real drums at hand, well, he would have to improvise with that glistening bald-head turned into a willing drum, all at his mercy, with folks happy and jumping about heartily!

Entertaining himself mentally at that spectacle, Yaya compulsively laughed inwardly. In fact, he made a silent note to check out the feasibility of a festival pronto, when he got close to the man; to celebrate his arrival in America. No sooner was he through with his inward prank, than his turn came at the check point.

"Next!" The bald-headed officer with a tired face looked at him. Then the officer bowed his head towards his desk, giving Yaya a profile, as if welcoming him to the task.

With his secret fun whirling in his head, Yaya's nervousness eased. Already he felt like he knew the man, and so he walked confidently to him.

"Good morning, sir." He gave his passport to an outstretched hand.

The officer looked at him sharply for a moment and opened the passport. "You have a B-2 visa, what are you in this country for?"

"Visiting. I'm on sabbatical." Yaya was studying the man's face; his long pointed nose and sparkling blue eyes; actually like most white people he had seen, either British, Russian or German.

"How long do you plan to stay?" the official asked with piercing blue eyes.

"About six months," Yaya said, holding his breath.

There was a pause, while Yaya wriggled his toes in his black patent shoes. The voice of the airport operator came through the intercom, to which the officer listened and then stamped Yaya's passport, declaring that he was given a thirty-day permitted period of stay. Then he must report to an immigration office for extension, should he have reason to stay longer.

Wonderful! Better than nothing. Yaya was joyous and shocked at the civility of the officer. *So you are kind, mister bald-head?* He immediately felt grateful to the man.

"Enjoy your stay in America," the officer said, returning the passport.

"Thank you, sir," he replied with a bow and a warm smile.

Wow, man! The officer that just processed him was not like the cold-hearted U.S. Immigration agents he had heard about. He felt guilty for coming up with that lousy joke about the shininess of the guy's head.

Okay, the man was not friendly; yet he was better than the dreadful demons that U.S. Immigration officers had personified in Yaya's mind since Munda's experience. But again, it might be his lucky day, so he hastened to the luggage area to claim his suitcase.

Even as Yaya stood waiting for his luggage by the luggage carousel, some fright still lingered, like the numb uneasiness from too much alcohol consumption, enough so as not to permit him to enjoy the excitement that swelled inside of him.

He decided it was better to contain his joy and wait until he was completely out of the vicinity of the airport, then he would really rejoice. He wasn't going to take any chances, just in case the officer offensively took note of him and decided to change his mind, and called him back, adamant and dead serious about canceling his entry permission. That would leave him certain to be booked for a return, bound like Munda, on the next flight. He sobered just thinking of such dishonor. He had to be his best.

The few minutes wait for his luggage seemed like hours, as Yaya's stomach tightened and bit inside, empty and struggling against anxiety and mounting excitement. Happily *bliss,* his small brown and white stripped Samsonite suitcase surfaced just about time, amidst others, going round and round on the carousel. With the air of one accustomed to such a mundane thing, he reached out and grabbed his suitcase, turning to go on, like some habitual traveler. Only, in this case, if Yaya had seen anybody jumping around, he would have jumped too. But that was inappropriate in such environment.

The next stop was at the custom control counter. By now Yaya was himself, friendly and the social bee.

"Hello, Gentlemen," he said with a big smile to the three nearest officers whom he judged to be about his age. They were white. One was standing by a luggage X-ray machine and two were sitting a few yards apart at separate stations opposite. He went to the friendly face, smiling, at the right counter, which had its own computer.

"Good morning to you, sir," he said, handing over his passport, and a completed custom declaration form: Form 6059B.

"Good morning.... Yaya LaTalé? Does that sound right?"

"It does, perfectly."

"I'm getting better at this."

"Obviously, sir."

"What do you have to declare?"

His total luggage comprised of a briefcase and a suitcase, with nothing to declare. The custom officer standing by the luggage X-ray machine scanned his suitcase through while the one at the counter inspected his briefcase, item-by-item. In less than five minutes he was free to go, and was through with entry regularities.

At this point, Yaya reflected on all that could have gone wrong. He felt thankful. God was on his side. He was now truly bound for America. Free! But was he free? Could he part with his secret past that had nagged and wrecked him and got him running here?

He sighed.

CHAPTER FOUR

"Welcome to America!" Sidi screamed across the lobby of the arrival lounge as Yaya entered the waiting area.

Sidi, Ahmed and two other friends, Abu Janneh and Barbar, all from Manika Kunda, had formed the entourage to welcome Yaya. All those people except Barbar, had obtained full legal status as immigrants in the U.S. They held the famous green card.

Barbar, on the other hand, was a law student on the F-1 visa. He had obtained his bachelors degree in the same school that admitted him to law school. It was a predominantly white school where he was one of two blacks in his class.

The other black was a young African-American lady, glowing to her toes, and well-mannered but reserved. Of affluent background, just like all others in the class, Barbar presumed.

On his part, Barbar supported himself. He worked as a security guard at a metered parking lot full-time, over the part-time permitted by his student visa status. But his needs were immense, he rationalized, hoping that Uncle Sam would understand why he worked a little more. It was not like he was selling drugs, he thought.

Almost six-foot tall, thick-chested and big-boned, and though not stout physically, Barbar looked like something just waiting to burst. He was argumentative, combatant and spoke in a loud voice, traits which Sidi and some of his countrymen thought could be hereditary.

In pre-colonial days, before the British came to Manika Kunda, Ambada, from where Barbar hailed, was a kingdom all governed by his name-sake and great-grandfather, King Barbar Keita.

When the British came and embarked on colonizing the country, some kings and chiefs willingly traded away authority to the Queen in England, but King Barbar, much the warrior and undisputed leader of Ambada, frowned at any such concession.

"An abomination, and an insanity," he exclaimed on hearing the news.

And then the cat-eyed messenger of the Queen and the man's black messengers came to the king's court with the plan: "Her majesty's government wants you as a subject. You would have to look to England and the Queen henceforth."

"Indeed? What insanity! To betray my hereditary authority?" King Barbar fumed at this effort to corrupt him. The warrior-king furiously stamped his specially carved elephant-tusk cane so hard on his mud-plastered floor that it broke in two. He discarded the lion head handle dismissively and stared at his lieutenants. A quick deliberation!

By now the Queen's emissaries were confounded, jittery and fearful for their lives.

"Let them go," the chief lieutenant murmured. "Just a warning to them this time."

Other members of the king's court with sad faces nodded, reluctantly agreeing. They knew it was the week of peace; before the soil was turned and the planting started. If the land must give its utmost, in this week everybody's heart must be clean and pure, and forgiving. So they could do nothing despite their anger.

However, the chief lieutenant and his men in unison beckoned at the trumpet man and passed a coded message. The trumpet man blew his carved-tusk horn; a short wail urging the sling men into action to scare away the crazy corrupting usurpers.

With stones hurling from slings, flip... flip.... flop...., the intruders ran away in a frenzy to their landrover—like destructive birds deserting a rice farm—leaving warning echoes behind them never to return.

"Just some nuts," the chief lieutenant joked to pacify his boss.

And despite his anger, the king laughed heartily at the running party who wanted him as a subject to some woman who sat ruling somewhere. "What an affront! Is she a goddess? Or can she kill a snake?" he wondered.

The flabbergasted warrior-king was said to have bragged then to his lieutenants that the only place he had for that woman, the Queen of England, was to put her among his many wives when he desired.

However, the following night, as in all cases of imperial rape for power in Africa, the British returned surprisingly, with cannons and bullets, and opened war on the land. Well ambushed and under-armed in combat with the superior artillery of the British, in that shattered night of thunderous eruptions of gun fire in Ambada, the elite infantry of King Barbar was devastated, discarding their spears and shields, their bows and arrows, and stones and slings, to live another day.

Barbar's great-grandfather, the warrior-king, who was the prized target, was captured and taken to England. And this wasn't the first time.

On the minds of the aged in Ambada, decades before, in the days of King Barbar's second predecessor, another group of white men had come suddenly. They spoke through their nose and were funny and friendly, but they turned out to be dangerous in the end.

They came in a big boat, like a house, which sat ashore of the salt-water, to the amazement of everybody. In their cunning, they crawled to the king, giving away enticing presents, like leaf tobacco heads, strange garments, and strong liquor. That won their way. They became royal guests.

Next, they prevailed on the jubilant king to lend them his drummers who had performed to entertain them. With the drummers on board their big boat, they lured with incessant music and potent liquor as many strong and healthy men and women that ventured joyously.

Once the Africans were onboard and drunk, the boat swept off, far into the salt-waters, with not a soul returning; like King Barbar, whom they said died in detention in England, while his territory became part of the crown colony, later known as Manika Kunda.

In their pranks, Sidi and Ahmed, dismissed Barbar in his aggressiveness as being probably mad at what befell his name-sake, King Barbar Keita. Sometimes, they alleged him to be the old warrior himself in a new flesh. And indeed Barbar validated them. For in his happy moments, he would say, someday, when he had completed his studies and established his law firm, he would take to court, England, America, and all the culprit nations in the West who partitioned Africa and exploited it unabated of its human and material resources for decades.

In fact, today, to make a point of his discipline, Barbar had insisted that they come in full force with him as the legal representative or watchdog, just in case Yaya had any problems. He had collected and reviewed legal journals and other pertinent laws relating to immigration and civil liberties in the U.S., with an itch to show his caliber as an articulate lawyer-to-be.

The need, however, for him as a legal connoisseur did not arise. Sidi was greatly relieved that there were no complications from the immigration people, and even more relieved for having no need for Barbar's expertise. Put bluntly, Sidi was uneasy with Barbar's egocentricity, and was happy that there was no chance for the self-proclaimed lawyer to complicate matters any further than they could have handled. Law student or otherwise, Sidi feared that half education could be dangerous, and Barbar's law education at that point was incomplete. Nobody but a fool would have counted on that as adequate legal representation!

Sidi was no fool, he knew he had his own immigration attorney, the same that processed his petition for permanent residency, and was with him until he got his green card. All he had to do was call the man if it was necessary. However, he had prayed on his way to receive Yaya that no situation developed that would warrant such action.

In the U.S., Sidi knew that one had better avoid any friction with the law, be it immigration, the police or otherwise. His rationalization was, no involvement—no defense! And like good health, he believed, that topped all. It was like Yaya making it safely. That was something to be thankful for, because he knew that it could have been a whole lot worse!

Now Yaya was approaching his waiting party, radiating with joy, like an astronaut just returning to earth. With hawk eyes and a drawn out face, they had spotted him in the crowd of arriving passengers and waved. Even before Sidi screamed the welcome statement, Yaya had caught sight of Sidi's towering dark frame and glittering white teeth, in the crowd ahead.

He had told himself he wasn't stranded; they were there. As he neared, Sidi quickly stepped forward ahead of the others to meet him. When they met, Yaya smartly stood his briefcase and suitcase at his side. They hugged and parted, and gripped hands, rushing greetings at each other. And then: *"Tana Tiyea?" "Tana Tiyea!" "Tana Tiyea?" "Tana Tiyea!"* That's an English equivalent in Mandinka of: "How do you do?" "How do you do?" They repeated this again and again, as the Mandinkas do when they meet after a long parting. With each *"Tana Tiyea?"* representing a greeting and an inquiry about a member of the family, with an answer, meaning, all was well.

When Sidi was through, the others crowded around Yaya with hearty smiles on their faces. And one after the other, they warmly shook hands with him—*the brother from home!*

Yaya, a little unsure, recognized Ahmed and called him by his name, hoping he was not mistaken, for Ahmed looked different. It seemed he had gained much weight since he came to America. Yaya looked at the others keenly, but was sure he had never met them. Sidi introduced them as Abu Janneh and Barbar Keita, friends of his and also fellow countrymen from Manika Kunda.

"Gentlemen, the mission is accomplished. We may go now," Sidi said, swinging his arms and excited.

"Time for pictures," Abu Janneh announced as they walked through the automated sliding doors of Terminal 5, which harbored British Airways at JFK, into an unusually bright day for the season in New York.

It was a Saturday morning, about eleven o'clock on December 29. Pleasantly, it crossed Sidi's mind that just after a white Christmas in New York when it would normally be snowing to overflow, on this day it seemed everything was in harmony with Yaya's uneventful trip.

For, like its counterpart in Africa which reigns supreme and in grace, the sun sparkled majestically above, to the bustling throb below, reaching those skins it could, soothingly, and going inside the pigments to drive away remnants of cold.

"Beautiful day," Ahmed uttered, looking up at the sun-warmed sky, like he was reading Sidi's thoughts.

"Fantastic!" Sidi agreed.

It was the sort of weather that one occasionally stepped out into and wished that all one had to do, was find a good spot and sit or lay down and stretch full length, basking all day long. Ancient photographers would say, "A perfect-picture taking weather!"

Among Manika Kundans, picture-taking had become a rite of welcoming new arrivals in America—the pictures served two purposes. Some were sent home to relatives to assure them of the safe arrival of the newcomer, and to show his or her reunion with kinsfolk away in the strange land. The remaining pictures were kept by the newcomer, as a souvenir, marking the beginning of a personal saga abroad.

They were walking along the pavement in Terminal 5, going towards the steps leading to the underground parking garage.

"Why not here with this British Airways sign overlooking?" Abu Janneh suggested.

They stopped, examining the spot.

"Sure!" Sidi okayed. He checked the film in the camera and clicked the flash ready.

"Here, Abu Janneh," he handed the camera over. "You start the clicking."

Getting ready, Yaya had stepped behind, straightening his coat and patting his hair. When the others started posturing, he joined them, with his briefcase in one hand, posed like James Bond, smiling all the way. His suitcase stood on the side, in view, near Ahmed who had quickly placed it there, as he posed.

"Barbar, you move over there. Yaya, come over here. Yes, good!" Sidi directed for a snap shot. He wanted his cousin next to him.

"Ready?" Abu Janneh prompted.

"Go!" Sidi said, posing.

"Everybody, say cheese, no cheese and never cheese." Barbar joked prompting. And they obeyed by their chuckles and smiles, while Abu Janneh went clicking and flashing shots, from different angles, with them in different postures.

Sidi handled the camera next. And after him, Barbar and Ahmed took turns. As the camera flashed, they were oblivious of everything. A few cab drivers honked at them, airport security staff looked, ignoring them, while the mass of people who busied to and from the terminal, sometimes briefly looked, but generally skirted them, and went about their business.

During their picture-taking spree, Yaya was looking at his countrymen and marveling at the changes in them. If he had not known Sidi and Ahmed, or had not been told that Abu Janneh and Barbar were from his country, there was no way it could have crossed his mind that they were Africans, not to talk about imagining them as countrymen. In his eyes, they looked American.

Yaya looked at Ahmed, standing about 6'1", next to Sidi in height, who seemed at least 6'3", about his height. They were all rounded, but Ahmed was bigger in flesh than all of them; and like Sidi and him, Ahmed had that dazzling blackness common with Mandinkas.

All of them were clean cut, with short cropped hair, Yaya noted, unlike his bushy Afro. Like all the others, Ahmed had on a sports coat. It was brown, over a pink striped shirt, with black pants and black shoes. On his wrist, he had a gold watch which was sparkling like everything else about him in that radiant sun. The collar of his shirt was pulled over his jacket in what was fondly called 'American-style' in Manika Kunda, as indeed all his other countrymen did, except Abu Janneh who had on a tie.

Abu Janneh was the shortest, about 5'7", with Barbar around 6 ft. Yaya placed them between the ages of 27-32, with Ahmed likely the oldest. They were all impressive, and in Yaya's eyes—with that American flair!

Wow! These are not Africans any more. They are just

*like those fabulous African-Americans who go to Africa as Peace
Corps, or those in the movies and the magazines. Even the way they
speak has changed. Hmm! America, Great America. Yea! It must be
a nice place to be. Just look at one time skinny Ahmed; Skeleet, was
his nickname everywhere until he left. You can practically count all
his bones then. But now, he is so well-rounded and so healthy
looking. Hmm! And they all seem physically rejuvenated. It must be
those chemicals we hear they put in the food in this country, and the
abundance of everything for good living. And of course, their peace
of mind, which makes them look so good and healthy!*

As Yaya stood by his well groomed and robust countrymen, he
inwardly felt embarrassed at his lean and hungry look. One would
think he was sick. But as the 'most successful' son in his
family—which was judged by some Western education and an
office job—it was his lot to reach out and share what little he had,
in terms of salary every month, with an ever-stretching extended
family, in those trying times at home.

But even more than the pressures from the general demands of
Yaya's extended family, there was this mentally exhausting burden
on him, hanging on him, tearing him apart, besides himself. It was
an unusual inheritance, handed over on a deathbed by a Grandmother,
who wanted him to follow in her footsteps, practicing what she lived
for and living the way she lived; while he and she were worlds
apart in thinking and everything before she died.

It happened one year and a half ago. Grandma Fatu in a death
wish chained him to a calling in his family, which so far he'd known
to be appropriate for only the old, the feeble and illiterates.

Yet he, Yaya, the most unlikely, the most educated and Westernized in his family, was woefully bound by a dead Grandma to the
most ancient of traditions, which he preferred to do without, and
which was in total conflict with his modern day dreams and
aspirations. That had started his mental agony.

Grandma Fatu turned out to be a nightmare even from her grave;
while he, on the other hand, struggled to live just an ordinary, normal
life, unburdened by what he knew not, but dreaded, and would rather
do without! That more than anything else bore his shrinking physique
in the past year and half.

He tried daily to be free, but didn't know how; especially not
when he dealt with a force that turned out to be determined and
furious like Grandma Fatu in her grave. He then learned that the
only option he had to be free and save himself was to leave the land
and go across the ocean. The opportunity of coming to America

existed among others. There was Sidi in America, a place he had looked forward to visiting sometime on a vacation. But it turned out that he became desperate, and had to hasten. However, after landing safely in America, he felt thankful to God in spite of everything. In fact he wondered, if this wasn't a blessing in disguise.

Well, Grandma Fatu, I thought you loved me. Evidently you didn't love me enough. Not at all. You shattered my world, hounding me. But I'm now far away. I had to leave for my sanity. Maybe now, you will rest. And please, select somebody else to follow in your footsteps. For I'm in a totally different world now, where my mind will be free and I will live a happier life—like these guys! Thank God! Wonderful America! You bastion of freedom—take me to your bosom—where everything is possible!

And as for you, my people, I won't forget you. I'll be back. Meantime, as always, I will help from here, whenever possible. But as for this sacred secret, I shall mention nothing of it to a soul, not especially to these guys, for as changed as they seem—they will only laugh at me!

Yaya noticed Ahmed handing the camera over to Barbar, who was now moving with the lens in his face, like a rock star with dark shades on stage, swaying to an applauding audience.

"Now, everybody change positions. Could you bend or squat for a quick shot, gentlemen." Barbar pushed a knob to advance the film.

The camera clicked and flashed—twice. Next, Barbar told them to get up and stand directly under the British Airways sign. Yaya did like the others, trying to enjoy this feeling of arriving in America and finding himself surrounded by countrymen. They had two more shots.

"Barbar, how many exposures do we have left?" Sidi asked.

Barbar got the camera from his face, and looked at the film counter. "Six remaining."

"Out of eighteen, we've taken plenty. Gentlemen, I think it's enough."

"More than enough," Ahmed teased. "Even if these are the only pictures Yaya ever took, he should have enough as souvenirs, with plenty left to send home to all the shattered hearts he left behind."

"If you mean my people, yes. I know it will make their day."

After the photo session, Yaya became a spokesperson, while his countrymen questioned him like some hot-stuff reporters.

"Tell us about Manika Kunda, Yaya," Barbar said.

"Man, there is a lot to say, what do you want to hear?" he retorted.

"About conditions generally." Ahmed offered.

"Not too good, at all, our people are hurting."

"That bad?" Barbar queried.

"Well, yes, for most of the people."

"Even with that mighty diamond they recently found? The star of Manika Kunda?" Sidi queried.

"Yes, we heard about that so called *star*. They said the third largest diamond ever found in the world. It was 989 carats. From the picture in newspapers, it looked like an egg laid by a hefty hen. But our human hens hatched it in their coops, and it died, I suppose. We heard nothing else about it. And it didn't touch the common man, like the two before it, each weighing over 950 carats, and all the others."

"Obviously some people are getting rich by hook or crook at the expense of the nation?" Ahmed observed.

"Of course, with no public accountability, our national wealth becomes private property, while the masses are scrapping pots and eating strange roots for food," Yaya reported.

"To say we can't take care of ourselves in that small country?" Sidi asked.

"At least not yet," retorted Yaya.

"Is there any hope?" Barbar asked.

"Maybe when you guys go back. You are badly needed over there, gentlemen."

There was a sudden hush, contemplative, as they looked at each other. Ahmed found his voice first.

"What about you, Yaya? Why are you running away?" he mocked, in retaliation. "You should have stayed there."

"Well, mine is a different story, altogether. I won't be long."

"Uh-huh," all the others said in chorus, as if to say we've heard that before.

"Yaya, you must first make this pilgrimage to America, right?" Sidi teased.

"Right, like you guys."

At this time, they were going to the underground parking lot below the terminals. They were almost at the steps that led below.

"Hey everybody, I don't know about you guys, but I'm mighty hungry," Ahmed complained.

"Me too, Ahmed," Barbar joined in the hunger cry. "In fact, I'm famished, since yesterday. It was from work to the library, and up and out this morning to the airport."

"That's like me," Ahmed added. "I skipped breakfast this morning, and it's almost noon."

"Sidi and gentlemen," Barbar called out. "I suggest that before we venture into that crazy traffic to Philadelphia, we have something to eat. My stomach is already rebellious from neglect."

"But you guys can't be so hungry that you can't wait until we get home?" Sidi said, glancing backwards in mock reproach. He was ahead of the others and they were all now on the steps.

"Of course, Sidi, you will say that," Barbar attacked. "You are taken care of, and don't get as hungry as single striving folks like us."

"There we go again," Sidi retorted. "As if I'm immune to hunger and have never been single." He was now stepping on level three in the parking garage, and looking about for his car in the dim light of the underground.

"Our situations are different, and you know that," Barbar screamed at him.

Sidi stopped momentarily, and looked straight ahead and laughed. "I know, Barbar, I'm married and you men are single, right?"

They were all off the steps now, with Sidi walking on one of the two driving lanes that ran between parked cars. There was a car coming on the other side—it was the entrance lane. He waited for it to pass, his eyes rapidly scanning the columns of cars parked on both sides. He moved into the next lane and saw his car, across, upwards to his left. He beckoned to the others to follow.

"Of course, Sidi," Barbar pursued. "If I may say so, we're all not yet as fortunate as you. Folks like us still sleep with only two legs, with nobody there in the morning to point to breakfast, not to mention dinner. But like you and everybody else, we still need to eat to keep on going."

"Don't over-flog it," Sidi snapped, stopping suddenly to survey Barbar. "Man, all you have to say is that you're hungry, and that we should find something to eat. But what's all this stuff about you sleeping with only one leg, or two, or less? Who's stopping you, or who's timing you? Not certainly me."

That silenced Barbar, somehow, as his mouth already in motion froze, to be closed without a sound.

Sidi laughed inwardly for warding them off from tormenting him, with their usual cries of woe—because we're single, my foot!

They got to his car. He opened the door for them and moved to the trunk where he placed Yaya's luggage. Joining them in the car, he was telling himself that he'd had enough from those three age-old single men, always showering him with guilt, or making a fool of him for being married.

Overgrown single men, always crying about their situation, and yet staying with one excuse after another without doing a thing about it, only to dump crap on him. Sidi told himself that he was not going to permit it today; certainly not in the presence of a younger cousin who had just arrived from home. It seemed his countrymen had the message, as nobody pursued the harassment. He started the ignition, and suddenly music filled the car. He lowered the volume.

"Gentlemen, I know there will be food at home when we get there," he said, and out of consideration added; "but if you guys insist, we may stop by some fast-food restaurant and get something."

"Sure," Ahmed said, unperturbed. "If only for the four-hour drive ahead."

"Say five hours," Abu Janneh offered. "We might as well get something to eat."

"Whatever!" Barbar said, twitching his lips, brooding.

Yaya, the Johnny-just-come, also decided to have an input. "Our people say, a man does not start any journey on an empty stomach, no matter how short the distance, for while you may know what you left behind, you may not tell what lies ahead."

"The stranger himself has spoken!" Sidi remarked. "Hey, let's go get a bite!"

The car in which they were exiting the garage was a high glossy black Cadillac Seville, four doors, automatic transmission, tinted windows, tan leather interior, sun roof and cruise control. An all-American car. A Cadillac was a rare car in Manika Kunda. Over there, the priced objects in cars were European and Japanese cars, like Volvos, Mercedes Benzes, Peugeots, Toyotas and Volkswagens.

Out of the reach of the masses in the country, cars could only be afforded by well-paid professionals, businessmen and the rich; and of course, the sudden-rich from diamond wealth.

With Sidi being in America for over six years, Yaya imagined he could own a car. He heard that cars were easy to get in America and that almost every hard-working adult who desired one could have one. However, Yaya never reckoned that a car as gorgeous and extraordinary to him as the black dazzling Cadillac they sat in could belong to Sidi.

It's certainly a borrowed car. Like those they rent for occasions even at home.

They were crawling along the winding lanes of the airport, towards the Vandyke exit, planning on a quick stop somewhere within Queens, en route to Philadelphia via Highway 95 south and the New Jersy turnpike.

Yaya was looking at the overhead signs by the roads leading to the terminals, which showed the airlines that went to each terminal, and which flights were arriving and departing. It was beyond him—the countless airlines that came to America. He observed that each of the terminals had more airlines and flights in and out per day than what Manika Kunda got in months, if not per year.

This car they sat in, Yaya was amazed. He wondered that as hard as things were back home, why did Sidi have to go to the extreme of renting such an expensive car—a type that he had never seen before—just to welcome him?

Barbar in the front next to Sidi turned facing the back seat. "Yaya, are you okay?"

"Yes, Barbar, I'm fine. Just a little tired." He smiled.

"That's understandable," Ahmed said, sitting by the other window, in the back seat.

Yaya leaned back in his seat, by the left window, and closed his eyes. *This big car. It rides so smoothly. Hmm!*

Could it be that Sidi got stuck with all that flamboyance in Kurudu where he grew up? Judging by this car, it seems so. Hmm! Kurudu, that diamond-crazed area in Manika Kunda. Funny to think of that.

A mere district, less than a tenth of Manika Kunda. Talk about diamonds for the taking, everyday. Yet what did they do?

After a good rain, almost everywhere, people stumbled upon quality diamonds, many worth thousands in British pounds, which they didn't know.

Maybe they got a fifth of the value, after being cheated, of course, by some hawking Lebanese diamond dealers and other mercenary merchants, who took the place of Her Majesty's government in preying on vulnerable people.

Still, most people got a decent sum. But in their short-mindedness, they believed that diamonds would grow out of the ground forever. Hence they lived for the day. The vogue was cars and ostentatious living for both old and young. Expensive clothes, jewelry, and lavishly furnished places, even if rented, though affordable, if not for car-craze. Yes, it was Mercedes Benzes, Volvos, Peugeots, et cetera, which took away all their money. Just living for the day, and no planning for the future or the unexpected.

Maybe that's what is still bothering Sidi. Or maybe he took after his spend drift small-father, his daddy's step-brother, uncle Brima. He was a one time wealthy diamond dealer who had three Mercedes Benzes, but lived in a rental house. Otherwise, why would somebody do such a thing just because your cousin is arriving from Africa? Obviously, some people never learn. Sidi must not have changed very much, it appears. He probably still has that diamond wealth mentality, that mere show-off that never endured.

Yaya wished Sidi had come in his own car, no matter how bad it looked, rather than wasting all that money on the *airplane* in which they were riding. He saw it differently.

After all, this is not home. Who can he impress in America? And besides, even in Africa, now the emphasis is on investments and not fanciful material stuff that depreciates so quickly, leaving nothing but empty memories.

"This is a mighty bridge," Yaya said of the Verrazano bridge, as they headed to 270 south.

"Yes, it is, Yaya," Sidi said. "It has two levels, one suspended directly over the other, and both constantly busy, even when they are six lanes each."

"Oh, America!" Yaya said. "From nowhere, they became a vital brain of the world, and in the leadership role everywhere."

"Well, yes." Barbar agreed. "America is a nation of all peoples, the proverbial melting pot, always having something cooking, if not at home, certainly somewhere abroad. Ask Saddam Hussein, he will swear to that!"

"The United States of America!" Abu Janneh hailed.

"The love of liberty brought us here," Yaya declared.

"And we hold these truths to be self evident that all men were created equal," Barbar said.

Yaya's eyes were roving and piercing through the smoked-glass window on his side. He was looking at the giant buildings, the incredible cars, and the seemingly happy-go-lucky people everywhere.

New York is a buoyant city and hectic; to live here, Yaya, you have to be alert and leave your eyes open all the time. He laughed as he remembered something he had read in some magazine about New York. It said, *"There is nothing you cannot find, or that isn't happening within a block anywhere of the Big Apple."* Yaya had found that statement intriguing, and considered it an exaggeration, but it stuck in his mind. And finally now he could say he'd been in the Big Apple, even if he was just driving through.

In the cushioned luxury of the Cadillac, Yaya was enjoying himself, breathing deeply the fresh leather scent, which mixed pleasantly with a variety of colognes creating a sweet fragrance inside the car. It was luxury, regardless of the obvious high cost. He decided to boost Sidi's ego.

"This is a great car, Sidi. It is luxury, first class."

"Oh, thanks," Sidi replied casually, though the huge smile on his face betrayed his pride. He polished the top of the steering with a palm smoothly, and slanted behind the wheel slightly. "Yaya, this baby is all fun," he said. "I've had it for almost two years now, and I love it."

Oh yeah? So this is his car? Two years, he's had it! Yaya consciously closed his mouth, so it wouldn't fall open. If there were diamonds in America to be picked as it used to be in Manika Kunda, he wouldn't have been surprised.

But in America? Again but ... aha! Well, Lord gracious! Sidi must have made it in America to own such a fabulous-looking car. In how many years? Six or less? No wonder, every dreamer wants to come to America. It must be a country of stunning possibilities, where dreams are fulfilled and lives are lived to the fullest.

"Sidi the great!" he hailed his cousin, now truly impressed. "Man among men! You are a doer, Sidi, and an inspiration! Wait till you take this car to Manika Kunda, man, you will be a star. Every one will think you've made it big. There are cars over there, but this car will be unique and definitely in its own class!"

"Yaya, you are saying that because you are new here," an amused Sidi responded. "We buy these cars here and plan to use them only here. I would never think of taking an American car to Manika Kunda, as appealing as that might be. They would be difficult to maintain over there, with no local dealers and spare parts outlets. Besides, except the trucks, most American vehicles may not fair well on our rugged roads."

"Sidi is right," Abu Janneh said. "That is why when many guys finally go home from here, they pass through Europe to get their cars. Because," Abu added, "European cars, like Japanese cars, seem better equipped for our scorching weather and creative roads."

"How are the prices in Europe?" Yaya asked.

"Reasonable," said Abu Janneh. "It depends on what you want. They say in Belgium, even with twenty-five hundred U.S. dollars, you can get a good used car, one less than four years old, which can serve you for a long time in Africa."

"That's right," Barbar stated. "It is true that in Belgium cars are much cheaper, and so is the shipping."

"Forget Belgium," Ahmed said. "I heard many people from Manika Kunda who bought cars in Belgium ended up regretting it. Didn't you hear about that at home, Yaya?"

"Well, not really. Cars were out of my mind, as they were out of my means."

"In any case, it is said that a bunch of hustlers and crooks who can practically sell you a goat for a cow have taken over the used car business in Belgium and that they are steadily duping unsuspecting Africans."

"From whom did you hear that, Ahmed?" Barbar asked.

"From the mouth of a friend in the used-car business who got burned. Since then he turned to Holland. He told me their trade secret; that the best thing to do if you need a good used car to take home, is to go to Holland and search in the newspapers. He said that if you are lucky to buy one from a responsible individual, you are likely to get a better car."

"Gentlemen, we will cross that bridge when we get to it," Sidi said. "Meanwhile, I know none of us is quite ready for such moves or preparing to go home finally. The issue here now is food. What have we decided to get?"

"Personally, I would say let us get some pizza," Ahmed said.

"Why not Chinese food?" Barbar asked.

"We don't have the time, Barbar. All we want is something fast to keep us going," Sidi answered.

Ahmed changed from pizza to suggesting hamburgers or fried chicken. They all agreed on fast food after sounding Yaya's opinion, who also suggested, "Fried chicken, if available."

"Let me warn you, Yaya," Sidi said, "the chicken here does not taste as good as the chicken we have back home. They are mass-produced here and fed with chemicals so they can grow fast. You will be lucky to eat one that is three weeks old. They don't give their chicken any time to let the sweetness come into them. So don't expect too much. The idea is to have something in the stomach."

"It's obvious you left home a long time ago, Sidi," Yaya stated. "Back home too, a few poultry farms have sprung up, producing similar chicken, almost tasteless."

"My man, if you consider those back home tasteless, wait until you taste the chicken here," Ahmed stated. "You will find a big difference between the two. They are like elephant meat and cow meat."

54

"Ahmed, I don't know about you, but I have never eaten elephant meat and I don't want to," Abu Janneh teased.

There was a Sunrise Fried chicken off 270 South on Rockingham Road in Queens. Sidi pulled up at the drive-in window where he put in an order for five, four-piece chicken dinners, each with French fries, and five medium cokes. They all contributed to pay for the order, except Yaya who was told not to worry since he had just arrived. *A-Johnny-Just-Come!*

Cultural shock number one for Yaya: "I have seen this type of restaurant in the movies where you drive by and buy your food, but I didn't know they actually exist."

"Of course they do. They are common here and they are called fast-food restaurants. This is a developed world, Yaya. Time is money, which makes restaurants like these necessary," Abu Janneh tutored.

Sidi received the order from the driver's window, gave everybody his share and drove off, promptly saying, "You guys better watch against dropping crumbs or making mess in my car."

"Yes, sir, Sidi, the boss," Barbar said.

The food became a distraction or an interruption in Yaya's appreciation of New York. Of course, he kept looking with the curiosity of a small-town boy in a big city, wanting to examine every structure they passed even though he was immensely limited by the food, the speeding motion of the car, and Sidi's warning about watching against making mess in his Cadillac. With the others, it was a grinding battle between the tooth and jaws, while occupied with their food.

Now they were well out of New York, on Highway 95 South heading for Philadelphia. It was four-lane traffic and Sidi was in the second lane, the first lane being the slowest. He was flanked by motorists all across the freeway. Suddenly a siren was blasting far behind them. Sidi's initial impression when he heard the wailing was that it might be an ambulance on an emergency of some sort, so he instinctively struggled for a chance to change lanes —to give way.

"The police!" Ahmed shouted.

Sidi had noticed that too from looking at his rear view mirror. The police car was barely inches away from them, still blasting and now flashing swirling lights from its top in blue, red and yellow. Sidi changed to the first lane, the police car followed and made no effort to pass. Shocked, it dawned on him that they were the target. He drove, looking for a safe spot to pull off the highway and did so at the earliest opportunity. The police car caved in on them.

"Your drivers license and insurance, please!" One of the two officers that had come out of the police car commanded, with his hand on his gun holstered to his hip.

Sidi frantically wiped his hands with a napkin that came with the chicken and reached in his back pocket for his wallet. With impatient hands, he handed his State of Pennsylvania driver's license and his auto insurance card to the officer who stepped back to the squad car.

Yaya, shaken and inwardly trembling by now, managed to turn with great courage and saw the officer sitting in the squad car, seeming to be talking into something black, which he held in his palm. The other officer, meanwhile, was towering over Barbar in the front passenger seat, looking him over, peeping in the back seat, scrutinizing everybody and looking on the floor of the car.

The officer that went to the squad car returned.

"Will you all step out, now!" he said.

The ill-at-ease Africans were shocked at the harsh commanding tone. Yet they stepped out.

"I want to see identifications for all of you!"

Ahmed, Abu Janneh and Barbar took out their wallets, pulled out their identification cards and passed them over to him. Sidi stepped in to explain to the officer that Yaya was just arriving in the country, that the only identification he had was his passport.

"Show them your passport," Sidi told Yaya.

"Search the car," the officer who had collected the identification cards told his companion as he stepped back to the squad car to check on the identifications he held.

"But why is all this?" Barbar the 'lawyer' asked. "I mean, I don't understand. What have we done wrong? And why must you search the car?"

The officer, who was already leaping into the open car, ignored him.

"That's okay, Barbar. No point arguing with them. Let them please themselves," Sidi said in an effort to deter Barbar from a verbal showdown with the officers.

"But this is totally uncalled for. Haven't you heard of the fourth amendment, the right of individuals to privacy, and against unlawful searches?" Barbar screamed for the benefit of the officer.

The police officer just kept prying. He stepped out of the car, after he was through with the inside, and asked Sidi to open the trunk. Sidi obeyed. When the officer saw Yaya's luggage, he asked to have them opened.

A completely tensed Yaya eagerly ripped open both his briefcase and his suitcase. The other officer who had gone to run a check on the identifications joined his companion at this point. Together, in a calculated manner, they searched through Yaya's luggage.

Ahmed, Barbar and Abu Janneh got their ID cards back.

"Mr. Sidi Béreté, do you know why we stopped you?" asked the officer who had taken their particulars.

"No, sir," Sidi replied.

"You were speeding. You were going at seventy-six miles on a sixty-five miles zone."

"But I am sure I was not..., sir? I had my cruise control on at sixty-one, and besides I was eating."

"Are you saying I'm lying, boy? I clocked you at seventy-five on my radar. There must be something wrong with your speedometer."

"I doubt if there's anything wrong with my speedometer," Sidi said, and with unflinching stare, he looked into the man's eyes. "Sir, if you were in my homeland, you would've had to produce a cow for calling me a boy. That name is for only *blakoros*—the uncircumcised. I became a man at fourteen in a big ceremony."

Talking back to me, eh? The puzzled officer's face turned pink. He bit hard at his lower lip, but otherwise showed self-restraint. "In any case, I am going to give you a ticket. Sign by the X."

As Sidi examined the ticket and speculated on signing, the officer continued, "Your signature is not an admission of guilt. You may appear in court and deny the charge, or you may send the fine in mail to the address shown on the back of this citation."

Sidi signed the ticket and returned it to the officer. He tore out two copies of the citation and gave them to Sidi saying, "Thank you sir, you may go. And drive carefully."

Sidi took off hissing. Everybody hissed in the car.

"Racists elephants!" Barbar said alluding to the officers who were both fat Caucasian males.

"Of course, just some typical racists," Sidi said, rubbing his forehead. "How else could they have singled me out in that traffic, and in the middle lane, with all those cars I had racing around me?" He sighed. "But..., they saw a black man driving a shiny Cadillac full of black men. They had to check us out," he said with a distant cracking voice.

"Really!" Ahmed screamed in disgust. "And check everybody's IDs? And search the car too?"

"They probably thought we are drug dealers or some criminals," Barbar declared.

"You are right. That's the price, buddy, for being black in this country and getting yourself an expensive car. Always expect harassment on the road," Sidi said, knowledgeably.

"It's to remind you of the burden on your color," Abu Janneh stated.

"Me, I'm used to it," Sidi said, leaning sideways to the window. "But this I say, nobody is going to rule my lifestyle just because they're hung-up on stereotyping. I work hard for what I get and I believe I should enjoy it any way I want, like anybody else. This is America—the land of liberty!"

As if dismissing the thought, he gushed a deep sigh and turned up the volume on his customized car stereo. Reggae music via four surround sound speakers vibrated in the air. A classic hit. *Papa's Land,* by the famous Nigerian singer, Sunny Okosun, was playing from a cassette. The song had something to do with old South Africa and its apartheid. Sunny Okosun wanted to know who owned the land in *Papa's Land?* This was followed by Bob Marley's *Redemption Song,* which Marley said he was dedicating to freedom fighters and black heroes all over the world; especially those leaders, he claimed in the song, that were wantonly killed while the rest of mankind sat by silently looking the other way. Bob Marley's record was followed by Peter Tosh's *Equal Rights.*

All through the songs the Africans were quiet, probably calming themselves or simply carried away by the music. As Peter Tosh in *Equal Rights* cried, rejecting peace and trading it for equal treatments and equal rights, Ahmed broke the silence.

"These records are old but they are classics," he observed, "and they carry a strong message for suppressed blacks everywhere."

"Quite true," Barbar said. "I find them thought provoking, and deeply touching. They're reminders any day of the struggles faced by Africans and black people all over the world."

"Right, man," Sidi said. "And personally that's what I like about Reggae music. It's a global black voice that has survived the odds. I don't only enjoy it, I also get a sense of pride and relief from listening to it. Do any of you guys get the same feeling?"

"Sure, I do," Abu Janneh declared. "It's the awareness it creates, like what some rap music do with vigor today." He went on to say how he had used Reggae and African music in the past to deal with his loneliness and sense of alienation when he was new in the U.S.

"I had dropped out of Bible college and was on my own," he said.

A HAUNTING HERITAGE : AN AFRICAN SAGA IN AMERICA

Among Mandinkas, which Abu Janneh was, to be a Christian was unusual. They were either Muslims mostly, or African religious worshipers. But Abu Janneh was a Christian and it ran in his family. That was from the point his great-grandfather, Lanfia Janneh, was up-rooted, and left disoriented and alienated. "Living in a world I didn't belong to," he reportedly said, in a toothless totter to his grandson, Lamini Janneh, Abu's father, who was just making ten.

Abu's great-grandfather, Lanfia Janneh, was one of the last slaves caught on the African soil, the year was 1850. Lanfia Janneh then was 21-years-old and was a rice farmer whose parents had wooed him a bride, to whom he was preparing to get married. Marriage ceremonies were big public affairs among the Mandinkas, so they required preparedness for the unexpected crowd that would certainly come. The groom and his family should be prepared with enough food to feed every guest all day long. And the abundance and variety of meat, instead of alcohol, was what thrilled the people. It was not unusual, in fact, to kill a cow and many did. But Lanfia and his father were poor, so that was out.

Two weeks before his marriage, he started going fishing, getting ready for the occasion. It was on one of those trips in a wooden boat along the salt water that Lanfia and a friend, Jejeh, were caught.

The ship was en route the Atlantic to America, the only viable market for slavery then. Britain had condemned slavery since Lord Mansfield's decision in 1772, and many other European countries were following suit. But some hungry slave merchants and stubborn plantation owners in the Southern states of America wouldn't let up.

However, Lanfia didn't make it to America, like the ship that captured him, with its crowded deck of shattered souls, stripped of their dignities. Floating in gloom for over six months in transit on the seas—within which Jejeh was murdered by the slavers because he would not obey their commands—the ship itself was attacked.

A British search party combing the high seas for slave traffickers to enforce the Emancipation Laws of the Atlantic Treaty—with the naval superiority of Britain—accosted the ship and seized it with all its human cargo. Now in British care, Lanfia was free. For starting from James Somersett's case in 1772, Lord Mansfield had declared in a landmark decision that any slave who set foot on British soil was free.

In the year 1808, several years before Lanfia was caught, the British had colonized a small West African country, Sierra Leone, which was used as a place for the settlement of liberated slaves from England. It took Lanfia two more years to get there, via Nova Scotia.

In Freetown, the capital of Sierra Leone, Lanfia met a lot of freed slaves, but nobody spoke his language, and the only words he knew in English were: "Goodam mornin, me, you, no, boss, beg, home, go, me place, thank you..."

Yet Lanfia Janneh knew that he came from 'Mandinkadu,' which means in Mandinka the land of Mandinkas. What Lanfia didn't know was that there were Mandinkas in over half the region of West Africa. In Freetown, he kept saying, "Me Mandinka, me go Mandinkadu." But nobody could help him. If there were any Mandinkas then in Sierra Leone, they were few, and in the interior, and besides, there were no maps.

However, ten years later, Lanfia Janneh found his way to Sobala, the capital city of Manika Kunda, another British colony. In Sobala, because of his little knowledge of English language, he had a job as messenger for the Colonial Administrators. Later he became a clerk; and through missionary influence, he became a Christian. That was when he found out that he was not very far from his place of origin. Mandinkadu had been renamed through the remapping of the land by Colonial Administrators, and was now Fardan; and the Colonialists had started calling the Mandinka people:'Mandingos.'

When Lanfia reunited with his people, it was like a miracle, a forgotten prayer answered. His sweetheart was already married with children. His parents were dead from a cholera epidemic, and the place was all dislocated. With his new Christian faith he didn't belong among a predominantly Muslim community. The people saw him as lost, if not out of his mind, praying to the white man's god, so they avoided him. With that sense of alienation, Lanfia returned to Sobala, sad at being rejected by his people. But he had found Christ, thanks to the missionaries.

In Sobala, Lanfia got married and had a son and a daughter, and maintained strong ties with the Methodist mission. His son, Kemoh Janneh, Abu's grandfather became a pastor. Kemoh had five children, four daughters and a son named Lamini. Lamini Janneh, Abu's father, became a pastor too and was a friend to many missionaries from England. It was within that environment that Abu Janneh was born. In the church mission where he lived, he lived with white people, went to Sunday school with their children, and played with them, even as they attended separate schools; because there was a special school for white children, mostly offspring of British administrators.

However, Abu Janneh's father wanted him to be a pastor like him, so they sent him on a scholarship to America to study theology. But once in America, he decided otherwise. He didn't want to be a pastor, so he dropped out of the Bible school and went about on his own. That was nine years ago.

Now Abu Janneh was making 28, with a first degree, which took him six years to complete. As an independent student, with a full time job, he paid his way through college. He finished three years ago, majoring in finance, with a three point grade average.

Abu's high hopes were marred by his father's death, two months after graduation. In the permanent state of emergency at home, under a sit-tight post-independence civilian regime, it was claimed that some political thugs—licensed to kill—mistook the simple preacher in an outdoor religious rally, for a disgruntled opposition stalwart rousing the people against the government.

Fearful of being another target, Abu Janneh decided to stay in America for a while. He applied for a political asylum and became a permanent resident. But even with the green card, and his mint diploma, he had no professional job. In the three years following his graduation, not a single door wavered open for him, even to beget the workaholic he'd become.

He delivered newspapers to residential areas in the morning and delivered pizza from a restaurant to hungry customers all over Southwest Philadelphia in the evenings. He claimed to work so hard because he supported a widowed mother, three siblings in school, and large group of extended family members at home.

"I was 19 and in junior college then," Abu Janneh recounted on his early days in America.

Sidi ejected the tape that was paying and turned off the car stereo.

"Our apartment complex was all duplexes," Abu Janneh said. "In the one I lived, my first neighbors, a young white couple were friendly towards me from the moment I moved in. They asked where I was from; we would chat; and when they met me occasionally in the parking lot with my car battery dead, they gave me a boost. The husband even invited me over for beer on weekends; he introduced me to American football. But his wife got transferred so they left town. And then a die-hard racist couple moved in next door."

"Quite a luck!" Barbar grunted.

"Real bad luck," Abu Janneh stated. "Really, even as a next door neighbor, those people would slam their door as I passed, or quickly pull their curtains."

"They thought you were a criminal," Ahmed said.

"Or worse! Talk about living amidst embarrassing unpleasantness, cold and uncaring," Abu Janneh remarked. "In the hallway, when I ran into them, if they looked my way at all, it was with eyes tightened and faces that seemed never to know a smile. Even when I greeted them, they just turned their heads away, snubbing me outrightly."

"You were in the wrong place," Sidi said.

"Yes, it was all hints to tell me I was. But I'd chosen that place for the convenience, commuting between my school and my job. That couple met me living there, for six months. I didn't expect anything like that; not especially as I was foreign and new in the country."

"Forget that!" Barbar exclaimed. "It was the color of your skin, brother. You're black and bad!"

"It's intimidating, when confronted with such hostility," Ahmed opined.

"Speak for yourself," Abu Janneh bluffed. "That is self-subjugation. I wasn't intimidated one bit. I was disappointed and indignant as hell.

"And with the people in the next two duplexes acting the same way," Abu Janneh continued, "I just felt like my great-grandfather would say; 'living in a world I didn't belong..,' and with nobody to turn to, yet surrounded by people. So, sometimes on weekends, I would take out all my records and cassette tapes, and select inspirational African songs and radical reggae lyrics decrying oppression and racism; and I'd blast my stereo to the fullest for hours, hit after hit."

"And your so-called racist neighbors didn't complain?" Ahmed asked.

"They did, indirectly. They called the police on me."

"I betcha!" Barbar snapped his fingers.

"Wait a minute, gentlemen," Sidi asked. "Did that sign say twenty miles to Philadelphia?"

"Yes!" Abu Janneh and Ahmed in the back chorused.

Yaya who was leaning in his seat, next to Abu Janneh, sat up and looked behind briefly for the sign, and leaned back listening.

"Indeed, they called the police on me. I could always tell by the way they banged on my door. So l would turn down my stereo lower, before opening the door for them. They would loom at my door, so like charging bulls with their eyes darting everywhere, and duly inform me about the complaints concerning the loudness of my music. I would gracefully apologize, hands down, all cooperative.

"Then they would ask for my identity card, which they checked through with their headquarters every time, as I laughed in my belly wondering which new crime they thought I might have committed since their last visit. Before leaving, they would warn me with menacing faces as to what they will do if they had to come again."

"Book you to downtown?" Ahmed asked.

"I guess," Abu Janneh chuckled. "As they left, I would say thanks, saying to myself, you are not going to arrest me if I can help it. My volume always stayed down after that, knowing somehow for that week, I'd made my presence and views known, in condemnation of racism and bigotry, which was the core of my being treated so disappointedly."

"Quite a way!" Sidi remarked.

"Yes, I deliberately used my music to bombard, in retaliation," Abu Janneh confessed. "Although, of course, I knew I was being a nuisance in the process. That was in Madison, Louisiana."

"Boy! You must have been in Peter Knight's territory," Ahmed said. "You should count your blessings you never ran into him."

"Who is Peter Knight?" Sidi asked.

"That was a man who believed in white supremacy and worked hard at spreading racial hatred," Ahmed answered. "He wanted all other races purged from America for a purer white domain, as if the land had solely or originally belonged to any of his ancestors."

"He should've lived in South Africa and rejoiced," Barbar said. "That would've been his heaven, to see where racism was at its heim and causing havoc."

"The shame of it.., that he found himself in America!" Abu Janneh said. "And more shame that the media calls his mentality conservative. When it is hating blacks, it's being conservative!"

"Yaya, we are almost in Philadelphia," Sidi said.

Yaya nodded and yawned. Abu Janneh and Ahmed yawned too.

"To think that the early immigrants came here running away from persecution in their own lands...," Ahmed observed.

"It's victims turned perpetrators," Barbar stated.

"But..., don't blame all whites," Sidi pointed out. "I've met quite a few good white people in America. In fact, they can be very altruistic and reliable as friends."

"Of course, like in any group of people, even among us blacks, there are the good and the bad, as well as the open-minded and the ignorant types," said Abu Janneh. "Yet it's when the bad decide to be vicious, alleging so on behalf of the good or the masses, that you find the *dubious honor* rubbing on the innocent, at least in the eyes of most victims."

"Quite true," Sidi said.

"My man, racism is a moral bankruptcy," Barbar expounded. "Like excessive greed and gluttony, it is a disease. In fact, it's a cancer of the mind which symtomitizes in insecurity and loathing. It gives birth to blanket prejudice and discrimination, exactly like that suffered by blacks right here in America."

"Yes, Barbar, that's saying it like it is," Ahmed commended.

"It's true, man," Barbar said. "Now, let me analyze racism for you. Like cancer, it is both malignant and destructive. There is the type that's similar to tumors. That's the blatant type as that which reigned in South Africa. In the Western world, one finds the gnawing kind, the slow killer, which creeps in, like lung cancer.

"In the West," Barbar continued, "Their type of racism is sometimes hideous and covert, which eats up its victims who are then left all feeble and broken, like the fate of many a black man in America."

"Doctor Barbar Keita!" Abu Janneh hailed.

Barbar ignored him. "In any case, one form of racism, whether blatant, subtle or hypocritical, can only be diabolically willful, and sometimes just as effective as another. As a pathological plight in society, what has fooled medical science from addressing racism as a mental disorder, and developing appropriate treatment for it, is the many guises it takes."

"Wow, Barbar, you really should have been a doctor instead of trying to be a lawyer," Abu Janneh teased.

"You bet!" Barbar snapped, sarcastically.

"I totally agree with you, Barbar," Ahmed said.

"Of course, Ahmed. Racism? It's very destructive. It undermines both the perpetrator and the victim. Most times, the victim invariably suffers the hurt, and deprivation, while the perpetrator suffers a psychological bondage, insecure within himself, and afraid of his shadows. Of course, his good sense tells him it's bad, but didn't Satan scorn goodness and settle to triumph in evil? And wasn't Icarus blind to his humanity and went soaring with waxed wings to the sun? It was his downfall! They call it hubris, or simply bigotry, which overwhelms common sense, basic morals and fair dealings!"

"Yaya, for a black person in the power establishment here, it's safer to make their laws your bible," Ahmed cautioned. "Or, be ready for selective justice, with all the odds against you."

"As if to be black is to be already guilty, where one has to be on the defensive always," Abu Janneh said.

"Exactly!" Barbar stated. "Take our case with those police officers who among all that traffic decided to pick on us. But my advice to all of you is this, learn to recognize the vice. There are many ways it can be dealt with.

"But whatever you do," Barbar warned, "don't share in the villainy by reacting stupidly. Usually, that's what you are pushed to do. Remember, just always try to stay calm.

"Learn to be positively assertive, and even be smiling, as you are dealt with. That way, you lure the perpetrator, like a hunter trapping a bush animal, into an open web with a rope lying where he can hang himself, legs up. If nothing else, that would be a spectacular sight for you to see, and a sobering feat for the fool who learns the hard way that with time goodness always triumphs."

"Barbar, frankly, we look forward to your lawyer days," Ahmed said. "And I would like to see you in court combining that native African wisdom with your legal training."

"You bet," replied Barbar, never quite the humble type.

All that talk about actual racism and bigotry and how to deal with the malaise was new to Yaya. His knowledge of racism so far had been only from news items about the outside world, particularly South Africa and its apartheid.

In Yaya's small world of Manika Kunda, where to be black was natural and good, racism simply did not exist among the many other problems. Over there, all people including non-blacks were at the least nice and friendly, especially the Peace Corps workers who got along just fine with the local people, as expected with host and guest, and equals in flesh and feelings.

CHAPTER FIVE

"We are now in Philadelphia, Yaya," Sidi said as he took the business road off highway 95 South to escape the busy downtown Philadelphia traffic. "We should be home in thirty minutes," he said with a yawn. "By now, only God knows what Pat is thinking."

At home Pat, Sidi's wife, who had waited for them longer than expected was fussing by herself and getting restless. Like a worrisome mother prevailed upon to permit her only child an outing with peers, Pat never felt at ease when her husband took off with that group he went to the airport with. She had stayed behind quite reluctantly. In fact, she felt almost left out.

The plan initially was that she and Sidi would make the trip to New York to get his cousin. Sidi himself had said it was to the boy's advantage that she went. Because he said, with all the problems that they usually get at the airport when they come, being a U.S. citizen, her presence at the airport could help. Like if any problem came up for the boy needing a guarantor before getting permission to enter the country. She was ready to go for the fun of it.

That situation changed, however, when Barbar, Ahmed and Abu Janneh showed up, getting clannish and bent on joining the trip—or rather simply taking over!

"I wonder how we are going to do this," Sidi had said. "I wanted Pat to come along too. Who knows, we may just need her."

"Man, with the four of us going, I am sure we can handle just about anything," Barbar the *macho* man had said, disrupting what was planned. And Sidi couldn't do a thing about it!

"None of us is a U.S. citizen, though, but Pat is," he had squeaked. Like that was telling them that he and Pat planned this thing from the start and they just came bursting in.

"We are not citizens, but we are all of valid legal status and that's what's important. Uncle Sam knows we are here and very legally too. Besides, I'm a law student, remember?" *Big-mouth* Barbar couldn't wait to say.

She had to hear this... "Yes, Barbar," that was Sidi, "but mister, for right now, you lack the power of attorney. There's not much you can do with authority if a problem arises."

"Oh yeah? Well, I will excuse your ignorance, but let me tell you this: I've done all relevant legal research and I feel quite capable. That's all."

"Sidi, if the man says he is capable, why not give him the benefit of the doubt?" Abu Janneh suggested.

"Okay, Barbar, you will be our lawyer, if we need one." Sidi had given in. "And Pat are you still coming?"

"That's okay, Sidi, I will stay," Pat declared with finality and a compromise that belied her disgust.

"But, Pat, you can still come if you want to," Sidi had fretted, after pleasing his kinsfolk.

"Nope, I will stay."

"Okay, baby, but I hope you won't feel bad?" he asked.

How could she make him understand? "Not at all!"

"Good, Pat. In that case perhaps, could you cook us some food. I think that would be better than us going out to eat. These gentlemen too may be joining us for dinner. And you know how they like your cooking. I hope you understand," Sidi pleaded.

Damn then, she muttered to herself, and yet grunted, "Okay!"

"Great! Well, we will be seeing you soon, darling. Sugar-pie, take care." Sidi said as they went out.

"Bye, Pat," the others chorused, filing out.

She got herself busy, and made her own plans to get over that.

As soon as they entered the car, and even before they took off from the driveway of the apartment complex, Barbar started lashing at Sidi.

"Sidi, the pragmatist," he laughed, his voice ringing sarcastically with the euphemism.

"What's your problem?" Sidi asked suspiciously.

"Nothing. I'm just amazed at what a wimp you act sometimes just because you are a foreigner in the U.S. It's ludicrous the way you clutch at your wife for protection, just like some terrified infant, dashing behind his mother's legs for a shield, whenever he sees a stranger."

"You think so, Barbar? Well, let me tell you now; as far as Uncle Sam is concerned, I prefer to play it safe. You can call me whatever you want," said Sidi, matter-of-factly.

"Indeed!" Barbar retorted. "What I don't understand is why you decided to doubt us because we are foreigners, even with my legal training, and yet believe that your wife would do more good than us in the face of an immigration problem."

"Who said I doubted you?" Sidi defensively asked.

"Oh, yes, you did, Sidi," Barbar pressed on. "But, man, look at us in this car and assess our caliber. We are foreigners alright but regardless, we are better educated and know more about immigration matters than your wife. And also, we are more capable of problem solving generally than she..., and you should know that!"

"But.., guys, must you argue unnecessarily? Pat didn't come. Why don't we just forget it?" Ahmed had said succinctly, and silence fell.

That discussion indeed was irrelevant, if they had asked Pat. As it was, she felt bad that she didn't get to tell those penny-and-dime friends of Sidi her mind that morning when their group showed up, butting in, leaving her out of the trip to the airport. Or they wouldn't have belabored the point.

They really need some straight talk, and I will do that soon!

That was as far as Pat was concerned. In fact, she had completely given up all ideas about going, from the moment they walked in, taking over.

The truth was, Pat couldn't stand that group one bit, particularly, as she would say: 'That rowdy Ahmed, or that big-mouthed Barbar!'

As for Barbar, she had always said, it was well that he was in school to be a lawyer; because she couldn't imagine any other use for his big mouth and his arrogant self. She detested their bond with her husband, the bunch of them. For they were only going to negatively rub on Sidi, and make him even more difficult, and acting exactly like them!

As Yaya was due any time now, Pat's only hope was that he too would not turn out to be like those two, Ahmed and Barbar, who were plain bad news, in her opinion. She had warned Sidi that Yaya, the guy that was coming, had better be a good one, especially as he was going to be staying with them. The previous day when it became certain that Yaya was on the way, she had spoken her mind on it again to Sidi.

"I cannot stand any other crazy African around here. It's enough to have to deal with your other friends. I hope your cousin ain't going to be anything like that Barbar or Ahmed. Cause I don't want any problems in my house than I can handle."

CHAPTER SIX

Pat was American, born and bred. She loved Sidi, and Sidi in turn loved her. That was in spite of their pronounced differences in thinking, cultures and values. They had met in a Pizza Hut some two years ago. Sidi was twenty-six then, with a mind of a sixteen year old when it came to marriage. He had stopped by a Pizza Hut to pick up an order, which was after clocking some twelve hours on the job. In that same pizza hut, Pat happened to be sitting alone, sipping on a glass of iced tea, and feeling confused and exasperated.

She had come on a blind dinner date and had been there for over an hour, but her date had not shown up. At this time, her legs were steadily pedaling under the table, her eyes fixed on the entrance and on the parking lot, through the many glass windows that lined the restaurant towards the parking lot. With disbelief, it was dawning on Pat that she might just have been *stood-up*. And she was inwardly boiling with rage and self-reproach for skipping dinner at home in anticipation of this date and worse, for bringing no money with her so she could order something, as badly as she needed to eat. She had been served a glass of iced tea but she wasn't sure how she was going to even pay for that.

It was early September in Philadelphia, and the fall wind was blowing cold that evening. Pat was gazing at a lone pin oak tree standing outside by the parking lot, with the wind shaking its thick shady branches. Some weathered leaves fell, nearly landing on a car pulling up in the parking lot. Pat noted, and tilted her head. She held her breath. With the eyes of a security guard at a bank, she shot through Sidi as he came through the door.

Could this be him? Pat asked herself, her eyes rolling and expectant. She noted this man had on a uniform. Ricky, the man whom she was supposed to meet, had not mentioned anything about either going to work or coming from it to make the date. She could tell this guy was just coming from work. His sluggish strides and the worn out expression on his face confirmed her guess that he was not her date.

Yet looking at the taller-than-six-foot man that came in, Pat considered him handsome, ebony black, with white shiny teeth and a fine physique. She clenched her fist and bowed her head thinking.

Winners and losers! And what the heck! With a sly curve on Pat's mouth, she looked at the back of the broad-shouldered hunk at the counter, and with a shrug, decided to flirt with him anyway.

The cash register was ringing, and the dark haired, big nosed cashier and waitress was taking orders from the *brother* at the counter. And then he turned, stifling a yawn, lazily looking at Pat. She held his gaze and beamed him a captivating smile. He noticed the wink. Her stark beauty struck him instantly, surging him alert.

He looked at the high-yellow, slim, dark brown hair, almond eyes and thin lipped female sitting there like a goddess, and wished she was waiting for him. With those thin lips, Pat smiled at him again, this time invitingly. His heart kindled with delight and he smiled back.

"Hi!" Pat said, still smiling, with a big twinkle in her eyes, as if to say, 'Come baby, come get me!'

"Hello, dear," Sidi charmed, betraying his accent, although now swept to high hopes. He raised his eyebrows. "So how are you doing today?"

"I'm fine, just fine." The accent shocked Pat. She didn't know what to make of it. She let out a huge sigh and leaned back in her chair. *I wish he were okay, like a real black brother. Then I would scream: 'Hey, come here baby! I could do a whole lot better!' But these Africans or Cubans or Jamaicans?*

"Your pizza will be ready in fifteen minutes, sir," the apron-clad cashier called to Sidi.

That news was just as well with Sidi, whose hunger had flown, now replaced with a yearning. He asked for a glass of Sprite, turned around and walked confidently to the table where Pat was sitting.

"May I join you for a moment, Ma'am?" he asked, bowing, and his eyes searching her eyes.

"Sure, why not. Take a seat." Pat smiled, cheering up.

"It's easy to see that you're just as nice as you're beautiful," Sidi flattered delightfully, sitting directly opposite Pat.

"Thanks," she said, with happy eyes. "My name is Pat, nice to meet you." She offered her hand across the empty table.

"Nice to meet you too, Pat. I'm Sidi." He engaged her in a firm handshake. Pat thought he didn't want to let go of her hand.

"Forgive me for this, but your beauty reminds me of *Mammy-water,* a kind-hearted goddess of the river where I come from."

"Oh, yeah? That's a new one, but thanks." Pat blushed. "Tell me about this goddess you say I remind you of."

"*Mammy-water?*" Sidi smiled. "She is folklore, but she is said to be very beautiful, very tall, with a smooth glowing complexion, long hair, diamond eyes and small nose. They say she lives under the water and comes out only occasionally to sit ashore, on some big rock, basking in the sun and combing her hair. It is said that she throws her comb at whoever catches her out there, and that's like a blessing; because by telling that comb any wish, it comes true immediately. In fact, quite a few people, we hear got rich that way."

"Lucky them. I could do with being rich myself."

"Me too," said Sidi, patronizing. "Nice place to eat. Do you come here often?"

"Not really. I'll say, every once in a while. You have an accent. Where are you from?"

"I'm from Africa. Manika Kunda is my country."

"Oh, that sounds nice. How long have you been in the U.S?"

"Three years, going on to four."

"That long? And you still have an accent? How do you like it here?"

"Great! America is a great country," Sidi replied, and he looked over his shoulder. "But it could still be a better country, the best in the world, if they started treating blacks right."

"You are right about that, baby. You are smart, eh? Are you married?"

"No, are you?"

"No! Do you see any ring on my finger?" she asked jokingly.

Sidi started shaking his legs below the table. He felt encouraged and decided to edge further into Pat's business.

"I see you are not eating anything. What have you ordered?"

"Nothing," Pat confessed, shifting her eyes. She smiled, and in an exasperatingly low voice explained how she had come on a dinner date, but her date failed to show up. "A fake he was, asking me out here, claiming to be treating me to dinner, when he knew he was lying." She sighed.

"But I'm more mad at myself than him. I should have known better than to come here with no money. Or, I would have fed myself and gone long time ago."

"It happens to the best of us," Sidi comforted her. "Don't feel bad. As they say, there is something good in every bad situation."

Pat smiled. "And some things happen for the best," Sidi said. "Look at it this way: for a starter, I might never have met you if that deceiver had shown up. So don't let it get the best of you."

"No, it ain't. I'm just mad, but I'll get over it."

"Great! The idea is to look at it positively. Maybe we can use this chance to get acquainted. You can be my guest, if you don't mind. I've placed an order to go. I will be happy to place another, to stay, this time for the best pizza that Pizza Hut can offer, if you can share it with me."

"Oh thanks, but are you sure you really want to do that? You don't even know me?"

"That is alright with me. We still have enough time to get to know each other. We could just say perhaps, this is the way we were supposed to meet. We may still be great friends. Who knows?"

Without giving Pat a chance to say anything else, Sidi called out to a waitress and asked her to place the order. Pat ordered a sixteen inch, thin crust original deluxe pizza, with pepperoni, sausage, mushrooms and green peppers and also a refill of her ice tea.

"Would you like anything in addition?" she asked him.

"No thanks, that will do."

Sidi's generosity impressed her. She studied his dark grinning face and assessed him as intelligent and open-minded. This made her feel attracted immediately to the African.

"You really seem to be a nice guy," she told him with a seductive smile. "How long have you lived in Philadelphia?"

"About two years, but before I came here, I lived in Washington D. C. for over a year. Then I moved to Maryland and lived there for another year. I came here straight from Maryland."

The pizza was served. As they ate, they explored their hobbies, their backgrounds and present situations. He learned that she had been engaged for nine months, had lived with the guy for three months but had broken up the relationship because the man told her that he liked her but wasn't sure she was the one for him.

"A silly, vain guy, who needed to grow," she said about her ex-fiance. And her face tightened briefly, as she reflected on the insult of the man's statement—putting her down like that!

"But it is all over," she claimed. "Now I'm living with my mother, only temporarily. And I'm dating nobody seriously. What about you?"

Sidi in turn informed her that he lived by himself, worked full time and went to school full time.

"Well, do you have any time for a relationship?" Pat asked.

"With the right person," Sidi replied.

At the end of their unplanned but pleasant dinner, in Pat's mind, she was clear about wanting to know Sidi better —to kind of check him out!

Sidi felt even more hopeful, especially with those promising looks that Pat kept throwing at him, *faire venir l'eau a' la bouche* —the situation made his mouth water!

He picked up his order, walked her out to an old Oldsmobile, which she said was her mother's car—hers was in the garage to be fixed. However, before parting, they both professed a strong desire to meet again. Telephone numbers were exchanged, and the following Saturday was agreed upon for a night out together.

By their mutual curiosity and consent to socialize, both Pat and Sidi were to eventually realize that they had far more in store than they bargained for. For what was to come engulfed them totally, leaving them wiser and making them pawns in life's changing stories.

Their Saturday night date turned out superb. They went to a disco club, of mixed races; a joint Sidi visited occasionally and felt comfortable because of its professional looking crowd. Pat was a good dancer and Sidi a natural, so they danced all night long. As the club closed, Sidi prevailed on Pat to tag along to know where he lived. Needless to say, he had been brewing a grand plan of his, to consummate their newly formed relationship. Pat, with much misgivings gravitated along.

Sidi's apartment was in the Southwest section of Philadelphia. The community where he lived was a grade or two above the *downtrodden* Northwest Philadelphia housing project where Pat lived with her mother. If things were different, Pat would have preferred to be living in this area and in the type of apartment complex where Sidi lived; but things were not different. All the same, she was excited at discovering that Sidi lived in such a nice area, just the type of upscale apartment community she longed to live in. But what she did not know, however, was the dramatic transformation ahead for her at Sidi's place.

The reality was, even with her African descent, Pat's perception of Africans up till then was low. In all her life, her disposition to Africa and Africans had been contemptuous and derogatory. She could never substantiate the basis for such attitude, except of course to say, that was just how she felt.

Like most Westerners, she had never stopped to reflect on where her negative perceptions about Africa came from. She might never have realized that such perceptions emanated from her own ignorance and prejudice, and were consequences of works by questionable sources who were woefully ignorant about the African society;

*in no less a manner, as early Western opportunists who visited Africa,
exploited it, enjoyed a civil and warm relationship with the people,
saw endless and radiant sunshine, then returned to their snow and
winter tormented countries, rich and happy, only to describe Africa
as the 'Dark Continent!'*

*Regrettably, even when Pat was lacking in personal experiences
and interactions with Africans, she held them in low esteem, with no
exception. That was how she initially looked at Sidi. She rationalized,
she had met him, he had been nice, but still, he was African, and that
made things different—he wasn't somebody she could think of for
anything serious.*

*As luck would have it, Pat, a victim of a wistful childhood
and eluded dreams, was a materialistic girl par-excellence.
In men, the possession of impressive material things counted
paramount—above everything else!*

Sidi, incidentally, happened to be generous and flamboyant,
with much credit to his upbringing in diamond-crazed Kurudu,
in Manika Kunda.

Even though a hard worker, he had this habit of being lavish,
with a passion for good things and good living; a blatant manifes-
tation of that idiosyncrasy showed in the way he furnished his one
bedroom apartment. Of presidential lounge caliber, the place was
a sizzling breathtaker for anybody that stumbled upon it, visiting
an average person like Sidi.

"So this is where you live?" Pat asked as he opened the door and
stepped aside to let her in.

"Yep! This is my crib," he said with a sheepish grin. "Come
right in."

She did exactly so. When Pat walked into the apartment and had
a full view of the living room, her heart seemed to stop, or so she
thought. Quickly gobbling some air and letting it out, her breathing
doubled, and her eyes wandered— popping in her head— while her
mouth fell and her legs refused to move.

Surprise! surprise! She sighed.

Noticing Sidi gaping at her, Pat gasped, and blew a sigh,
focusing her eyes sharply on him. She had in those eyes a look
of wonder and fascination, genuinely beaming and viewing the
African, now in an entirely different light.

"Wow, Sidi!" she uttered between rapid breaths. "You have
quite a beautiful apartment here."

"Thanks. So you like it?"

"Do I like it? Sidi, I love it. It's gorgeous!" she said, sounding grateful, like she had been handed a present.

Cannily, Sidi made his welcome statement, about how she should relax and feel free. And he excused himself to the bathroom.

Pat sat down on the loveseat, crossed her legs and posed, with the euphoria of a person relishing the relief and realization to have finally arrived.

"Isn't this style and elegance?" she asked herself, leaning in more *elegance,* and looking around. The furniture she sat on was part of a five-piece sectional, with recliners, high backs and thick armrests, all generously upholstered in a smooth black material which Pat judged to be leather and got crazy about on sight.

She gently laid her purse on the center table, which she thought was a beauty. It was round and crafted with gold-brass frame and smoked-glass top, with a bottom shelf, and it had three matching end tables. Her eyes wandered to the dinning room table, which was gold-brass and smoked-glass top, with four revolving chairs nicely in the same material as the sectional pieces.

It must be nice! Pat laughed. She pushed her hair back, a finger touching her hair bow to check that it hadn't fallen.

The boy's crib is all gorgeously laid out. He has everything. And he is single too. This rich African!

Next, Pat marveled at the wet bar in the left corner of the dining area. On top of it was an assortment of bottles of liquor, wine and soda, neatly arranged in a row. She was detailing those when Sidi came out. He had changed into blue boxer shorts and a white T-shirt, which, if Pat noticed, she didn't show.

"Sidi, I thought you said you don't drink?" she asked, leading his eyes.

"Oh, that? No, I don't. But I entertain guests, occasionally," he said, coming over to her, smiling indulgently. "By the way, would you like something to drink?"

"I better not have any more drinks, Sidi. I had enough at the club. Some coffee maybe?"

Sidi went to the kitchen.

Pat kicked off her shoes, relaxing, and gazed at the black lacquer entertainment center facing her against the wall. Her eyes rested on the stereo system. It was a complete Sanyo system. She quickly scanned the units individually. A compact disk, a tape deck, an amplifier, a turn table and a radio receiver with equalizer. On the other side of the entertainment center, a Sony VCR, and a 27-inch screen Magnavox television set stood.

She just loved the setup. The boy had everything she needed.

Sidi brought the coffee, drew an end-table near her and sat the coffee mug down.

Pat asked to use the bathroom. It had connecting doors to both the living room and the bedroom and all the doors were open. Inside the bathroom before she closed the doors—the bedroom last—her eyes made a calculated sweep at the interior, and she shook her head, acknowledging it as another case in style: The massive dark pine waterbed, with a multiple drawer pedestal-mirrored headboard and shelves with doors; then the two mirrored high-boy night stands with designer lamps on top of each, standing on both sides of the headboard. The bed was neatly dressed and sharp.

Enticing! Pat smiled.

In Sidi's apartment, those furnishings were his priced collections. In a four year period, he had diligently saved, sacrificed and worked hard to buy them, so as to accomplish such standard of living in his home away from home!

To Pat, the African's place was an inviting set up, all ready and waiting for a woman like her. So she didn't see herself far from jumping in that big fanciful bed and lying there —like that was where she belonged.

Actually, it was a joke among Sidi's friends, Abu Janneh and Barbar, that Sidi's place had just the right touch to sway a few undecided girls into suggestive and willing partners. They claimed it was for many home-scouting spinsters, "a please-marry-me set-up."

And it made an instant convert out of Pat. A sucker for good time and posh life, Pat resolved promptly that she had found her prince, and this came with a flaming desire to have Sidi there, then and forever. For no more than her vanity in unity with that cozy atmosphere, she instantly discarded all scruples about a lady not giving herself up to any man on the first date. Rather than scruples, it was passion and stooping to win which reigned when Sidi came and sat next to her.

On this night Pat had on a black dress, the top of which was cut in a big-U, providing a succulent view of her cleavage. When she stood the dress stopped a few inches up her thighs, emphasizing her height and slenderness. But sitting as she was on the couch, the hem of her dress had come mid-thigh, exposing some exquisitely fresh flesh, which Pat made no effort to cover. Instead, her eyes roved on Sidi's dark glaring flesh, thick thighs and firm muscles outside of his shorts and T-shirt.

Sidi was excited, yet trying to be a gentleman, though his eyes kept lingering at Pat's chest and on her fresh thighs. When their eyes met, she was smiling with ardent warmth. This was as he acted cool, with his hands locked under his thighs, even as his wiggling thumbs and forefingers ached for an okay, to reach out to her delightful breasts, to lift them to freedom.

He released a hand, to stroke hers. They gripped and smiled.

The glint in Pat's almond eyes sparked more fire in Sidi; his red tongue flickered like a cobra's, and he licked his lips, making a slight watery sound. Then he pulled her closer and she came, throwing her glorious self into his arms, pressing her firm resilient breasts to his chest, and kissed as she was kissed.

Now with Sidi's fine morals loosened, he dipped a hand into the top of Pat's dress and filled it with an ample tit, which came tumbling out between his stroking fingers. He gazed at the full lustrous flesh which he nibbled and bowed to suck on while his fingers closed in on the other. Meanwhile one of Pat's hand had found its way into his shorts where it was cuddling and tracing the contours of his throbbing massive manhood.

Sidi's last sex was over five months ago. With Pat's acquiescence, and already nearly sex starved, he couldn't wait much longer. He picked her up from the living room and graciously transported her to his waiting waterbed. Trembling with excitement, he undressed her, each piece followed by gentle strokes, until she was naked. He then undressed himself and out of habit—as this was a casual relationship—he got his condom.

While Pat with wide eyes struggled to put the rubber on him, one of Sidi's hands was busy down the split softness between her thighs, to where Pat directed him when she was through. As Sidi lowered himself into the quivering Pat underneath, she gasped and moaned, encircling him with her hands and feet.

"Do me, baby," she said. And indeed he did, sliding, pumping and humping all night long. Pat voluptuously flapped her head from side to side, giving herself to him, all and more, and through and through, until rays of the late morning sunshine cascaded through a crack in the window curtain of the bedroom, making intricate patterns on their entangled nude forms in bed.

Pat stayed for the *Sunday* with Sidi and all day long they explored and shared themselves to total satisfaction. Then she left Monday morning.

"Baby, it occurred to me...." Pat returned a few hours later with a suitcase full of her things. Her eyes traveled over Sidi as she stood at the door. Then she noticed he was holding it open for her.

Pat entered and put down her suitcase. "Okay baby, I mean, I thought that I should come back," she said to a shocked Sidi. As if to buttress her point, waving both hands across the well-furnished but disorganized apartment, she declared, "I've got some work to do around here, putting everything in order, and I'm starting right now."

"Is that right?" Sidi asked confused, digesting the situation.

"Yes, baby, wait till I finish, you'll see the difference. I'm going to add a lady's touch to this place. That's what you need. As classy as you are, I bet you'll like it, and be happy too!"

Taken aback, Sidi fondled his watch thinking. He realized that he was now under a siege of some sort. *Yeah, man! But why not tell her, Pat, thanks for the thought. Really. But please.., I'm fine, as it is!*

He looked at her face and looked down at her suitcase, and felt embarrassed. *Such a delicate looking woman. What has gotten into her?* He looked into her eyes and felt touched.

"Well, Pat, okay. I hear you."

"Oh, baby, you're going to be happy. You know, you men are all the same, just big babies. I'll show you, Sidi. You really need a woman! Wait, soon you will be wishing I'd stay here to be your wife."

What? That amused Sidi. He looked at Pat and felt more stunned than ever. *This girl has guts, eh? Now woman.., don't bet on that!*

Puzzled and divided on how best to handle the situation, Sidi wanted to ask, 'Did I say I need this? Or did you come only to help, and if you did, why bring your luggage?'

Sidi knew it was an invasion —an old game—and that Pat was feeding him that soothing idea of him needing a wife, or some woman to look after him, only to coax him, and to get him where she wanted. Yet claiming courtesy, he refused the urgings of his rebelliously independent self, which wanted him to tell her, *no dice,* and to make his position known immediately.

Instead, his soft spot prevailed, which said, he didn't need to hurt the lady's feelings, or at least not yet. And so, he relaxed and permitted her a field day.

Sidi prided himself to be a hard core and an unrepentant bachelor. But even after admitting to himself that Pat's enticing schemes were designed to grip and definitely orchestrate his life, his reaction was to put on a countenance common with rebellious teenagers who laugh inwardly, if not openly, at any serious resolve to make them conform.

Strangely, Pat reminded Sidi of his childhood, of bouts then between Barrie, a delinquent friend of his and the friend's mother about tidying up his room. He always sought a chance to be at Barrie's house every Saturday morning and observe as the mother, piously serious, went picking, packing, and putting, in her words, some sense into the chaos here—which was a constant situation in Barrie's room. During those fond escapades, when Barrie's mother toiled, he and Barrie anticipated her every move and bet on it and watched, scoring points. By the following Friday evening, everything was back *wizzy-wazza* for the Saturday sport. And who said life doesn't replay itself? Too bad Barrie missed this.

Occasionally Pat threw him a sweet smile, without stopping her work and her display of refined feminine antics, which came with intermittent lectures about the proper care and place for items around the apartment. To those corrections, he nodded, and raised his eyebrows in amusement, and mumbled, to mean, 'Well, Baby, ride on, and just keep going on...'

"This woman must really mean business," Sidi found himself lamenting in the bathroom when he went to empty his bladder. Legs apart, standing over the commode, and letting go, he sighed.

Well, for all I care, let her knock herself out. I hope that makes her day. But, at the end of the day, reality will come. She will know, that I, Sidi Béreté, have no intention of getting married now. Not today! Not tomorrow! Not yet, period!

Then a fart escaped him loudly, as if to agree with him totally; he thought about that and felt good in that privacy. Now relieved somehow, he came out of the bathroom and went smiling to Pat in the bedroom, where she was busy straightening the sheets on the bed.

"How does the living room look?" she asked coyly, lips curved up in anticipation.

"Great. You are just great," he bestowed.

"So you like my work so far?" she further coaxed.

"Of course, very much," he said. "You're doing a good job!"

Yet he told himself to stop the double standards. He knew he was creating a situation of misunderstanding. Without anybody telling him, he could see that Pat was not fooling, and that she had that wistful outlook, which marriage oriented women have when they see a potential for settling down. To think that he now embodied such potential, bothered him very much.

He liked Pat. He enjoyed her love making and appreciated

her efforts in tidying the apartment. But by no means was he sure he wanted to be a serious candidate for her. Sidi decided he might have fun, but like many chronic bachelors, he had so much to take care of before getting married. Because of that, he felt absolutely convinced that he was not only *not* ready for marriage, but also *not* ready for any kind of live-in situation with either Pat or any other woman. That would be too much for him and just complicate life.

Sidi's attitude towards women had been one of splendid isolation, that was of course, after the usual: *Wham! Bam! Thank you, babe. Whew! See you later.* Commitments of any serious nature or relationships with the tendency to tie him down were specters that scared him stiff. So naturally, marriage or anything marriage resembled was completely out of his scope and vocabulary.

Several of his flustered lady friends had dismissed him variously as, *"a wimp, a conceited fool,"* and, *"a macho man who thinks he's God's gift to women."* They had called him, *" a no-good man,"* which meant—*a heart-breaker*—not someone to count on for marriage!

Sidi never minded. He kept to his plan, knowing that they always got over their frustration with time. He had his goals, his tight schedule of work and school, and wanted no encroachment. But if so, he wondered, knowing what Pat was up to, why was he putting off coming out straight to her, so that she would know exactly where he stood?

Or why wasn't he mustering the courage to tell her, 'Thanks, but no thanks, Pat, please go. I will clean my own apartment. Please take your luggage. Please, Pat, let's be friends, but.... Here, if you are broke, I will give you my last forty dollars, but please go. I will call you, sure! G'bye! See you later.' And never call her again, like all the others that had come with similar designs on him, that he had successfully kept at bay.

Why was it, in fact, that Pat's take-over demeanor sat well with him? And why was he feeling weakened in his usual defense that puts matters to rest? Was it nostalgia? Or, was it the innocent beauty on Pat's captivating face, and those almond eyes that sparkled with warmth? Was it her sweet smiles on those beautiful lips of hers that struck him with a pang? Or, could it be he was falling in love? No, it couldn't be. Sidi strongly dismissed the latter. The strong untamed Mandinka man that he thought he was, a feeble sentimental flurry like falling in love was the last thing he would own up to, even to himself. Yet, he let Pat carry on.

Meanwhile, with the tenacity and resolve of a cork on a wine bottle, Pat kept on. Needless to say, she had no intention of stopping. In her mind, Sidi was an unborn babe and a toddler altogether, tote in a cradle, ready to swing to a different tune, even if he was blind to see it coming.

Like a captain and a ship, Pat made the options hers not his. She rationalized, if Sidi couldn't by himself make up his mind to settle down, she would make it up for him.

Armed with the covetousness of a head-strong woman, she played to win. She luxuriated in mesmerizing and cajoling him in a manner that not only intoxicated him with passion, but actually got him longing and singing. From the cleaning in the apartment, to cooking and dining knee to knee, followed with more teasing and love-making. Soon Sidi's chronic bachelor's guard went flying, taking with it all reservations about the invasion. He justified it as settling for *en couleur de rose*—the bright side of things!

With Pat around, things got so convenient that Sidi would come from work, meet his meal ready and waiting, his laundry done, the apartment clean and everything in place.

Also, instead of his usual routine of running around, with roving eyes for the feminine kind, now there was always a pleasant and stimulating companion waiting at home, with cheerful eyes and a seductive smile, saying, "welcome;" and coming close with her sensuous figure to lean on and do things with. Naturally, their relationship blossomed into trust, then commitment, culminating into marriage.

In the eyes of Sidi's strong-headed bachelor friends, all these happened so fast that they were swamped with disbelief and left open-mouthed and completely flabbergasted.

At the time Yaya was due in Philadelphia, Pennsylvania, it was slightly over five weeks since Pat and Sidi had celebrated the second anniversary of their marriage. Over the period, their relationship had seen good and bad times, and survived it all. Their cultural difference remained, however, to be their main problem.

Sidi, with his traditional extended family and communal oriented African culture, could neither comprehend nor relate to the whopping individualistic tendencies of Pat, whose focus in everything seemed to be centered on herself and what affected her personally.

To Sidi, the welfare and realities of his kinsfolk and town's people were as important as his own. He would do anything for them except if it posed the greatest danger personally, as was in the case of Munda, in whose situation Sidi felt regretfully handicapped, because he was himself then on a shaky status in the U.S.

Such constraints aside, in Sidi, the African will prevailed, such that he regarded every person from his homeland that lived in Philadelphia or anywhere in the U.S. as some extended relative. They were always welcome at his apartment, and when they came in need, they shared what was available.

Also, he could wake up in the middle of the night and rush to their call for help, wherever it was, as long as it was not a case of intentional infringement with the law. As a principle, he kept away from any of his countrymen who toyed with and deliberately violated U.S. laws. Such misguided fortunes, he believed, the culprits must own singularly, knowing well that playing with fire, you get burned, with the chances of some fires running wild, and making deep scars—way into the hearts and minds of those left behind in Africa.

Otherwise, for Sidi, like many of his towns men in America, sharing and mutual support was a strong and long cord that had no end. That was an ingredient of happiness abroad, as it was back home.

Pat, however, had her own beliefs. Like most people haunted by a painfully neglected childhood, and evolving out of a classic case of communal impersonality encountered in the West, she would say, "I look out for myself number one, 'cause folks just don't do nothing but bring you down, if you let them."

Pat resented to the swing of her hip, what she called, "Sidi's simple - mindedness and lack of experience," which she claimed, he reflected in his, "foolhardy willingness to share with, and help, every Tom, every Dick and every Harry, who comes bursting..." At this attitude, she always gasped and jerked her fists to show her frustration.

"They just see you as somebody to get over on, and there ain't nothing to it but depending and depending, like parasites!"

Pat could never understand nor accept that any of Sidi's friends could come to their apartment and expect to eat or drink, as if they lived with them, and have contributed something financially to anything in the house.

"They make me sick, your *peoples*! And they're silly to think that I too will run to their calls, or dance to their wishes like you do, as if we are all from Africa. Not me, baby. I'm an American, and I ain't going to take it—not here in America!"

CHAPTER SEVEN

Pat incidentally, was born in Mansfield, North Carolina, as she told Sidi not too long after they started living together.

"Oh, baby, I grew up in Fifth Ward, a very neglected part of Mansfield," she stated. "We were five in my family, myself, my mother, two brothers and one sister."

She informed Sidi that she was the youngest and was barely two years old when her parents got divorced. Then her two brothers, fourteen and thirteen, were the oldest, and her sister, who was next to her, was eight years old.

"Our father left us high and dry, baby. He went and never came back, not even to see us, his own children."

Pat said that between the limited welfare assistance that the State of North Carolina offered and janitorial work in a nursing home for the aged, their mother struggled and pinched every penny to support them.

"We thought the world was mad at us, as we grew up having to do without many simple necessities. You hear me? Yet we were born in this society blessed with plenty. Sidi, really..., you know, we knew even as children that we were on the wrong side of the fence, where winters grew colder, and summers steamed souls; and with most folks in the community looking out only for themselves."

Pat claimed they endured severe hardships and deprivations to barely stay alive. And she said, there was so much frightening reminders of danger ever present in their suffering neighborhood. That as kids, they were taught to keep away from strangers and trust no one. And they had no hand of the community come forth, to embrace them, to draw the line, and say, "We are us."

In fact, she habitually pointed out to Sidi that when growing up, they basically received no assistance from anybody, be it relatives or otherwise. And that was why she came to see the world as a cold place, where *nobody* could either be trusted or might seem to care, not even her own father.

According to their mother: "He ran away leaving his manhood behind, because what he has between his legs ain't nothing but a stud, if he cannot support his own children."

With quivering lips and wet eyes, she told Sidi that as she grew up, her frustration and disenchantment increased when her two elder brothers enlisted in the Vietnam war and got killed in that hellish jungle. Then she was ten.

At twelve, Pat's elder sister took off with some Cuban man. Like their father, her sister too got preoccupied with herself and never came back to see either her or their poor mother. This got Pat even more disillusioned, because she really loved her sister and knew her mother did too. But it seemed her sister decided to act like she fell from the sky, not in the least caring about either her or their aging mother who struggled to raise them all.

Pat said that when she was sixteen, her shattered graying mother decided to move back to her home town, Philadelphia. She brought Pat along. And from the moment she arrived in Philadelphia, she fell in love with the city, even though her basic realities did not change much. She and her mother stayed stuck in a *downtrodden* welfare housing project in Northwest philly. They depended on food stamps and other welfare assistance offered to them by the State of Pennsylvania.

Fed up with such a fixed state of deprivation and hopelessness, Pat said she decided to drop out of high school at seventeen. She left home in search of a better life, the kind that she saw all around but had never had.

However, bouncing in Philadelphia, in *the city of brotherly love,* she claimed to find no *brotherliness,* other than loneliness and threats of danger lurking on the streets. So she ran home several times, only to leave again, convinced there was some big chance out there waiting for her in the brightness of the city.

"I had so much bad luck and met only the wrong men. Sidi, I could have had a nervous wreck out there."

Sidi agreed, thinking of a lone girl, struggling between menial jobs with a congested catalog of exploitation and disappointments with various men, and a better life that kept being elusive.

However, now as Sidi saw the light in Pat's eyes and sensed her excitement, since they started living together, he felt good. He hoped things would work out between them.

The fact that Sidi was African and Pat was American, and they got married, fell within Sidi's range of expectations. He had tasted love—American style—frantic, uninhibited and fulfilling.

However, had Pat been sounded, she would have testified that their marriage was one of those sharp twists in life, like the amazement of stumbling upon the most mischievous boy in high school—*Now a pastor?* For if anybody had hinted to Pat, a few years back, that she would get married to an African, she would have either cursed them outright, or thought they were way out of their mind.

Like many Americans set astray about Africa, Pat was misinformed, confused and contemptful about the continent and its people.

Despite the fact that her ancestral background sprang from Africa, for Pat, the word Africa brought only dreadful and negative images. When she thought of Africa, she saw mainly poverty, worse than her's. She saw—as depicted on American television—starving babies and seemingly homeless people; thin and half-naked women gathered in groups on open fields with their flabby breasts exposed, holding sickly babies with flies hovering over their heads.

Supposedly missionary agencies that mostly show such hair-raising pictures depicting the ravages of war and famine to solicit help and pledges from the American public —yet create the *havoc scenario!* Those brief T.V. *slots-of-woes* usually form a partial basis of perceptions about Africa for many Americans and Westerners, and Pat was no exception.

Whatever the other culprits might be, Pat's mind had been programmed to look down on her African heritage, in just the same manner that the never-easing-odds against her from birth—disproportionately common among her race—had rendered her paranoid and stripped her critically, making her doubt herself and look at her race as even if not inferior, but somehow, inadequate.

While Pat, as expected, had fallen victim to self doubt since childhood, and battled with a positive identity crisis, as an adult, unfortunately, she stayed alienated from the *best of her own people.* And she deliberately blocked out all later attempts to reach her with cultural awareness and other corrective measures diligently designed by relentless African-American activists, intended to assert a positive black image in confused minds like hers.

In Pat's mind, instead, she made suspect of all cultural awakening efforts. As for those who came to her claiming to be happy and confident because they were *aware* and *proud* of their heritage and themselves, she would say: "It never rained on them. And because they got lucky!" This she held against any African-American who appeared to her to be *above* the negative mental images created about their race and their ancestry.

In such limbo, naturally, Pat had no link with her heritage and it held no meaning for her. On that issue, if she spoke, she would say, she was black and she was born in America. Period.

When asked and pressed about her racial history, she would say that she was Indian mixed, and that somebody in her family, some great grandparent was reportedly brought to America as a slave from somewhere in primitive Africa: *"A place where people lived in jungles and ate each other."* Anything to do with Africa beyond that did not interest her; that was until Sidi came.

Yet, Pat and Sidi hadn't been in matrimony for even six months, before Barbar who was always running his mouth started saying that Pat got married to Sidi, purposely seeking a welcome break from her lingering insecurities, and as a way out of her vicious circle of destitution. Ahmed hushed Barbar! But as Pat ran off more and more of Sidi's buddies, they formed similar opinions—upon knowing her obsession with material things above warm human relationships; her constant complaints and concerns about only *herself;* her sudden transformation and her instant crowning of Sidi as her prince; from the moment she got to his place—all against her testimonies of a lifelong elusive craving for similar betterment and a backdrop of solid contempt for Africans!

Sidi dismissed his friends' notions about his wife as lousy. Though sometimes as their relationship got older, Pat made him wonder, even as he claimed to be happy and felt good that the marriage happened.

By marrying Sidi, the African crowd that Pat discovered taught her new lessons about a people she had always taken for granted. As Sidi treated her with respect and more reverence than she had ever got in a relationship, she felt hard pressed to accept that a man as decent and as intelligent as Sidi could, in fact, have come from, *"..back there in backward Africa!"* as she blurted a few times.

"You must be a Prince or one of those special tribes with all the riches back there in Africa," she told Sidi on one occasion, her voice ringing with sarcasm. Then she winked and quite characteristically ventured further: "I mean, like the selected few over there where all the rest still may be running about naked and sleeping in trees and caves with snakes and monkeys."

She learned fast, however, in living together with Sidi, to better keep her distorted notions about Africa to herself. Sidi made it quite clear to her from the onset, sensing her negative mind set about Africa, that he did not entertain or care for such *ignorant misconceptions* about his background.

"Pat, let me be frank with you," he said, in a bid to correct her erroneous opinions. "I want you to know that I'm nothing but an average African. I'm neither a Prince nor somebody from a wealthy family. In fact, my background is poor, and very poor. And let me say, I'm where I am today because I strive and work hard, and because I've learned to believe in myself. But it's not been easy.

"However, I want to let you know that you offend me very much by your remarks about Africa. I can excuse your ignorance but please don't be stupid. Remember, I'm an African and proud of who I am just as much as you probably are about being an American—if not an African-American!"

"Don't get so worked up Sidi, I don't mean any harm. I was just telling you what I've heard."

"I'm not worked up or angry, Pat," Sidi remarked. "I've heard derogatory stuff like that about Africa from various people around here. Most times I've ignored them, but not when it comes from my wife, and moreover another black person. You may not know this, but generally your lack of respect for your race, and your lack of cultural pride comes from such terrible miseducation and misconception. And you're permitting it, sort of, and thereby robbing yourself of your heritage, only to stay confused and open to mental slavery."

What are you saying, boy? Hey, shut up, nigger! You are lying!

Sensing Pat's lack of interest, Sidi's dark face got even darker now.

"But Pat, please tell me, how can one claim to be anybody without pride in your people or race, your culture and your ancestry? Look at the Jews, the Italians, the Irish and even the American Indians. Do you see them recklessly looking low down on themselves? Or, can you imagine them discarding their cultures? Never! Because, culture and values make a man, without that you are lost!"

"Maybe." Pat shrugged, very bored.

"There's no maybe about it!" Sidi said, enthusiastically. "Pat, it's like your ID card, without which you are Jane Dow out there!"

"Now, Sidi, be real." Pat laughed.

"Of course, I'm as real as I can be. What I mean is this, Pat, one's culture is something to hold on to; because there are times when it's the only thing you have left..., just look at the American Indians! Our people say, if you don't know where you are going, you should at least know where you came from."

Talking in circles again. "Sidi, what are you saying?"

"I'm speaking English, right?" Sidi got up. "Okay, Pat, think of most of my countrymen you know. In spite of our educational levels, don't you see that most of us can only get menial jobs around here? Yet, don't we survive and succeed in many ways—beyond sinking in this system? Do you know why?"

"No, you tell me!"

"It's because we draw strength and pride from our background. It makes us refuse to succumb to the hurdles, the hopelessness, and the discriminations that we are confronted with constantly. Basically, our beliefs, values and pride keep us aloft."

"I know you people are strong," Pat conceded. "I really admire you Africans for that. I always wonder how you guys come here, and in a short time seem to be doing so fine."

"That's no magic, or anything unique. It's all in the mind. It's called variously perseverance, determination, or self-esteem. Simply put, it's being aware of who you are, and working hard at what you want regardless of the odds."

"Yeah, Sidi." She raised her chin up at him. "That's easy for you to say.... You've not lived in America all your life. You don't know what black people have been through here!"

"Com'on, Pat. I'm not an illiterate! Why do you think I have that—?" Sidi pointed to a narrow five-inch long wooden bookshelf in a corner of their living room. "I have over there a wealth of knowledge, about black experiences and realities from ancient times to now."

"But Sidi, those are books; I'm talking about living it, as we blacks in America have."

"Baby, I'm African, remember? The dehumanization, destabilzation and exploitation of blacks started not in America but Africa. We were invaded, subjugated, divided and exploited from the days of our ancestors to present times. How do you think Africa got divided into several little countries, such that you find Mandinkas in Gambia speaking English as their official language, while those in neighboring Senegal speak French?" Do you think we gladly decided to be so?"

"I wouldn't know, I've never been to Africa."

"Pat, that's why I tell you to read to open your mind. I have a book up there in which an African-American scholar, Dr. Naa'im Akbar talks about, *'The chains and images of psychological slavery.'* Or simply put, mental shackles: We started fighting that by getting rid of the Colonialists in Africa; that was what the civil rights struggles sought to accomplish here too; yet sadly, like a cancer, those shackles are still gnawing at the morale of quite a few people of our color in this country."

"No, Sidi, our problem here is racism."

"I know so, Pat. But.., what does racism do to its victims? Besides the alienation, doesn't it drive self-doubt and destructive thinking in their minds? Yet baby, how would those obstacles be defeated?"

"By people themselves!"

"Okay.., through self-empowerment, as Dr. Akbar says. But also, just as innocent black men now pay for the damage done to their image, somehow; so also is any black problem a collective black problem. It's not enough that one individual triumphs. A general never wins a war when all his soldiers are fallen. If you're alone standing, when all others are down, who is going to catch you when you fall?"

"Yet Sidi, here in America everybody is out only for themselves."

"No Pat, that sounds hopeless; not everybody thinks like that. There have been and there are still many committed black people out there seeking the interest and making way for people like you, and everybody. It is you that has to realize or appreciate that and change. You will be surprised what good it will do for your self-esteem.

"And that is where culture comes in. It gives you a positive identity and a sense of pride and belonging. In fact, it becomes a unifying force and makes you defy the odds, because it is all in the mind. And you owe it to yourself to free your mind from all negatives about yourself that had been injected in. Do you agree with me?"

"Well, Sidi—"

"Yes, well, Pat. Baby, for crying out loud, take charge. Check out your beliefs, as to who you are, what options you have and what you hold dear. And think about whether anybody is going to look at you as somebody if you don't look at yourself as one. Not certainly the white man!"

"But I know that."

"Good. That is why you have to face the challenge and free your mind, because nobody can do that for you. And remember, a positive mind is an able mind."

In spite of Sidi's seeming lectures to Pat about Africa, about culture, and about freeing her mind, she still was at a loss as to what to expect from Sidi's cousin Yaya, who was coming straight from Africa. In her mind, she assumed he would not look any way as decent as the Africans she had met in the U.S.

"But you guys have been Westernized," she told Sidi when they were discussing picking up Yaya at the airport. "For all I know, he might look just like one of those homeless people who live under the overpass of the freeways, or like somebody just stepping out of the penitentiary."

Sidi felt really frustrated by that speech. He realized that Pat seemed stuck with too many *distorted* notions about Africans and the continent, which had been ingrained in her mind over the years. He looked at her and shook his head, trying hard to suppress a rising anger.

"Pat, stop!" he said. And in his usual painstaking manner, he warned her: "The boy is a decent fellow, and you'll be surprised at his intelligence!"

"Well, we will see," was all she said.

Pat had cooperated with Sidi to bring Yaya to the U.S. with great reluctance and frankly, she was the least excited about his coming. As far as Pat was concerned, Sidi was being lavish with the money he used to buy that expensive airline ticket just to get Yaya over. She had told Sidi on several occasions that there were better things he could have done with all that money.

"I would like to go to Las Vegas, for instance, and you know it. You've been promising me all the time. All my friends have been there. Yet, I can't get to go. But it is okay for you to spend all that money for some damned soul to come from Africa."

"But, Pat, there is no reason for that attitude. And please cut out the curse words. As I've always told you, I'm just trying to open the way for a brother. It is something I have to do. I hope you will understand," Sidi had pleaded with her.

"Damn that, I am tired of hearing all that sorry stuff," Pat had yelled in protest, just before yielding to Sidi's plan. "But, okay, Sidi, I will go along with you on this one. Yet after this, no more of that sorry stuff of, 'let's help this or let's help that.' I need some help too."

Sidi who was pleased that the matter was resolved, even if fragilely between them, just did not say anything. He was grateful that things were going according to plan for Yaya to join them.

CHAPTER EIGHT

"We are home," Sidi announced, as he pulled into a vacant space in the apartment's parking lot.

"They are all out of it," Barbar said, about the others in the back seat who were stretched and flung, dozing.

"Wake up, gentlemen. We finally made it," Sidi said, coaxing the sleepy heads.

"Time to unload, folks. Bundle yourselves and step on your two legs," Barbar commanded, taking his seat belt off, as Sidi turned off the car's ignition and took his seat belt off too.

Everybody was yawning as they got out of the car. Ahmed got Yaya's luggage from the trunk and together they went to Sidi's apartment.

Pat was lying on the couch in the living room, reading advertisements in the classified section of the *Philadelphia Inquirer.* The stereo was easing some soft soul in the air. In spite of that, she did not miss the footsteps outside her door. When a key turned in the lock, she knew they were home. Anxiously, she folded the papers and sat up. The moment the door opened, she stood up, staring aghast at them as they walked in.

What greeted them at the door was a tantalizing mixture of fresh opium fragrance and a rich beefy-brothy onion smell, rising and enticing their nostrils and watering their mouths. They were quick to see that food was ready from looking through the transparent lace material spread over covered dishes, plates and glasses on the dinning room table—as Pat always did when expecting guests. The prospect of eating one of her delicious meals stirred a silent hubbub in their stomachs.

"It's about time you guys made it! I thought ya got lost, or something!" Pat yelled, with her eyes swiftly scanning the others, and resting on Yaya, whom she scrutinized like a commodity of controversy.

"Welcome!" she said.

"Thank you," Sidi said, going over to hug her. He felt even proud of her today, for food was ready; and in tone with the elegant furnishing of the apartment, it boasted the gratifying appearance of a place well kept.

Obviously, in their absence, Pat had done one of her special cleaning jobs. Even the rug had been recently vacuumed. This Sidi appreciated greatly.

"So how are you, darling?" he asked, his love for her burning hot in his eyes.

"I'm fine, sugar," she told her husband.

"We were delayed on the way, Pat," Barbar elected to say. "You should be thankful we are here after all."

"Sure!" Pat retorted, shooting him a hostile glance.

"Barbar is right, Pat. We got stopped by the police, they claimed for speeding, but I know better. It was just the usual harassment, you know. In any case, this is Yaya. Yaya, this is Pat, my wife."

Yaya instantly bowed slightly and stood straight at attention like he was going to salute. Hesitantly but cheerfully, he took Pat's hands. "I'm very pleased to meet you," he said.

"I'm pleased to meet you too. Welcome!"

"We've heard so much about you at home," Yaya said, still shaking Pat's hand, and grinning from ear to ear.

"Oh, really? Isn't that news?" Pat pulled her hand. "Well, later you will tell me some of those things you've heard about me. But... welcome, and feel free. Did you enjoy your trip?"

"Thanks be to God I'm here. The journey took so long that I thought we were heading for where the world ends, but it ended okay."

Barbar, Abu Janneh and Ahmed were already seated and leaning back, unwinding in the coolness inside the apartment.

"Yaya, let's take your things to your room. Excuse us, Pat, and gentlemen. I'm showing Yaya his room." Sidi grabbed Yaya's suitcase which Ahmed had dumped by the wet bar. He opened a door from the living room, to an average size room, and they entered. The room had a queen size waterbed, with a solid pine headboard and a night-stand with a lamp on top, the umbrella shaped shade of which still had plastic wrapped around it.

"This is your room," Sidi said closing the door. In a low tone, he warned Yaya. "Watch what you say around Pat. She is very paranoid about what she imagines my people think and say about her. It's the cultural difference, I guess, or just basic insecurity. No big thing, but you just know that."

"Sure, Sidi. But, believe me, I didn't mean anything bad. I just blurted what I said out there just now out of excitement. Anyway, all I've heard about her are good things, and that's what I'll tell her."

"Good. Now, this is your closet," Sidi said placing Yaya's suitcase in a little compartment cut off from the room by two sliding wooden doors. There was no room to stand inside, even empty as it was. He looked up at the two metal bars running at the top from wall to wall, and said, "I will get you some hangers later, for your clothes."

Yaya was looking all over the room and sighing with contentment.

Sidi moved across the room to another door. "This is your bathroom. It's all yours." He opened the door to a clean self-contained room of full-bath. "We have ours. It's connected to our bedroom, just like yours."

"This is a nice place," Yaya said, observing the convenience. He thought of his flat in Sobala, which was modern as this—where everything was alright with him! That was, until his grandma died and left him a mystical inheritance on her deathbed; and because he wouldn't do as she said, she haunted him out of the country.

Sidi was wondering why Yaya suddenly had a sad look on his face. "We moved here purposely because we were expecting you," he said impressively.

"Thanks, Sidi. Really, I don't know how to thank you."

"That's okay, man. This is my obligation; to make you feel at home and happy."

While Sidi was showing Yaya his room, Barbar and Ahmed seized on the chance to engage Pat in their usual conversation. Most times, this had the tendency of turning into a heated argument. Somehow, it always had to do with a tug-of-war over values, African versus American.

As a habit, Ahmed and Barbar always tried to browbeat Pat into accepting some aspect of African culture, some of which she found utterly shocking. On this occasion, as usual, it was Barbar that got Pat the jitters.

"Well, Pat, now you have a second husband," he teased. "You should really count yourself lucky, like some queen. Now you can truly sit back and relax and be sure that all your needs will be met promptly."

"Look! Why are you saying that? I don't need a second husband, right? Sidi is enough for me. In fact, he meets my needs very well. And you, Barbar, don't you start any mess by suggesting anything, right?"

Ahmed laughed, and Barbar fitfully fell laughing.

"Relax, Pat," Ahmed said. "Barbar is not suggesting anything outrageous. He is barely making a statement of culture."

"What culture?" Pat snapped cynically.

"Our Mandinka culture, of course," Ahmed retorted. "Don't you know that if you were in our country, and God forbid, Sidi dies, Yaya could be your next husband? Bestowed with all rights to take off from where his brother left?"

"You mean they do like in a political office, when the deputy takes over if the boss dies?" Pat asked, standing sullen, hands on her hip, eyebrows narrowed and pupils wandering.

"Yes, if that's how you see it!" Ahmed retorted.

These guys aren't lying. They don't normally lie about their culture. As Pat thought of that, a tremor of shock waded through her, followed by a charged silence. Meanwhile, the Africans with amusement stood watching her reaction. Suddenly she twisted her lips in a saucy smile. *Bull come,* her mind said, *I don't want to hear it!*

"Hey! You Barbar and you Ahmed, this is not Africa. And you see? That's the whole problem with you people. You leave Africa and come here and think you can act like you're in Africa. But this is America, baby. It does not work like that here. And—"

The door opened, bringing Yaya and Sidi.

The argument instantly stopped like a halted motor.

"Munch time," Sidi announced going towards the dining room table.

His countrymen filed behind him, like recruits after the sergeant. All the men got seated as Pat leaned back in her seat, browsing through the newspaper.

"You guys go ahead. I had mine, after waiting forever."

For dinner, there was a large casserole dish of parboiled rice, and another of beef stew, with a medium bowl of mixed vegetables, full to the brim, the sweet peas and carrots sweating and standing out in their crowd.

Without words, everybody had healthy servings, and were scooped in earnest, clattering silver on plates between mouthfuls.

Yaya decided to make an impression, to compliment Pat, for her effort. "You cook great, Pat," he said.

"Yes, Yaya, Pat is a good cook," Barbar remarked, even before Pat had the chance to accept the compliment. "I may disagree with her on most things, but I concede that she's good at putting the pieces together to make the stomach happy."

"You bet," Pat said, with a sly smile on her lips. "And Barbar, you happen to have quite a large stomach to be made happy. Don't you?"

"Well, I make no qualms about that. I'm a whole six foot standing and robust. What do you expect, Pat?"

"Some money sometimes. Food costs money you know? We don't buy it here with stone. Maybe you do in Africa, but then, that is Africa."

"Pat, please stop," Sidi appealed. "And hey, people, I wish you'd let us enjoy the food. Please, Pat, these are guests. I don't expect anything from them, and you should not either."

Pat hissed silently, and frowned to register her point. She then sat tight-faced, which Yaya noticed. He gave her two bows, one for courtesy and the other to show concern.

Sidi too caught Pat's face. He tried eye contact but failed, and gave up, knowing she was boiling with anger. The others were preoccupied and seemed to care less, with spoons scrapping plates. When they looked up, it was to the radio, in a listening mode, to happy voices chatting.

"Damn free loaders, how I wish I can tell them. They come here all the time and stuff themselves without leaving a dime. All I hear is big empty talks; Africa this, Africa that. I wish they would stop depending so much. But I don't blame them. I blame that fool, Sidi. He thinks he's still in Africa. They don't know there are no free lunches in America! But I will tell them one day. And oh! I'm so sick of it? But I'll wait. There will come a better time. Next time!"

While Pat was boiling within herself, the meal was over. Following Sidi, everybody said thanks to her—an excellent cook. She barely shook her head.

Sidi and Yaya took the dishes to the kitchen. "We will see about these later. Let's join the others." Sidi said.

However, shortly, Ahmed, Barbar and Abu Janneh left, promising to stop by later in the evening to chat with Yaya and hear the latest news about home.

"Thanks again, Pat, that was a good meal," Sidi said. Pat didn't respond. He tried soothing her. "Pat, you are a good woman, and a good wife too." Still no response. To save face, with Yaya sitting there, he added, "It's okay to get mad sometimes, but don't mind those guys. I wouldn't worry about them."

"That's you," Pat said. Her face didn't budge from the radio, and she continued her humming to Whitney Houston's, *I Have Nothing*, playing on an FM station.

"Pat? Since everybody is gone, let's talk for a minute, please. It is important."

Pat turned towards him. "Okay, you have my attention."

Yaya sat hearing, yet distracting himself with an old issue of *Ebony* magazine that he picked from among other journals on the bottom shelf of the center table.

"Pat, this is about Yaya," Sidi stated. "As you know, he is a blood relative, my first cousin. If we go by our custom, he is your brother-in-law. And with him coming here, he is an addition to us. Our responsibility now is to get him adjusted to the American society. We would have to do that together. Most importantly, I look forward to seeing you two get along. That would make it easy for us all, as there is no telling how long we may be staying together."

"I'll do my best," Pat responded, and in afterthought, she snapped. "You tell him to watch those ones that just left here. He should not join them or start acting like them, especially that Barbar and that Ahmed."

Yaya's mouth opened in a wide smile. Sidi noticed and winked, to caution him. He then turned to his wife.

"Com'on, Pat, that's the least I am worried about. I would rather we talk about better things, about ways of helping the guy. He's an adult, you know. He can decide for himself what's good or bad for him."

"Sure!" Pat retorted, rapidly chewing her upper lip and looking away, frowning.

She was boiling afresh. It was statements like those from Sidi that made her think he paid no attention to her words. Here, the boy was new in the country, she was advising him against those *devils*, yet there was Sidi saying something else!

Pat thought of several reasons to contradict what Sidi had just said. She knew of many adults who could not tell the difference between what was good or bad for them. Sidi himself happened to be one—as far as she was concerned! However, she declined to comment, not to get started, with the guest and all that. Besides, she had other things on her mind for this day.

She gave Sidi a not-too-pleasant glance. He got up and left for the bedroom.

"Tell me about your trip," she told Yaya.

"My trip? It was very exciting but tedious." Yaya said, warming to Pat. "It took a total of eighteen hours flight time to come from Sobala to New York. And that is apart from our stop in London.

We were in London for six hours, our flight connecting time, they said."

Sidi was on the telephone in the bedroom. "Yes! Yes! My cousin. My first cousin. He just arrived from Africa. This morning! He is h—"

Hear him, no telephone manners, screaming like they're squeezing his balls. Pat hissed silently at Sidi.

"I didn't know where to go in London, so I made the best of my stay at the airport," Yaya said, cheerfully smiling at Pat. "I visited the duty free shops, talked with some English people and even met a man from Manika Kunda, my country."

Uh-huh, so you people go there too? Pat wondered, or was that what she heard? She had to intensely listen, wanting to scream—slow down, so I can understand you. Now she watched Yaya's face keenly as he spoke, trying to read meaning into his words from the movement of his lips.

"Yes, I didn't believe it," Yaya excitedly babbled. "A man from my country. He worked at one of the snack shops at Heathrow airport. He was so happy to see me, like I was by stumbling on him. He offered me a table and waited on me while we talked about home, about politics and the situation in our country. He told me about life in London. He was sad.

"About black reality and progress in the UK, unlike America, which has many great blacks like Andrew Young, Jesse Jackson, Julian Bonds, Ben Hooks, Farrankhan and all the black stars, who stand committed to black welfare."

Oh yeah? Pat was impressed. *So he knows about all those people?*

Yaya looked at her and smiled. He felt proud just from calling all those big names—of great African-Americans! That would let Pat know that even though he was just coming from Africa, yet he was informed.

"Manjo, was the fellow's name. He claimed he had an M. Sc. in Mathematics from Cambridge University, but since graduation all he had done was calculate the tables to clean in that snack shop.

"He said he didn't want to go home either, because all he could do there is be a teacher and do worse —if they cannot even pay him when the month ends—like they're doing to other teachers in Manika Kunda. He told me I was fortunate to be coming to America, which was where he wanted to come, but had no help.

"I was with him for three hours, watching him cleaning the tables, welcoming customers and waiting on them. I felt sad for him, doing that sort of job with all his education; so I told him I had to leave before I miss my flight. He gave me his address and telephone number. I wore away the rest of the time wandering about the airport. But overall, I will say, I enjoyed the trip. And thanks be to God, I made it safely."

Sidi had returned, and was sitting on the recliner, smiling happily, seeing those two communicating.

But it was with resignation that Pat waited for Yaya to finish or stop. All the while he talked, she was telling herself how thick his accent was: *"Stronger than even Sidi's. He's probably mixing English with Mandinka or Swahili or some African dialect. What? He talks fast, like he's got a hot potato in his mouth!"*

When Yaya stopped, Pat could only smile and sigh, and look at him.

"Yaya, Pat is a wonderful wife." Sidi complimented his wife, happy at the smile on her face, not knowing she was looking at Yaya because she was amazed and puzzled at the speed with which he talked.

"Yes, Sidi, I can see that already. She is really a good woman."

Pat smiled widely at Yaya. She decided she had lingered long enough, or shown enough hospitality by her presence. She got up, excused herself and went into the bedroom.

"I heard Grandma Fatu died, over one year ago, is that correct?" Sidi asked.

"Yes, she did, in fact this month makes it exactly one year six months since she died, and it happened right in my arms."

"Oh, no! That was some luck, wasn't it?"

"Really. They sent me a telegram that she was seriously sick. I went to see if I could bring her to the hospital in Sobala, but she died the moment I got there."

"Some timing right? But at least you witnessed it."

"I more than witnessed it. I was part of it and it was I that broke the news."

"But she was quite a legend. Wasn't she?"

"Yes, she was, in her own rights."

Suddenly, they heard Pat screaming from the bedroom. "Sidi! Sidi! One minute please."

"Whom did she choose to take up with her work?" Sidi asked Yaya, ignoring Pat's call.

Yaya cleared his throat, as if suppressing an itching cough.

Pat appeared at the doorway frowning. "Sidi, I was calling you!"

Sidi saw the checkbook in her hand and got up instantly.

He joined her in the bedroom.

Good timing! Yaya heaved a long sigh. He couldn't have honestly answered the last question that Sidi asked, and didn't want to lie to him. Yet he had no intention of disclosing to either Sidi or anybody in America, that it was he, whom Grandma Fatu appointed to take up after her with her work as a bone healer.

What would be the point? They won't believe it. I still don't, either. But as sure as the sun shining outside, I was the one that she picked, just before she died, to be her successor. Me, of all people. I never opened my mouth about it in the family. Because, even though they would have felt bad, knowing I'm the most wrong person she picked, still they would've pressured me to do as she said; for fear of the sky falling on my head certainly if I ignore her words.

Defiance in such a traditional matter has been unheard of; nobody in the family could either imagine the price or wish it for an enemy. In fact, but for one man in whom I confided, only God knows what price I could have paid. Yet, I can't talk about it as he advised me, and as Grandma Fatu always emphasized. For though I'm safe now, there's some big secrecy. A great risk, I know, and many taboos, which can't be broken!

Yaya could hear Pat and Sidi in their bedroom talking in hushed tones. He thought of Grandma Fatu, and couldn't believe that she died less than two years ago; because the heritage that she left with him and its aftermath had tormented him so much that it seemed like ages since it all started.

He had such a big dent in his memory—caused by what transpired between him and Grandma Fatu on her deathbed—that by Sidi simply bringing up her death and asking about her successor, it sort of just brought the images flooding his mind afresh, like it all happened only yesterday.

Even now, sitting in Sidi's living room in Philadelphia, with Sidi and his wife in their bedroom, Yaya's mind was gone. It had flown to Wuyadu, his maternal ancestral home, a wooded village about twenty miles away from Taényadu, his home town.

It all started one year, six months ago, he thought, now vividly having the incident in total recall.

He was involuntarily recasting the scene, once more, like a person blurting under hypnosis before the widening and glaring eyes of a psychiatrist.

"Yaya, are we alone?" Grandma Fatu had asked, with faint eyes, on her deathbed. *I was on my knees feeling her pulse.*

99

"Yes Grandma, just you and me, please sleep. I'll be here by your side."

"My time has come, my child. I am glad you made it." She strenuously moved her other hand, reaching back under her pillow. She pulled out a leaf, almost withered and all crumpled. She sighed, and then slowly slanted towards me, groaning. "Here, hold this leaf." She coughed. "Do you know it?"

"Yes, Grandma." It was her secret leaf. I loved Grandma Fatu dearly, since childhood, but I dreaded that leaf entirely, and those people it brought, bloody, groaning and crying all the time.

Even as an adult and far away in the city, I could sometimes see the blood and hear those groans in my mind. And that was how that stayed with me, all because of this leaf. I wished Grandma Fatu had nothing to do with it. But she cherished it, and had always confided in me about it. When she did this, I always had my eyes open but my mind away—so far away!

Now she was showing me that awful leaf again. "Of course, Grandma," I said, "you showed it to me several times and said not to tell anybody."

"And you didn't?" She seemed to be holding her breath.

"Never! Grandma, never!"

"Good!" She sighed. "That was on purpose. It was a test." She coughed fitfully, and smiled at me. But I could feel the pain inside her, by her irregular breaths. Her face was now serious. "I want you to rub that leaf into liquid in your palms and put your palms into mine."

The brown of her eyes had enlarged and seemed burning red. I did as she said, all confused, while she was gasping for breath like her life depended on this.

Then she gave me her thin palms. As we held palms, suddenly her whole face was glowing, as she said happily:

"You have been chosen after me, my child; and just as my grandfather passed on this heritage to me, I shall now pass it on to you and you alone in the family. You must represent, cherish, and continue to your dying day, this infinite blessing that is a tradition in our family. Or I will see no rest in my grave." Then, she blew out like a busted balloon, and laid still.

Thunderous shocks streaked through me. This wasn't happening.

"What, Grandma? No, Grandma! Why me? Oh, no! wake up! No, no! I don't...." It was so useless. She was not breathing. I checked her pulse. There was none. I couldn't believe she died right off! And to leave me so stuck without giving me a choice?

As the image reeled off Yaya's mind, he recalled yet again, how then he had sat, open-mouthed, and was shaking like a leaf and drenching in his sweat as if somebody had spitefully poured a bucket of water over his head. He was confused and sad for two reasons. His beloved Grandma had just passed away in his arms and her corpse laid in front of him. To make matters worse, she had left him an inheritance he hated and the demands of which he wouldn't accept, not at his young age and with his ambition.

Sidi came back to his seat. "I'm sorry Yaya, Pat kept me in there."

"I understand, man. That's what it means to have a wife," Yaya responded.

"Okay, we were talking about Grandma Fatu. Who did you say she asked to take up after her?"

"I really don't know, Sidi," Yaya said and closed his eyes. He placed his hands behind his head to prop it and leaned back on the couch. "As far as I know, nobody has come forth to make any claims," he said, without opening his eyes.

Sidi was watching him. He thought about that and knew it didn't sound right.

"Isn't that strange? Her work was a special inheritance in the family, since when I know not. I can't believe she died and did not pass it over to somebody. " Sidi shook his head and said, "That is sad. It's all because of Westernization! Things are changing and we are losing our values."

"Yes, Sidi," Yaya said. He looked at his cousin and smiled sarcastically. *You can say so, Sidi. But I wish you had been there so she could have left it with you. Big value indeed. I don't see it that way. In fact, that was why I ran away to here.*

Pat emerged in tennis shoes, tight-fitting jeans, and a cashmere blouse with a purse under her arm.

Her husband looked up at her as she stood over him, while Yaya studied her from behind. Pat's jeans laid exquisitely on her shapely thighs, her long legs, and her round behind, stretching it to the limits in curves. *These sexy American women,* Yaya thought, giving her credit for her figure.

"I'm going to meet Brenda. I need to take her to a store." Pat said.

"Why can't Brenda go to the store by herself? I don't see the point," Sidi babbled.

"Well, I need to go too. There's something I want to get from there."

"Then, I guess you are going to the store."

101

"Isn't that what I said?"

"Bye-bye, Pat. Don't stay too long."

"I won't. Yaya, I will be back soon. Feel at home. Okay?" And she swung out.

"I didn't know your wife is black. The news we heard home was that you married a white woman," Yaya said.

"But of course, any woman you marry here is a white woman to our people," Sidi retorted. "In fact, as soon as you say she's not from home, they say you've decided on a white woman. That's even if the woman's complexion is darker than yours."

They both laughed at that.

"Quite interesting how our people think," Sidi said, still grinning. "Tell me, what's the general condition with them?"

"They're living. And for right now, that's the best one can say about their conditions."

"Hardship, right?"

"Yes, hardship."

"When last did you visit Kurudu?"

"About three weeks before I came. Your parents and the family are doing well. I went to say good-bye to them. Everybody was appreciative of everything you are doing from here. They told me to greet you, that they will be writing soon. Remember, what you said about letters being opened at the airport?"

"Yes, it beats me why. But let me ask, is it true what they say, that things have deteriorated so badly in the country that survival for most people is an ordeal?"

"It is worse. Like it is humorously put, many are sucking air for food."

"And they say the salaries of government workers are squandered, left and right, with all forms of corruption going on?"

"Yes, quite true," Yaya confirmed, strongly nodding. Then his face dropped. "In fact, the style now is *checkgate,* a scheme by which some of our ministers and their accountant-cohorts are having heydays, with ghost workers on payroll in most government departments. Manika Kunda is swindled sweating, foreign aids and all, while the people are starving."

"That's what I heard. That the masses cannot afford even yams, the basic food any more? What happened to farming?"

"Farming? It became old. All the youths that helped on the farms went to school, and now, everybody wants office jobs. They are all in the cities."

"Isn't that pathetic?" What's in the cities for them?"

"They're finding out," Yaya stated.

"It reminds me of our other countrymen who some years back flooded the diamond mines in Kurudu; in their youths, deserting schools and sweet homes, for quick riches!"

"Yes," Yaya said. "And many missed that quick bus to riches. And now with the diamonds gone, most of them are thinking all over."

"Any sensible person could've predicted such dilemma," Sidi said. "Yet pretty soon, some of them will be blaming the system and taking to arms, and preying on innocent citizens."

"As armed robbers?" Yaya asked.

"What else? Or, if they are led by some disgruntled high profile personality or a confused idealist, they would stylishly call themselves *rebels*—overhauling the system!"

"Thank God that rebel wave has not yet got to Manika Kunda as it has in some African countries," Yaya said.

"But Yaya, from the news we get here, while in places like Eritrea, rebel activities might have been justified as a struggle for freedom, in many other countries it's just anarchy upon the land. And the destruction and holding to ransom of poor defenseless people by corrupt and disillusioned individuals, lured by greed for naked power and unearned wealth. So with access to arms, they manipulate a group of vulnerable youths and call themselves rebels, seeking to change the system, and yet go looting and raping pregnant women like it's been in Chad, Liberia, Sierra Leone and Somalia."

"I've heard those shocking tales, too." Yaya said.

"And yet, in history, all worthy political revolutions were by the peasants, the suppressed and the working class who united and fought to improve their conditions," Sidi stated. "But heartless atrocities against rural people and peasants to change a system?"

"It's anarchy by the people to the people!" Yaya said with cynicism. "If not.., democracy all misunderstood."

"To me, Yaya, those vexing wars in Africa seem more like the inter-tribal wars in pre-colonial days, but they're even worse now with Western technology and ammunition. Yet the sad thing about it all is the destruction of innocent lives and the hardening of youths who slay each other like fowls."

Yaya shook his head. "Really, in Manika Kunda, I hope that doesn't become the fate of our disillusioned white-collar youths of today, whose primary occupation is parading on the streets in the cities, crying hard times and no jobs."

"When many could be having large peanut farms and getting

rich," Sidi said. "Does the government encourage farming or give any incentives to aspiring farmers?"

"Yes, by lip service. And let me tell you how they show it; a few years ago, a generous country gave us fertilizer for free, instead of giving it to the poor farmers who badly needed it, some big shot diverted it to a neighboring country for sale, to get foreign exchange, for his personal use. The newspapers got wind of that and it made headlines. Now, most international agencies have started delivering their assistance themselves to the people, since they've realized some of our leaders don't believe in delivering."

"That's an awful situation," Sidi cried. "And what about education? Yaya, I think what we need in that country is more technical and occupational training. People should be trained with essential skills to independently survive. That could be the core of any foreseeable middle class. If a man can make ends meet, he can aspire to anything. Is the government doing anything about that?"

"Yes, they've made some inroads; we now have a few technical schools."

"That's good," Sidi said. "Indeed, with this global recession and the extreme hardship in the country, it's good that the government is owning up to the people, for once."

"For where? Instead, some are just getting worse. Sidi, the recession might be an international crisis, but our unique problem has been selfless leadership. It's evident that all what some of our leaders learned from their colonial mentors was how to steal and channel our money out of the country, to their next homes, where they end invariably in exile, as the case with most bad leaders."

"Quite sad," Sidi cried.

"A daring journalist once said, 'By all descriptions, we are a nation of economically abused people, and by none other than our leaders.' The poor journalist was thrown in jail immediately after that."

"But so far, those are our gains from independence. If our politicians are not strangling some poor journalist, they would be killing themselves for power, or robbing the nation clean. Yet when will it end?"

"Only God knows, Sidi. Maybe when they learn to stop being greedy or when people in leadership realize that their positions are not meant for them to enrich themselves at the expense of the people. And when they realize that they have limits and must opt out when they can't deliver."

"You are right. To imagine the riches we have and yet the

degree of poverty plaguing our people. It's disheartening to think of the way our people are suffering! Indeed, the sad letters I get. Talk about letters dropping tears."

"What else do you expect in that situation, when hardship grays the youths and withers the old?" Yaya asked.

"Just a rotten deal!" Sidi said. "But a time will come for reckoning."

"You bet it will. And if it's happening right now in other places, those corrupt ones in Manika Kunda would be fooling themselves to imagine that they are invulnerable. Didn't a historic figure once say, 'You can fool some of the people some of the time, you can fool some people all of the time; but you can't fool all the people all the time'?"

"Yes, that was Abraham Lincoln, if I'm not mistaking," Sidi said.

Yaya yawned and nodded in agreement.

"Hey, man, I know you are tired, after all those long hour you've been cramped up in the air. Why don't you go get a shower and get some sleep? I bet you need a lot of catching up on that."

"Right. I'm as fatigued as one who just finished ploughing rice seeds in a large farm all alone." Yaya stood, stretching himself and yawned again. "Excuse me for that, Sidi." He stood still. "Man, I'm sorry.., I wish I could bring your letters...."

"No problem. At least the postal system is still functioning, and those who want to write will still write."

"You can be sure of that," Yaya said going towards his room. As he stepped on the cold tile in the dining room, it struck him that he was barefooted. He came back and picked up his shoes which he had kicked off under the center table to flex his feet. Barefooted, he walked to his room.

CHAPTER NINE

It was 9:30 p.m. when Yaya woke up. He had slept for six hours straight, compensating for his sleeplessness in the past twenty-four hours through the journey. When he opened his eyes, the room was totally engulfed in darkness. Yet, Yaya felt thrilled beyond measure. Like one creeping gratefully out of a smashed automobile wreck, he thanked his stars, and shoved blissful sighs of relief, for waking up to find himself where he was.

In his sleep, it seemed he was bound hands and feet, and yelping, in an embarrassing and disturbing scenario. He had ventured out alone on his first day in the country, just getting to know his neighborhood. On the sidewalk a block or two away from where he lived, a van had suddenly pulled up beside him and swerved to a grinding halt.

Immediately, two husky white males had jumped out of the van and charged at him in sprints that shook the ground. Yaya sensed trouble as his mind raced to tales of kidnapping that abound in American news and crime stories. The men were instantly upon him. Next, Yaya, with pounding chest and cringing stomach, imagined guns pointed at him.

Aghast, transfixed, and dismayed, Yaya swallowed dry saliva, and closed his eyes expecting to be swept off his feet and thrown into the van to be taken to some underground outfit, blindfolded, and awaiting further instructions. Who would pay the ransom money? That confounded him. In hopeless despair, he opened his eyes only to be confronted with flashing badges and the men claiming to be agents of U.S. Immigration.

What? Oh, no! This is just as bad. Yaya's knees knocked.

"What is your name, mister?" The two officers proceeded to question him, alternately.

"My name? Yaya LaTalé," he said with trembling voice.

"Show us your green card."

"*Waeyoo! Awaar!*" Yaya uttered a typical Mandinka panic cry.

"Green card? I don't have."

"Show us an I.D."

"I.D? *Awaar!* I don't have."

"What about your passport?"

"My passport? It's at home."

"Great, as if that does you any good. What country are you from?"

"When did you come to America?"

"Manika Kunda. I'm from Manika Kunda. I just came today, this morning."

"Bingo!" one of the officers said. "Then you must be our man."

The other officer informed him that he was arrested and that they were taking him to New York Immigration for questioning.

"Wait! Wait! No warrant?" Yaya asked, delaying the arrest.

"We don't need a— "

Yaya took to his heels.

"What? Hey!"

The officers chased, quickly catching up with him. They grabbed him, pulled his hands behind him and slammed a handcuff on his wrists. He struggled to say something but his mouth was heavy, and the men didn't want to hear it. He felt partly carried and partly pushed, and swiftly swept into the front seat of the van. The officers sandwiched him and the van took off.

He was taken straight to the tallest building he had ever entered. The lift went up forever and stopped at what he thought was *Level 96* or *Level 69* written on the wall in front of him. Out of the lift, the officers took him to a long rectangular room that was divided in the center by a thick net of iron bars, forming a cell on the other side, with a narrow door in the center and a big padlock on it. On the side of the room towards the entrance, a long table stood with a few chairs around it. Yaya was told to sit on one of the chairs.

One of the officers that brought him left briefly and came back with a round, forty-something white man. This man was dressed in a blue suit that seemed exquisite. Surmising the new arrival to be an important person, Yaya stood up to greet him but was commanded promptly by the agents to sit down. Still, as he sat, Yaya greeted the man. He looked at Yaya and in that gaze, Yaya saw a chilling contempt in his deep, pondy green eyes, spelling doom. Indignation and fear such as he had never known further cramped his stomach.

The man, with a hint of a frown, informed Yaya that he was a judge. He said that Yaya was charged with perjury and fraud for submitting false information to immigration with intentions to enter the country to become an illegal alien.

"Anything to say in your defense?" the informal judge asked. He whistled undertone, like he was enjoying the torment.

Yaya wished he could melt and vanish, rather than sit there answerable to that man. Because he now felt miserable like a person stripped stark naked and put on parade to be jeered at!

Leaning forward and frowning condescendingly, the man asked again, this time harshly, "Anything to say in your defense?" And he started stroking his mustache upwards with a finger.

Yaya sat silent. The shock and blatant spite on the man's face had gotten the best of him. And due to an upsurge in his ingrained aversion to humiliation, he made no effort to speak. Though his visa was valid and he had a million defenses in his mind, he deliberately uttered nothing.

The jolly posturing judge was taken aback and obviously interpreted the silence as guilt. Without much ado, he thereby informed Yaya that he was declared, *persona non grata,* which meant, Yaya could not live in the U.S. any longer. He was to be deported promptly! Yaya was told all arrangements were being finalized to that effect, pending the arrival of a plane that was to take him back—*same way Munda was sent!*

Immediately, one of the arresting officers opened the iron cage and commanded Yaya in, slamming the door behind him. Yaya heard the lock click and turned to see the men leaving. He called out to them to please get him out, but they were gone.

In that mental pandemonium, Yaya broke out in tiny beads of sweat that drenched him to the toes. Like a certified lunatic, he kept shaking his head wildly and stamping his feet, as he stared vacantly through the iron bars of his cell at a blank wall.

Grandma Fatu, did you do this? Must you destroy me completely? What did I do to deserve this? Was this caused by my enemies back home? And why? The questions were endless, but there were no answers. Tormented by the situation, he tossed and turned in his sleep.

Somehow, a crowd of laughter filtered in this nightmare, live from the living room. This suddenly jerked Yaya to reality. When it dawned on him that he must have been dreaming, he bounced and rolled sideways, and rolled over on his stomach, luxuriating in the waterbed, which he altogether thanked Sidi for providing him.

Recalling the dream, he laughed his head off in silliness. And then, he decided to keep the weird dream a secret. Now in absolute control of himself, he thanked The Almighty again, and prayed silently to Mighty Allah, for his blessings and guidance, after which his spirit soared.

Feeling invigorated, Yaya got up abruptly, happy with the world. Now accustomed to the darkness, he located the switch and turned on the light, blinking at the brightness. As he surveyed the room, the voices in the living room diverted him again. The noise he heard sounded like a Boy Scout meeting without order, except that in this case there was music in the background.

Wow, there must be a crowd out there, probably fellow Manika Kundans. Sidi must have told them about my coming. My God, I must have slept too much. Let me bathe quick and join them.

"And here he is!" Barbar shouted characteristically the moment Yaya stepped out of his room.

"Surprise!" Ahmed prompted, screaming.

"Surprise!" It seemed everybody in the living room screamed in chorus, with Pat's voice distinctly screeching in the bawling clamor.

Whew! Yaya instinctively stepped back, wondering if he was indeed awake or in the right place. By now, he was a silent spectator to a speeding contest between his heartbeat and his mind. His mind won, making sense of the situation. This must be some practical joke, he thought, but he knew he was awake and in the right place.

He could see Sidi, Pat and Ahmed, and the others that picked him up at the airport that morning. But there were many strange people present too, and they were all dressed up. Some were dressed in African styles, like Barbar and a few others who had on safari jackets and matching pants. Others had on double breasted suits, sports coats and different kinds of Western apparel. The crowd was mixed. There were as many women as men, and even a few white people.

Instantly, it became obvious to Yaya that he had stumbled on a party scenario, and that the party was for him. However, the shock, the strangeness of the faces and all those eyes that were focused on him made him self-conscious and had his feet unsure as he paced to where Sidi was standing.

"This is your welcome party, man," Sidi said, in response to Yaya's bewildered look; as if that information was necessary. "It was nothing planned," he said in half truth. "But hey, relax and enjoy."

Yaya felt a tinge of embarrassment, topped with a sense of elation. And although still confused, he felt excited and joyous. Yet he decided to exercise restraint and look dignified, knowing he was the guest of honor.

"You've got to relax, man, and mix with the people," Sidi whispered in his ears. "Everybody here is a friend."

Yaya fretted a little, but moved, smiling and exuding cordiality, and embarked on a greeting spree. He was shaking hands, nodding and waving as he saw fit. He estimated forty people at the party.

After the lull that greeted Yaya's appearance, the music picked up volume, and soon people got busy. A few people jumped on the dance floor, partners were drawing closer, or engaging in conversations, with the singles acting single.

Now that the party was going, Yaya felt immensely at ease. There were less eyes on him, so he quickly returned to his position near Sidi, from where he indulged his eyes. Laughing in his belly with excitement as he watched the people, most of whom he didn't know, he commended them for the party. And he gave them *excellent* for their success at surprising him so neatly. A perfect conspiracy—not even Sidi had given him a hint!

Image conscious as Yaya was, though, he wished he had had the faintest advance notice of the party, if only to present himself appropriately dressed for the occasion, and in total control of himself. Yet as it was, he reflected on his appearance, and decided he was okay. His better instinct had forewarned him that first impressions count and he knew that goes with being presentable.

When he heard those voices from the living room and knew he would soon be joining them, he had put on black wool blend slacks, with matching socks, and a pointed-toe black leather shoes, topped with a half-gown. The half-*buba* flowed to his elbows and came down to his knees. It was of native *gara,* which was made from tying and dying a light colored garment in one or more colors. Yaya's gown had multiple designs of rounded-rainbow, from cycles in brown, mauve and gold.

His choice of the gown was essentially ethnic like the gown itself. It was an assertion of cultural allegiance as to who he was. However, for a party, he would have dressed differently, in something much comfortable for partying, especially partying American-style. But that was too late. He decided he didn't want to appear vain to everybody present by changing clothing in the middle of a party. Besides, he told himself, undoubtedly in that conspicuous gown, he looked like the guest of honor; even as he wasn't sure how he was going to swing in it—come dance time!

"You are the center of attraction, " Barbar materialized behind him, breathing hard behind his neck. "Mister, just see all those beautiful women here. You better start enjoying."

"I am, already," Yaya responded evasively.

"Well, get down with it. This is your party. And hey, who knows, it may be a long time before you have another like this thrown for you."

Yaya thought Barbar was belaboring the point. He decided not to pay any attention to the incitement. He knew he would let go and have fun when and if he got ready. Meantime, he decided to let his eyes do the enjoying, the marveling, especially at the lustrous beauties that abounded the place. The ladies in their flashy dresses and short skirts, leggy and all flesh, were assembled, it seemed as if cut out of some big sexy catalog.

Yaya wondered which of them were single, or if, indeed, they would consider a penniless and baffled newcomer like himself. Quickly, he dismissed his wistful thinking—that womanizing thought—and told himself that he should be concentrating on reorienting his life and getting over his setbacks since Grandma Fatu's death.

The party scene was like many Yaya had been to back home. With chairs against the walls, the center of the living room had been cleared to make room for a dance floor. And with the music jamming, many people were dancing and watching a young man about 21-years-old who was getting down in a frenzy to, *You Can't Touch This*, away from his partner, as if he was M.C. Hammer himself. He wore glittering blue pants and a shiny light-blue rayon long sleeved shirt, buttoned to his wrists, with Jeri curls on his head. He could have been mistaken for an American, except for the facial tribal marks. The young man's deserted partner, a tall slim lady, was stepping backwards farther and farther from the spotlight into the crowd, while he just went on getting more room and twisting himself like a cobra wrapping on a tree trunk.

On the sides, people sat, and stood, and moved about, socializing and mellowing out. Some seemingly unattached men, working on dates, or seeking dance partners, or just being nice, could be seen going about, charming the ladies. A few of their counterparts stood in the corners, arms folded, shaking to the music.

Barbar, Abu Janneh and two others—the debaters—were passionately engaged in an argument near the bar.

And like everywhere, the defiant 'I'm single if you're single, and ready to go,' were inadvertently making a show of seductively looking pretty, and saying it all, with their daring grins, provocative countenances, and hard flesh.

The unencumbered couples, the happily married and lovers stood out, crowding themselves, even as others excused their partners and moved about in temporary freedom—as if they were by themselves—with angry eyes following them, watching for the first sign of when they would start getting into some mess!

In Yaya's eyes, what he saw different was the ostentation and the affluence which smacked among youths in this party as compared to similar parties in Manika Kunda. Everybody here looked sharp, from head to toe, as if they came competing for a Mr-&-Mrs-Well-Dressed. Their cheeks were full, their faces glowing and heads shiny, like the jewelry worn around their necks, fingers and on their wrists. They showed not the least suggestion of worries as to where their next rent, or next meal would come from.

Boy! These guys are enjoying life in this country. Just see how robust and relaxed they seem, when their contemporaries back home are—

"Wake up, Yaya!" Pat came to disrupt his thoughts.

She grabbed him by the arm and ushered him to the dance floor. Yaya forgot about the limitations of his gown, which swung with the music like it had no other use. Dancing with Pat to Michael Jackson's *Black or White,* he moved with the music like everybody else on the dance floor. Pat was totally amazed.

"You dance very well," she remarked.

"Oh, do I? Thanks." Yaya smiled. He thought, when somebody doesn't know you, they don't know you. "I'm a quick learner, Pat."

Yaya went on dancing like he always did. Those who cartooned him in college said he was a 'self-styled soul brother.' Because he was the social secretary and organizer of the Alpha Phi Laborers' exclusive parties. And indeed, music of all kinds was his thing, while dancing was his past time, through college and even after. With that background, he felt confident on any dance floor and quite a few social gatherings. In fact, that was why tonight he quickly pulled through the shock with which the party came.

Most of the people at the party were from Manika Kunda. In their characteristic vein of solidarity, they had thrown the welcome party for Yaya just like they would cluster around him and boost him, at some of his worst periods in the U.S.

The moment word went around that Sidi's brother was coming that morning—for among Manika Kundans, cousins are considered brothers—there was no need for any coaxing in the community to rally support. It was immediately presumed there would be a get-together to welcome the stranger. Like always, it was a freewill thing, where nobody was tasked anything. But in tune with the occasion, everybody brought what they could afford. Some brought six packs of beer, others brought cartons, while those that wished to bring hard liquor and wine did so.

Mostly, the women contributed the food and each brought enough to feed a crowd. There were indigenous African dishes like *fufu* and *egusi* with *bitterleaf, Jollof rice* and beef stew, *fried plantain* and beans, *ricebread cakes* and *roast beef*—Manika Kunda style! There were also various foods common to Africans and Americans, such as fried chicken, barbecue chicken, different kinds of stew and salad.

This was all done in good faith, as a means of sharing and rejoicing together; and also, as a way to impress the stranger from home with the positive spirit that prevailed so far away from home among countrymen abroad. After all was done, they danced, in the spirit of their goodwill shown.

Despite the stampeding pace of the party, Yaya went around meeting people, and everybody made some effort to be nice to him, and to make him feel like a chief, if only for that night. He stopped to talk to all the American guests in the party—the two white couples and a few African-Americans. They bid him welcome, and asked one or two questions about Africa.

At 12:30 AM Ahmed was on the microphone. He was a *Mandinka Dein*, which is the actual way Mandinka youths call themselves when speaking of their ancestry.

Ahmed Karankay was a grandson, great-grandson, and great-great-grandson of cobblers. In Manika Kunda, before the onslaught of alien civilization and confusion, society was such that principal occupations were carried out by particular families.

When musicians were needed, they called the Kuyateh family, or the Jibateh, or other families that sprang from them. These were the Jaylebahs, or praise singers and musicians. For a big ceremony, where cows were needed to feed the guests, they headed to the 'Woreti'—meaning owners of the ranch—who reared cattle.

Like most African names, 'Woreti' got corrupted to be Waritay or Warratie—as transcribed by Europeans—to be used as surnames for original Mandinka ranchers. When their family tree is extolled by the Jaylebahs, Waritay is also sometimes referred to as Jabbie.

And from the days of Mansa Musa of the ancient Mali Empire to Sundiata Keita of the Kingdom of Songhai to today, in some West African countries, such as Guinea, Mali and Gambia, to name a few, the Mandinkas had distinguished themselves in leadership.

Through the legacy of their great ancestor Kings, the Keita family which was royalty bore 'Mansa Dein.' 'Mansa' for King and 'Dein' for offspring—now simply Mansaray and Kakay as offshoot—with the lineage extolled as Keita or Tayea for 'dignified gallantry,' an unflattering honor shared with the Touré family. The griots still say that these were some of the ancient ruling families among the Mandinkas; same way that the Karankay family were known for cobbling.

Ahmed Karankay's father remained a cobbler, and Ahmed too was earmarked to be one. He never went to school in Manika Kunda, and instead, studied the Koran since infancy. Because, besides his predetermined profession, his father was a staunch Muslim who identified Western education with Christianity. To send a son to school was to make him a Christian—and that would be over his dead body!

Yet at 16, Ahmed drifted to Sobala, the capital city, and became a cook in a hotel. From there he joined a crew of a ship at 18. And because he studied the Koran at an early age, which he had to memorize, he had developed a sharp memory. This helped in his self-education.

About the time he dropped off his ship, which was on a stop in Miami, Florida, Ahmed was almost 21-years-old and had read enough to obtain a high school diploma. Two years later, he took the G. E .D. or high school equivalency exam and passed it with flying colors.

He had lived in the U.S. for eight years, with seven of those years in Washington D.C. There he attended Howard University, a premier black institution which showcased black intellectuals into a tight-knit American mainstream, way before desegregation hammered its way into classrooms across the country.

From his second year in the country, Ahmed had been married until three years ago, to an African-America lady he dearly loved. She was a school teacher who propelled him to Howard, her alumni institution. Before that, she had helped him legalize his stay in America. And it was a big dream—for a family with children, success and security—with hopes of even someday returning together to Africa. But their marital bliss was cut short by a 17-year-old vagabond who had dropped out of school for the streets, and thought his manhood and success in life lay within the barrel of the gun.

25-year-old Tracy was killed, while visiting her mother on a Sunday evening in Southeast Washington D.C., by this drug-damaged misfit. It was a drive-by shooting—a vogue in gang-infested, impoverished neighborhoods of urban America!

Tracy's murderer was sent to some youth detention center

instead of the gas chamber—to be paroled in a year or two —in the bereaved and enraged husband's opinion; a flaw in the judicial system that killed him every time he thought about what happened; especially when he reflected on the rampant black-on-black fatalities, which seemed to carry less weight than killing a stray dog gone crazy with rabies.

A chubby six-footer, who showed his weight in his voice, Ahmed was 29-years-old, and claimed now that the only thing that interested him was a career break. This he sought in all ways. Descendant of cobblers, since time immemorial, he wanted to be a corporate executive! And he held an MBA with excellent communication skills. Yet some of his countrymen mocked that he was of the wrong color in an alien culture, which his unfavored African accent further detracted from in corporate America—a seemingly exclusive enclave—where he had three strikes off.

A determined Ahmed, however, moved to Philadelphia a year ago still searching, but now drove a cab, sticking a resume in the hands of every passenger he picked up that had on a tie or a suit. If they said they were not employers, he asked them to please give the resume to their bosses. His unconventional means were starting to pay off, somehow. He had a second interview pending at a major manufacturing company for a position he'd always wanted and believed could make all the difference for him.

Presently on the microphone, Ahmed had earned that M.C. status from past performances, and he took absolute liberty now because of his kinship with the guest and the host.

"Attention please, people in the party, hear me," he bellowed in his usual baritone voice. They gave him the benefit with silence. "Thanks," he acknowledged. "Now, ladies and gentlemen, we all know why we are here today."

There was some murmuring in the crowd.

"Yes. By our coming together here, we show that we still care for each other, despite the distance from home and all the challenges we face by living away."

The crowd got mute. Ahmed cleared his throat.

"As our people say, let us all join our hands firmly, but not because anyone is afraid of the wind blowing them away. The wisdom of that adage is, oneness; for us to be together and stand together. If there is any need for that at home, there is an even greater need for it among us in America or anywhere abroad, where we are strangers and where we are almost nobody, it sometimes seems.

"But suffice it to say, we are somebody to ourselves, because we know who we are, where we came from, and why we venture out.

"Each of us in America, I'm sure, came here with a goal, and I have no doubt, in my mind about that goal being geared toward something worthy. And whatever these goals may be, when obtained, they become a fulfillment for us, in the form of happiness, progress or success. And still, such fulfillment becomes an asset and pride to our origins and communities. For what it boils down to, is for us to empower ourselves to contribute our shares, as best as we can, to the many needs back home.

"That is why, we are happy whenever we are joined by one of us. That is also why we have occasions like these to welcome them in our fold; to show them that they have kinsmen here who wish them well. That being so, now, on behalf of the Manika Kunda community here in Philadelphia, Mister Yaya LaTalé, I speak with our collective voices to say, we heartily welcome you into the fold.

"As you start your saga in America, we say may your dreams come true, and whatever your goals may be, may you reach them. May all news about you that go home be good news. This I ask with the blessings of our Lord, The Almighty Allah, and the blessings of our parents and our ancestors."

"Amen!" the people in the party answered.

"May your steps be guided in America by the values of your heritage and may you go home proud."

"Amen!" they answered again.

"Thank you. Thank you, ladies and gentlemen. I would now give the microphone to Yaya himself, so he would make a short self-introduction." Ahmed then stood aside holding out the microphone to Yaya.

Yaya did not expect this, like all developments of the night, so far. *What's this style they've got here? Does everything come in surprises? Oops! Yaya, now remember this: You are just an average guy who has come to the U.S. to better himself like everybody else. No worrisome details—say nothing about Grandma Fatu and the heritage! Just be yourself and stay confident. Okay?*

He got to the microphone, and all eyes were focused on him. He smiled and blew at the microphone as if to make sure it was functioning. He looked around the room, through the guests, and decided to see nobody in particular.

"Thank you, Mister Ahmed for that excellent effort," he remarked.

"Also thanks to everybody for being here for me, and for the goodwill you have shown. As most of you know by now, my name is Yaya LaTalé. I'm from Taényadu in Manika Kunda, and Sidi is my cousin.

"I went to University of Manika Kunda at Sobala and had an honors degree in Greek and Roman History and Civilization. But why am I telling you that? Actually, maybe, I'm doing so for one reason; so you would know the direction of education where I come from, as to how archaic and out of touch it is for a developing country.

"My major, Greek and Roman History and Civilization, like Biblical and General Studies, happened to be the most accessible of the few majors available for us at the University, and that's a legacy we inherited from our British colonial masters, which to many young minds today, is no more than a handicap, leaving us technologically unskilled and dependent.

"But worse still, while other African leaders with foresight have evolved educational systems in line with their needs, the leaders in Manika Kunda are still clapping their empty hands and crying, hoping for handouts from the outside world, if many a youth should ever have that relevant technical and professional training that we badly need. Yet, they triumph at master plotting to be wealthy and die in power."

"They will pay for it one day," Barbar screamed, tiptoeing from behind in the audience, alluding to the leaders in Manika Kunda.

"Sure, they will," Yaya responded. "However, back to myself. After college, I had two options, to teach or join the Civil Service.

"I decided to join the Civil Service, and started as an executive officer at the Ministry of Interior, and worked my way to the position of an assistant administrative officer. I was there for almost three years. But my last year was troubling, not quite what I wanted; the bureaucracy and the incompetence of our Civil Service quite apart—"

"Yes! Yes! Yes!" A lean dark man with bloodshot eyes standing alone in the back was loudly clapping. All eyes turned towards him, and murmurs could be heard in the crowd. It was obvious that he was drunk. Another man went to calm him, yet the well-dressed but unsteady man, whose hair was falling all over his head, kept clapping loudly, and nodding with dim eyes.

Meanwhile, Yaya paused, and was feeling totally sad. He was thinking of what got him here. And if he could, what he really wanted to say was: *"Ladies and gentlemen, forget about*

*that Civil Service baloney. I was happy at home as it was. But my
grandma died, and left me bound to an ancient tradition in
my family. That totally complicated my life, and threatened to
undermine my ambition and render my education useless. When I
refused to succumb to her death wish, she came after me, wrecking
my world—even from her grave! But you guys won't understand
that. And I won't tell you. "*

The crowd had gotten quiet and were again looking at Yaya.
He smiled.

"Ladies and gentlemen, to be frank, the shortcomings of the
Civil Service apart, I had always wanted to further my education
and to go into an area that is fulfilling, beyond just warming a
desk and staring at the walls in some big office, simply to make
a living at tax-payers' expense. To make a long story short, that
is why I came to America, thanks to Sidi. As we all know, at this
point, I can only hope for the best. Once more, I wish to thank
you all very much."

The guests in the party applauded Yaya after his speech. He
immediately won several hearts. Like he had wondered early on in
the party, now it was the single ladies wondering if that eloquent
and ambitious African hunk was single. As he shook hands,
mostly with men that came forward, now with a little more respect
in their eyes, he had become a hot commodity to possess for a
few lonely hearts.

"Isn't he handsome?" a small woman with dangling earrings in
a pink dress asked her companion.

"Yes, like something to kill for," retorted her attentive round-
figured companion with a wicked grin, as she wet her lusty raspberry
lips.

And they got themselves busy leering at the physique of the
towering African, whose mouth now was absent-mindedly open,
enough to reveal sparkling columns of well formed teeth. The
slight sweat breaking on his skin seemed to be oiling it, and asserting
even more, his Mandinka blackness.

Graced with what could be called a black blessing—which
makes many black people look younger than their actual age—at
25, despite his 6'4" frame, Yaya looked like a teenager. That fact
coupled with the low expectations about him, considering he was
just coming from Africa, was why most people were stunned
after his speech.

Sidi observing in a corner, saw from admiring glances adorning his cousin, that Yaya could have a field day with the single ladies in the party, be it Africans or Americans. Supposing, he knew how to play the game! As crazy as Sidi knew some of those women were for new arrivals, and especially for promise, brains and muscles in a man, all of which his cousin had. He decided he would just throw some rubbers in Yaya's hand if he had a catch.

With the party in full swing, the single African women in their characteristic vein of traditional inhibitions, barely smiled at Yaya; and those that yearned for him, did so only with their eyes, which rolled flashing with flame and passion. Meanwhile, their bodies stayed put, posturing, waiting for him to make the move. The interested American ladies, on the other hand, with their sense of liberation, took matters in their hands. They would stop by him, offer a hand and say their names with a sweet inviting smile and go. Others who cared less about propriety, would push off whoever was in their way, to grab him for a dance, to crowd him and edge him for private conversations.

Like most single African young males that newly come to America, Yaya's fascination with African women was tentatively on the hold. His interest laid in American women, and this showed in the way he carefully selected his dance partners. They were all Americans, in spite of the frowning faces of his African sisters.

Through Pat's maneuvering, Yaya ended up being taken and spoken for by one of her friends, a fleshy full-figured African-American lady with a big behind—quite a lustrous catch for an average African! However, that didn't stop a couple of other women from dropping notes of admiration with telephone numbers in the open pocket of Yaya's gown as he danced.

Quite unlike most African parties in the U.S. that usually stretch till 5 a.m., the party ended abruptly around three, because the police came and demanded that the music be stopped. It was learned that Sidi's neighbors had called the police and reported disturbance by the noise from the party.

CHAPTER TEN

It was Monday, about noon, and Yaya was at home alone. Sidi and Pat had gone to work. Before leaving, as always, Sidi reminded him to keep the doors locked at all times and to open for no strangers—on no account!

"Just a safety measure," he had volunteered, in answer to the lingering question in Yaya's eyes. "We don't take any chances here," he simply stated. "Watch the five o'clock news on television and you will know why."

This was new to Yaya; a person coming from the laxity of a place where front doors were closed mostly to keep out flies and mosquitoes or to maintain some coolness indoors. However, from the first day that he stayed by himself, he did exactly as advised by his cousin. He kept the doors locked, and started intently watching the five o'clock news every day. After a few accounts of violence on people turned victims in the illusive safety of their homes, he had less doubts about the need to bolt all doors, and to peep through the windows and in the front door's peep-hole, several times, before speaking to anybody outside, not to mention opening for them.

The past weekend following this Monday made Yaya one week old in the U.S. In his dreamland—*where a man can be himself, and think only of progress, and make it big. Yes, man!* A feast of that reality was unfolding in his mind, dream-coated with hopes and high hopes.

The dual curtains of his bedroom window were pulled apart and he was standing in the center of the split by the window. Outside, there was a burst of shower. Yaya couldn't help staring blankly through the misty glass window at the rain; the intensity of it making him think that it seemed to be pouring with spite. Instantly, he thought of the fabled seven days rain—an active myth in Manika Kunda passed by folk-lore from generation to generation. He laughed as he reflected on the myth. *A seven days rain?*

Never in his life had he witnessed a phenomenon as endless as an uninterrupted rain, day and night, for seven days. But that notwithstanding, never had he seen a torrential rain as that which was throbbing outside, without the myth crossing his mind.

Yaya wondered if there were similar myths in America. "But this is a white man's country," he told himself. "They dwell in science and technology, not superstition, witchcraft and repressive traditions. No wonder they are so progressive!"

Gazing through the mad rain outside, Yaya reflected on himself, Grandma Fatu and that heritage which was thrust upon him. Until that incident at Grandma Fatu's dying bed, and the torment it opened for Yaya, he had loved Grandma Fatu dearly. She was his mother's mother, and the one towards whom he staggered his first steps. He was left in her care when six-months-old because his mother was sick and was seeking treatment. They struck a bond which lasted through her life.

Grandma Fatu was a success. She was respected and admired far and wide in Manika Kunda. Living by tradition, she was a slave to her heritage, with a chunk of that heritage being a special inheritance, of which she was the sole custodian in the family. Also, it was her calling, and that was the incredible feat of patching together broken bones in members of the body, by simple and natural means, it seemed.

It was a wonder which, to believe, one had to see. Simply, she would say, "It is just putting back a wholesome smile on the faces of shattered people."

After the people had left, mended, bowing in gratitude and awe, she would put her hand under her chin in contentment and say to members of her family present that she wondered what other better use she could have made of her life if her grandfather hadn't passed down that blessing to her.

Throughout Grandma Fatu's life, she was a sedentary woman, who stayed where she was born, in an ancient and obscure village that didn't grow. She never saw a modern city, or a telephone or even light from electricity. She heard of Sobala, the capital city, but didn't care to go there and nothing about the place aroused her interest.

Yet people of all nationalities, white, yellow and black, at a certain period, paid her homage. They came in doubt and curiosity, but stayed in belief in her humble surrounding, watching and fervently wanting her knowledge. Desperately, they made cash offers, and promises, and pleaded to let her share her knowledge with them.

She was warm to them and treated them as guests; yet she showed and told them only what she wanted disclosed. After some time, she stopped all such visits from people who came to pester her to reveal something that was an ancestral secret—and a sacred thing to her!

Grandma Fatu had three children, Sidi's father, Foday Béreté, Yaya's mother, Iye LaTalé and a last son, Wusu Béreté. Grandma Fatu became widowed when Wusu was ten years old, and just when Yaya was born. That was also when her grandfather died and left her the heritage.

Two links of the heritage were gone and two links of the heritage were created. Yaya was specifically claimed and anointed by that incidence, but nobody knew, except Grandma Fatu. The secrecy surrounding the heritage was such that she could not make a disclosure of it to even her children.

It was all in one leaf, and the uncompromising eyes of the ancestors and their laws. The story in Manika Kunda was that nobody in this life who breathes the common air would ever find or see that leaf growing in any bush—even for those who claimed they knew it and sought it—without it being handed down to them. And as far as anybody could remember, that story had never been disproved.

Besides Grandma Fatu's house, there were only three other cement-block houses in Wuyadu. The rest were mud houses, many already changed to zinc top, with a few still roofed with thatch. It was a village of sixty or less houses, and a population of less than two hundred people, mostly subsistence farmers.

For streets, Wuyadu had flat grounds with footpaths, and a dusty motor road that passed by, serving as the modern link to the outside world. For Grandma Fatu, life in wooded Wuyadu was fulfilling and the best. There were no schools in Wuyadu, and so of course, Grandma Fatu never went to elementary or secondary school, not to talk about anything beyond. The only use she had for a book that strayed on her turf, was to tear out a sheet of paper to put some salt in or wrap her snuff. Industrial pollution, scientific discoveries and plane crashes occurred not in her planet.

In her line of work, which was demanding and restrictive, she obeyed the rules and felt comfortable with the awe that surrounded her. It was a dream met, where she didn't have to debate anything; for their was nothing to debate about fulfilling a dream, till the end of her life.

"You have been chosen after me, my child. And just as my grandfather passed on this heritage to me, I shall now pass it on to you and you alone in the family. You must represent, cherish, and continue to your dying day, this infinite blessing that is a tradition in our family. Or I will see no rest in my grave."

That was where it went wrong for Yaya. Why did it have to be him in a large lineage of immediate and extended family multitudes? And with all the demands of that inheritance? And its restrictive life? That was not his dream. He was a modern man. A crop of enlightened Africans that was emergent. The first generation in his family to go to the white man's school.

At two years of age, when his mother was well, Yaya had left the wooded village of Grandma Fatu to live with his parents in their family compound in Taényadu, which was three times the size of Wuyadu, and twenty miles away. Taényadu had an elementary school which Yaya attended. It was the only school in that area. At 13, he was away from his small village of Taényadu at a boarding school on the outskirt of Sobala, due to a British Commonwealth scholarship for meriting students completing elementary school.

The secondary school was opened by the British, during colonial rule, and was patterned on the British Public School System. Here to be English and *civilized* Western style was the ideal, with religion and native culture taking the back seat. Nobody changed that through Yaya's school days.

In his five years in secondary school in a boarding home, Yaya spent every quick break in Sobala, like many other school mates, fascinated and excited by their discovery of the city, glittering and dazzling in their village eyes. With a few friends being natives of the city, with generous boys' rooms and accommodating parents, Sobala became home, in Yaya's transformation, as Taényadu and Wuyadu became dull, to be visited more out of necessity.

When he went home on holidays, to his parents in Taényadu, or to see Grandma Fatu in Wuyadu, there was always a time constraint. He was in a rush to keep their minds at ease, doing quickly whatever was required of him, just so as to have time left to spend in the city, his new found haven, with stimulating peers.

The city and school became one to Yaya's uneducated parents, who thought that such high education had to have its price. They let him go whenever he asked, and for consolation, they held with pride onto his impressive grade reports, even if those had to be read to them. It was proof he wasn't straying self-destructively.

That was how it was until he finished college at 22, unusual, considering his background. But he was lucky. By now educated and exposed to modern life, Yaya's aspirations and hopes for fulfillment were nowhere around Taényadu, and of course, by no way near Wuyadu.

Yaya knew where he wanted to be, and got a job immediately

at graduation in Sobala in the Civil Service. As it was the vogue among college graduates, he had a flat, which was electrified and well furnished in an elegant two story building, the likes of which Taényadu lacked.

His social life was perfect, with respect among peers, in the fast and glorious life of the elite that he was. He was doing well on his job, where he was liked, respected, and was groomed for upward mobility.

With his achievement seen as a mighty feat among his people, he became a doctor to their monetary woes and their desperate cries for help. That was expected. There was no escaping it, so he played along, conceding that it was his responsibility.

Half of his salary every month went into various forms of assistance to members and friends of his family, extended family members and others, who came thanking God because a son of the land—one of theirs—has made it; even if to simultaneously lay out their problems and ask for assistance. Yaya did his best. And that in itself was his happiness.

Then he had that telegram at work which said he was needed because Grandma Fatu was seriously sick and could die, any minute. He left work immediately, and jumped into the first available vehicle heading that way. After a night in transit, where an old couple fed and sheltered him, he reached Wuyadu on foot at noon, hours before any transportation would have been going that way. He was just in time, to see Grandma Fatu die, with other members of the family outside the room at the dying woman's request.

To Yaya, the situation in itself was sad, but what made it lingering and imperative was the deed that transpired.

Grandma Fatu knew she was to pass on the heritage to Yaya, for it was obvious. It showed by the timing of Yaya's birth, a new link coming to replace the old, which had died. And when Grandma Fatu dreamed of her deceased grandfather, who handed her the heritage, laying hands on Yaya's newborn head, it symbolized the betrothal for succession.

Showing the leaf to Yaya, some two years before her death, Grandma Fatu had hinted to him without saying so, that he was the one to take over from her. They were alone in her room. She had pulled her rattan stool close to him as he sat on a bench, and held the leaf up to him, declaring with her native pride and ambiguity: "Behold! For this is your heritage; it is like a snake, and you are its skin. A snake never dies because it has shed its skin. It lives on, vibrant and alert with the fresh gleaming skin. For it is only when the snake dies, that the skin dies with it and rots. Yaya, you are just such a skin."

"Great, Grandma, I know," he had said, to oblige her, just with his ears. It was more out of deference, but he paid no attention to the message, among his many distractions boiling in the city. They were worlds apart, with a wide generation gap.

However, as far as Grandma Fatu was concerned, she knew that when it was time, Yaya would know, and that was what mattered. In her eyes, Yaya's successes in the white man's world, going to the apex of their school, living and working with them in that big Sobala, proved even more that he was the right choice, the best. And besides, he was not like a few boys around—the-do-nothings—who had only been to the little school in Taényadu, and thought they were better than the rest of the people who farmed, yet had no trades, except to steal from people's corn farms and sell stolen goats to crooked motorists that flew past.

In fact, by the act of showing Yaya the leaf every year, and demanding secrecy about it, Grandma Fatu was grooming Yaya for his role after her, which she presumed was best for him, as it was for her, and her grandfather—with or without the white man's education! That was why she held on for him! *My time has come, my child. Am glad you made it.*"

And when she handed the heritage to Yaya, her task was done.

After Grandma Fatu's death, even though Yaya's mind was yoked, he said nothing about anything to anybody. He took part in Grandma Fatu's burial, and stayed for the seventh day burial ceremony, and came for the 40th day ceremony, both events being vital burial rites among the Mandinkas as with many other ethnic groups in Africa.

Grandma Fatu's 40th day ceremony went fine. It was well attended. There were almost all relatives, and many elders and personalities, from everywhere in Manika Kunda. She was a Muslim, so the occasion was observed in an Islamic manner—with a Mandinka affectation, which was little—because Islam had been a part of the people for ages, like a grandfather to the first Christian effort in the region.

For Grandma Fatu on this day, after *Salatul-Zuhr*—the two o'clock afternoon *Salfana*—prayer, the elders read the Koran sitting on mats in the center of her parlor, while the people sitting on benches and squatting around in the parlor and in the Verandah, answered "Amina."

The readings and ensuing prayers were blessings poured on her, and supplications to Allah on her behalf.

After the prayers, the Jaylebahs or praise singers recounted her many deeds, which were attributed to the wonders performed by her ancestors, in whose steps she walked.

Numukeh Kuyateh, the famed Jaylebah in Manika Kunda, had the crowd transfixed when he took the floor. With his rich soothing and captivating voice, he started by proclaiming *Jam-mare-woohh* with Grandma Fatu's name—which was an act of invocation—as he glorified her:

Jam-mare-woohh, Fatu Béreté! Jam-mare-woohh, Fatu Béreté!
Daughter of Salu Béreté! And granddaughter of Brima Béreté!
Of the Béreté family, whose good deeds lay in wind that we breath.
Jam-mare-woohh, Fatu, daughter of the Béretés!
Your deeds were done!

Jam-mare-woohh, Fatu Béreté! You, who everybody broken ran to.
And the white man with all his knowledge came seeking.
Without whom many broken human bones would have rotted.
The medicine man and the white doctors would say, 'Cut it!'
But did God make people to go about any less?

Jam-mare-woohh, Fatu! God wanted people whole.
Not with one arm, or a broken back or limping.
Yet with Satan and his havoc, anything happens.
So God made you and blessed you.
To work wonders, and do what many cannot do.

Fatu Béreté, you who spoke to the wind and it answered.
The leaves in the bush bowed and called you, 'Boss!'
Jam-mare-woohh, Fatu, you who succeeded where others failed.
And in the worst case, you said, 'Welcome....'
Doing good deeds, strengthening, mending—
(.......And so Numukeh went on.......)

The ceremony ended with feasting, and plenty of meat to take home, from two cows killed in Grandma Fatu's honor. This was to mark her final departure from the human world.

Throughout the gathering, even though Yaya overheard discussions from people wondering as to whom Grandma Fatu appointed to take up after her, he kept mute. And of course, nobody suspected him, so he didn't have to answer any queries. He was considered a white man to them anyway, because of his Western education, and his big job in the government; one of the few sons of the land who had gone that far; a novelty that they both respected and had hope in, but which they still felt some uneasiness about.

That night, however, even after the community had marked the 40th day of Grandma Fatu's death, she came in Yaya's sleep. It was in her compound where everything seemed normal. The sun was still rising, hovering over the large mysterious baobab tree with its thick ominous branches. The town was empty; people had gone to their farms. Grandma Fatu was sitting outside in the verandah of her cement house, on a rattan stool, with Yaya sitting legs-crossed on a wooden chair close to her.

It was like on one of his quick visits in his college days when Grandma Fatu would put everything aside, to sit with him, inquiring about his progress, and glowing at the good news about him.

She was reminiscing about the Bérété family and its connection with the LaTalé family, which she said were one, like the Jabbies and the Waritays, the Kakays and the Mansarays, and so on. She said that the LaTalé family were cousins of the Bérété family and they came from the Bérétes. So Yaya's mother was married to her first cousin, Åñsorn LaTalé. They were of the same root, which the ancestors believed was best in wedlock, because then it unites the family even more, with everybody caring for each other as brothers and sisters.

Yaya was listening. Being a *modern* man, he was battling internally with some of what he heard. Yet he cherished these trips into his ancestral background. And Grandma brought everything to light.

She told Yaya that their immediate forefather, Kefinba Bérété at one time lived like an outcast in the land of the Felakas—a group of Mandinkas who speak a slightly different dialect—which covered both Taényadu and Wuyadu.

That as a young man, Kefinba had come from Atiyae, his home town, to Taényadu bound by love. Grandma Fatu said the story was that Kefinba and a young girl Kaday had fallen in love when he was twelve and she was eleven. They had met as students

127

while studying under a Karamoko—whom, among Mandinkas, is a scholar of the Koran—who teaches youngsters and some grownups how to read and recite from the Holy Book. And from that early age, Kefinba and Kaday had nursed their love through puberty.

As they grew, their relationship became more like that of a brother and a sister, such that Kefinba went and worked on Kaday's mother's rice farm and performed masculine services for her, like cutting wood for cooking, catching bush animals for meat, and mending her hut. For Kaday's mother, who did not have a son, needed the help, living—in a big cantankerous polygamous home of five wives and over forty children—with a husband that was a kolanut trader and was gone all the time, hawking from village to village. Kaday's mother very much appreciated Kefinba's services, saw him as the son she did not have, and so encouraged him for her daughter.

It was with that impetus that love grew thick between the two youths. However, at seventeen, Kefinba became concerned as he watched Kaday's father practically sell his older daughters to the highest bidders for marriage as soon as they became sixteen.

A worried Kefinba feared losing his lover to some rich man who might come with cows and bags of kolanuts. So he convinced Kaday, who was nearing sixteen, that they should visit a learned psychic—called, Bolon-Mafendehna, meaning a palm reader—who was passing through the village, and had people rushing to consult him, so as to know their future and fate.

The fortune-teller told the teenage lovers that he saw big clouds in the way of their love. He said that they would have to tackle numerous difficulties if they would ever be husband and wife. As the sad couple left the house of the Bolon-Mafendehna, one of his students, a youth about Kefinba's age, approached them and told them that he knew something they could do that would bind them together forever.

"And what is that?" Kefinba asked anxiously.

"Cut a wound in your finger and cut a wound in her finger, and join the two wounds together, so that your blood will become one, thereby uniting you forever."

"How is that supposed to work?" the youths inquired in chorus.

"It is a vow, by nature and your blood, if any of you should break the relationship, the other person's blood would fight you and kill you. And most lovers are doing that, so that if anybody decides to break you up, just tell them that you have sworn by your blood to stay together. That would stop them."

Kefinba and Kaday thought about that. Desperate and knowing no better, they decided that they loved each other enough to commit themselves that way. As they joined their wounded thumbs, Kaday swore that even if she was forced to get married to somebody else against her wish, she would always love Kefinba. Kefinba swore that he would be Kaday's man as long as she lived and that even if her father were to give her hand in marriage to somebody as far as in Egypt, he would go after her. That sealed their bond.

Kaday turned sixteen and there were talks about her beauty as she got plump and ripe. Together they went to bathe in the river alone and saw their nakedness. Kefinba saw that her breast were plump and shooting out and her body had formed fully in series of smooth curves. While Kaday saw that he had a stiffness between his legs every time they got out of the water or when he came close to her. Yet they were both virgins and would not think of doing anything beyond touching, because sex before marriage was taboo in the culture. Also it was customary and a major pride to mothers to display a blood-soaked cloth to other women as testimony that their daughters lived right and were met virgins by their husbands on the night of their marriage.

Not long after Kaday's sixteenth birthday, suitors started competing with Kefinba for her love. Her mother warded them off, claiming she was spoken for by Kefinba, but her father would hear nothing of it. And just as Kefinba feared, a wealthy farmer in Taényadu heard of Kaday, and came with a cow, two bags of rice and a bag of kolanuts seeking her as a wife. Again as expected, Kaday's father happily gave her hand to the man, even amidst her cries about some vow she had made to Kefinba, and his blood in her vein which would kill her.

Her father was not willing to listen to such silly talk, and so nothing could stop her from going away. But that did not stop Kefinba from following her either. He left Atiyae as soon as Kaday left, bound by his vows. In Taényadu, Kaday found herself unhappy in a polygamous home where she was one of six wives, and the youngest and the most hated by the other women. But she had Kefinba on the side.

As luck would have it, not quite three months after Kaday got married, her husband got sick and became incapacitated for a whole year. This gave Kefinba ultimate access to her.

About the time the husband got well, she was pregnant, going on to six months. When the husband saw her protruding belly, he was furious, knowing quite well he hadn't touched her throughout his period of illness. He asked Kaday whom the man was, but she insisted there was no man, which made him think she was taking him for a fool. The irate husband—who worshipped only at the shrine in his house—then decided to bring a dreaded witch doctor to put a curse on whoever it was that went to bed with his wife.

The then King of Taényadu, even though a Muslim, but a friend of the husband, reluctantly gave his permission. The famed witch doctor came from afar, and there was no secret that he was a witch and heathen no less than the devil himself. It was said that when he shouted, a burning flame erupted from his mouth.

By mid-afternoon on the day of the curse, as a crowd gathered in an open field, an aged man in tattered clothes stood at a far end alone. Those who knew him were whispering in dread. He had laid out a dried leopard skin on the ground, on top of which he had his paraphernalia: of cowry shells, all sorts of animal horns and eyes, some dried skulls and bones, and a talisman—his idol—which was covered with white cloth, now reddish with stains from kolanuts that he chewed amidst incantations to spit the dredge on his deity.

In a hot tropical sun, everybody was sweating and watching as the witch doctor started his work. He flashed a little mirror in his hand against the sun, inviting the sun as a guest of his deity, on which he spat a watery kolanut dredge, calling it 'the mysterious one.'

He then made his announcement. "The mysterious one is summoned here today, to render justice in a case of adultery. Some devious person in this town, took to bed the wife of Bala Sewa, while he was sick.

"And that person is here. I can see him. You know yourself. I command you to come out right now and confess, so that you may be saved. Or you may stay in the dark, hiding, where the mysterious one would seek you, and get you, and crush you, like it has done to many like you. So come out right now, I say!"

There was a rumbling in the crowd. The witch doctor stood still and looked, his red fiery eyes darting as he waited for the culprit to come forth and own up.

But nobody showed up. The witch doctor was frowning.

"Again, this is your last chance." He stamped his feet. "I say come out now before I do what would never be undone." His eyes were furiously roving through the crowd.

With still no response, the witch doctor then chewed some more kolanut, murmured some incantations and spat the reddish dredge all over the white cloth.

"What I'm saying is, that you cannot hide. Don't fool yourself, because the mysterious one here will seek and get you anywhere and everywhere to iron it out with you. And let me tell you this secret: when he smiles, it rains; and when he laughs, it is thunder that descends; and you will find out what he does when he is angry. That is, if you don't come out now! So come out and confess, if you don't want to be doomed. "

As indeed the witch doctor said, Kefinba was present as was Kaday. They were, however, apart. Kaday was with her vengeful husband in the front row, while Kefinba stood in the far back watching like anybody else.

Even with such dreadful threats about the powers of the so-called mysterious one and some impending calamity, Kefinba had no intention of confessing. He had told Kaday that he was never going to humiliate himself before that pagan, even if the man were to spit fire through his nose and his ears; and that Kaday should insist if asked anymore, that her husband was responsible for the pregnancy, which rightfully Kefinba considered himself to be, by their bond; before her father traded her for wealth.

Besides, both Kefinba and Kaday were Muslims by birth and upbringing, who believed in nothing but Allah, seconded only by their love, which was natural and to which they felt bound till death. At this point, they were more concerned about the public anguish and disgrace or humiliation which they would face by disclosing their relationship rather than the prowess of the witch doctor and his mysterious one.

Feeling challenged, the reddish teeth of the witch doctor glared with scorn as he screamed: "So you won't come out at all? Good! Very good! Now the mysterious one, this issue is yours! And everybody present will bear witness of your powers. They shall see!"

The witch doctor took a small bell that was painted white which he rang: 'gbelian.., gbelian.., gbelian.., gbelian...' He dropped the bell on the leopard skin. And took his mirror which he flashed all around him, chewed some kolanut, said some incantations and spat on his talisman.

"Mysterious one, I now call on your powers, which never fail just as night always follows the day, and humans always bear humans, and as fire always burns. May you manifest your powers now!"

Suddenly, by some coincidence or unexplained reason the sun had receded under a dark cloud which now covered the sky. The crowd got awestruck and mute. All eyes were focused on the witch doctor, who was getting more jubilant, chanting, chewing kolanut and spitting the dredge on his deity. He patted his idol.

"Let it be as I stand here to curse whoever it was that impregnated Bala Sewa's wife when he laid sick, that the name of the mysterious one shall linger in this land. May—"

A trumpet sounded close-by. "P'uugn-gpor! P'uugn-gpor! P'uugn-gpor! P'uugn-gpor!" Everybody turned. A messenger of the King came running towards the witch doctor.

"Wait!" The messenger was breathing heavily. "The King said to tell you that you should not invoke thunder or any natural calamity in his land. He said you should limit your curse to the will of Almighty Allah in this matter."

"What?" the witch doctor hollered frustrated. "What?" he screamed again, and a flame like a serpent's tongue shot out of his mouth. He was trembling with rage. But he knew the law; he was in the King's land and had to do as ordered, or both he and his mysterious one would end up without heads.

He took his bundled stuff, which was still wrapped in the messy white cloth and hugged it like a whipped child with a doll, looking all pitiful.

"Mysterious one, we were summoned here for nothing!" he cried. "Their King said let the will of his God be done. May his wish be!" The witch doctor then mumbled some incantations which nobody heard. "Go away everybody!" he said angrily. "Go! It is all over!"

Not quite one month after the witch doctor left town, Kaday had a still birth and died in the process. Naturally, there were rumors in the town that it was the curse, and that she had fallen first, with the man to follow soon.

Kefinba was shattered and almost went insane. At Kaday's burial, he frantically attacked her husband whom he accused of killing his sweetheart. He was joined in the attack by Kaday's mother who was wailing and telling everybody that it was Kaday's father and Bala Sewa who killed her daughter. She went about explaining how poor Kefinba had struggled together with her daughter since their childhood only for her husband and his endless greed to give her daughter away to that heathen for him to kill her.

Everybody saw Kefinba as being out of his mind, and with his *complicity revealed, he was deemed cursed and doomed with no future left; so even Kaday's husband did not see it fit to fight with him.*

It was with that stigma that Kefinba, at eighteen, left Taényadu, immediately after Kaday's burial, as he took off guilt-ridden, bereaved and lost. His family looked for him in vain for two years and presumed him dead. Yet twenty miles away, in the thick forest that Wuyadu was, he had found a home and a retreat in his grief.

Living in that dense forest inhabited by monkeys, baboons, lions and all sorts of wild animals, he desired no human contact. And drawing on his manhood training like a lost warrior, he survived on wild fruits and bush animals. It was said he was fasting and praying to Allah all the time, for forgiveness for himself and Kaday.

And then in the third year, he started going to town in Taényadu on Fridays to join the Muslim Jamaat for the Friday afternoon Jumu'a or congregational prayer. Nobody could believe it when they saw him. In his tattered clothes, and with his bushy hair, people were afraid to approach him, presuming him to be as insane as a wounded lion, even if he had stayed alive.

Now 21, Kefinba still kept to himself, but would journey the twenty miles distance every Friday on foot.

On one Friday that he came to pray, there was so much sadness in the town, and the crowd was smaller than usual. It was said that the King's first son, his heir, who was fifteen, had fallen while riding a horse three days ago, and broken a leg.

The chief medicine man felt hopeless and miserable because the bones in the injured leg of the prince were sticking out, severed and shattered in some areas, with not much holding the limb together. In fact, the foot was starting to fester, and there was fear that the Prince was likely to die.

Kefinba Béreté went with the crowd that afternoon after the Jumu'a prayer to sympathize with the distraught Royalty. But with his stigma, he was turned back at the gate. So he quietly went to his little hut in Wuyadu. That night, however, he had a revelation that changed his life. His Grandfather whom he remembered only as an infant appeared to him and told him he could cure the prince, and showed him how.

Kefinba left early the following morning for Taényadu and declared to the King, for whom he had waited several hours to have an audience, that he had come to cure the prince. The King laughed in disbelief, but as desperate as he was, he gave Kefinba a chance. Amidst scorn and threats, Kefinba made the prince well, and up on his feet, as if the accident never happened. A grateful King instantly rewarded Kefinba with wealth and granted him nobility in the land.

Grandma Fatu was now recounting with pride to Yaya that since then, when the gift of bone healing was given to their forefather Kefinba, the power had always manifested itself in the Bérété family, and that she made the fifth generation to sustain the heritage.

But suddenly, there was wailing and groaning in the distance, so Grandma Fatu stopped talking. Both she and Yaya looked in the direction from which the cries of anguish were coming.

A group of people came through the bush path; the one which ran in the coffee plantation next to Grandma Fatu's compound. They were about ten, with four men carrying a plain raffia hammock that had four protruding wooden handles, two before and two behind, which laid on their shoulders.

The hammock contained a groaning man, yelling like he had just been lynched by some irate mob. And it seemed so, from the blood caked in dripping lumps at the sides and bottom of the hammock. As they came, the three women in the party, whose faces were dripping with tears, cried in sing-song manner —oh! oh! help us, oh!—with their arms outstretched in front of them, while they fell over each other sideways, in staggering steps.

Yaya got up, following Grandma Fatu who stepped out of the verandah, steering the wailing party around to a back house, which harbored her treatment room and guest rooms. Deliberately, Yaya slowed his steps, and came behind the group, his stomach already in turmoil from the sight of all that blood.

A gray-haired man hopped and caught up with Grandma Fatu who was leading in quick strides. "Please, great woman, help me!" the old man said, his face in total grief as he pointed backwards. "That is my son. He fell from a palm tree. Please, great one, help him!"

Grandma Fatu gestured to the crying women to hush, as she opened a room which had in the middle several individual goat skin mats spread, adjoining each other, and a wooden bed towards the wall on one side.

"Bring him in here. And I want you all to stay outside," she said, motioning to the frantically weeping women. "Lay him over there." She pointed to the center of the room, where the mats were.

The men relieved themselves, carefully laying the injured man who seemed suffocated by choking gasps.

"We are from Limbadu. It happened early this morning," the father said. "We passed five villages and crossed several rivers to get here."

The son was no more than 21, lanky, with big eyes and mouth that were open, telling the excruciating pain he felt. He had bruises all over. One leg was wrapped in a native cotton-cloth that was blood-soiled.

Grandma Fatu bent down and removed the cotton-cloth around the wrapped leg, to reveal a foot traumatized and fit for amputation, with whitish cartilage sprouting in threads, and blood-specked bones glaring naked, around the thigh, where the knee used to be. The knee was now twisted completely, such that if the man were standing, the toes on his left foot and right foot would be facing opposite directions; and no telling which way his dangling kneecap might have gone flapping.

A chill of fear surged through Yaya. Sicker than ever and horrified at the sight, he turned sharply away; only to be confused further by the wailing of the women outside, and the groaning of the old man and his son inside the room.

In a flash, Grandma Fatu got to a cane woven basket sitting in a far corner, almost invisible. She brought a bottle, removed the dried leaves that corked it, and knelt by the groaning man, pouring a greenish liquid in her hand and rubbing it all over the man. She generously poured the content of the bottle directly on the shattered knee.

The man twisted in jerks, his face a picture of convulsion, whitish saliva pouring out of the corners of his mouth which was shut tight by clenched teeth. His hands and head pounded ferociously on the floor.

Yaya wanted to hurry out, to run and keep running. But he couldn't. Grandma Fatu bore heavy on him, worse than a butcher's hold on a cow awaiting to be slaughtered. Now standing like a statue, his whole insides froze in astonishment when he involuntarily looked at the injured man and saw a dark greenish cloth forming over the bruises on the man's skin, with all the blood drying up.

Grandma Fatu emptied the bottle over the man's face, rubbing it in, forcefully opening his mouth, so some of the liquid would drain inside.

Yaya saw that for some reason, the man was now calm and lying so still that he had to look at his chest to see if it was moving, to be sure he was not dead.

"Did you come prepared?" Grandma Fatu asked.

"Yes, blessed one," the old man answered.

Grandma Fatu opened her palm.

The old man reached into his gown and brought out four kolanuts, two red and two white. "Bori, bring the cock!" he yelled.

A boy with dusty feet, in khaki shorts but with no shirt on, came forth. He gave a red cock tied at the legs with a raffia string to the old man, who passed it over to Grandma Fatu.

"We got all of these on our way here," the old man said.

Grandma Fatu moved a little away from the ailing man and dropped the cock on the floor, its legs still tied. She asked Yaya to go bring a cup of water and a plate, which he did. She placed the kolanuts in the plate and sat the water next to it.

"Where is the white cloth?" she asked.

"White cloth? We didn't bring any," said the old man, his eyes apologetic.

Grandma Fatu got up and walked swiftly to her main house, and came with a piece of white cloth wrapped in her hand. She sat down and beckoned to Yaya and the others to come around. They formed a circle where she was sitting, by the side of the stretched-out man. Grandma Fatu placed her hands on the items before her, and raised her head up in prayer. Everybody followed suit.

"Allah, the Creator, the Almighty, this is your servant praying to you, and it is for you that I have sat this clear and cold water. Also, you the good spirits of my ancestors, this is your daughter Fatu Béreté calling on you."

"Amina! Amina!" the group intoned.

"Grandpa Kefinba, I'm addressing you. This cock is for you and these are your kolanuts. They are also for you, Grandpa Soriba, you who passed this blessing down to Grandpa Backari who passed it to Grandpa Brima. And they are for you too, Grandpa Brima, you who passed down this heritage to me."

"Amina! Amina!"

"In your kindness, you saw it fit that I should carry on with your work. Yet, no work I do could be done without you, without your guidance and your blessings."

"Amina! Amina!"

"A man fell from a palm tree today, he is lying here. His leg is broken and twisted. They came to me and as you wished, I'm here to do as you did."

"Amina! Amina!"

"But Grandpa Kefinba, as you told Grandpa Soriba, who told Grandpa Backari, who in turn told Grandpa Brima and who told me, before I accept this work, you must give your approval and show me that I can succeed, and that this patient will recover completely."

"Amina! Amina!"

"Therefore, God Almighty, and you the spirits of my great forefathers, as this rooster has two legs, and this man has two legs, if I can cure this man, let me break a leg of this cock, representing the injured leg of this man. And let me put these two injured creatures, and your kolanut, and the water, under this cloth. When I raise the cloth, if this cock gets up and walks, I will know that you have accepted the case and granted me the power to heal this man; for it is with your blessing that I work."

"Amina! Amina!"

"And now Almighty Allah, the creator, forgive me for injuring this poor animal so."

"Amina! Amina!"

And swiftly, Grandma Fatu broke the cock's left leg, at the knee, corresponding to the injured leg of the man. She gave the frantic cock to Yaya to hold; the feathers flying all over as it flapped its wings in anguish. Next, Grandma Fatu spread open the white cloth, and moved the water and kolanut to each side of the man's head, and tapped him on the shoulder to wake up. She handed over to him the crowing rooster.

"Hold onto it tight," she said. And then she covered them with the cloth. "Let us all stand over them," said Grandma Fatu preparing for another prayer.

Everybody was up, and in a circle over the covered bundle.

"God Almighty, and the spirit of my great ancestors, please show me that you are with me, as I now depend on you."

"Amina! Amina!"

"The injured cock and the man underneath are now spiritually the same. When I uncover them, may the cock fly out and walk without a limp, just like this patient will, after I have healed him with your permission."

"Amina! Amina!"

"By the grace of God and the blessings of my ancestors."

"Amina! Amina!"

"Thank you everybody. Let us all leave them alone now," Grandma Fatu said, turning away. And then she turned to the strangers. "I will open those two rooms for you now. You can go in and rest, or you may sit outside. My people will be bringing food for you soon. I have to leave you for a short while. And Yaya, you come with me." He followed.

"Now, we are going to get prepared!" Grandma Fatu said. She headed for the bush behind her compound. "We should know when we come back if this injury is not a curse or some act of witchcraft. And if it is not, the bird will walk firmly. Then we start the healing."

"What if the injury is caused by some witchcraft, Grandma, and the cock does not walk?" Yaya asked, disheartened and puzzled.

"Then, I simply tell them that the case is beyond me. I'm not a witch doctor, my child. I'm a bone healer. If there is anything mysterious underneath, I'm sure they know where to go."

She looked at Yaya, who looked confused and lost. "Watch it, mister white man, you city boy, don't fall over that tree trunk. Somebody must have cut it down for wood."

Yaya stepped over the fallen log and moved away from the grassy area to the footpath. Just then he caught a zigzag movement under the grass a few feet away from he where was.

That's a snake! Yaya felt disheartened as a trickle of sweat ran down his back as if it was the snake on his skin. He jumped.

Grandma Fatu ahead missed that sight but she suddenly stopped and turned towards him. "Here, these are what we need." She started counting with her fingers: "The sacred herb, some wooden planks, a string with which to tie the medicine on the foot, and some goat oil. I have the goat oil at home."

Getting those items, Grandma Fatu walked Yaya through that bush, telling him which trees were planted with whose navel and by whom. She would stop to talk to some of the trees, and she had a story about most of them in that bush.

To Yaya, this was like passing through a village with a native who meets people, greets them or stops to chat with them, and insists on narrating their background to you. As the babbling went on endlessly, Yaya couldn't help getting concerned and wondering if his gray-haired Grandma was not losing it or getting senile.

On their way back, Grandma Fatu had the herb bundled in her head-tie, which she held under an arm. Her scanty gray hair like listless grass swayed with the wind, laying bare her skull. Yaya held the wooden planks and the palm leaves from which she said strings were made.

At the back house, she dropped the herbs on the floor of the verandah and sat down on a little wooden stool. There she made strings from the palm leaves with everybody watching her.

Yaya could feel the anxiety in the air, from the people who came with the patient. They had some sad looks on their faces, which depressed him. And he only felt relieved that they had their eyes focused on Grandma Fatu and not him.

"Now we are ready." she said, picking up the strings. "Yaya and Pa, you come with me." She meant the old man. "And I want the rest of you to wait for us out here."

They entered the room. "Leave the door open," she said.

The people outside crowded the doorway.

"Stand back and don't block the doorway!" Grandma Fatu shrieked.

The man underneath the cloth was groaning; the cock was struggling too.

The group outside were murmuring, seeming impatient, playing cats and dogs with their heads finding space to have a better view.

Inside, the old man was pacing. Meanwhile, Yaya now felt all the hair on his body standing straight. He kept clenching and unclenching his fists.

Grandma Fatu was calm, without a flicker of expression on her face. Perhaps she was meditating or bidding her time. Finally, abruptly, she pulled away the cloth. The cock shook its beak, squeaked, pecked at the hands that held its feet and stretched up, as high as it could go, flapping its wings and squeaking some more. Simultaneously, the lying man was hollering, though holding tight onto the cock. Grandma Fatu bowed by them and removed the cup of water and the kolanuts. She put those farther aside. She then reached for the rooster, held it by its wings, and circled it over the man four times. Then she dropped it on the floor.

The cock jumped, flapped its wings, crowed and ran out through a cheering crowd—without so much as a limp!

"Praise be to Allah!" Grandma Fatu said.

"Praise be to the Almighty God!" the old man said, with both of his hands in his face.

The people outside were dancing and singing thanks too, to God.

Yaya smiled with admiration for his Grandma, although not still a convert or present at the scene by choice.

"Now Yaya, go get the mota and pound the herbs with the goat oil in it. And remember, this patient is yours. All yours. He should be up in four weeks, if you are good! I'm gone."

But wait, not so fast, old woman! Yaya's frown was a mile long as he vacantly stared at Grandma Fatu going inside her house. *By the way, who said I want to be good at this? Or to even get involved?*

In that plight, Yaya looked around to meet sharp eyes on him, from the restless relatives of the patient. And promptly, he moved. He got the mortar and the pestle, and got some water in a bucket, with which he washed the inside of the mortar and the tips of the pestle. With those utensils, and the herbs, and goat oil, he maneuvered himself out of view, to an open space, where the back house stood adjacent to the front house.

There was a mango tree in the center of the sandy strip, a few feet behind the houses. Its branches extended over the tips of the roofs, forming a shade beneath about two yards in circumference. That was where Yaya got busy, pounding the herb. As he did, his hands took off with a mind of their own, his fists tightly clamped around the pestle, which went up and down into the mortar, with such energy that it amazed Yaya. He pounded like one possessed, ignoring his sweat soaking body.

Then inexplicably the pestle broke in two. One half stuck in the mortar while he held the other. Neither was useful for any more pounding. Now, Yaya wondered whether he applied too much pressure, or if the accident came from being carried away —or was it the old stick saying it's had enough?

"Grandma Fatu, the pestle has broken," he called out.

"What, brother? Which pestle? Grandma Fatu is dead!" said one of his younger brothers, lying with two others on a mat in the room with him.

"What?" Yaya sat up in bed, unbelieving and frowning in puzzlement. He looked at his brothers. The one who spoke was sitting, looking at him with wild eyes. The others seemed sound asleep.

Then Yaya remembered. He had come for Grandma Fatu's 40th day ceremony which had taken place in the day, and it was now the following night. He was lying in a room in her back house, with his brothers crowded on the floor.

He could feel the boy's wondering eyes peering at him.

"Just a bad dream," he said to the youth, not to alarm him further.

He laid back thinking how it all seemed so real. He then laughed it off, welcoming the educated notion that it was his mind playing games with him, because Grandma Fatu was dead. In that dream, what he experienced was something concocted by his own mind, just how the mind works. And he fell off asleep.

Shortly afterwards, Yaya had another conference with Grandma Fatu. It was just like he had been on a recess. They were at the

140

back house, in the room with the patient. She was sitting on her rattan stool with the pounded substance —greenish and oily—in a pan on the floor before her.

"Now Yaya, take this *moryoh...*" Grandma Fatu placed a handful of the substance on the mat near Yaya. "Squeeze the liquid out of it unto that man's foot."

Yaya looked at the ailing man's shattered leg and cringed.

"And remember, Yaya, the potency of this *moryoh* could be destroyed if it ever goes directly from one hand to another. If you must give it to somebody, always put it down like I just did, so they can pick it up."

"Thanks, Grandma," Yaya said. Though if he had the freedom, he itched to tell her, '*Big deal, slave driver! I want out!*'

Yet, he went on to draining the liquid out of the substance over the man's knee. It was obvious that this was having a soothing effect on the patient who was now breathing deeply with his eyes closed. The wounded area got coated with a dark-brownish-messy-green color.

"Straighten his legs and form his knees."

Mighty Allah, and Holy cow of India! Man, do I really have to put my hand in there?

As Yaya deliberated, Grandma Fatu shot him a fierce glance which made him bow immediately and start feeling his way in the man's knees.

When he watched her face—his hands on the knee-cap, touching some chopped human bones, and thinking he was getting sick—it seemed she was smiling.

"Enough! Now take this, and plaster it all around his leg." She pushed the *moryoh* in the pan towards him. "After that, take those four wooden planks and lay them around his leg, and tie them with these—" She was pointing to some ropes that were lying in a neat row on the mat, which she had made out of threads from the palm leaves they brought.

Yaya looked at her for a moment, still absolutely rebellious and not imagining himself in that position. But as spellbound as he was, he went on to apply the *moryoh* generously over the knee, up the thigh and down the leg. He then laid the four wooden planks around the leg and tied them firmly.

"Good job," Grandma Fatu said. "Enough for today. You will let his leg stay like that for one week, and after that, you should start dressing it twice a week. After a while the *moryoh* will be dried, of course. But all you have to do is to mix it with fresh water and goat oil every time you apply it."

Yaya felt relieved somehow, thinking that any break at all would be highly appreciated. With that feeling he decided to show some interest. "Will that make him well?"

"I have never failed, my child, or we wouldn't have touched him."

"And what do I do——"

Grandma Fatu was gone.

A shocked Yaya woke up immediately. This time he was definitely terrified and shivering. That was not a dream, he reflected. But he was in bed and had been sleeping. He looked at his brothers on the mat. They were all covered to the neck.

But what? This bizarre dismay couldn't be happening!

Sitting up in bed that night, in Grandma Fatu's back house, Yaya, however, was intensely concerned. His mind in disarray and his heart jumping like he had a kangaroo in his chest. Years of resentment and dread for what Grandma Fatu did as a calling awe-struck him. Also, his more than fifteen years of continuous Western education, and his modern perception of himself, with his career aspirations in the civil service, all compounded matters.

And frankly, Yaya preferred the lifestyle he was living in Sobala, which he had no intention of giving up. Even with all that Grandma Fatu had said, and especially with what he had been through for one night.

In the wee-wee hours of that night, he wished he could disclose those dreams to somebody. But to whom? Stating a word of it to anybody in the family, even his mother, would just start an uproar and create a sense of panic.

Then the whole family would know that he was Grandma Fatu's appointed successor—a square peg in a round hole! More so, when they knew quite well that he was the wrong person for such work. This was like him picking some *uneducated* relative and putting her in his office in Sobala and expect that person to perform even some simple clerical work.

"That would be senseless, quite senseless!" Yaya told himself. He reached up to the plank of the wooden window over the head of the bed and got two recent copies of *Newsweek* and *West Africa,* magazines that he had brought from Sobala. He read those till day break, by a little kerosene lamp he had wound completely up and placed next to him on the bed. As he read, he leaned against the wall facing his sleeping brothers, whom he envied in their innocence.

Daylight was a relief!

Yaya went out, got a bucket of water and went for a bath in a two-room zinc enclosure behind the house. There was a pit toilet in the other room. Here, it was just a flat ground, cemented, with a drainage, where one brought water in a bucket to bath. It was quick with him. He got out and put on a shirt, slacks and shoes, and went greeting people inside the house and around the compound.

It was 7:00 a.m. Most of the people had awakened. The women wore long *gara* and cotton gowns with chopsticks in their mouths. They stood and sat in a group chatting in the center of the backyard, around big pots on huge stones set in triangles that had burning flames underneath, from chunks of wood stuck in-between.

There were many strangers from yesterday. Some people were returning from offering *Salatul-Fajr*—the early morning *suba* prayer— at the mosque. They were mostly middle-aged and elderly people. Many had a *torsorbear*-rosary in their hands and were rolling the beads as they came. The men wore white caps and light colored *bubas*-gowns. The women had their heads tied up and wore gowns too, though more colorful and variously cut.

Yaya stood in front of Grandma Fatu's house, bowing and greeting everybody as they came in or passed by. After making sure he had said the morning greetings to everybody that he should, he returned to his room in the back house, where he packed. He then swallowed some *mornee*—an oatmeal-like porridge made from rice flour rolled into tiny balls and boiled in hot water and sugar. He liked the sour-sweet taste, which came from some green lemon squeezed into the *mornee*, or perhaps it was *tombii*—another sour fruit.

After breakfast, Yaya went around again, saying good-bye and explaining that he had a long journey ahead. At 8 a.m. he was in a Mazda mini van, bought cooperatively by the produce farmers of Wuyadu and Kankalay, the next village, to transport their products to buying centers in the big towns.

Yaya stopped in Taényadu—some twenty miles away from Grandma Fatu's village—just a customary homage to the family compound, to see members of the family who couldn't go to Grandma Fatu's 40th day ceremony. After two hours of seeking everybody, listening to complaints, demands and problems, a produce truck came along heading for Sobala. He jumped into it, lying on top of bags of coffee beans and not particularly caring where he was taken.

143

CHAPTER ELEVEN

"Hey, mister, are you there? We have arrived," the truck driver's assistant hollered at Yaya.

He looked at his watch; it was 9:45 p.m. The two hundred miles journey from Taényadu to Sobala in the loaded Toyota truck nonstop had taken ten hours, which was expected on the rugged roads that characterized the highways of Manika Kunda. The truck was in a drive-way in the eastern section of town, some five miles away from the northwest where Yaya lived. Yet he didn't find it necessary to ask if he was going to be taken home. The finality in the voice of the man who announced their arrival implied enough; that the truck had reached its destination with no plans to move an inch further.

Yaya jumped down and dusted himself. Even with the hard stuffed bags of produce which had cushioned the impact of bumps and gallops along the way, he felt sore all over. He paid the fare, said thanks, and saddled his little traveling bag and stepped on the street.

Sobala was beautiful, the *London* of Manika Kunda. Lights were on everywhere. As Yaya walked towards home hoping a cab would come along soon, he thought that it was interesting how the British developed this country: *Because the colonial Administrators lived in the capital and the provincial and district headquarters, those were the only places they saw fit to provide with modern amenities. Towns like Taényadu and a multitude of others lacked even tap water, not to mention electricity. And yet for countless decades, they were digging all over the country for diamonds, gold, and other minerals, which were exported along with all sorts of produce to the 'home' country.*

A cab was approaching; Yaya flagged it down.

"King George Road."

"Come in."

Yaya laid back in the cab. *Indeed, King George Road! Why not King Mansa Musa Road? Or King Sundiata Keita Road? They just came here and twisted our mind and got our wealth and left us high and dry.* He closed his eyes and went dozing off.

144

But suddenly the cab stopped. Yaya opened his eyes to see a rough looking man standing over the driver. The man outside was dressed in the bewildering colonial police uniform of a breast-shaped hat and an ill-fitting dark gray khaki outfit. It seemed as if some rats had been eating holes in the shirt, or something dug out of an overseas archive.

"Where is your driver's license?"

The cab driver folded his fist and laid some crumpled notes into the palm of the officer.

"Okay, driver, go!"

Yaya felt sick thinking of what transpired. *Going on to 10 p.m. at night, and the police still hustling these poor drivers for handouts?*

"That is the story of our lives," the driver stated.

"That's bribery," Yaya said. "You should have refused to give him anything."

"Aha! Mister, you don't know anything! He would have kept us there, and found every sort of problem with my vehicle. These police or our politicians, I don't know which is worst."

Yaya refused to even think about that, except to concede to himself that since Independence in Manika Kunda, the politicians had proved to be no better than their colonial predecessors. They all behaved in the same way, got what they could, and took it out of the country. Why else would a small country like Manika Kunda not have basic electricity and water supply in every nook and corner? No wonder every educated youth yearned to live in the cities.

The cab was on King George Road.

"The yellow two story house by the electric pole," Yaya said.

He got down, paid his fare and went upstairs to his flat.

"Welcome, sir," his house boy said. An illiterate youth who had wandered into the city seeking some fortune. Yaya had employed him, because of the cheap labor in the country, to do his cooking and cleaning, and run his errands. That was how the colonial expatriates of his standing lived.

In his flat, Yaya felt happy to have made it back. He knew this was where he belonged. The burnt brick building in which he lived had four flats, two up and two down. His was a two bedroom with a living room and a bath, all tiled and brightly painted in light yellow. He had just completed furnishing the place with a locally carved contemporary bedroom and living room set. He also had added a gas stove, a refrigerator and an air conditioner, with the latter installed in his living room window barely three weeks ago.

To many people, possessing those items was a sign that Yaya was progressing, because they portrayed a living standard that was considered a luxury, not affordable to many. If he had a car, they would have considered him rich. But Yaya knew that would take years of savings, and that those were privileges of his white counterparts—young and college-educated civil servants in the colonial days—who would get one as soon as they sat at their desks.

He barely nodded to his house boy and went straight to his bedroom. He dropped the traveling bag, and laid on his milk-colored framed bed, which, with its customized headboard that had a magazine rack and six drawers, occupied most of the room.

"I'm warming your food, sir," his house boy said, standing in the doorway.

"Thanks, Kortu, I'll be right out."

"Madam was here early on today. She said I should go tell her as soon as you make it back."

"Good, leave the food alone and run over to her. Say I said, she should come tip-top."

Yaya was planning on a night out with his girlfriend to further unwind and be himself.

He showered and dressed in a brown short-sleeve safari suit, over his black, made in Italy, leather shoes. He then had a quick absent-minded meal, and was back in the kitchen dumping remnants of rice from his plate in a garbage can when he heard Abie's high heels clicking gracefully in the verandah like she was marching through some hall to receive an award.

His house boy, who was with her, opened the door, so Yaya met her in the living room. "Hello, country boy!"

"Hi, darling." They hugged and kissed.

"How did the trip and the ceremony go?" He suppressed a sigh and she saw it.

"Fine, babe, everything went fine. The ceremony turned out bigger than I expected. And how have you been doing?"

"Really fine. But you look worried and seem down. Did something go wrong?" She was worried about the pressure she sensed in him.

Yaya looked at the tall slender figure and sighed. Abie with her silky copper-toned face, and her rabbit nose, full lips, radiantly raspberry, striking splendidly with the big round gold earrings on her small ears. She held a black purse in her hand and wore a gold embroidered mauve-and-white *gara* top and matching pants, in perfect harmony with a pair of mauve high-heeled shoes. He thought, beauty, brains and class were what Abie had. One minute with her and she could tell how he felt.

She was smiling at him as she stood swaying her purse, her long dark hair in braids hanging down to her neck. He cherished Abie, so beautifully black and sensuous, with just about enough Western sophistication that he liked in an African woman—not pushy or too meek—just level-headed, with a rational sense of humor.

Abie had graduated not quite six months ago from a nursing school and was working at the government hospital where it was Yaya's hope that one of those hot-stuff doctors would not steal her before he got round to marrying her—if ever! First, there was the hassle he expected to face coming from a family which believed in fixing marriages or putting two total strangers together. But now, added to that concern, he worried how or whether he would survive Grandma Fatu's grip on him—such a bewildering threat—which was overshadowing every other problem.

Yaya didn't know that his worries were showing on his face. This got Abie wondering about what could be darkening his thoughts.

"Yaya, darling, is there something bothering you? Did anything go wrong while you were in your hometown?" Abie's tone sounded so pitiful to him.

"No, baby. I'm just exhausted." He smiled to charm and disarm her. Then he decided to bluff it off. "But you know how it is, when I go back there, the only time I'm left alone is when the last person in the town sleeps."

She laughed at that. "It sounds like you're pretty important over there then," she said. "I envy you, Mr. Chief. I just hope they didn't push some woman at you."

"Well, we didn't get to that this time."

"Look at you, maniac. But at least you knew better than to let them show their fat faces up here with you."

"You can bet on that. I wouldn't, not especially with you camping around the corner."

She puffed her cheeks at him. "What's the plan?"

"Partying, if you have no objection. It's Friday night."

"And I thought you were worn out."

"Try me."

Socialite that he was, Yaya was well known in the nightclub and was hailed the moment they entered, by friends, colleagues and acquaintances. The manager of the place was a friend too, from high school days, who ran up to meet them as they got to a corner table. He greeted Abie who wasted no time in sitting. Then he turned to Yaya.

"Hello, Mr. LaTalé. How nice of you to come."

"Indeed, as if I'm not here every weekend," Yaya joked.

"That's the point," the manager said. "I admire your courage. To imagine that you compulsively come here and just watch others doing all the drinking, while you sip Coca-Cola all night long. Abie, is it true that he gets drunk on only sugar and water?" They all laughed.

"I mean, I've seen you holding him tight out of this place a couple of times," the manager of the club further teased. "Or am I wrong?"

"Get away from here," Yaya said. But the man had started going away anyway. *Sinners are always seeking partners,* Yaya thought, reflecting on what he saw as a ploy to get him drinking. Because he saw absolutely nothing wrong in coming out and partying without bathing in alcohol or losing his head.

There were warning signs pasted outside at the door and up a wall inside this rendezvous that said, 'No Shoes, No Shirt, No Service.' On this Friday night as most times, it was a crowd of primly-culturally-attired and Westernized wannabees. They were an elite group of young businessmen and professionals, and their seniors, the *sugar daddies* with their pot-bellies and salt-and-pepper hair.

The place had an air of a private club where almost everybody knew the others. As usual, the ladies outnumbered the men and were younger than their male counterparts. But not surprisingly, the women made up for the difference in age, by outdoing their partners on the dance floor and with their restless mouths at the tables.

A pot-bellied man, almost gray, with puffed cheeks and round bags under his eyes was leaning in his seat and smoking steadily. He seemed totally ignored by three younger and provocatively-dressed ladies sitting at his table. They talked to themselves endlessly, like they belonged to some all-female fraternity, while their male partner gaped chimney-like.

With the lights glazing in signals and assorted colors over the dance floor, and with music swirling from powerful speakers that reached his soul, Yaya kept dragging Abie, and whichever lady that was willing for a dance, until his shirt started sticking on him.

It was all in a bid to purge his system completely of the ordeal with Grandma Fatu in his sleep—just yesterday in Wuyadu.

Abie and Yaya had a ride from the club. As usual, they ended at Yaya's flat. Abie was twenty-one years old and was an independent adult in the city. There were things she would do in Sobala that she wouldn't dare think of in her hometown, Gbepehme, in the Western Region of Manika Kunda. That was like being in the room of a man, way past the middle of the night, as she was with Yaya at this present time. In Gbepehme, she would have felt so naked and weary that it would not have been worth the try.

To start with, nothing went on in that small town that somebody didn't see. And for an unmarried girl like her from a competing chieftain family—with all the rivalry, name-calling and bull-fighting that went on between the ruling families for the crown at each succession—she had been taught that an amoral exposure or scandal about her was all that was needed to break the bone out of the well deserved chance of her family's grab on the staff or throne. So, over there she was careful. She dated nobody and lived like a native girl by traditions and expectations.

But in Sobala it was different. This was the city, and she lived a long distance away from anybody that came from her hometown. Besides, when she left home tonight, she didn't have to explain to anybody where she was going and when she would return. She shared a three bedroom flat with two other girls she had met in nursing school. They did pretty much the same things. None of them might be at home now or if they were, they would be with their boyfriends.

Yaya and Abie met over three years ago. She was in her first year in nursing school and new to the city. Yaya was in his final year in college and his fraternity was throwing a non-exclusive ball. So they sent a bus to the nursing hostel to lure the needed women from over there with a free ride to the party. As social secretary of his fraternity, Yaya played host to Abie and others. And from that night on, he fell in love with her. But it took two more years before he could know her as a woman. When he did, it was just two months to her twentieth birthday, the same time she passed to go to final year. It was to his credit that he made her a woman. That was slightly over a year ago.

When they had sex, he always used a condom. With Abie, it was not so much from fear of the hovering AIDS epidemic, which many Africans believe started in the Western world but which got blamed on Africa.

Because Africa among other continents in the world could be likened to a desolate old woman living with no relative in some backward village, at whom everybody comes pointing fingers, when inexplicably their child dies and they must find a *witch*. So when AIDS came, and was initially a lifestyle trauma among distinct segments of the population in the West, they still blamed it on Africa. African physicians were stunned, saying that clearly that ill-wind blew from the West.

Yaya knew his society, his limits, his goals, and his fears. Ambitious and undecided at 23, he used the condom on Abie like other girls he had dated since high school to avoid an unwanted pregnancy and the liability of fatherhood which he didn't feel ready for. More so, as he dreaded the scandal and uproar that some men have gone through from impregnating people's daughters in Manika Kunda without properly seeking their hands in marriage.

Now, Abie was in Yaya's bedroom and he had gone to the bathroom. When Yaya returned, she was in nothing but scanties. Her maiden breasts were entrapped in a pink bra, which held them high and pointed, yet revealed the silky fullness of their tops and inner curves.

Abie went to the bathroom next. As she left, Yaya was feeding his eyes on her beauty, from her elegantly healthy legs, to her full, firm and fresh thighs, and then to the sheer nylon briefs clinging sumptuously on the rounded cheeks of her behind.

Yaya went and laid on his bed stark naked with his shaft shooting up like a rocket launching into orbit. Abie liked to be dominated and this was one night he wanted to be in control. He closed his eyes, mellowing out like he was getting ready for some world championship bout.

Then Abie came back, with her exquisitely tailored body exposed and gyrating plumply, and threw herself on him like one diving into a backyard pool. He grabbed her and planted a kiss on her full raspberry lips. She cuddled into his arms and clung at him as they laid sideways.

One of his hands went stroking in the front, going downwards between her legs, while the other struggled to unhook her bra. Succeeding, he let loose a pair of full, round and pointed tits crowned with thick black nipples. He stroked, toyed and teased the dormant nipples alternating between two and three fingers. They quickly grew tall and radiant. The sight making his mouth water, he proceeded to lick, suck and chew on the nipples, one after the other, as Abie groaned and moaned, thrusting one breast after another into his mouth, going wild, from the passionate contact with the sensitive areas surrounding her trembling nipples.

There was no thought of Grandma Fatu when Yaya mounted the soft craving form of Abie and delved into her happy velvet vault, filling her with his throbbing length, making her shudder and utter a deep sigh of passion. She lifted her legs and hooked him over his lower back. Then they moved together with the bed, which cracked rapidly and relentlessly in rhythm.

He stayed on top this time, servicing her from the front, sideways, and bowing, as she yelped, twisted and grunted until she started sucking her breath in sharp little gasps and rocking her hips out of key, but steadily wiggling and going out of control. When he came, it was with such a warm sensation that sent blissful stars into his head, as he got lost, and found himself in her tight embrace.

When he looked at the clock on the wall, it was 4 a.m. They were at it for a full hour. Afterward, laying there next to her instantly sleeping self, he told himself it was a gigantic relief and he needed it.

On the following day, Saturday, Abie and Yaya woke up at 9 a.m. They went to the bathroom together. But Yaya stepped out first and came to the living room to find the tiled floor sparkling from the doorstep of his room all the way to the kitchen. The cushions were neatly arranged against the back and sides of the two long couches sitting in an L shape, with the brown velvet upholstery on them seeming almost lint free. The center table, a tall squared unit made completely from mahogany wood, stood glowing, like the matching dining room table and its chairs.

"Good morning, sir. Breakfast is ready," Kortu said, cleaning the refrigerator.

"Good morning, Kortu. Thank you, good man."

Yaya went to the dining room table and opened the two covered dishes sitting in the center. Breakfast was ready. Kortu had boiled some cassava, and to go with that, he had made a palatable stew from fried liver, fresh tomatoes and onions in vegetable oil.

Abie came out as he was covering the dishes. She was in one of his thick robes and was walking barefooted. Yaya went and turned on the radio, a Sharp radio/cassete unit which he gave Abie some money to buy on her trip to London at her graduation from nursing school. The unit stood equal in height with his 13" black and white T.V. on top of a unit like the center table. The radio was on the National Broadcasting Service of Manika Kunda. An attention grabbing Jazz rhythm was playing in the background over which a heavy masculine voice reassuringly spoke, claiming that *Hollywood* cigarette was the best brand for strong men. It said nothing about the health hazards from smoking cigarettes.

After the advertisement, the voice of the radio announcer came through: *Good Morning. This is the National Broadcasting Service of Manika Kunda. And this is Battilloi Waritay, reading the 10 o'clock news. According to a news release from the office of the President this morning, a special tribunal has been set up, comprised of judges, government representatives and members of the armed forces, for the treason trial of Sitafa Cibin and others rounded up in a foiled coup plan against the legitimate and democratic government of Manika Kunda.*

Yaya hissed. He went right back to the radio and switched the unit to tape. He thought: *Manika Kunda and our treason trials, they never end. Every six months there is a new treason trial and a bloody execution of persons who purportedly tried to overthrow our most beloved President and his most beneficent government.*

This President who came to power through the electoral process fourteen years ago. But since then, he has used all tactics to perpetuate himself and cohorts in power, at all cost, even by undermining all integrity of the voting system and the wishes of the electorate, and nobody can say a thing! Because, to oppose him is to line up on the list for the next treason trial or eternal detention. Yet they say a legitimate and democratic government!

The tape was playing a nice Congolese music in Swahili. Neither Yaya nor Abie understood a word. But they liked the beats and at least preferred that to the depressing news about some innocent people on their way to the gallows. Abie was even wiggling in tune with the music. Yaya went to the dining room table and started helping himself. Abie went to meet Kortu in the kitchen. He was cleaning the stove.

"Good morning, Kortu."

"Good morning, Ma."

"I see you're doing a good job. You're really taking good care of your boss."

"Yes, Madam, I try Ma."

"Guess what? Why don't you take the day off, and for today, I will do your job."

"Okay, Ma, if you say so, Madam." Kortu bowed with a big smile to show his excitement. He immediately washed his hands and went into his room. Abie joined Sidi at the table. And soon Kortu was out saying good-bye.

Immediately after breakfast, Abie threw off the gown and stayed in a light gold transparent nylon wear, with nothing underneath; her exquisite body showing through, seeming on her like her parts were crafted to be assembled in series of smooth flawless curves.

The rest of her chore that morning was washing the dishes, cleaning the table and sitting on Yaya's lap to get him back into the bedroom. There, they did what they did the previous night for three hours continuously. Then they slept off, with plans to go to the beach later, where they would have dinner.

Abie said some doctors and nurses were throwing a send-off party for a colleague from the nursing staff who was going to London to study medicine.

At 4 p.m. in a cooling afternoon sun, the reggae jamming, private-car-turned-into-taxi which took Yaya and Abie to the beach pulled up at the party house. It was a round mud-plastered hut, painted green on the outside with a thatched roof, which seemed like an umbrella. Some smart Lebanese merchants had constructed this unit and a few others around the beach to capitalize on the emergent tourist industry and the elitist desires of young 'well-to-do' Manika Kundans. Each hut had a bar, a few toilets, a well-furnished common room and recreation rooms with TV screens fed with videos.

The units always felt cool inside, possibly from the thick layered mud walls and the palm leaves up on the roof. They were open to patrons indiscriminately, as long as one afforded the high price of the drinks and eateries which short-skirted waitresses served.

Occasionally, these units were leased for private parties like the one Yaya and Abie came for. It was a small party of about thirty people, half of them doctors and nurses, and the rest like Yaya, with a friend from the hospital. Abie introduced Yaya around. Of course he already knew most of them, particularly the prominent doctors, like Dr. Douda who studied under Dr. Denton Cooley, the famous heart surgeon in Houston, Texas, and Doctor Bayoh who studied in Germany and who some sources in the hospital claimed could do 'fifteen surgeries a day.'

Abie went ahead, mingling in the crowd. The jazz music playing was barely audible in the background, because people were mostly socializing. The crowd here was as somber as a social gathering of college professors, except that the latter were known to rant about their frustrations in funding while doctors would rather talk in jargons.

Yaya was sitting on a barstool at the bar, letting Abie live up to her reputation as Ms. Popular. He looked at Dr. Lundy and Dr. Bayoh, both in their middle ages. They stood surrounded by other doctors, all Manika Kundans, most of whom had trained and specialized abroad. Yet they sacrificed everything they could get for practicing in those advanced countries to come home and serve their people. He respected that. In his opinion, the silent heroes of Manika Kunda were those doctors and the teachers across the country, some of whom hardly even got paid when the month ended.

The short-skirted waitresses serving drinks were now asking people if they wanted food.

"Yes, please," Yaya said to a waitress that came.

"What would you want, sir?"

"What is there to offer, Madam?"

"Roasted chicken, *jollof rice*, mixed vegetable salad, fried plantain and chips."

Yaya thought, that's all? He wanted some thick African food, like *fufu* or some kind of yams. *But gosh! These Westernized Africans, even the food at their parties now have a Western bent!* "Okay, give me some chicken, jollof rice, and some fried plantain."

The waitress went and brought him a plate. As Yaya ate, he noticed a couple of doctors no more than thirty-years-old, busy with their eyes, inspecting the shining thighs of the waitresses. They would whisper to themselves with raised eyebrows, while their eyes stayed fixed at the behinds of the girls. The waitresses too seemed to enjoy the attention as they went up and down swinging and giggling with a mischievous glint in their eyes.

Doctors and women! Yaya thought; he wondered if it's their in-depth knowledge of the human anatomy which made some of them into chronic womanizers.

There was that one, Dr. Kuma who studied in Russia, who had been running after Abie forever; since she started going to the hospital for her clinical; yet he was married or lived with some woman. Yaya couldn't even tell who the Dr. Kuma came to the party with as he moved around clowning and talking to one woman after another. As he headed towards Abie, Yaya called her over.

He was not going to sit there and let some leech steal his woman before his eyes, particularly when Abie looked so beautiful and sexy in her T-shirt and tight fitting-jeans. As she came to him, walking gracefully with her braided hair dangling around her head, he thought she was the most beautiful woman in that crowd, if not in the whole of Manika Kunda.

Yaya chatted with a few of the doctors and nurses, and they left the party in the middle of the endless speeches. He wanted to smell some fresh air from the sea, and Abie wanted to see the band playing at an outdoor concert on the beach.

The average Manika Kunda came to the beach fully dressed as they would to a party. And indeed most of them came to band shows and all kinds of parties that went on constantly on the various beaches surrounding Sobala.

At the bandstand on the other side of the long stretching-beach, Abie and Yaya were just in time to hear the band leader announcing that they were playing their last record. He said they had an engagement to play at the Safari Club later that evening. It was the club that Yaya and Abie had gone to the previous night.

The band was a group of young adults on their way to stardom in Manika Kunda. They could sing any hit or mime any artist anywhere in the world. All they needed was to hear a record and go to work on it. Like they'd done with M. C. Hammer's *Too Legit To Quit,* which they were singing now. If you heard it, you would clap for them, even if you didn't get ecstatic like the massive crowd of youngsters and adults who stood mesmerized and hailing.

As the record came to an end and people started leaving, Yaya and Abie got away from the crowd. They held hands, both of them kicking the yellow sand as they walked towards a set of rocks along the shore. The rocks had been beautifully arranged by nature in a quarter of a mile distance with enough room between each for personal space.

These smooth sun-baked rocks were hot spots for lovers. They sat here, leaned on each other, or laid down. Also some white tourists spread their towels on top of the rocks, where they laid between the rays of the sun and the sensual heat beneath. Abie and Yaya sought a vacant rock and sat shoulder to shoulder.

It was 6. p.m. The sinking sun loomed farther down in the deep seas. The waves were flapping at the shores, bringing objects that fluttering sea birds clattered at. Abie was talking excitedly to Yaya but his attention was focused on the sea, and his face was clouded. She followed his eyes, and as she looked at the deep blue sea, it reminded her about Yaya's mind, which seemed to be holding a mystery from her.

"What are you thinking about, Yaya?" Abie asked.

He looked at her; he was thinking about Grandma Fatu and the inheritance that had been handed to him. But he couldn't tell her.

"I was just admiring nature," he said.

"Yes, nature. You've been having this cloud on your face since you came from your hometown. Did your people ask you to marry some woman over there? You know, that's how you Mandinkas do."

Abie and Yaya were from different ethnic groups. She was a Temnaé, a minority ethnic group from the Western region of Manika Kunda. Yaya would have sworn to Abie that it was nothing to do with some woman. But he didn't. He was taken aback by the tone of her last sentence. *"You know, that's how you Mandinkas do."*

"Frankly, Abie, there was no situation about any woman, so lets forget that."

She didn't believe him, but didn't feel like saying anything. Or what could be so bothering him?

They went out again that night to the club where the band was playing and rested on Sunday.

With the weekend over, life went on as usual with Yaya in Sobala, his preferred surrounding. He would go to work, come home, go play tennis or hang out with Abie and friends. This went on for one week. However, on the following Friday night after Yaya's return from Wuyadu, even though he went to bed in Sobala, somehow he found himself busy in Grandma Fatu's back house in Wuyadu.

"Get some fresh water and moisten the *moryoh*," Grandma Fatu had said.

The patient was lying on the mat with his foot propped up on a pile of some old blankets. One of the women that came with him was by the fireside in the center of the backyard cooking. The little boy, Bori, was running around tossing and catching a ball patched together from raw rubber, very likely from one of the rubber trees scattered all over the village.

"Where are all his other relatives?" Yaya asked Grandma Fatu.

"It's been one week, Yaya. They went back and left the woman that's out there and the little boy. But go on and do as I say." She willed him with her eyes.

He went to the big clay pot in Grandma Fatu's parlor, got some water and came back.

"You forgot the goat oil and the grinding stone. Go to

my room, they are standing at the foot of my bed!"

Yaya went and got them.

"Now, before you even touch that man, go get that bottle—" She pointed to the basket in the corner. "That's the first thing you will put on his wound when you remove the dressing. Also, be ready with the *moryoh* by mixing it with some goat oil and water."

Yaya fetched the bottle and grounded the dried *moryoh* with water and the goat oil. He let that stay on the grinding stone as he removed the man's dressing. Staring at the raw dripping sore, he shivered and cringed, but the flesh on the knee was forming. The shredded cartilage that were standing were now lying, with the bones not so exposed as they were last week. He poured the greenish herbal lotion from the bottle on the wound, and applied the *moryoh* until the man's leg was all plastered with it.

"Rub it in by stroking your hand over the knee six times."

Yaya did so, and Grandma Fatu nodded. He then carefully laid the planks around the injured leg and tied it with the string. When he looked up, Grandma Fatu had disappeared. He gaped.

This procedure went on twice a week for four more weeks, until the man started standing and moving with the leg. Grandma Fatu was there every time. After each occurrence, Yaya would wonder how he happened to be traveling at some appointed time in his sleep from Sobala to Wuyadu to perform the service. Also he wondered how come he would not resist and speak his mind to Grandma Fatu. Yet, like a zombie, he went through it all.

And yet every time afterwards—when he found himself in the same pajamas he slept in, on his luxurious bed —he would dismiss the experience as some nightmare, *a bad dream*, even when something kept telling him that everything was real. Or, how would he know step-by-step the details of what to do? Never in his life had he observed Grandma Fatu at her work when she lived. He never went even close, because he couldn't stand anything about the whole thing by mere thought. Those patients, their pains, the sores, stale and raw blood, all made him sick.

But now about nine times he had done that work, even without knowing. Obviously Grandma Fatu was not resting in her grave, like she told him before she died. It must be her spirit that came taking over him and transporting him and making him do all those things that he did. A few weeks ago, he had thought about tying his leg to the bedpost when he slept to see if that would make a difference. But suppose Abie or his house boy walked in on him sleeping in such form? *That would be really ridiculous!*

Already, Abie was accusing him of changing, not being the usual Yaya she knew, because he was brooding all the time and uncommunicative, and not going over to see her. He wished she knew what he was going through.

Well, it will soon be over! Yaya cheered himself up. The man was getting better. Grandma Fatu herself had said in their previous meeting that there was only one more treatment left for the patient, and the knee seemed to be healing fine and the man had started standing and even moving on it.

She had said that, as for the patient learning to walk perfectly with that leg again, he would have to do so at his own pace in his village. And anyway, Yaya thought, even as he went to work sometimes exhausted and sleepy, at least Grandma Fatu had, so far, not interfered with his days, which he spent as he liked in Sobala.

"Yaya! Yaya!"

"Nar'amu! Nar'amu!" Yaya found himself answering in the usual Mandinka way to a loud call of his name by Grandma Fatu. It was the day of their last treatment for the patient.

She was inside her front house, while he was tossing Bori's self-made rubber ball with him between the houses.

"Grandma Fatu is calling me," he told the kid.

But Bori who was standing at the far end, behind the houses, was running away towards the front yard, shouting, "Grandpa, Grandpa."

Yaya went to bid Grandma Fatu's call. They met as she came out of the back door holding the grinding stone and the goat oil wrapped in a dry leaf. Yaya rushed to get the grinding stone from her.

"No, you go get the water," she said.

Yaya went into the parlor and fetched the water. In a haste he filled the cup to the brim only to have water splashing on his pants as he walked outside. Chiding himself for being so careless, he met Grandma Fatu standing in the middle of the backyard with the old man who had come with the patient a month and a half ago. He was with a woman and a younger man, and all their feet were dusty, obviously from the long walk on footpaths through the bush. The old man held a rope that was knotted around the neck of a goat. The woman had a hen in her hand, while the man had on his head a loaded sack.

Yaya bowed in greetings to them.

"They even brought us some presents," Grandma Fatu smilingly said.

"Yaya, show him where to put that bag of rice. And Pa, please come with me and tie the goat on one of these poles in the verandah over here," she was walking towards the back house.

The water still in his hand, Yaya led the man carrying the sack to Grandma Fatu's parlor. He pointed to a corner where the man dumped his load. They returned to the back house. Everybody was in the treatment room. Yaya could see the patient, all excited, standing between his father and the young beautiful woman who had recently arrived.

"Oh, Mama, I thank you for such a wonderful job," the old man was saying.

"That's the man to thank," Grandma Fatu said, pointing to Yaya as he walked towards her. She was sitting on her stool near the mat with the hen in her hand.

"You've done a great job, young man. God bless you," the old man said.

"Thank you, Pa. Yet the honor is Grandma Fatu's," said Yaya in a self-effacing manner.

"Oh, really, you did a good job, though," the young woman said. She was holding the patient's hand and admiring the leg that was injured. Meanwhile, his eyes on flame roved all over her, while the other woman who had stayed to nurse him was shooting both of them hostile glances as she stood by the door, with her arms down Bori's shoulders while she talked with the man who was totting the rice.

Yaya watched the exchange of current between the two women and the man. He presumed that the women —who could not wait to vent their jealousy, and who seemed to have no love lost between them—were wives of the injured man.

"Okay, everybody, Tamba will be ready for you to take home today," Grandma Fatu declared. "And now, please excuse us so we can do our work."

With that the relatives of Tamba filed out of the room. He sat down on the mat and stretched his legs, still excited and leering at the wriggling figure of the just arriving young dark lady who walked out last.

"Yes, Tamba, you will be going home today," Grandma Fatu declared again.

"Oh Mama, I thank you so much. I know my family will be so happy. Did you see my wife who walked out just now? She had a baby who was not even three months old when I had this accident."

"Well, you can say thanks to God, that at least you have recovered," Grandma Fatu stated.

"How many wives do you have?" Yaya asked out of curiosity.
"Just two," Tamba said.

Just two? Yaya laughed inwardly at that. He was older than this guy and still single. *I hate to ask him how many he's got when he makes thirty. Such die-hard polygamists! A boy twenty or at the most twenty-two with two wives? And in this day and age?*

But again, Yaya thought, what do you expect from such an illiterate palm-wine tapper? "The more women you marry is the more problem you will be creating for yourself, mister," he warned.

"I know!" the fellow stated matter-of-factly.

"Let's get to business," Grandma Fatu prompted. Yaya looked at her, and thought that as far as she was concerned, Tamba could have professed to have five wives and it would all have been in place.

"Tamba, you take the dressing off your leg, and Yaya will mix the *moryoh*. Because after today, you will be doing it for yourself." Grandma Fatu then concentrated on tying the legs of the hen, after which she dropped it on the floor!

Yaya got the grinding stone and traced the dried *moryoh* over it; he then added some water and goat oil and mixed everything together.

Tamba had undressed his leg and was marveling at his knee, which had some scars, but otherwise looked perfectly healed from the outside.

"You have healed fine, Tamba. You won't need to tie it up anymore," Grandma Fatu observed. Then she turned to Yaya and started smiling. "Yaya, are you not proud of yourself for doing this curing from the start all by yourself while I only watched? Didn't you do it like you were supposed to?" And she laughed big, showing all her missing teeth.

Next Grandma Fatu said: "Yaya, you have passed-out!"

"Passed-out?" Yaya couldn't help laughing inwardly, wondering from where she learnt that word. Maybe from some soldiers she had cured—recruits who got injured in training and were rushed to her. They used that word for graduation from training. He reflected on what she said and acknowledged silently that indeed he had just graduated from Grandma Fatu's school of bone healing, to be known as Yaya, the bone healer. *Quite a title!* He heartlessly laughed, nodding to her and thanking God that Abie knew nothing about this!

"Master, finish your work," Grandma Fatu prompted.

Yaya rubbed the *moryoh* over Tamba's knee and all over his leg. Then he gathered the wooden planks and wrapped the strings around them, and he put those away in a corner.

"Well, Tamba, we are done. Go join your folks. Later, before you leave today, Yaya will give you some *moryoh.* You will mix that with some goat oil and water to rub on your knee every morning."

Tamba got up, groaning. "Thanks, Grandma Fatu, and thanks, Yaya," he said and left the room with a slight limp.

"He will be alright in a week or two," Grandma Fatu said.

Yaya was on his knees, still on the mat, rubbing his *moryoh*-soiled hands together and gazing apprehensively at Grandma Fatu.

"What's next, Grandma?" he asked.

"What's next, Grandma?" she mimicked Yaya and smiled broadly at him. "My child, that is what makes you special. We're now going to seal your new carved bond with the ancestors who passed down this gift to us. And then I'll leave you in the hands of their spirits for companions."

Yaya quickly looked at his hands on which the *moryoh* had dried up, with a frightful alarm ringing in his head at the words Grandma Fatu had just said.

Not quite yet, Grandma Fatu! He tried to get up, to run and free himself. But he felt glued and had no control over his body, even as his mind kept telling him: *'Run, run, run, Yaya!'* He realized it was hopeless. He tried to speak but his mouth was heavy. There were tremors in his temple, yet he couldn't utter a word.

Yaya wished to scream: *'No, Grandma, no! Please let me go! I don't need this gift or any bond! I love my ancestors and that's enough! Now, can't you see, this is not for me? I already have a career in the Civil Service and I live differently in Sobala. Please, it's a big family. Give it to Wusu, your son, or anybody, but—'*

Grandma Fatu had gotten up. She came to stand over him, casting a shadow over his body like a cage. Yaya was shivering and feeling an eerie chilliness all over. His armpits were dripping with perspiration and beads of sweat like twinkling stars glittered on his forehead as he agonized in earnest. She placed her palms on his head.

"Yaya, you are now sacred and must know the scared secret, for your life will henceforth be by the dictates of the kind spirits of your ancestors. You will communicate with the spirit world, and until you are permitted, no man that is different from you should know what transpires." At this, Yaya sighed heavily, and felt some wetness around the corners of his eyes, out of powerlessness and despair.

"Now listen carefully and remember these, for you will need them....." Instantly, Yaya winced at the hot musky air at his ear from

Grandma Fatu bowing and mumbling—it was four phrases—she repeated them three times.

"You should never say those aloud to anybody's hearing." Then she folded her fingers and started counting. "The first is for wisdom from the spirits when you need it. The second is what you say when a patient is brought to you. The third is when you go in search of the sacred leaf. And the last is when you refuse a case; you must say it seven times to keep the evil spirit that has been cast on such a patient out of your way."

Yaya looked at her still wanting to say: ' *Oh, Grandma, can I be left out of this?'*

Grandma Fatu probably thought he was confused, because she told him, "Don't worry child, it will all be clear to you in your sleep."

Yaya gasped and dropped his head, sinking farther in silent despair! Now overpowered, even the false hope that he had entertained about being free after tonight was gone. Grandma Fatu must have noticed, because she laughingly patted him on the shoulder saying, "You will do fine and very fine, just do exactly as I've taught you."

And then she walked away towards the door. At the threshold, she turned to face him with a stern look in her eyes.

"Now you have it, Yaya. When it is time for you to pass it on, you will know. But the heritage must not stop at you. And you cannot transfer it but to whom that is chosen. For to do so is to kill the snake." With that she was gone.

"Knock! Knock! Knock!" Kortu, Yaya's house boy was at his door.

Yaya woke up jerking and sat up with the shirt of his pajamas wet and sticking to his skin.

"Boss, are you alright?"

Yaya ran to the door. "Yes, Kortu?"

His house boy couldn't miss the heavy breathing, the frightened look in his eyes and the soaked pajamas on his body. "Sir, you were screaming just now, and saying something like, 'Oh no! Oh no! Please let me go...' as if somebody was attacking you."

"Was I? I'm sorry, it must have been a bad dream."

"Yes, sir. I've been noticing you saying things like that more and more in your sleep lately, about once or twice every week. Maybe some evil people are fighting you."

"I don't think so, Kortu."

"Well, sir, you are a book person. But if it were me, I would go see a diviner. There is a good man in my village. He will tell you everything, from witchcraft to bad people who may be after you."

"I don't need that, Kortu. Goodnight."

"Well goodnight, sir. I'm sorry."

"That's okay."

As Kortu left, Yaya looked at his watch, it was 4:30 a.m. He took off his damp pajamas and went naked into the bathroom. He urinated and cleansed himself with water the Muslim way, as he was taught since childhood. He told himself that if he had a bath now, he wouldn't sleep anymore; so he dampened a towel and ran it over his body to get rid of the stickiness of his sweat.

He went back to his room, tied a little loin cloth around his waist and laid on his back, reflecting. It was close to four months since Grandma Fatu died, and from the time he went for her forty days ceremony, things have been getting worse, and yet seeming real everyday.

He thought of all what transpired regarding Tamba whom he has just completed healing in his sleep together with Grandma Fatu, as if she were alive. The whole experience had ended in more disappointment. The fact was, whether this ordeal was real or not, Yaya had hoped and prayed it would stop and he would be free from it. Yet he was getting in deeper and deeper.

He regretted that he couldn't recall the village from which Tamba and his folks came, or he would have made a trip to investigate. To know if indeed that fellow Tamba was in existence, and if it was true that his leg got injured and was cured recently.

He thought of how he would put it: *"Hello, Tamba, do you remember me? I was the one that cured your broken leg. Tell me, while you were in Wuyadu, were you aware or in control of yourself? Did you find things around you to be normal? And how did you happen to be there in the first place? Because I can't tell you how I got there. I only found myself doing those things under Grandma Fatu's command. And, Tamba, by the way, she is supposed to be dead. Do you know that?"*

But then Yaya remembered how Grandma Fatu had said he shouldn't tell anybody about what transpired. And for all he knew Tamba, too, might just have been a spirit anyway; an accomplice in Grandma Fatu's grand plan to teach him her work.

Didn't she say, "... And then I'll leave you in the hands of their spirits for companions?" But..., did Grandma Fatu really hand him over to some spirits? What snake was she talking about just now?

Yaya closed his eyes thinking. *Snake.., snake.., snake and heritage!*
The memory came back like he did a fast rewind on a video
cassette. Two years ago, on a visit to Grandma Fatu, she was sitting
on a rattan stool in her room, with him on a bench next to her. She
had the leaf in his face and was looking into his eyes, as she said:

*"Behold for this is your heritage. It is like a snake and you
are its skin. A snake never dies because it has shed its skin. It lives
on, vibrant and alert with the fresh gleaming skin. For it is only
when the snake dies, that the skin dies with it and rots. Yaya, you
are just such a skin."*

'And this new one tonight?' He rubbed hard at his forehead
to recall Grandma Fatu's last words—not quite an hour ago! He
shivered thinking about the eerie feeling he had as she stood over
the threshold, speaking, with her compelling eyes on him.

*"Now you have it, Yaya. When it is time for you to pass it on,
you will know. But the heritage must not stop at you. And you
cannot transfer it but to whom that is chosen. For to do so is to
kill the snake."*

"Oh, Grandma Fatu, can you ever understand?" Yaya cried out
aloud and felt stunned by the echo of his own voice in the stillness
of the night.

Kortu in the other room had quickly sat up in bed at the cry from
his boss. He listened intensely for any more sound. There was
none. So he felt no need to get out again.

Kortu told himself that he knew what was happening. Some evil
people were messing with his boss. Because, though he might not
come from the same town with Mr. LaTalé, yet he knew enough
about people envying and hating other people—particularly a
progressive young man like his boss—to want do evil things to
him, to harm him, to destroy him, through fetish. But his boss
wouldn't believe and won't listen. These book people!

Well, Kortu reflected, he didn't get much education. He left
s c h o o l in Standard Four—the seventh grade—*because of no
school fees!* But even if he was educated like Mr. LaTalé, he would
not blind himself or pretend that native mysteries never occur.

Kortu knew better. *Because they happen all the time. Like
when there is a big light that comes from nowhere in my village
and shines broadly and brightly under the ageless baobab tree.*

Kortu was concerned and worried. *Mr. LaTalé is a nice man,
almost like a brother.* He prayed silently that those people fighting
his boss—don't succeed! He laid back, with his ears open.

CHAPTER TWELVE

"I'm sorry, sir," Yaya apologized to his boss. It was 2:00 p.m. in Sobala. The heat he was feeling inside was even more than the 99 degrees outside, which was baking both him and his boss as they talked. The archaic air conditioning unit in the window opposite him had stopped working and there was no telling when it would either be fixed or replaced.

"Yaya, you are sliding," his boss said. "You were a promise here but you are turning out to be an embarrassment and you are putting me in a bad position."

"I regret that very much, sir. I do accept that it's all my fault, though, honestly, I cannot tell you why all this is happening to me."

They were in the office of his boss, the permanent secretary of the Ministry, a stocky middle-aged man from the Northern Region of the country. He went to Oxford University many years ago. He was one of the lucky few who had a colonial government grant to study liberal arts abroad. Since he returned home, he had been in the Civil Service.

"Yaya, I've worked in this Ministry for over fifteen years, but I have never seen any staff here deteriorate like you." The man looked at Yaya who shifted his eyes down. "Knowing you are capable, I put you in charge of a project for a whole month, and ask you to write a report. But what do I get? Disappointment and embarrassment!"

"I'm really sorry, sir." Yaya was thinking that he wished his boss knew what he was going through.

"Do you know how I felt when I took that file to meet with the Minister and found nothing but blank pages in it?"

Yaya could only look at the balding head of his boss as if that would solve the mystery. He knew he had written the report, had it typed by a clerk and had put it in the folder himself. He even kept a copy in his desk drawer, which, also, he could not find anymore. And yet he kept the only key to the drawer. He felt sad that these days it seemed everything he touched got messed up somehow.

"Yaya, I know you don't drink, do you?"

"No sir, I don't even smoke cigarettes."

"And you are not smoking hemp?"

"No, sir. I have never touched that stuff!"

"Then, Yaya, tell me what's happening with you? I guess you know I had hope in you. You had always impressed me as a serious boy, and there were times I could see myself in you when I was your age. Our backgrounds are similar. From a massively illiterate family we made our way to such an enviable position through hard work and ambition. And yet you are slipping."

Yaya's stomach tightened. His felt his boss' words like blows from a hammer to his guts. One thing he had prided himself on was not to leave himself open for a reprimand about his work from any source. To be careful was a creed to him in everything, even as a teenager. Which was why, his teenage friends called him Mr. O. M. for "over meticulous."

But suddenly, like his boss said, he was going down —a simple, silly, series of blunders! And the worst thing was that he was not doing it. And even as he could not say this, he knew some force greater than him must be leading him to this chain of personal turmoil. He looked up at his boss.

"Last week, we were in a meeting with representatives of UNESCO, and you bowed your head down right there on the table and slept off and started snoring. Now tell me, what can be more embarrassing than that, both for me, you, the Ministry and the country? Do you realize what impression that gave to those white people about us? That we are incompetent! A whole senior staff dozing off in such a critical meeting!"

Yaya thought of Grandma Fatu. She was the one about whom he was dreaming. Now she came to him both day and night, and regardless of where he was, he found himself sleeping, and being nagged with: "*We are waiting, Yaya, for you to heed us. You should be the one after me; go back home and undertake what is your heritage. It is a special call and you have no way o-u-t!*"

Now, it was three weeks to make it a year since Grandma Fatu died. He had gone on with life as usual and as he liked after those incidents with Tamba's leg. He had refused to even think about the heritage that Grandma Fatu left with him. In fact, since his return from her 40th day ceremony, which was over ten months now, all he had done was send letters and money to the family at home.

So far, he had canceled all trips to both Taényadu and Wuyadu, until he was free from all the torment and be sure as to what was happening.

Yet, in the past three months Grandma Fatu had been coming

166

regularly in his dreams in all kinds of nightmares that he made no sense out of. Yet every time he dreamed of her, something went wrong for him. He either lost something important, or got embarrassed in a way that made him look stupid, like now as he stood before his boss without any explanation.

"Things have to change, Yaya. I cannot keep covering your back while I expose mine. This is a government Ministry. And remember, we are under constant scrutiny by an idle press and I have people to answer to. Do you really understand the seriousness of what I'm saying?"

"Sure, I do, sir. I'm sorry."

"You can go."

"Thank you," Yaya said feeling sad. He didn't know whether to promise that things would improve or that they won't happen again. Because he knew he was not in control, but he could not say so, that would be like opening a can of worms, and besides, Grandma Fatu had warned him not to disclose what was transpiring between them to anybody. Thus he walked out with his head down.

Three weeks after Yaya's encounter with his boss, Abie had stopped by his place to pick up her china dish for a guest she was inviting for dinner. It was 1 p.m. She knew Yaya would be at work, but she expected Kortu at home.

Kortu was cooking diner. He had a late start and so had three fire places going on the gas stove. Some sun-dried lima beans were cooking in one pot, meat was steaming in another, while he had rice boiling in the other. He planned on cooking some sweet potato leaves together with beef chunks and condiments in palm oil, to eat with the rice.

He was sitting on a stool in the kitchen, busy over a tray which had heads of fresh potato-leaves tied in bundles. He had loosened a bundle and taken out some, which he held in his folded palm, the tips extending outward between his forefinger and thump. In the other hand he had a knife with which he was chopping thin slices off the leaves.

Creengh! Creengh! He heard the door bell ring. Kortu sighed in frustration. This was one time he hated being disturbed. He was rushing to finish this thing. Who could that be? He laid the knife on the leaves, washed his hands and ran to the door.

"Hey, Madam, so it's you. How are you?"

"I'm fine, Kortu, just a little sleepy. I worked last night."

"Madam, you work too hard, oh!"

167

"I guess so. But, Kortu, I came for my china dish. Do you know where it is?"

"Yes, Ma, let me bring it." Kortu went to the kitchen and brought the dish.

"What are you cooking for your boss today?"

"Potato-leaf stew."

"Ummh! I can almost taste it. Bring me some when you are through."

"I will, Ma."

"But, Kortu, tell me, hasn't Yaya been acting strangely lately?"

"Yes, Ma, since he came from his village—"

"Right! Kortu. That was when I noticed him getting sort of strange, like one with a burden on his mind."

Kortu stood silently, scratching his head and thinking about his boss. "It must be some problems he had at home, Madam."

"I thought so."

"Don't you see, Madam, he hasn't been there since he returned, for almost over a year now, which is unusual? He's talking in his sleep too. I hear him say, 'Fatu, Fatu,' most times."

"Who? 'Fatu, Fatu?' Kortu! That must be the woman they found for him!"

"No, Ma, I thought that was his grandma's name."

"Which grandma, the one that died? Why would he call her name in his sleep? No, Kortu. It's the woman that they found for him. Trust me!"

"But why should they? He has you."

"Kortu, Yaya is a Mandinka. I know them. Their men? Nobody is right for them. No matter which woman they have, they must get a Mandinka woman; or if they don't, their people will find one for them. They believe in marrying only to themselves."

"Ma, yet, Mr. LaTalé is different."

"Yes, he is different now, but isn't he changing? Well, wait till his people increase pressure on him. He will look like that Mandinka *Karamoko,* the one that is teaching the Koran to those children, in his big gown and many wives down the road. You will see! The more money he has, the more women they will be arranging marriage for and bringing for him."

"But Mr. LaTalé is a modern man, and he is educated."

"Then you don't know a Mandinka. What is the Western culture to them? They think the sky of themselves; and because they are mostly Muslims, they claim that according to the Koran, they can have four wives. But don't you see those big and crowded

Mandinka compounds all over this country? The men in their big gowns sitting in the front, with their many wives in the backyard, and their numerous children grouping around?"

"I see them, Ma. I wonder at their women with those big gold earrings, hanging all over their ears. Their men must be good to them."

"Yes, they must be. But I don't want to live in a polygamous marriage! And I don't know what Yaya may do! But I hope I'm not wasting my time on him."

"You are not Madam. He is a modern man, and he loves you."

"Bye."

One month after Abie and Kortu discussed Yaya, which was thirteen months since Grandma Fatu died, Yaya was sitting in his office talking to himself. He had dreamed of Grandma Fatu last night. And that made him apprehensive. He just knew something would go wrong before the day was over. It always had. Just then, his typist, a young lady who had worked with him for two years, brought some papers she had typed.

As Yaya bowed his head glancing through the report, the typist, who was standing by his side, looked at him from head to toe and rolled her eyes.

She had never seen anybody deteriorate so much. Really! To think of Mr. LaTalé when she started working with him, always charming, smiling and dressed smartly. His body was full, fresh and shining. But now look! This thinning and ruffled man was not the Mr. LaTalé she knew, his hair uncombed and shirt all wrinkled. What could be bothering him? She hoped he was not going out of his mind—*because he is even talking to himself these d—*

"It is fine. You did a good job, Jarreu." Yaya looked up at her, and she forced a smile.

"Thanks, sir, I'm going for lunch now."

"Sure. See you later, Jarreu."

Yaya carefully read the report again. To be sure that everything was alright. He could not afford another degrading encounter with his boss. After he had scrutinized the report and felt satisfied, he took out a sardine-sandwich which Kortu made for him that morning and poured a cup of coffee from a flask on his table. As he ate, the phone rang. It was a female colleague asking if he wanted to go to lunch. He apologized, "Sorry, Amie. Too much work today, maybe tomorrow?"

"Sure, Mister Busy!"

Yaya went back to eating while reading some documents before him on his table. The phone rang again. He almost didn't pick it up. But as he did—his heart seemed to leap out of his chest!

It was Kortu on the phone, crying, sobbing, telling him that his flat had caught fire. That he just came from the produce market and wanted to cook. But the moment he struck a match, the house erupted into flames and a big fire was burning, and people were coming.

Yaya just dropped his sandwich and leaned back in his chair. He blew out a long breath, and looked straight ahead. Strangely, he felt relieved. At least now he knew what was going to go wrong. It was the shelter over his head.

Yaya lost everything in the fire that burned his flat. It was a gas leak from an interchangeable four-gallon tank used for the stove. The landlord, a smart Lebanese business man, had insurance coverage for his property but Yaya had none. So he found himself starting all over.

Luckily for Yaya, in the same month that his flat burned, a friend of his was leaving for England to take up a one year course. The friend offered him a place, living with his family, while he was away on study leave. That had been nearly a month ago, and now it was fourteen months since Grandma Fatu died.

Kortu too was living with some friends, until Yaya could get himself together and rent another flat. If they didn't transfer him to up country, just to make things worse for him.

Thoughts about that transfer was what was bothering Yaya this Friday evening. Because, besides the lack of basic amenities in most rural districts, already he had too much haunting him from up country to feel excited about moving to live and work there.

He thought about Abie. Previously, on Friday evenings, they would be together, getting ready to go partying. But things had changed. It seemed like ages since they had gone out or done anything together. And Abie was getting scarce these day. *Poor working girl!* He decided to go see her.

The distance between where Yaya now lived and where Abie lived was much farther, and there was no telephone at her place. Yet he decided to take a chance on meeting her at home. He took a mini-bus that shuttled in his area, to where he could get a taxi. He met one of Abie's roommates at the taxi park returning from work. They shared the ride.

He was let into the parlor by the roommate. Right from the verandah, Yaya heard Abie's happy voice talking with some man inside her room. He almost didn't knock on her door. But he thought, of course, she could have male friends. Or it could be some relative visiting. He knew she wasn't seeing anybody but him. He knocked.

"Who?"

"Hello, Abie, this is Yaya."

There was sudden silence inside her room. And then it stretched. He could hear nothing, not a sound. Yet Abie was in there with some man. Yaya quickly looked behind his shoulders to see if Abie's roommate had gone to her room. Because this was embarrassing! It was not happening...

He decided it was best to leave. He was turning around when Abie's door opened by a crack. As she slanted her body through the narrow opening, Yaya had a slight view of the inside. In that partial darkness, he saw a stocky dark-skinned man in white pants, with no shirt on and a towel thrown over his shoulder sitting on Abie's bed. He looked like Dr. Kuma, the womanizing doctor at the party who had been after Abie since her clinical at the hospital.

When Yaya's eyes met Abie's, she looked at him dismissively.

"I'm sorry, Yaya. I have a visitor."

He noticed how she stood determinedly covering any chance for him to see inside the room. And she had just a flimsy cotton wrapper hanging on her, covering her only from her breast to the tip of her thighs. And all her thighs were exposed, her hair ruffled. She had stale makeup on, and probably had nothing under that wrapper.

Yaya couldn't believe this. Disappointed and humiliated, he stood there tensed and perspiring. Furious for his folly, he wondered, has she been doing this all along? Out of impulse, he put his hands in his pockets.

"Com'on, Yaya, you should know we're not like we used to be."

"But Abie, do you know how long it took me to get here?" he heard himself asking.

"Again, Yaya, I'm really sorry. I just thought it wouldn't work between us."

Quite interesting, Yaya thought. "Since when, Abie?"

"I had been thinking about it for a long time. I just made my decision."

"And with Dr. Kuma, right?"

"That's my private life."

Yaya sighed. His looked at Abie's stone-set face, showing

171

no emotions, like an estranged wife who had just slashed off her unsuspecting husband's genital and was cold-heartedly enjoying watching him bleed.

Yaya mustered all his strength, and said, "Thank you, Abie."

He then turned and left. As he walked in the dimly lit area where Abie lived, his mind couldn't resist saying, *Thank you, Grandma Fatu. Now I lost my love too!*

Haunted, jilted, and down, Yaya went to work the following Monday and was called by his boss to a conference. There were three of them in his boss' office; he, his boss and an executive officer, a young man about his age who had joined the Ministry last year straight from college. Yaya was given a letter to read, but before he could go through it, his boss started speaking.

"Yaya, your transfer has been approved," his boss declared, as if it was he, Yaya, who had requested a transfer. He laid the letter on the table around which they sat, and listened.

"We are posting you as an Assistant District Officer to Kebay District. That's your home district, isn't it?"

Yaya nodded.

"You will live in the district headquarters, Limbadu." His boss smiled though Yaya thought he saw nothing funny in this.

"I know that will serve you right, considering your present circumstances."

How much of his circumstances would this man know? Yaya wondered. He knew his boss engineered this transfer. A man that was his mentor. Yet looking at the cold calculating eyes starring at him, belying the occasional hollow grin, Yaya couldn't believe that their relationship had actually gone sour. What was he doing to deserve all these?

"Your transfer will be effective in December, which is four months from now. Before then, you can take a leave if you want. But meantime, I want you to confer with Sidique here, whom we are promoting to your position."

"Thank you, sir." Yaya felt mute.

"If you have any questions or need anything, feel free to ask me," his boss said.

"Sure, sir, I will." The shock and gravity of the situation was shattering Yaya. He knew the finality of bureaucratic decisions, and the blood shedding and ill will that lay ahead in trying to avert his impending transfer. This was something he had to do some serious thinking about.

"Mr. LaTalé, I will depend on you to fill me in before you leave. I'll be doing two jobs now, because I'll be doing my present job, and working a few hours with you everyday."

Lucky fellow! "Sure, Sidique. It will be my pleasure," Yaya said.

"You gentlemen can go back to work now. And here, Yaya, don't forget your letter of transfer."

Yaya went back to his office and thought about the transfer. To Limbadu? Wasn't that where that fellow, Tamba, came from? The guy whose leg he cured in his sleep with Grandma Fatu overseeing? It must be. *Oh, no!* Yaya lamented. They were now sending him closer to Wuyadu. Things would only get worse for him, once he got to that district.

He looked at the letter of transfer. It was not even a promotion. In fact, it was a demotion, because he was leaving the city as an Assistant Administrative Officer, and going to a remote area which lacked modern amenities, as an Assistant District Officer. Same position. And what was in it for him? *Only more torment!*

Then Grandma Fatu would be before him every minute nagging him about being a bone doctor.

Restless and in a tormenting agony, on the second day after he was told about his transfer, Yaya sent a note to his job reporting that he was sick. It was on a Wednesday. His plan was to take the rest of the week off. He had decided to seek in another town, 400 miles away from Sobala, the custodian and practitioner in another family—in fact the only other family that he knew in Manika Kunda—that had the sort of inheritance Grandma Fatu had left with him. It was Yaya's belief that the laws against disclosure wouldn't apply to the man he planned to see, since he did the same thing as Grandma Fatu.

After traveling for two days both on foot and in three different vehicles, Yaya got to his destination, Korkordu, late in the afternoon.

The sun was burning hard and everybody was under some shade. Many women were sitting on short wooden stools in their verandahs; some were weaving rattan baskets, while others spindled heaps of cotton wool into intermittent strands of thread on sticks, stuck between their index and big toes, which they spun with their hands. Some men could be seen at the sides of the houses weaving the cotton threads into cloth on intriguing fixtures of sticks through which they pedaled and pushed the threads with their hands and feet. The completely gray-haired men were laying in hammocks in the verandahs and under thatched courtyards. Most people in sight were elders. The able-bodied men and women were probably sweating it on their farms.

Korkordu turned out to be a much bigger village than Wuyadu, but seemed behind, judging from the standard of the houses. While looking for Kondorfili Bunsor, the man he came to see, Yaya counted only one cement house and six zinc tops. Wuyadu had four cement houses and countless zinc tops. As for Taényadu, it was a modern city compared to this village.

Now they were sitting in Kondorfili Bunsor's hut, on separate sheep skin mats. He was an older man in his sixties, with a back like a camel when he walked, and the protrusion was even more pronounced when he bowed in his sitting position. He waited patiently until Yaya finished explaining his problem, then he laughed.

"Yaya, tell me, besides the inheritance your grandmother left with you, have you been having any problems lately?"

"Yes, Pa, all kinds; and worse, I get nightmares on a daily basis."

"When was your last nightmare?"

"Last night, on my way here, at a village called Sinor, where I stayed the night with a family. I slept for only three hours, that was when I had it. It was Grandma Fatu with a giant cobra in her hand running after me."

Kondorfili Bunsor shook his head. He got up and went to a white cloth pasted in a corner of the hut. It was a square piece, about a yard in circumference, which was his calendar, where it was moons for months and rains for years, with nothing for days. The calendar had in thick black, thirteen parallel lines in four rows—representing fifty-two moons in a four rain period. Every time an old moon went and a new came, he would cross a line, making a slanted X, with his *Kala*-a grass quill pen, which he dipped into a bottle containing *duba*-a black ink made from herbs boiled with coal to perfect blackness.

When Kondorfili Bunsor accepted a new patient, he put a dot in the lower section of the X for that moon. And when the patient got healed, he put another dot in the upper section of the X for the moon in which he was through with that patient.

In his business, Kondorfili Bunsor started marking his calendar at the onset of the harvest moon with its festivals, just when there was plenty in the land and when gifts were generously poured on him for his services. Strictly going by when a new moon was sighted, after he had crossed thirteen lines for thirteen moons, he knew one rain was gone; then he started the next rain with a new

174

harvest moon, and continued until all lines on the four rain cloth were crossed; this he took to the burial ground where his ancestors lay, to present to them as testimony that in the past four rains, he had lived according to their wishes, carrying on in their footsteps by doing the work they did. He buried the old cloth with his ancestors, and asked for another four rains of blessings, which he started with a new cloth.

When Yaya's grandmother died, Kondorfili Bunsor had put a circle around the X for that moon. That was because it was important to him. She died in the seventh moon after harvest moon in the second rain on his current four-rain calendar.

Looking at the cloth, Kondorfili Bunsor noted that following the moon he had circled when Yaya's grandma died, all the remaining five moons in that line had been crossed. And in the line for the third rain, after the last harvest moon, it was now the ninth moon. He quickly did his calculations, then held his breath, and came back to his seat where a worried Yaya sat.

"Your grandmother died fifteen moons ago by our count," he said casually.

Yaya's mind went sharply to the difference between calendar months and lunar months, and though he was not limited to counting the revolutions of the moon in the sky for time keeping, like this man, yet from Yaya's study of Ancient Greek and Roman Civilizations, he knew the origin of the modern calendar, which was initially based on the activities of the moon. From those studies, he knew that there are 27 days and about eight hours between one complete circle of the moon and another.

Also, Yaya knew that for somebody like Kondorfili Bunsor who lived by the sequence of moons in the sky, usually it is thirteen moons from one yearly event to another; as compared to the twelve months in a calendar year, say from one Christmas to another. His grandmother died on the 29th of June last year, and now it was August 28, of the following year, which made it almost fourteen calendar months since then, but about fifteen cycles of the moon.

Yaya sighed. The man was right. But how could this man tell so quickly and correctly how long ago his grandma died? How did he know? Did he mark it on that cloth? And how did he read it? He was full of awe for the man.

Kondorfili Bunsor arranged the blue *buba* gown he had on, straightened himself and looked at Yaya with eyes that were red, deep and tight like that of a serpent. "Your situation is peculiar," he said, his mouth splashing spittle as he spoke.

175

He reached back and scratched his hunchback.

"Yaya, your grandma will never rest in her grave until you take up her work. And by the end of the second rain, which is the twenty-sixth moon following the day that she died, if you've not gone to do as she said, the wrath of your ancestors will fall on you." He paused, to see how he was affecting Yaya.

"And the curse will be insanity, or blindness or deformity or all. Nobody can change that!"

"A curse? 'Insanity or blindness or deformity or all?' Oh, no! That can't be. Why? Tell me why?"

"I cannot answer that question for you. I did not make the laws, I follow them, and sleep with them, and I have no problems with them."

"But that suits you. You like it the way it is. And this is life for you, and a choice."

"And so it is for you, young man. A choice to walk in the path of your ancestors or get cut down by their wrath. Isn't a storm through a forest more likely to break a stiff tree before it breaks a flexible one? Make up your mind, young man!"

"But can't I continue with my job in Sobala, and attend to this task that has been cut out for me?"

"No, if you must do this work, you must be dedicated to it, and must live where your grandmother and your grandfather lived, or you can't escape their wrath anywhere in this land."

"So, if I have to escape the curse, I cannot use my education, after all?"

"That's like taking a bath and hoping the water doesn't wet your back."

"And there is no way out for me?"

"No, none at all!" Kondorfili Bunsor looked at Yaya, battling a rising bitterness in him. *Such confused descendant of saboteurs!* He looked away in disgust and scratched his hunchback. Then his face lit with a scheme to avenge.

Meanwhile, Yaya sat with his arms crossed at his chest like a person coming down with fever, as he patiently looked up to the old man for a solution to this dilemma created by Grandma Fatu.

With a counterfeit grin masking the evil plan he had brewing on his mind, Kondorfili Bunsor looked down on the mud floor in the space between him and Yaya.

"Aha! Young man..., wait! I think there is a way out!" He nodded vigorously. "Yes..., I think so...." He traced his index finger on the floor drawing some invisible lines like a diviner, which he wiped off with his palm.

"You may leave the land, if you can, for a while, and stay away until it is two complete rains after your Grandma's death. You will be free of all torments and the curse." His eyes were all along fixed on the floor.

"You mean..., if I go away from here, like far away, and go about with my life, I will not be haunted anymore? And nothing will happen to me when the two years are over?"

"Yes. If you cross the ocean, where the land breaks from here, you will be free. For the leaf will never grow there. They will pass it on to somebody else. And when the time is up, you can come back and live in peace. Nothing will happen to you." At last he looked up Yaya.

Yaya smiled feeling relieved, somehow. *At least that's a break.*

Kondorfili Bunsor too was rejoicing inside, because what loomed in his heart now for the young man sitting before him was worse than darkness in a lagoon.

Ironically, when Yaya approached this man, whose eyes reminded him of a serpent, he knew immediately that his patronage suffered, for he seemed poorer than he should be. He was just now rebuilding this mud house with cement bricks; and he was in a business from which Grandma Fatu had built a big cemented compound long time ago. It was obvious that Grandma Fatu was more sought after when she was alive.

However, while Yaya was busy explaining his constraints and concerns, Kondorfili Bunsor had simply seen the issue as a perfect chance to nail the coffin in rivalry and the desecration of such a venerable heritage. Now was the time to stop the unnecessary distraction that somebody like Yaya would be to him, if he were to do as his grandma wished.

Kondorfili Bunsor, with his jittery eyes rolling in his head, was thinking of how good his business had been since Yaya's grandma died; and the new cement house his mud hut would soon be!

Well...., nothing would stop that now. Because even though this heritage originally belonged rightfully and only to the Bunsor family, when Yaya's Grandma, Fatu Béreté was alive, things were difficult for him. But that wouldn't be again!

Kondorfili Bunsor saw himself doing much better soon, in absolute control, famous and respected as sole owner in Manika Kunda of this miraculous heritage. Yes! For he knew that when Yaya left the land, there wouldn't be any continuity of the sacred heritage in Yaya's family. And by the end of the second rain following his grandma's death, if Yaya didn't use the leaf, it would be total insanity for him—no matter where he went!

Of course, Kondorfili Bunsor was sure of that! He had seen it happen before, same calamity as Yaya's. Alpha, another youth, with fried hair on his head and a chain on his neck like a woman, came one day looking miserable; because his grandfather had died and left him bogged down with the heritage, as in Yaya's case.

Kondorfili Bunsor simply told the boy the same thing he told Yaya. "Leave the land, go somewhere the leaf won't grow, and keep your mouth shut. You will be free."

The boy ran away to a place they call *Urssia* on *Sukuwarcip*. Yes, he came to say good bye—he was going overseas to become a white man. But as had been certain, news came of him as the two rains cycled. The people in *Urssia* sent Alpha back and he now roamed the streets with all rubbish circled around his head. That was one less distraction and desecration of such a venerable heritage.

Next, if Yaya went and became a *fatorkeh* like Alpha, he, Kondorfili Bunsor, would henceforth be the one and only. And when his time to die came, he would never leave this sacred heritage to somebody like Yaya or Alpha. To him, they were a lost group anyway. Instead, he would hand it over to a serious-minded adult; one who valued the ways of the ancestors.

After that visit, however, Yaya was jubilant. He had at last talked to somebody, the only person he could have such talks with, except Grandma Fatu who pestered him in his dreams. And the great thing about it was that the man had been in the business for a long time, like his grandma, and he knew all the laws so much.

Grandma Fatu should have told him the risk involved and how to escape it, if she really loved him. Since she knew he was not going to do as she said, with all the time she had been bothering him in his dreams.

Poor Grandma Fatu, Yaya lamented, reflecting on her anger; she had been so disappointed that she was getting vicious. But she wasn't going to win this one.

"..If you cross the ocean where the land breaks from here, you will be free. For the leaf will never grow there. They will pass it on to somebody else."

Across the ocean, where the land breaks from this land? No more nightmares? No more Grandma Fatu coming in his dreams like last night, all furious and fierce, with a split-tongue cobra, wrapped around her, and putting it in his face? And that green slimy pond he found himself stuck and drowning in on the night before his flat burned down, with the faint shape of Grandma Fatu walking away with a ringing laughter? And no more inexplicable and embarrassing mistakes on his job that bring him humiliation and disrespect? To go somewhere he would completely forget about Abie and all the loss he had suffered?

Yes, indeed, he would go to a different land, for his peace of mind and his fulfillment. For why else did he go to school and college if he should settle for being a village wonder like Grandma Fatu? Of course, he would go, for a while, for his sanity and to be happy. It would be a place utterly different from Manika Kunda, and far away, with more opportunities, where he would be free and could better himself. And he would come back when all this was over, as an even better person!

There was Sidi in America, his first cousin. They had always communicated. Wonderful America! Sidi was making it, from the pictures that came—nice flat, beautiful American wife—and the occasional but massive financial support he sent home. If Sidi could make it in America, supporting himself from scratch, Yaya could make it too.

They say everybody makes it in America!

Immediately Yaya got to work on the following Monday, which was September 1, he applied for a month's leave to be effective on the 10th of November, one month from his transfer. He didn't hope to be in the country by the end of his leave in December, which was to come up in four months; as that would make eighteen calendar months since Grandma Fatu died, which was nineteen lunar months.

And Kondorfili Bunsor, the man he talked to about his problem, had warned that the curse would fall on him, if he was still in the land by the *'twenty-sixth moon,'* or what made two complete calendar years since his grandma died.

The leave was okayed. Without really explaining to his people the real reason why he must leave, Yaya came up with a master plan, about a chance in America to study for a short time and come back as a boss on his job. Then, of course, he would rebuild the family compound. He prevailed on his mother to pressure Sidi, her brother's son, for a ticket, which was all he needed. And Sidi had made that promise just before he left anyway.

It worked. Sidi sent the ticket. Yaya had his visa and was bound for America. He shared his private savings among members of his family and left. He hoped Grandma Fatu would pass over that heritage to Wusu, her last born who needed it more, as he was already living in the house and had nothing to do.

Wusu had dropped out of school in the fifth grade because he was looking forward to taking over from his mother. And indeed so was he now accused, though he denied it vehemently.

When Yaya made it to America, it was exactly eighteen months after Grandma Fatu's death. He had crossed the vast Atlantic ocean, and from his high school geography knowledge and all the maps he had looked at, he was sure about several breaks in the land between anywhere in America and Manika Kunda. He counted himself lucky to come out with six months remaining, without some calamity befalling him or being forced to return to the restrictive and shattering life chosen for him by Grandma Fatu.

Today, as he stood by his bedroom window where he lived with Sidi in Philadelphia, Yaya reflected that he got to the U.S. on the 29th of December which was a Saturday, and that now it was Monday, the 7th of January. Grandma Fatu died two years ago around 6 p.m. on a Friday, June 29; the coming June 29 would make it two complete years. Then he would be free!

As he had done since he consulted with Kondorfili Bunsor, early this morning, Yaya noted in his diary the time gone —counting one year, six months and nine days—since he was handed the inheritance which became a nightmare. However, now he felt good. Because there remained less than six months for Grandma Fatu to give her problem to someone else. And for that he couldn't wait!

By Yaya's watch it was now 3 p.m., Sidi and Pat should make it home in the next hour. The rain was still pouring. Yaya went and sat on his bed, the waterbed, and laid down in that luxury.

A whole week in the U.S.A.? In America? Bon vivant! Indeed! Thank God, a man is free at last, from Grandma Fatu and her torments. Really.., to say no more horrible consequence for a person being himself? Free like a bird and in America too? Not bad! This is just the right place!

Yaya, however, only had a visiting visa and his permitted period of stay in the U.S. was barely one month. In this period, he was neither permitted to work, nor even to seek employment. In fact, he was required to depart from the country, prior to the expiration of the date on his I-94, which was the entry document he was given specifying his permitted period of stay. And that bothered Yaya.

He recalled the letter Sidi wrote to him when he sent the ticket. He said: *"Please return this ticket to me before its expiration date, if you cannot get a visa, so I could get a refund. Sadly, Yaya, I know that America's visa policy for African countries suffers.*

It is unlike that of Europeans and citizens of other favored nations, who may hop in-and-out of America at will—some with life term visas. For you guys in Africa, and only the lucky at that, the common visas issued are the B-1 or B-2. That is, of course, besides the F-1 or student visa; but that is beyond you, as I cannot presently afford to pay your tuition for a year or more in any college here. But even then, you cannot be sure of a visa. However, good luck!"

When he had his visa, Yaya counted himself lucky, knowing that generally, for the few Africans who ever made it to America, sometimes it took years, and the most stringent form of screening and scrutiny mustered by the Consuls at American Embassies in the regions.

As a Senior Civil Servant in his country, it took Yaya three months and four rejections to get a B-1, visiting visa, like Munda's, and that materialized about a week before his departure. The period he had applied for vacation was over and he was due to assume the position in Limbadu, which he delayed, desperate for a way out of the country as Kondorfili Bunsor advised.

However, with the 'almighty' visa in his passport and Kondorfili Bunsor's words ringing in his ears, he happily told his boss to give somebody else his new position— *that precarious transfer*—because he was going to *AMERICA!*

Yaya knew that by this trip, he was killing two birds with one stone: running to save his head and performing a dream pilgrimage to the *Garden of Eden* known as the United States of America.

Quite an important milestone in his life! And now with Yaya in the country, the radiance of the American dream circled in his head, with Grandma Fatu's haunting deed and threats, gradually fading into the background.

Instead, in Yaya's mind, the statute of Liberty rafted, beaming triumphantly, eyes upon him, touching his heart and soul, and holding him in a trance. Telepathically, in their silent communication, the great custodian whispered: *"Yaya, Thou Brave Believer In Freedom And Lofty Dreams, I Say Stay. Stand Up,*

Join My Flock, And Be My Disciple. "
Yaya felt elated at that message. Indeed, quite a golden chance. He got up and went to the window and looked outside, up at the sky; the cloud was clearing and the rain was ceasing.

It seemed, though, that immigration authorities and the Statue of Liberty spoke in different tongues. Because before Yaya knew it, the thirty days he was given to live in America was gone, and he had no idea, or the nerve to go to an immigration office for an extension of his visa. Actually, what he needed was a green card, or any status that permitted him a little lengthy stay, and at least a work permit. But those chances were nil at this point and in his situation. He knew that, and Sidi knew that too.

However, in the past one month, Yaya felt like a *born-again,* from experiencing the *joys of the American way of life* as seen through his shock-ridden native African eyes. At home, cable television with its numerous channels became his main attraction. He got to it at every chance and stayed glued, flipping from *CNN* for regular news to *BET* for steady entertainment; and to the local stations for local and prime time news. As the major television networks dished out world news, Yaya with the remote control would flip from Peter Jennings on *ABC* to Tom Brokaw on *NBC* and to Dan Rather on *CBS.*

Then there was the famous *NIGHTLINE* with Ted Koppel and his cogent interviews, which he had read about in *TIME* magazine when *NIGHTLINE* won the DuPont-Columbia award in 1981 for its coverage of 'America Held Hostage' during the Iran hostage crisis; when the American Embassy was under siege in Tehran—for 444 days, from November 4, 1979 to January 20, 1981—by the followers of Iyatollah Khomeini. Now, Yaya saw *NIGHTLINE* live and Ted—*oh, Americans and their liberalism, as they addressed the TV guru*—every weeknight at 11:30 p.m. on channel 6, a local ABC affiliate.

As he watched one program after another on American television, they all depicted to him the wonders of America and the distant pace of life in the U.S. as against his country.

Like most immigrants, Yaya was eager to be Americanized, so he had his ears and eyes open for anything that would help. When Sidi and Pat could get together on outings, they took him around and showed him the *City of Brotherly Love,* where the founding fathers from the thirteen original colonies, signed and sealed the American Declaration of Independence. On all the outings, almost everything Yaya saw that was uniquely American thrilled him. The accent and affluence of the people, the heterogeneity of the society, the general sense of freedom and even the rat race he imagined in their rushed life.

From the word go, Yaya convinced himself without any doubt that there was total convenience and ease in every facet of life in America. Also, he believed that besides the apparent luxury Americans enjoyed, the system worked to make everything easy for them. That was compared to other systems that were intentionally designed to make things difficult for their people, like in Manika Kunda, for example, where even education happened to be by elimination and not inclusion.

But Yaya felt good that he was now in America and in his second month, even with his handicapped immigration status which seemed like learning to live with a vampire.

Some evenings and at least one day on weekends, Sidi took him to meet friends and their countrymen. On these visits, what Yaya saw was situations that told success stories of good living, nice cars and fine apartments. Among those countrymen that he met in Philadelphia, he knew a few hardly made it through high school at home, yet they had big cars and were enjoying such luxuries in America that he, an employed college graduate, could not enjoy back home.

Because they are in America! Truly, America is a wonderland!

Yaya felt gratified that his decision to come was the best; and as for staying, it was a *fait accompli,* at least for a few years ahead.

While his visa was valid, Sidi had taken Yaya to obtain an identity card, issued by the State of Pennsylvania, and a Social Security card from a local Social Security Office, a branch of the U.S. Department of Human Services.

"Those are vital documents," Sidi had told him. "One cannot over stress their importance in America. They are like birth marks and they go hand in hand; without them you are nobody in the system."

He assured Yaya that as a non-immigrant, and even for somebody like him, the documents were an important step. But that was over one month ago. Now Yaya was approaching the end of his second month in the country. So far, his only accomplishments were an ID card and a Social Security card.

Barbar, his countryman, the lawyer, had warned him that those documents could not be used for anything substantial other than for identification purposes or perhaps opening a bank account, especially with his Social Security card marked with: 'Not valid for employment.'

That left Yaya nowhere. He thought that those documents were nice to have, but wondered, of what help they were going to be to him if he couldn't work. And as for banking, he knew that was a remote stage yet, because he had no money.

Even without a work permit, if the Social Security people had not boldly written the disqualification on his S.S. card, as restless, eager and bored as Yaya was, he would have been looking for employment all over the city.

But both Sidi and Barbar had warned him bluntly that he dared not present that Social Security card to employers, because some might not only refuse to hire him, but might also trap him to be picked up by immigration for deportation. And Yaya dreaded that, for he knew what kept him at bay.

Incapacitated in America by a new set of constraints, Yaya depended solely on Sidi for everything, from toothpaste to snacks at bed time. Like a blind man, Sidi was his eyes, his cane and his way into the society. Consequently, if he were to work at all, he looked up to Sidi for a way to his first job; so he pressured him. Sidi never minded.

With the understanding of one who had been through Yaya's route like any newcomer in America, and as one who lived as an illegal alien for many years, Sidi was patient and constantly informative, when not consoling. Sensing Yaya's disillusionment one evening, with just the two of them in the living room, Sidi felt compelled to put things in perspective.

"I wouldn't tell you it's going to be easy," he said to his flustered cousin. "And Yaya, unlike the general belief back home, nothing comes easy in America, particularly not for us. But the good thing is, there is hope, and somehow things will work out for you, as long as you keep hoping. Meanwhile, just take it one step at a time. If a job comes along that suits your condition, good, otherwise be my guest and relax. A chance is bound to come for you."

"That's my hope," Yaya said, raising his head up and looking at Sidi. Sometimes he didn't know what to think of Sidi, because he knew that if Sidi was really aggressive, as big as Philadelphia was—and for as long as Sidi had been in America—he would have found something for him by now.

"Sidi, any chance I get will be a big help for me. But the big question is, when will one come?"

"Time man, time."

Yaya sighed. He moved forward to the edge of the couch, rested both arms on his knee and looked pointedly at his cousin sitting on the reclining chair next to him. "Sidi, as you know, I'm going into my third month now, and honestly, I'm going crazy from lying around idle. I've never felt so useless in my life."

Sidi nearly laughed even as he sympathized with the pleading look in Yaya's eyes. As if he, Sidi, had any control over things. It just showed how naive Yaya was in his thinking about America.

"Now, Yaya, believe me," he said, sounding serious, "I know how you're feeling. It's all part of the game and nothing unusual, but things will get better."

"That's all I can hope, Sidi." Yaya moved back in the couch and leaned. "It's just that I can't wait to start doing something. Then, I'll actually feel like I'm in America."

"Oh, yes, you will," Sidi said almost sarcastically. "Have no doubt about that. And remember, in America, once you start working, you must stay working, constantly. Take it from me. In my six years in this country, I have worked more clock hours than I could have worked in my entire life time in Africa, and it has all been on menial jobs. I hate them. But can I stop?

"No, because living in America is all bills. They pile and flow on you like bees on a honey comb. You will see. As the Americans say, 'You've got to bust your butt working everyday to make it.' My friend, my best advice to you presently is to eat, sleep and get healthy."

"I'm in top shape," Yaya snapped. "Man, after sitting around all this time I'm well rested and ready to take up any job, or face any challenge. Sidi, I was a busy man in Manika Kunda. Sitting all day doing nothing is not for me. And really, Sidi, I'm sure if we intensify efforts, I'll find a job. I have no doubt about that."

Looking at the seriousness on Yaya's face, Sidi struggled not to laugh, as he thought of something to say that would silence Yaya and put him in his place.

"But of course, Yaya, yet..., don't push your luck!" Sidi mockingly muttered. "Because man, don't forget..., you're just an illegal alien!"

Yaya's eyes popped out in disbelief and his jaws sagged. He became absolutely quiet. Sidi looked at him laughing, judging that he was probably nursing the shock. If he became mad at Sidi for tormenting him like that, he said nothing. Yaya only gushed a deep sigh—avoided his cousin's eyes—and leaned in a corner of the couch where he folded his arms, stretched his legs and stared up at the ceiling.

Sidi was practical. He knew that if Yaya thought lying around for two months doing nothing was enough frustration, deeper levels of frustration awaited him. And indeed Yaya's third month came and left him no better than his first month did in his quest for something to do, or in his words—to be useful in America.

Meanwhile, Sidi could tell that Yaya had started pitying himself. He now talked in rhetoric, about how it was challenging enough for any ambitious young man to be unemployed, but worse when, on top of that, other handicaps were imposed.

Sidi would only listen. In his view, that was a situation Yaya created for himself by electing to come to America. Sometimes Sidi felt baffled and wanted to laugh at Yaya's folly.

Really, from the position of a stable civil servant in his country, and a productive member of his community, he has successfully transported himself to this agonizing situation he now finds himself in, living with vain hopes, from day to day.

Sidi wished Yaya would cry his problems to Ahmed, who would say, "Welcome to America!"

In the past month, which was Yaya's third in the country, it was dawning on Sidi that due to the setbacks his kinsman was having, he was starting to get disenchanted with his self-Americanization. Yaya would no longer be watching programs on television, and go about screaming: *"Wow! Oh, great! Fantastic!"* In fact he had stopped making all those flamboyant exclamations that expressed his infatuation with America. Rather, in the mist of captivating and dynamic programs like *OPRAH,* the comics and musicals on *BET,* and during prime time and other newscast, he would bow his head in his hand, or sag back on the couch, lost in thought and brooding.

At such moments, Sidi knew Yaya was going through a wake-up trauma, his illusions about America versus reality. Wondering why Yaya left his job and came to America, Sidi believed that evidently, Yaya had been misinformed by some countrymen.

Those who live in America and go home on 'borrowed' money and show off, and paint rosy pictures over there about how one barely needs to get into America and makes it straight away, living fine, having your own car, working two jobs, or going to school, or doing all—and whatever!

Also, Sidi knew of the affluent American image in Manika Kunda—all intrusive—an image suggestive of America as an easy path to success and the fulfillment of all one's wildest dreams. Some Africans who had lived for some time in America would say, like many Americans, that 'it's all *B.S.*' And now, Sidi thought, Yaya was learning that in real life, rosy tales might only be good to hear.

CHAPTER THIRTEEN

As Yaya faced his new challenges in far away America, thoughts about Grandma Fatu and the inheritance turning around to fight him surged from time to time. Due to his ordeal at home, he found it hard not to recall the tormenting vow that became his predicament.

"... You must represent, cherish, and continue to your dying day, this infinite blessing that is a tradition in our family. Or I will see no rest in my grave."

Could Grandma Fatu have finally rested in her grave? In his third month, Yaya wrote a letter to Kondorfili Bunsor, the serpent-eyed man that he had consulted, who advised him to abscond from the land or prepare for the consequences. That was, if he stayed and didn't dedicate his life to the heritage his grandma lived for. The man couldn't read; somebody would have to read the letter for him, so Yaya coded his message, as below:

Dear Pa Kondorfili,

I'm writing this letter to you with much pleasure. I left the land after all, and came to America. And now, I'm in my third month. So far, everything is quiet and fine here, no sleepless nights or anything. I hope so it is over there as well.

Maybe somebody has been found to replace me. I'm really hoping so. And then maybe those sleeping will stay silent without anybody worrying in their sleep. That will make me happy more than anything. That is my prayer now.

Please, Pa Kondorfili, write to me soon, to keep me informed. I promise to send something for you as soon as I start earning anything here.

I will always be grateful to you for saving my life. Many thanks from me, and may The Almighty Allah bless you.

Best wishes and more greetings to you, your family and everybody.

Yours truly,
Yaya LaTalé.

Kondorfili Bunsor received the letter in his village, Korkordu, about the time Yaya was in his fourth month in the U.S. The letter was read to him by Demba Conteh, a graying man in his mid-fifties who was the headmaster at the elementary school in the village and the postal agent in that area. Of course, the contents of the letter were vague to the headmaster, but the man that it concerned knew the meaning behind every word.

The poor headmaster left immediately, and after shouting thank you after him, Kondorfili Bunsor went to the white cloth in the corner—which was marked with lines and slanted Xs—his four years calendar where months were moons and years were rains and every year started with the harvest moon.

He is now in America, eeh? How long more? Wait! His grandmother died seven moons after harvest moon in the second rain by my count here. Yes, I know so, by this circle! Since then, two harvest moons have passed. And now, it is five moons after harvest moon in the fourth rain: five moons in the second rain, and thirteen moons in the third rain, and six moons in the fourth rain; is it twenty-four moons now. After this moon, and two full moons, it will be two complete rains since his grandma died! Yes, only this moon and two full moons remain!

Shshsh! Did he say everything is quiet over there? Yes, so will it be! So will it be! Until the twenty-sixth moon, and before the sun goes down on the twentieth day of that moon, he will know that there is no escape for him from the curse. By sunset it will be, ugh..., total insanity—like Alpha's!

We will hear about it in the wind, like we hear everything here. I will be the only person on earth who knows anything and why. Oh, I like the secrecy! There will be nobody to ask me. And nobody to compete with me again. They will know only me for this wonder, everywhere.

In fact, now, they all come here, for I'm the only miracle bone mender in this land. Even some white men have started coming. I don't know for what? Those wizards! Do they want to steal my knowledge? Well, not this one, because it is sacred.

Yes, there will be no more competition. As for you, Yaya, I'll write to you tomorrow, to keep you fooling yourself. You good for nothing lost lots of today!

The following day, Kondorfili Bunsor went to the village headmaster. They met in the verandah of the headmaster's small two-bedroom mission house, which came with the position. The floor was cemented, but now cracking all over, in forms similar to shapes of letters in the alphabet; as if some kindergarten kid had gone wild on it, getting educated. At one end of the verandah, swaying slightly with the wind, was a raffia hammock suspended by its two edges with ropes from the ceiling. At the other end, near the front door of the house, stood a coarse wooden table with two raw-pine chairs tucked under. The headmaster offered Kondorfili Bunsor a seat and pulled a chair for himself. They sat amidst squeaks from the table and chairs.

A pinkish sun was sinking and the farmers were returning home along footpaths running through the bushes surrounding the village. The day's work done, they came with bundles on their heads, of herbs, dry wood, loaded sacks, etc. The men hurrying ahead, with the women and children following.

"Headmaster, I came so you can write a letter for me, to a young man in America. "

"Okay." The headmaster had suspected that. He got up, went into his room, tore out some sheets from a writing pad, got an envelope, and sat down, pen in hand.

Kondorfili Bunsor handed a letter to the headmaster. "I'm writing to the young man who wrote this letter to me. It is going to the address on his letter."

"Okay."

"Say: it is me Kondorfili Bunsor of Korkordu that is writing this letter to him."

The headmaster started by writing the man's address and the date on the top right corner, and on a line below to the left, he wrote: *Dear Yaya,* and raised his head up. "Okay?"

"Say: I greet him plenty, and my body is fine and my whole family is fine."

"Yes?"

"Say: I have received his letter."

"Okay."

"Say: it is good news to me that his body is fine too, and he is sleeping well."

"Yes?"

"Say: I've not heard anything from over there, his home town. But I do not expect anything yet either, until two moons from today. That will make the death of his grandma two complete rains."

"Okay?"

"Say: at this time, as long as he is not having any problems, he should not worry. Everything will go on smoothly. And he will be free soon."

"Okay."

"Say: there is one thing I have to warn him about. And that is this: he should not disclose our secret to anybody, be it here or over there!"

"Okay."

"Tell him that if he observes that, everything will be fine. But he should not mistake and do otherwise! For then, I know not what will happen! Tell him to remember that and he will have no problems. And say, I greet him well, and we are all fine here."

"Yes?"

"Say: this is from Kondorfili Bunsor."

"Okay."

"Thanks, headmaster, when can you post it for me?"

"Tomorrow."

"Thank you, good man."

According to Yaya's diary, he received that letter on Tuesday, April 26, towards the end of his fourth month in the U.S.

Now, at 2. p.m. on Wednesday, May 14, he just wrote his third letter to his mother and made entry of that in his diary, because there had been no reply from her to any of his two previous letters. In this letter, like the others, he told her he was doing fine and that everything was great with him, even when they weren't.

Sitting on his bed, he glanced through the diary in his hand, and reflected that counting till today, it had been twenty-two months and two weeks since Grandma Fatu died on the 29th of June two years ago.

He was now in the second week of his fifth month in America. He has kept the law, because he hasn't told a soul. Yet, he wondered, why such bad luck?

It couldn't be Grandma Fatu and the inheritance still fighting him, or Kondorfili Bunsor would have told him. Such a nice man, Kondorfili Bunsor, so helpful. Wait, as soon as he has a job, and starts making money, he would send Kondorfili Bunsor something really impressive, like a Seiko watch or a big radio, in appreciation.

But why such bad luck?

Yaya closed his diary and placed it in the night stand next to his bed and sat brooding in this room, which now looked like a cell.

The strong believer that he was in America, in his fifth month since making it to his dreamland, Yaya was hard hit by the cold realities he confronted. First, for breaking no ground at all in employment, and consequently being far from surviving on his own in the society.

A victim of chronic delusions and misconceptions about America, Yaya brooded in disbelief that he, Yaya, the academically successful, he who got a job in the Civil Service of his country straight from college, and he who also declined various job offers, could come to the uncontested land of plenty and be shamefully stuck in a situation where he could not fend for himself?

Always on the receiving end like some beggar, for five months straight? Even when he could take any job? Yet, not even a lowly street sweeper job? When everybody else in their big cars and bright faces seemed to be doing fine? No, Yaya agonized, this couldn't be happening to him in America —*where everybody makes it!*

CHAPTER FOURTEEN

"No big deal Mister, everything will be alright," was what a disgruntled Yaya kept hearing from Sidi, as he and his wife ran in and out from work, talking about their days on the job. Among other things, they talked about discrimination and the prejudice of coworkers.

This was ridiculous to Yaya, who thought they should be grateful that they had jobs at all. As far as he was concerned, let them give him a job, and if they must, let them put all the discrimination they could in that job, and see if he wouldn't take it happily.

All that discrimination stuff was alien and meant nothing to him anyway, because, what he cared about was making headway into the society and being independent; if he had to encounter discrimination in the process—he resolved—so be it! This was not his country. He was not going to try to change the white man. By the way, he wondered why Sidi from Manika Kunda wasted so much time in complaining about discrimination. Doesn't he have a fine car, a nice apartment, and a job? As if Sidi didn't know what big progress he had made by being in America. Or how the whole family at home was now looking up to him, Sidi. He would gladly change places with Sidi any time and would care less about discrimination. In life, Yaya consoled himself, to survive and succeed, one must overcome obstacles and strive to be victorious, always.

He wished Pat and Sidi would quit nagging so much about something that didn't do them any good, and start helping him get a job.

"I don't believe it, Sidi, that after all this time, you cannot help me find a job anywhere in Philadelphia," Yaya attacked his cousin one day as they were returning from watching a play at the Institute of Contemporary Art, University of Pennsylvania in West Philly. Their car was at a traffic light at 34th and Walnut street. Sidi was waiting for the green light.

"I'm now in my fifth month here, and yet for all this time in America, I haven't earned a penny of my own."

Sidi looked up at the light, and on that one, and with that

192

trend of thinking, he deliberately refused to respond. But for the several pedestrians that were crossing the street at random, Sidi could have pressed hard on the gas pedal when the light changed. He refused period, to let Yaya get to him. He decided that if the guy liked, he could do all the self-pitying he saw fit.

What Sidi knew for certain was that he was doing his best, considering Yaya's situation. "Mister, I wish you would realize that America is different from back home, where one may bribe for a job, and where laws are looked at by many as some sort of nuisance to the community," Sidi commented, after they had gone for a few miles in silence.

"Yaya, in America, the general tendency is to obey the laws, for every violation comes with a consequence. That is how the average American thinks, employers alike."

"But how do other people come here and get jobs easily, like those who run across the borders or get smuggled into the country?" Yaya asked, flustered.

"Many of those people are Mexicans or Orientals. They're of a far lighter skin color, Yaya. And candidly, they're more accepted here than a black African like you. Besides, I don't know what network they have or how they do it."

Yes, you know. Yaya frowned. *You're not just aggressive enough!*

It was obvious to Sidi, though, that there was no way Yaya was going to get any *reliable* job with his invalid work status. Of course, he knew that with luck, there could be some small businesses, like a janitorial or construction contractor who might care less about work permit regularities and hire Yaya. But even those had proved hard to get. For indeed, the daily Mexican exodus into the U.S. and the constant migrant boat people along the coasts of America had culminated in saturating those areas.

As far as Sidi was concerned, with Yaya planning to stay in the country, the only solution was to have his status changed to a legal residency with a right to work. In that case, he could both work and go to school, should he desire. But also, that solution was far fetched, not an overnight matter, not particularly for a struggling African youth. And in such a situation, no amount of determination or zeal could do much.

Sidi was no stranger to the fact that to be black in America and to have an accent on top of that, could only be likened to having to walk on a thorny path with no shoes on. And to have come from Africa, too? As Sidi's friend, Ahmed would say, "It's a case of triple odds in multiples."

Now, Sidi was on his back porch, just returning from work, waiting for his food to get warm. He had his hands in his pocket and was looking afar.

Yaya was inside, uncommunicative and a pity to look at, like a frustrated medical doctor whose license has been seized. And yet he was not even five complete months in the country.

Thinking about Yaya's dilemma, Sidi couldn't help reflecting about his own reality. There he was, making seven years in America, and he could call it home.

Two years after high school, drifting, he had stumbled upon a diamond in Kurudu—his home town—the diamond area. He sold it and instead of buying a car and cruising like all his contemporaries, he found a school in America, bought his ticket and came.

He came with mighty dreams and strove hard, all alone.

His father, a polygamist, with three wives and thirty-two children could not sponsor him in college. In fact, he could not even put him through high school, like any of the other children. The man played it safe, dismissing Western education as corrupting the world, especially with stories of the white man going to the moon. But also, not rich, he couldn't afford paying school fees for his many children.

However, Sidi felt thankful that his father permitted his wives to do as they wished for their children. Being an only son, his mother put him through high school by doing petty trade. But that was all she could do. Ambitious and fascinated with the promise in America, Sidi had taken the first chance, and risked, in search of the golden fleece.

In America, he had struggled his way, living by the rules, working hard and seeing himself through school. He had finished college, Summa Cum Laude, with a degree in civil engineering. He went to a mixed school, predominantly white. At graduation—when the economy was healthier—most of his colleagues, particularly the white boys in his class, all had job offers. Many starting at twenty-seven thousand a year. Some as much as thirty.

Now a permanent resident in America, he had followed every job lead from the week of his final year, to graduation day. And after that, he kept in touch with the placement office of the University and searched independently. They told him at the placement Office about the essence of a continuous search, ready resumes, customized resumes, a clean cut and positive first impression. He did everything the white boys claimed they did and more. He invested in suits, ties, white shirts and shiny shoes, and knocked on doors until his hands had calluses.

He only had to greet in offices and ask for job listings to see clouds come over the previously unclouded faces of secretaries and personnel staffs. For almost two years following graduation, all his zealous efforts and hard earned job interviews led to dead ends.

The best he had had so far, professionally, was a move recently from his housekeeping and cleaner position to maintenance man in a hotel where he had worked for the past three years. Yet, he was the most junior in that crew of basically high school graduates, most of whom bossed him all day. But he held on, and was contemplating going for a masters degree.

But does anybody back home know his frustrations? Or the rejections he dealt with? No, they wouldn't understand. However, Sidi reflected, that if he could help it, he would prefer to encourage aspiring youths back home to stay there, and explore opportunities or develop worthy trade there, rather than migrating to America. Already, he was stuck. He was married to an American woman and had no money to go start a decent life with her back home. That is, if she would consent to go.

Yaya's situation really touched Sidi and got him thinking afresh about his being in America and the pressure from home to help others to join him.

It's like the cigarette smoking paradox, where a chronic smoker fearfully warns a delinquent youth who fondles a cigarette against smoking, because of its addictiveness and health risks. Of course, such a warning would only sound hollow to the youth, because of the adviser's own smoking habit.

For an African, as long as you live abroad, no matter how good your excuse or how honest you may be, your advice to youths encouraging them to hold on to home, and not fool themselves about heavens abroad, could not be taken seriously.

You could tell them the intrinsic price of your experience away, or you could warn them that it is better for them to seek, and to cast their roots where they would be more accepted, but they won't listen to you. Statistics prove it is a waste of time. Again, Yaya serves an example.

Of course, Sidi knew nothing about what hurried Yaya to the U.S. To him it was just the American craze common at home.

Reflecting on such illusions and the reality, Sidi wished it could be believed back home what it took to survive in America. But they wouldn't.

America is not only exotic to many people over there, it is also the true land of milk and honey. Many believe that by one simply living in America, one has made it. It is garbage by truckload for them to hear anything otherwise.

Try telling them that behind the opulent facade lay an unaccustomed dehumanization in stock for the average African—along with the pains and frustrations in the will to survive as a black foreigner in America—selfish minded, you would be accused, wanting all the heavenly goodies, and wishing a share for nobody else. So you attempt to turn them off.

Why else would Yaya, at 25, a college graduate, a senior civil servant in his country—with all the prospects of upward mobility—decide to desert his position and drift, blindly, seeking the American gold mine. To Sidi, Yaya was just another eagle lured by the attractive American pastures, propelled by a dream which countless Americans wish, but find elusive, especially most black people!

It was true that immediately Sidi got his visa to come to America he promised his favorite aunt, Yaya's mother and Yaya himself, then completing high school, that as soon as he, Sidi, got settled in America, God willing, he would help Yaya to join him. But Sidi did not know then what he knew when he got to America.

As he battled with his personal trials, feeling his way in the U.S., and compared notes with Yaya's smooth development at home, Sidi felt compelled to dissuade Yaya from giving up on his chances at home for America. But that was to no avail.

Both his aunt and Yaya had lately held him captive to his commitment; letter after letter of urgent and fervent pleas and wailing, topped with a threat of a curse from his aunt, gave him no choice. So he brought Yaya over. But with him now in the country, they were both reflecting. Looking at Yaya's heavy eyes, bowed head and broken shoulders, Sidi could have said, " *I tried to tell you, but you wouldn't listen.* "

He had known that once Yaya came such stressful periods were bound to come and he also knew that if mishandled, such situations could cause irreparable damage to his reputation in the family, and even all over Manika Kundan. He didn't wish that. No *Mandinka Dein* would wish that.

Sidi had seen many families from Africa fall apart in America, simply because somebody failed to understand that coping in the American society would not exactly be like going on a honeymoon. And that, far from what they thought, their benefactors, whom they came idolizing, might themselves be only pawns in the daily American roller-coaster.

Obviously, like most newcomers that join relatives residing in the U.S., Sidi knew that Yaya had erroneously presumed that by him, Sidi, simply living longer in America, nothing was beyond him in situating a newcomer within the American system. As far as Sidi was concerned, that was wistful thinking, and he treated it as such.

However, with the coach rolling and Yaya onboard, he realized that he had to steer to a safe stop, if only for how it might be seen back home. It was now incumbent to seek and search for a foothold for Yaya. As expected of a good big brother, Sidi preached hope, provided for Yaya and assured him that things would open up.

He regularly told Yaya, in casual conversations, that the experience he was going through was not peculiar, but a rite of passage for the average African when new in the U.S. To keep Yaya busy, he had taken him to get a driving permit for learners, which he followed by giving Yaya occasional driving lessons. When Sidi couldn't, Pat helped.

Yet for Pat, Yaya's stay with them had lasted long enough. She felt invaded, with no privacy. It used to be that she would come from work, get settled into the house and slip into something comfortable and revealing. Proud of her figure: size eight, firm in the chest, slim waist, round behind, with great legs and thighs, Pat knew she had a great body, and she liked to flaunt it, like *a private dancer,* at Sidi.

And she loved those sexy night dresses into which she used to get him yearning. To her, it was the fun of being married; to entice your partner and make him long, way before you are ready. But no more of even that. She dared not do that, with Yaya living with them. *And as jealous as Sidi is!*

"Pat, make sure before you step out in the living room you are properly dressed," were his stern warnings now, regularly; as if it was she that invited the guy and created such an imposing situation!

In fact, as far back as Yaya's fourth month with them, Pat was already disgruntled, because Yaya was like an ant crawling up and down her spine. And she fretted daily.

197

Really, as if Sidi is not enough to live with, and those other crazy domineering Africans who pop in at random. To have another who permanently lives with us and doesn't work, and who is in trouble with the immigration folks? No, baby—not with this girl! They ain't going to get over me. Because my mama had no fool!

One evening at bedtime, over five months now since Yaya had come to them, Pat was stretched on her back in bed with Sidi.

"Sidi, I am tired of this shit," she flared in rebellion. "You didn't tell me it was going to be like this."

Sidi had expected that. And knowing Pat, next he knew she'd start raising hell like crazy. Confronted now, and laying next to her, it crossed Sidi's mind to divert her, by arousing her wilder passions, to the point where all that came out of her were her demanding wailing of: '*Oh yes, baby. Oh yes. Oh, you're killing me!*'

But no, Sidi thought, that was no solution for this. He told himself that he had to be frank, to make Pat understand, and even plead with her, or things would blow out of proportion.

In the faint light of the bedroom, laying on his back like Pat, with the comforter pulled to his chest, Sidi clutched at the edges and waited in a thoughtful silence, sensing Pat, before speaking.

"Pat, I know this is my doing and that it's been tough for you." He turned to face her. "And I'm sorry. But please, exercise some patience. It's not like he's going to stay with us forever. Things will change. He will soon find a job and move to his own place."

"But when?" Pat turned away, facing the wall. "The man has been here going on to six months now, and all he does is wear out the couch. He acts like you owe him something."

She turned on her back again, now looking at Sidi from the corners of her eyes. "God knows, I am being patient. If he can't find something here, why don't he go back to Africa, with all that good job he said he had there?"

Sidi was looking through a crack between the curtains of a window opposite him, at the branchy shadow of a tree outside. He looked up at the ceiling briefly, thinking of how best to put what he wanted to say; then he rested his eyes on Pat.

"Baby, you have to be an African to understand why Yaya can't just go back as you said. If he came on an ordinary visit, just to see America, it would be easy for him to go. In that case, there is nothing at stake. But he did not. When he left Africa, he came to the U.S. with a goal, just like I did."

"Big deal! And so?"

"Well Pat, he left his job and his whole family with a hope to better himself. If he should go now without achieving anything here, the whole society will look at him as a failure; and they will cast the blame on me too; and no matter what, they will say I refused to help him because I've lived here longer."

"But you ain't nobody here," Pat said frowning. "How can they blame you? You are barely scrapping to survive, too."

"I know that, but back home they don't see it that way. Why do you think I get all kinds of letters from people asking for help? That is why I am happy that some of them get a chance to come and see for themselves. Now, Yaya knows better. But please Pat, bear with him. It won't be too long."

"I've heard that before."

"But, baby, I want you to believe me. Let's just give him some time. Okay?"

Pat knew she was not going to take it much longer. It had been hard enough for them before Yaya came. Sidi had insisted that she must work, for the extra income to let them stay above the poverty line. And she was working, eight hours, almost everyday, lifting, bathing, changing soiled diapers in a nursing home for the aged; only to come home and face another stress.

A sad-faced African sitting in the living room, wanting this and wanting that!

CHAPTER FIFTEEN

Sidi's gem. It so happened that Yaya had a windswept admiration for Pat, and also a considerable deference for her; partly because she was Sidi's wife, but mostly because Pat was American.

In all Yaya's life he held everything American on a pedestal. The word superpower attributed to the nation had, since childhood, ingrained in his mind ultimate respect for Americans, which showed in his relationship with Pat.

From where Yaya came, he never had to touch a broom or wash his clothes, or even wash a dish that he ate from. He didn't have to. When growing up, there was always abundant help to do those things. Besides, Yaya was a man, and in his family compound women performed such chores.

In Sobala, Yaya lived like a boss in his own flat with a house boy, where he had no need to do any physical work. He just had to call and somebody would run answering, "Yes, sir?" And that person, of course, was ready to do whatever was asked.

Yet the moment Yaya got to America, he knew things had changed. He changed along too. Without anybody telling him, upon waking up, he would wait until Pat and Sidi leave for work, then he would go into the kitchen, wash the dirty dishes in the sink, clean the stove thoroughly, take the vacuum cleaner and run it everywhere in the apartment. After that, he would dust all the furniture in the living room and take out the garbage.

He never picked what task to perform or what not. Like ever ready, Yaya was always on the look out for what to do, to please, and to contribute in terms of services in the household; he did that whether his hosts were in or not.

In fact, on one Saturday in his first month, after a healthy meal together with his hosts, Yaya even offered to cook sometimes if Pat would teach him. But Sidi discouraged that notion on conception.

"No, Yaya," he told him, knowing well how his cousin bowed to his wife. "Me and Pat will handle that. You are a guest. We very much appreciate what you are doing around here as it is. But really, you don't need to cook for us."

"But, Sidi, I don't mind. I'm doing nothing presently. It would take away the boredom," Yaya explained.

Sidi pulled him aside, so that Pat who was in the kitchen wouldn't hear what he was going to say. "Look, if you start cooking around here, Pat will leave everything to you. I know her. You could watch and see how it is done, but never take it upon yourself to cook, except of course for yourself, or you will regret that you started it."

With that insight, Yaya gave up on his idea of helping with the cooking. He settled instead, on cutting the meat whenever that service was required; he also defrosted it at Pat's request, while she was at work. On those accounts, he got along with Pat.

But Yaya misjudged Pat. To him, she was his brother's wife, and as customary back home, being younger than Sidi, he thought he could take liberty with her, within reasonable limits. This was due to an age old tradition which bestows the right upon a young male in the family to marry, if he wishes, the wife of an elder brother, were the elder not alive.

And despite Yaya's education, he was alien to the individualism that underlined Pat's frame of mind. Like the African he was, he mistakenly believed he could dump his concerns on Pat, as he would Sidi. He also expected her to empathize with him, and, in fact, be a bulwark in those trying times, especially as she was family and an American.

What Yaya did not know was that he was treading on Pat's nerves, totally encroaching on her space, and creating considerable inconvenience for her. For how long she would take it, she didn't know, but she resented it altogether. Thus she held back on anything that could have created a rapport between her and Yaya.

Just so that he gets going soon, out of here!

Defying Pat, Yaya had strongly linked with Barbar and Ahmed, people Pat considered a bad influence, and by that chumminess, he succeeded in positioning himself squarely in her mouth, making Pat let out her five months of frustrations....

"You, Yaya, I see you didn't listen to me about that Ahmed and that Barbar." She stood in his face, fuming vehemently. Yaya had just been dropped off, after being away for a whole evening.

"You're going to be just as bad as they are. I hope you get a job soon or something, and pack out of this place."

Yaya, who was in the process of sitting on the couch, froze in mid air. He stood up, slowly. As the weight of the words registered on him, he felt extremely sad, reflecting on the hopelessness of his situation. And while still bracing the insult, Pat, who had stepped away, came back and stood in his face, posed like she was ready for a physical fight. "You heard me, didn't you? I said, I wish you would get your ass out of here!"

The anger, shock and hurt tempted Yaya to slap the living soul out of Pat—*and go anywhere!* But he thought better, not to come to the disappointing level she was now stooping. In total restraint, he turned away from her. Since Sidi was out, he went quietly to his room.

Sitting on his bed in his room, Yaya felt bewildered and weakened. He reflected sadly that only bad situations bred humiliations of the sort Pat now directed at him. He who, if he'd desired, could have married the likes of Pat in doubles, and maintained them adequately. Yet now being insulted anyhow, by a woman whom he highly respected and who was neither his mother nor his wife, or even a girlfriend.

Yaya wondered, how could Pat tell him not to associate with his countrymen, when indeed he needed them so much. And when, in fact, for him to stomach most of the frustration he was going through, those same people were his pillars.

He knew Pat and her husband gave him shelter and fed him, which he appreciated. But did that mean she would take it upon herself to determine whom he would be friends with and whom he wouldn't? And particularly when it was his kinsfolk?

Yaya reflected that Barbar and Ahmed, like most of his other countrymen in Philadelphia, had been nice to him. What they'd not done so far, was to get him a job, which was from all indications, beyond them. But in these trying times for him, they'd given him money and presents, like clothes and shoes. They were constantly in touch with him, to boost his morale and keep him hoping. Several of them had invited him to their homes, and entertained him, and told him their own experiences, just to inspire him. Would he desert them just because Pat desired him to do so?

"No!" Yaya hollered, with a defiant frown. Moving to the edge of the bed, he bowed his head in his palms over his knees, lamenting, and he caught himself at it—a silly thing to do—he berated himself. He decided not to let that action by Pat depress him any further. But he would tell Sidi about it when he returned. And in spite of Yaya's anger he laughed at the woman's audacity.

He wondered, why didn't she try that with her husband? It was through Sidi, after all, that he met Barbar and most of the others. In fact, those same men that Pat didn't want him close to, were the ones that picked him up at the airport the very day that he came, and he did not ask them to be there. Sidi brought them along, and Sidi still maintained a good relationship with them.

Why not Yaya? Maybe, Pat should try to control Sidi, and not Yaya!

He was lying on his bed reading a recent issue of *Newsweek* when Sidi came home. Yaya looked at his watch, it was 10:15 PM. He had the urge to go meet Sidi in the living room immediately and tell him about his wife's misconduct that evening. However, he decided to continue his reading. He was all absorbed in a piece about new talks in the Isreali-Palestinian catapult. It seemed some hope for peace had finally emerged.

"Where the hell have you been?" Yaya heard Pat querying Sidi.

"Didn't I tell you I was going to see the Kakays? You know they had a baby this past Sunday. We didn't get to see them at the hospital, so I though it's about time one of us went to visit them now, before the baby starts walking."

"Yeah, damn sure you went to see the Kakays, pretty soon you will go see the kukus."

"In that case, maybe so. But, Pat, I'm tired and hungry." Sidi seemed to plead.

"I don't care one bit how hungry you are. You should have eaten where you went. I bet they worked you good."

"And what exactly do you mean by that?"

"You shut up, boy! Don't get me started. You whore. As if you don't act like you're God's gift to women; always running out with one excuse or the other. But I'm ready for you. The day I catch you, we'll both be on TV."

"Pat, don't threaten me. And don't make me regret this relationship."

In his room, Yaya missed nothing. He shook his head: *Whatever does America do to a woman's respect and fear of her man?* He could not imagine a wife speaking to her husband in that manner back home. She would dare not. Besides, where would she have that audacity, when she knew, it was the man's prerogative to be with her or be with another woman, who might very well be his other wife. *But this is America.* If he had any inclination to go meet Sidi in the living room, it all vanished.

Yaya was in the bathroom brushing his teeth, about to call it a night, when Sidi knocked at his door. He hastily gargled the tooth paste out of his mouth and ran to answer.

"Mr. LaTalé, are you still up?" Sidi asked fondly.

"Yep, come in." Yaya opened the door.

"I saw the light on, and thought you might still be up."

"I was. In fact I was reading. You know I seldom go to bed early. Are those letters for me?" Yaya was referring to some airmail letters in Sidi's hand.

"Yes, here. I stopped by the mail box on my way back. It seems everybody at home shifted to you. Nobody writes to me anymore, for which I can only be thankful."

"I bet everything in these letters is a request for something or the other," Yaya said, fondling the letters he was holding.

"Tell me about it. I've had my share, now it's your turn."

Yaya briefly looked at the return addresses, and laid the letters aside on his bed, towards the wall.

"Sit down, man," he told Sidi. "I need to talk to you."

Sidi noted the seriousness in Yaya's voice and slightly raised his eyebrows, curious. He looked at the letters and the bed with its crumpled sheets, and sat down.

"Yes, man."

"This is about your wife."

Of course, why didn't I guess that? Sidi looked at Yaya as if to say, what could it be now?

"Sidi, since I have been here, I have respected Pat, and treated her as best as I could."

"Yes." Sidi nodded

"I don't think I have done anything deliberately to upset her. I thought we had mutual respect. But this evening she shocked me. She was rude to me in a way nobody has ever been."

"No, man, don't tell me she went-off on you."

"Yes, exactly. You know, I told you that Ahmed and Barbar were to pick me up. They came and we went to see a Nigerian guy who has a janitorial service. The man did not have any openings, but he promised to call me as soon as he gets one.

"He made me fill out the application form and everything. From there we went to see Spike Lee's movie, *Malcolm X*. Sidi, immediately I came in through the door, Pat was at me, for going out with those fellows. She even said outrightly that I should pack and leave. As a matter of fact, she said, she wants my ass out of here."

"No, she didn't!"

"Of course, Sidi, she did. I wouldn't lie on her."

"And what was your response?"

"I just ignored her, and came right into my room."

"That was smart, Yaya. To be frank, I'm not really surprised that she behaved like that. Didn't you hear her threaten me when I walked in this night?"

"Yes, she was speaking so loudly I couldn't help but hear. She said something about you two being on TV?"

"Yes! What she meant was, after she has killed me, or did something violently bad to me, enough to bring the media. Can you imagine that? Sometimes she makes me really fearful of her."

Yaya barely looked on. *If you are afraid of her, what am I to do?*

"I didn't know African-American women behaved so? I thought they were more sophisticated than that. Is Pat's behavior a common thing with them?"

"No, Pat is different. I would confess that she isn't one of the best representatives of African-American women. I've known that, but I like to think positive. It seems it's some personal problem with her. Let me tell you this, man. And I'm being open with you. I care for Pat, but she is too outrageous for me sometimes. My feeling is that her upbringing is taking its toll on her.

"Yaya, Pat grew up in a place where it was rough and so violent that kids matured fast, and lived by their wits. She had no father to care for her. And despite the plentifulness in this country, according to her, even survival was a battle."

"Really?"

"Yes, she did not even finish high school with all the potentials that she has. It was hardship, I guess. In any case, I looked over all that, and was hoping I could influence her for the better."

"Sidi, are you telling me she didn't even finish high school? I thought she was highly educated."

"Not quite. Over clouds and thunder, I drilled her, and made her take the G.E.D., which is an equivalent of the high school diploma. Yaya, if you visit where she grew up, and see the environment she lived in, you would really sympathize or understand why she behaves the way she does; her being comfortable with confrontations."

"Is that so? Where was that? Here in Philadelphia?"

"No, in Mansfield, North Carolina. It's a place called Fifth Ward, and it seems like it's in a fifth world, because it is even worse than some villages in Third World Africa."

"Sidi, tell me you're exaggerating," Yaya pleaded.

"No, I'm stating facts. We went to Mansfield for a wedding, and Pat took me through Fifth Ward. We went to a house, where she said she lived, the sort I've never entered, even in Africa. In the neighborhood, what confronts you is hopeless poverty and misery."

"What? That's shocking to me!"

"It was to me, too. Yaya, when I looked at the faces of the people over there, what I saw were sadness, strains, and pains, obviously born by deprivation and subjugation. And what you feel among them is a sense of desperation."

"Sidi, man, don't tell me it gets that bad here in America too?"

"Then you got a lot to learn. Go to any big city, and you will stumble upon the scenarios. Inner-cities, they are excusably called, or ghettoes, otherwise. They are like a civilized jungle, where the rule is survival and self-preservation at all expense."

"But why is that so, with all the advancement and opportunities in America?"

"I can't tell you exactly," Sidi said, shaking his head. "But, of course, it has to do with an imbalance in opportunities. Visit some places, you'll think the system works to keep in check people of our kind—the African-Americans. For every successful one you see around, there are hundreds in the ghettoes, broken.

"In these ghettoes, Yaya, about ninety percent of the inhabitants are blacks, some Hispanics and other minorities; some are so destitute, you would think they just arrived on their feet at a refuge camp."

Yaya's face had tightened like somebody jolted by a surprised visit from a disagreeable mother-in-law. He was looking at Sidi with both hands under his chin.

"Sidi, I'm confounded. But this is a developed world. I thought almost everybody here was reasonably well off."

"No, buddy, that is not conceivable yet, not even in America, at least not for a majority of black people."

"That's sad. It sounds like economic apartheid at work."

"Yes, even if not officially. Of course, Yaya, some people blame black poverty on black attitudes, and say things have changed. But that's looking at it with blue, hazel or green eyes. Look at the society and see the black lot, and you'll wonder if everybody breaths an equal opportunity breeze."

"Sidi, man, we must really have the wrong impression in Africa. The impression over there is that African-Americans are doing much better here, like everybody else. In fact, with so many superstars and celebrities that are black like Micheal Jackson, Oprah Winfrey, Bill Cosby, Eddie Murphy, and others, and the glamour and glitter of their image worldwide, you wouldn't think other African-Americans could be so limited."

"Yaya, aren't you now in America? Well, wait, you'll see. Of course, as a black African, you'd be hit worst by it all. For whenever you step out on the street, you're first of all, black, and then your Swahili accent, as they say, registers another rebuff."

"Really? Sidi, back home, you should see how white people from here and Europe mingle with us. Americans, particularly, are greatly admired for being so down to earth; you would never think that in their country the color of a person's skin still matters. In Manika Kunda our whites don't relate to us on color basis."

"Of course. Yaya, do you think those that go home believe in racism or if they did, would they behave that way over there? They wouldn't. They know racism went away from those lands with British, French and Portuguese Colonialism. Now we give respect and expect it, period. That's why you cannot meet a racist in Manika Kunda."

"But frankly, I never met a racist over there," Yaya confessed.

"True. When they get there, we respect them as strangers with no attitude barriers," Sidi said; "so they have to forget about their color difference. Yet you meet them in their countries. Of course, some that you socialized or became friends with, would still be nice and happy to see you; some may even talk of fond memories. But others wouldn't so much as let you into their houses just because of your color."

"You don't mean Americans, because they are by far liberal," Yaya stated.

"I live in America. I don't know about Europe. But I guess it could be much worse there. From what I hear, thanks to the civil rights movement, things are considerably better in America."

"I thought so too."

"Yaya, racism as a black misfortune is like a chameleon and its many colors or the legendary spider and the endless tales about it. What's your time now?"

"It's 11:25"

"Gosh, I've had it for the day. It's time for me to go to bed." Sidi stood up, and moved towards the door, then turned. "Hey, Yaya, about Pat, please bear with her. At least, you now know something about her background. You will know where she's coming from the next time she confronts you."

"Sure, Sidi."

"At the first chance tomorrow, I'll have a serious talk with her. But meantime, please, just learn to ignore her."

"I will."

"To be frank, of course, you will find some shocking behavior in her for a woman. That's bound to be. Sometimes it's the Western culture, you know."

"Yes, I know that."

"Good night."

"Good night, Sidi, and thanks."

After Sidi left, Yaya laid in bed, baffled. He folded his hands behind his head, trying to take in what he had just heard. Bewildered, he sat up and propped his pillow upright against the headboard and leaned against it. As he turned over in his mind the information Sidi had dumped on him, the waterbed pulsated beneath and went unnoticed, like a casual wind blowing on one's skin outdoor.

He was wondering when it would all end, man's wanton subjugation of man, and all the stories about people stripping others of what they themselves could not do without. Seeing no end to it all, he felt additionally despondent.

Exasperated, he turned to the letters Sidi had brought. They were five, all from home. There was one from his mother, this he anxiously read. She said she had received all his letters but had not replied till now because she always told his father to say in his letters everything that she wanted to say. The rest of the letter was the usual communication as from most mothers: concern for him, news about the family, some advice about taking good care of himself, with prayers and wishes from his father and her, and on behalf of the family.

Of the four left, he opened the next one he was most curious about. He could tell from the return address that it was from an uncle who was crippled with his legs amputated at the groin. Yaya remembered the terror he felt as a child when he saw the man once in Taényadu, with his big gown gathered around him like a heap.

Uncle Alieu, they called him. He had come on a visit to Yaya's father and had to be carried and set down, always calling on people to help him out. Maybe that was why he never traveled. Yaya had never seen him after that visit. His letter went as follows:

Dear Yaya,

I greet you plenty, and my whole family greets you many many times. If you don't know this, I want to tell you that I am your uncle, and I live in Madiala. We are all of the same blood. Your great forefather, or your grandfather's great grandfather, Kefinba, and my grandfather's great grandfather, Jibrila, were of the same parents. It was my great grandfather Jibrila that was weaned by their mother before your forefather Kefinba could be conceived.

There were three of them to their mother, the third one was a woman; she died as an infant. That left two of them to their mother. But your forefather migrated to the lands of the Felakas, which was why your great grandfather was born there, and mine was born here. In the family, I'm in line with your father, we are brothers, like our forefathers were; so you are my son and nephew, and a brother to my children.

The last time I saw you, you were five years old. I'm sure you cannot remember me, that is why I have told you our family connection. Yet everybody in the family had known that you were gone to the white man's land but me. One of your uncles, Tejani LaTalé of Juladu stopped by here for a few days; he told me the news and gave me your address.

My son, I am happy for you. I'm more happy because you went there in peace time. I was in England and Burma too, when I was your age. We were taken to fight in the big war on the British side, during colonial rule. That was where I lost my feet. A hell-fire from Hitler swept me off my feet, since then I have never stood. The next thing I knew I had no feet. But I'm lucky to be alive because everybody with me that day died.

For you to go over there to better yourself is fine. I know that the Lord has answered our prayers. For that has been our wish, that somebody rise among our children someday and be someone great. All the family here is sure you will be that, and we are praying for you.

Yaya, my son, now that you are over there, I want you to buy me a wheelchair that will be carrying me about, so that I don't have to sit all day in one spot. And please don't forget your cousins that are with me here. Backari my eldest son finished high school two years ago. He is a teacher at the elementary school here in Madiala. He is very serious, and wants to further his education. I want you to bring him near you, so that he will follow your footsteps. Please try to do this soon.

Also, I want to tell you that the big house in the family compound here has started to leak. The roof is old, and we are old and poor, and besides I'm crippled. Even my land has to be farmed for me by the kind people of this town. And that is hardly enough for me to feed my family year round.

So it is the responsibility of you, the children, to rebuild the big house, because that is where your great forefather lived. If you cannot rebuild it now, at least maintain it. That is why I am writing this letter to you. We cannot let that house fall and have that disgrace on the family. If that happens, it will be like shaming our ancestors and asking for a curse from them; may God forbid.

For that reason, I want you to send one thousand U.S. dollars immediately, as your own contribution. And please send one more thousand dollars for me too. All your sister's here are grown women now; I am planning to let them join the womanhood training and initiation ceremony in this coming dry season. Everybody is looking forward to that. With your help, and the blessings of our ancestors and Almighty Allah, it shall be.

As for you, you will be a success like a wild fire in Harmattan. And just say amen always, because we are always praying for you; for your success, your prosperity and long life.

Please send your reply and the money to this address:
Alieu LaTalé
c/o Post Master
Madiala
Atiyae District.
Manika Kunda.

Many greetings from me, the family and everybody here to you and your friends.

I am your uncle
Aleiu LaTalé

When Yaya finished reading the letter, he felt sorry, and didn't know whether to laugh or to cry. He did neither. But his recent recurring array of helplessness, frustration and depression, overwhelmed him. Confused, he flung his hands wide open, as if he was going to address somebody: *Man, now, tell me, how can I do anything for anybody when I cannot even help myself? Just look at the shape I'm in and tell me, eh?*

Hard pressed, Yaya took a deep breath, held it and let it out. He repeated this five times; a habit he had formed to cope with demanding situations, and now it had a lulling effect on him. His lips parted, and a gush of laughter escaped him, fascinated by his reality. *Oh, buddy! So much hope pinned on me and no headway in sight.*

He turned to the other letters and took one of the three left. It was from an old girl friend before Abie. He reflected with surprise to hear from her. Yaya's relationship with this lady had been like steel and magnet, tumbled into current and water. They met in college, in their first year, and hit it off like Siamese twins separated at birth. By final year, they were drifting with different persuasions.

The young lady became a liberated convert. For an African woman, she characterized such a gigantic sense of freedom that would mock proponents of women's liberation even in the West. Hers was of a sadistic edge, leaned to making him suffer in the name of love. Everything had to be her way. She wanted him at her heels, gyrating without a mind of his own, while she wriggled and stuffed him with her overblown sense of importance. That was beyond Yaya who took it for a while, and let go, for his sanity. His assertive lover spit fire at his insolence for dumping her, but she realized it took two and cooled off. They struck an understanding and stayed friends, with occasional relapse, and no commitments until Abie came.

In her letter, she regretted what Abie had done to Yaya. Now, she sounded a changed person—sweet, humble, caring and wishful—wanting Yaya to bring her over to join him, as a wife, of course.

Yaya felt touched, but in his situation he wasted no time thinking about her proposal; because that was out of his plan completely, even if he could afford it. One, he needed to see the new change in this lady for him to believe it, and he didn't want to take a chance of committing himself, to let her join him as a wife. Two, he didn't think bringing her to the U.S. would be the best thing for her.

She had a job at home as a Public Relations Officer for an Insurance Company. Yaya would be the first to tell her that it made no sense for her to leave her job to come to the U.S. for the heck of living in America. If he should advise her, it would be that she should count her blessings with what she had. As for her mister-right, he hoped one came along soon. And he thought, the sooner the happier for all. And then there was a letter from Abie!

Dear Yaya,

I know you probably don't want to hear from me, because you are angry at me. You have all rights to be.

But please understand why I did what I did. First you became a changed person for a whole year while we were still dating. You were hiding something from me. I learnt that your people found you a woman called Fatu and I didn't want to take a chance.

That was more so as I know that as a Mandinka, your people believe in polygamy which I was not prepared for. But now that you have gone to America and you are alone there, I'm starting to think that I was probably wrong about second guessing you.

I broke up with Dr. Kuma the very month you left, which makes it almost five months now that I'm not seeing anybody.

I'm your woman, Yaya, I want to be your wife. What do you have to say to that?

I'm ready to join you anytime and please make it soon. With love from your wife,
Abie.

Yaya hissed. *Indeed, 'your wife!' After she jilted me and went with that womanizing doctor who obviously in turn ditched her!*

Abie was one person Yaya refused to think about, period. The way she disappointed him, when he needed her so much, at such low points in his life—when his flat got burned and he lost all his possessions.

So, she wants to come to America now, right? So that she can take off with the first man that she stumbles upon with a shining car and a nice flat?

Yes, indeed, Yaya thought, he would bring her in a hurry, especially as he was in such a bad shape. Because he was destined to be the greatest fool on earth!

Yaya went to the last letter. It was from a good friend, Sam, with whom he entered college the same year. They had lost contact after final year. Yaya later learned that when he went to the Civil Service, Sam returned to college to get a diploma in Teacher Education.

In his letter, Sam was saying he was a teacher at one of the secondary schools in some village in the Eastern Province. As usual with most teachers in Manika Kunda, he was grumbling about no pay, poor pay, and the frustrations of the teaching field. Sam wanted to come to the U.S. to do his masters, and wanted Yaya to help him. He said he had no money, and no hope for scholarship, but that he would appreciate any help Yaya could render to get him in a school in America. He promised to pay back, of course, in due time all expenses incurred by Yaya, after he'd made it to America.

"Now that I have your address, I will do all I can to stay in touch with you," he said in the conclusion of his letter. "But please try to reply to this letter. You are my only hope presently, and I am looking forward to your brotherly assistance."

After reading that letter, it fell out of Yaya's hand without him knowing; so also did his mouth fall open. His other hand had found its way to his head, unknotting his tangled natural hair, and pulling from it a few long strands, which he stroked up and down his forehead. A smile formed on his lips, as void as an overworked cashier's grin born by courtesy only in line of service.

Even as hard hit as he was, Yaya felt amused: *So this is what it means to be in America, right? To want, and wonder, and wish, while folks at home think you are making it, and have all the solutions to their problems?*

Every week, Yaya received at least twenty letters from friends, relatives and acquaintances at home. Most sounded like bill collectors, and worse—because they made unrealistic demands! If one person didn't want the White House, they wanted the Empire State Building, or so to speak.

He wondered how would anybody expect someone that had newly gone to better himself in a strange country, to be able in less than six months, to buy you a car, a drilling machine or a tractor? Those were the letters Yaya was getting.

Everything is there in America, they seem to think, just for the taking, and only waiting for a willing person to send it. So, since Yaya, a simple and nice guy, perfectly fits the picture, why not plague him with letters upon letters of requests?

Reflecting, Yaya found it intriguing that his mother, who should be asking him for everything, had yet to ask him for anything. And yet every obscure Manjo and Musa immediately wanted a piece of his American pie. A pie he hadn't even whiffed a scent of, not to talk about tasting.

Yaya made the entries in his diary: May 20:—*I received letters from Mom, Abie, Gbongapay, Uncle Alieu, and Sam. And oh, Pat showed her true colors today, by shockingly insulting me, and letting me know she wants me out of here. Yes, I've got my cue.*

It was past midnight, but Yaya couldn't sleep. He decided to step out on the back porch for a breath of fresh air. Not to wake up Pat and Sidi, he quietly inched his way out of the apartment. The porch was covered and carpeted and had a wooden fence of about five feet high. Yaya leaned on the fence and had a partial view of the street, the sky, and a picturesque Southwestern Philadelphia at night.

He felt good that he had come out. The bright sky and the gentle wind against his body had a settling effect on his mind. Looking up at the wild expanse of the sky, and marveling at the wonders of nature, Yaya remembered how as a kid, he thought the sky fell somewhere in some big ocean that surrounded the earth, where the world ended, and where the moon and the stars went into hiding, to shoot up at night.

In Philadelphia that night, the moon was three quarters full, and the stars were few, but shining their worth. The illumination was of the sort that every small town without electricity longed for in Manika Kunda. It was the kind that kindled the spirit of the old, and enticed story telling in the front yard, while cutting loose the children in games of different kinds.

Yaya remembered his favorite game, hide and seek. The mere thought of his excitement in those blissful periods flickered memory of his first romance. He laughed, wondering if a first kiss and a relationship that didn't go beyond that, qualifies to be so called. He recalled that he was twelve then but didn't know the girl's age; maybe she was older by a year or two.

The sky of Taényadu had been clear, and it was playtime in the moonshine. He had escaped from his companions seeking him and wandered from his compound, and passed two compounds more. As he approached the fourth, he saw a lone girlish figure sitting in the verandah of a back house. He diverted to her in hopping strides, all curious. She was a strange girl in the neighborhood.

"I have never seen you before," he said.

"I know."

"Do you live here now?"

"No, my father is sick, me and my mother brought him to a medicine man."

"Oh, I'm so sorry."

"That's okay, he is getting better." And then she giggled and folded her arms across her chest looking up at Yaya. Sitting there in that posture, and with the story of a sick father, Yaya sympathized with the girl; he even went on to empathize by sitting close to her and putting an arm across her shoulders. Little did he know that that was dangerous. He almost jolted with shock when, suddenly, a kiss was planted on his lips. Wild eyed, and with an instinct of an animal, he quickly indulged, to satisfy his sprouting ego.

The kissing was a mere touching of the lips, and the emission of the smooching sound. But it was enough to get Yaya elated and to put a spring in his walk like a man. He told all his friends about the girlfriend. And waited for two days to perfect his skills, only to go there and learn that she was gone.

The family had left that morning, returning to their hometown, but unfortunately robbing him of a perfect romance. He never saw or heard anything about her anymore. Yet, he still remembered her face and wondered from time to time how she was doing and where she could b—

Yaya shuddered. He heard an emergency wailing! He counted the second screamings of sirens in the distant night, since he had been standing out here on the porch. He couldn't tell whether it was the police or an ambulance; they seemed to be busy in Philadelphia this night. He thought again about his love life and felt relived that he had no serious relationship to worry about. Not after all that he did for Abie, and what she did to him.

Funny, since he came to America, the women he dearly loved in Manika Kunda, all of whom turned around and poured pepper in his eyes, now claimed to be his wife by some destiny. *Good for them!* But at such a point in his life, when nothing seemed to be going right with him, of all dreams, romance was farthest.

For a man who liked to be in control and comfortable with picking the tab, Yaya felt that engaging in anything intimate just then, would only put him in situations where he would have to make excuses and plenty of them. Instead, he decided to make none—at least for a while.

"Getting involved with somebody? No, sir! I don't really care for any relationship or any involvement, right now," he told Sidi one evening when Sidi tried talking him into showing some interest in the young single ladies they occasionally ran into. "That's way-out for me, presently."

"Com'on, Yaya, we all need that. Face it and make it easy on yourself."

"Sure, I accept. But a man has to be up to it, and for now, I have no room for that. Besides, personally, I prefer being comfortable first before thinking of anything like that."

"If that's how you feel, buddy, what can I say?"

"Nothing. There is nothing to be said, Sidi, I'm okay."

Yet, Yaya felt worse. In his present situation, he saw himself like Kortu, his house boy in Sobala, who after he had squandered his pay as fast as he got it, then went about crying for the rest of the month, 'Boss, I am broke, flat and down.' Yaya thought that if he had a girlfriend now, he could imagine easily telling her, 'Lady, I'm broke, flat and down.' And which woman would like that? he wondered.

Yaya reflected that his luck in America had so far left him short, because the obstacles just proved to be entirely different. Now, he was no more the Civil Servant and role model that he was in Manika Kunda, and apart from having no job and no sense of belonging to the society, he must also keep looking behind his back, fearful of the mysterious hand of immigration officers. He heard they could snatch an illegal alien from any hiding hole in the country.

Sidi and his careless talks! Because he has a green card and is married to an American woman!

"For them to get you, it's easy!" he had told Yaya when he was in his second month, just when his visa had expired. "Do you remember the forms you filled out on the plane? It's how they pick you up, from the address you gave as your U.S. residence. But don't worry, they won't start looking for you until you are here for six months. By then things would have changed."

But he came on the 29th of December last year, it was now the 20th of May. In about nine days, he would be in his sixth month, yet nothing had changed.

Yaya sighed, realizing that there was no telling when his luck would run out, when mysterious immigration would track him down and come to book him, and put his hands behind him for being an illegal alien. Would they really deport him?

Of course, Yaya, don't fool yourself, you are taking a big chance—was his answer to that question.

".... I think there is a way out." Those were the words of Kondorfili Bunsor, the man whose advice partly got him here. *"You may leave the land, if you can, for a while, and stay away until it is two complete rains after your Grandma's death. You will be free of all torments and the curse."* Yaya remembered how happy he felt when he had that first ray of hope.

"If you cross the ocean where the land breaks from here, you will be free. For the leaf will never grow there. They will pass it on to somebody else. And when the time is up, you can come back and live in peace. Nothing will happen to you."

Well, Yaya thought, Grandma Fatu died on June 29th, two years ago, which this coming June 29th would round up to two years. And since he came to America with just six months left for the two year cycle to be completed, now with only nine days left of his fifth month, he figured that in less than two months this whole ordeal would be over. So, Yaya wished that if the immigration people were coming to get him, they should wait for at least two more months; one month and some days for the ominous two years which followed Grandma Fatu's death to be completed. And he needed the remaining days after that, to know if the inheritance had been handed to someone else. Then he would be relieved in a big way!

Before Grandma Fatu's ordeal, he was happy and had freedom, status and a life in Manika Kunda. It all vanished just like that. But things would get better for him again, by the grace of Almighty Allah. In fact, with time, he would get back everything he'd had, and do even better! Yes, he had to keep on, he must, because of all his responsibilities at home.

Yaya thought of his family—the whole family—his mother and siblings, his step-mothers and their children, and his father himself.

In Yaya's immediate family, he was the fifth son, even though he was the first born to his mother. Next to him was a brother who was 18, and then came two sisters who were 16 and 14 years old. While his mother had only four children, his father, on the other hand, had a total of 59 children. His old man fathered them all through the years of his virility. The man was a classic polygamist.

As far as Yaya could remember, his father always had at least four wives. When one left, a new one always came to replace the one that left. He had seen that happen twice, but his mother stayed through. It seemed she did not have a choice.

Like a typical African woman, his mother was a downright traditionalist. Even when it was apparent that she was sad in the marriage, she stayed, according to her, for two reasons. One, that it was the choice of her parents that she be married to the man, and she could not disobey them by leaving. She surmised that that would be an unforgivable dishonor to her parents. Two, the future of her children mattered greatly to her.

In her traditional frame of mind, she believed that the only way her children would be blessed or grow up to be anything in society would depend on how she treated their father, her husband. Those thoughts made her stay in the marriage, and made her stoop even when it meant taking all the downpour she suffered.

It was obvious to Yaya that even for polygamy, the marriage was far from the ideal. There was no fairness. His father had a way of showing favoritism to his newest wife, with only his first wife coming anywhere close in terms of better treatment. The other women, besides those two, were somewhat like step-children in the marriage. Yaya's mother was one of them. She had ascended to the position of the second wife, after the two preceding her had left. That did not make matters any better.

Supposedly, there was a time table where every woman had her time. It was an unwritten eight day-roster; each woman had two days. On those days, she cooked generally for the whole family and shared her husband's bed. But it was no secret that his father reshuffled the schedule at whim, particularly when it came to deciding who to sleep with, and always tipped in favor of his new wife. That discrepancy in his behavior always led to confusion, and just left the women at each others' throats.

Yaya noticed the scuffles and hated them. But as an offspring in the family, it was unimaginable that he could either intervene or comment on what was happening. That would be a blasphemy.

Like the other children, should he be present at the onset of such reckoning, all he had to do was distance himself and find something to occupy him, regardless of whether his mother was involved or not. Yet, as he grew up, he found out that he could not bear it and so escaped to the city during his high school days, claiming some class project or the other.

Being the first generation in his family to go to school and obtain Western education, even as a teenager, Yaya maintained serious reservations about his father's life style. But under the heavy arms of tradition and fear of provoking a paternal curse upon himself, Yaya had decided not to ask questions or debate anything, or even hold it against the old man. That was the norm in his father's world. In fact, the man's life-style symbolized success, the community counted him worthy and granted him due status.

Yaya knew, however, that there were actions by his father which flawed polygamy, and cracked the walls of family unity. For example, his father's over attachment to one woman and his habit of rocking the schedule. That not only compounded the rivalry among his wives, but also led to fights and animosities.

Those negative feelings among the mothers, inevitably boiled over to their children, offspring of the same father in a big family compound, who got stuck in-between but were left on their own to deal with pent-up emotions. Naturally, they fought among themselves secretly to settle scores, as their mothers, blinded by jealousy, battled in the open on simple issues.

By tradition, the children were expected to accept and respect all their step-mothers and love them, and their offspring as well. In fact, that was the cardinal rule in Yaya's family. Everybody was expected to show love to one another, both by actions and words, even after their periodic and compulsive outbursts!

Indeed, what could be more nerve-wrecking than polygamy? Yaya asked, reflecting on the reservoir of courage and discipline that was needed to witness one's mother being jumped on by a co-mate; and to feel the anguish of the incident and to have to block out all memory of that and still have to relate to the assailant with trust and affection, bearing no grudge absolutely, ever thereafter. Those hard realities underlined the basics of a typical polygamous family, the type he came from.

Inherent in the tradition was the customary practice, instilled in all offspring, that in a family, oneness superseded personal emotions in all matters. It was like a band-aid that plastered all wounds, with a bond that demanded nothing but loyalty and pride in the lineage—

Wow! Another siren wailed desperately, this time nearer. Yaya counted it as the third, since he had been standing out here. He leaned out, looking towards the street but couldn't see which vehicle was the source. There was a young white couple strolling towards the apartment complex. They seemed fastened together as they came.

Nice match! To Yaya the lovers were just like him and Abie, when it was as if they were made for each other. He laughed when he remembered Abie and her unconvincing and silly excuses for jilting him. "*Because you were hiding something from me... I know that, as a Mandinka, your people believe in polygamy...*"

She should have known him better. If he could have discussed Grandma Fatu's issue with anybody, Abie would have been one of the first people to know. But he couldn't tell even his mother, who was almost next door when Grandma Fatu died and handed him the inheritance. Because he couldn't. That, however, didn't stop him from loving Abie and it wasn't as if he was messing around.

Yet, Abie left him. It depressed Yaya to think that she entertained such skepticism about him being a polygamist—just because his people were.

Reflecting on Abie's faulty reasoning, Yaya couldn't help laughing. He was 25-years-old when he left home and had been living in his own place and working for over three years since college. If he wanted to do like his people, he would have married one woman every year in those three years. Many people in Taényadu were offering their daughters to him for marriage, and his parents were constantly parading their choices of beauty before him. That didn't affect him.

He wanted one wife, somebody he loved, and he thought Abie would do. He dated only her since they met. Indeed, nobody needed to tell him about the evils of polygamy. From what he saw in his family, he did not only detest that style of life but would advise against it for anybody.

But, by the way, who was Abie to question the lifestyle of his people? Okay, they believed in polygamy, but it had worked for them. Or, why did the traditional wisdom of generations permit it? Or, how could society have thrived and rejoiced in it? Like everything, he knew there had to be bad cases of polygamy and good cases....

There was Pa Bayoh in Taényadu, for instance. He had four wives. They were the only four he ever had.

The wives or co-mates treated one another like sisters, while their offspring collectively acted like a team, with one stand in all aspects. They had different mothers but the same father and all of them lived in the same compound. And they had love and respect for each other, underlined by a general trust and constancy of faith in the family.

Even as teenagers the offspring performed chores like farming or mending the houses where each of their mothers lived, together. They were welcomed and fed heartily at all times in the private homes of all their step-mothers. And the credit went to Pa Bayoh who was as fair in dealing with his wives and children as he was a disciplinarian. He stood against divisiveness and malice in his family.

Like a true apostle of family unity, Pa Bayoh's leadership centered on peace, love, respect and loyalty. And seniority ruled among all. The youngest child obeyed the next ahead, even if minutes accounted for the difference in age. It was the same with the wives; ascendancy and clout in the family was by who came first and who came last, with all being treated with maximum and equal regard.

In a situation of severe quarrel between two wives, Pa Bayoh would call all the women and some elders together. They would hear the grievances and the elders would 'hang their heads'— or confer—and render judgment by traditional rules.

If the junior wife was wrong, like a trouble-maker, her act was condemned and she was verbally lashed by all. Depending on the severity, she would be banished from the household, for as long as Pa Bayoh desired; such a woman was sent with an escort to her parents for them to know their daughter's character.

Were it a senior wife in the wrong, her mistake would also be pointed. Sometimes, she could be stripped of her status and ordered by Pa Bayoh to be limited in activities and movements in the compound. She could not share her husband's bed or partake in family affairs and meals for a stipulated time. And in either case, for a proud African woman, that disgrace wasn't worth a discord, so they avoided friction and arguments that got them on the quarter-deck.

With the children, it was obey and report, where a younger child was hardly ever right. That notwithstanding, Pa Bayoh and all others in the family lashed at errant seniors with tendencies to be bullies. Thus, there was no day when one would go to the Bayoh compound and see a fight.

The women cared for themselves and looked after all the children as they would their own. The children, in turn, bowed to all mothers and looked after themselves like they were all born by the same mother.

Should you go to the Bayoh compound in Taényadu at moonshine, you would meet those women sitting together and entertaining themselves with story-telling. They would be eating freshly boiled peanuts from a big bowl sitting in the center of their circle. And as they laughed together, with them falling on each other like one happy family, you could not help but be happy for them.

But that would be speaking of almost perfect polygamy, and only few men accomplished that; just like only few men could actually adhere to perfect monogamy, where a man would marry one wife and never sneak out to fool around, cheating on her, and vice versa. Not with the various accounts of marital infidelity common everywhere.

Yaya wondered why Abie left him for Dr. Kuma. Was it because Abie's mother was English and her father was married to only her, or because Dr. Kuma was of the same ethnic group with her and more of their people were monogamists and Christians?

Well, didn't he ditch her? She should have known better! That in every relationship, what matters is personal principles and preferences. And as for polygamy, one cannot hold the customs of a man's ethnic background against him, like Abie did—because your people are polygamists!

And yet, Yaya knew that almost everyday one heard on television or read in newspapers and magazines of the Western world, the cradle of monogamy, that some member or the other of a royal family, or somebody of renown was cheating on his or her spouse.

Quite amusing, he thought, because as the so-called monogamists are caught cheating and exposed, their counter-parts in Africa, the pronounced polygamists, perhaps should be pouring scorn on them for hypocrisy.

Thinking of a classic case of monogamy gone wrong, Yaya reflected that while in high school, he saw for himself four boys, schoolmates, each from a different mother, but fathered by the same man, who got married to only one wife, and yet none of those boys was hers. In fact, until they met in high school, none of the boys knew the other existed, not to mention knowing that they were related.

With pride, Yaya reflected that as large as his family was, at least he knew all his brothers and sisters. His father didn't have to hide any offspring, and he did not stumble on an illegitimate sibling on the street. They all grew up in the same tumultuous compound.

But..., who was Abie to question and hold against him—

Whew! Yaya jerked and quickly ducked. *Phew!* There were sounds of firecrackers or gun shots somewhere close by: ' *Paw! Paw! Paw!* ' In less than two minutes another siren went wailing. The fourth. Suddenly it occurred to him that it was not safe standing out in the porch at that time of the night. He went inside.

Yaya threw himself on the bed and reached out to read his mother's letter again. After reading the letter, he thought of her, her tales and her tolls of surviving in a polygamous marriage. In his mind now, he vividly visualized her, walking tall, always with a ready smile and a pleasant face, even with her line of worries under her eyes, which she held up gracefully.

He sighed, reflecting that even without hinting, he always saw through his mother's dignified meekness, and could tell the tales of pain her dark eyes concealed. And though worlds apart, physically and in thinking, he instantly empathized with her; a victim of polygamy at its worst.

Of such magnitude was the pain he felt for his mother, as he imagined what she had been through, that he wondered if she could ever be compensated enough for her selfless sufferings through the years?

Yaya decided that whatever it might take, he would give it a good shot, especially as the dark days were almost over for him. In a month, he should be completely free from all worries about Grandma Fatu and the haunting heritage. As for his luck in America, he believed that it would shine anytime, in this land of abundant opportunities where every ambitious or hard working person could make it. With that in mind, he resolved to succeed and slept.

CHAPTER SIXTEEN

"You sorrow boy, hey, you nigger, don't ever tell on me again, you hear?" A furious Pat attacked Yaya the following evening. She was standing over him in the living room and retaliating for the argument she'd had with Sidi that morning, concerning her misbehavior to Yaya the previous day.

"I don't know what you're talking about," Yaya said, his eyes down at Pat's feet, hoping to avoid further argument.

"You sure do! Smart ass!"

"But..., but, Pat..., please. You don't have to insult me, eh?"

"I damn well can do anything," she barked, with her arms swinging over Yaya, as she looked into his skull. "Yes, this is my place and not yours!"

"Of course.., I know that," Yaya looked up at her. "But we can at least respect each other."

"Folks like you don't deserve any respect." She turned and started to step away.

"But suppose I were to treat you in the same way?"

Pat turned with her mouth wide open, looking at Yaya. She placed her hands on her hip. "Then I'll curse your ass out some more. And I'll kick your damn African ass out!"

"I see," Yaya said. "But if you feel so bad about Africans, why are you married to one?"

"That's none of your business, knuckle head, kinky-haired African. I am through with you, boy! You better never talk about me behind my back again." She went and sat on a barstool, by the kitchen bar, her usual position when on an affront.

In distress, Yaya recalled what Sidi told him the previous night, about Pat growing up where most people had a gun, and where to be shot was easier than being offered a glass of water. He thought of the rampant violence, fueled by desperation and anger from hardship. And he remembered Pat's threatening vow in her attack on Sidi just last night —*we will both be on TV!* He only raised eyebrows, and didn't feel insulted. But he was very uncomfortable.

As Sidi was not at home, Yaya decided to go out for a walk. It was early evening, around 7 o'clock. Beams of light were already shooting from passing cars, and the street and security lights were on. There were also twinkles of light from bulbs in most of the apartments. Yaya took the sidewalk by the parking lot in the complex, and seeing nobody outside, it dawned on him that people mostly kept indoors in that neighborhood.

He walked through the length of the apartments, about 150 yards, with the buildings in two straight lines facing each other and the parking lot. He would stop to admire cars, learn their names, and even peek at the interior of some that he fancied, telling himself he would get one soon. *Because everybody has a car in America!*

On his way back, Yaya saw people from the apartment windows peeping at him. He noticed that they watched him pass and when he looked behind, he saw them still looking at him. As he walked he felt more eyes on him, noting every step he took. This made him nervous and uneasy. But he held his head up high and looked straight ahead, increasing his pace. Suddenly, an expensively dressed white lady, glittering to her high-heels, was taking off with great speed when she got out of her car and saw him coming towards her. Stunned, Yaya felt more frightened than humiliated. He prayed to make the remaining 20 yards home and tried not to run, so somebody won't come chasing him.

Sidi was home. Pat had snubbed him and gone into the bedroom, where she got on the phone. Sidi had no response from her about where Yaya went. But he knew Yaya was safe, perhaps with some countryman who took him out. Or being bored, he'd probably gone out for a stroll. After a quick meal, Sidi sat on the couch in the living room, staring at the TV. He was alone with his wide hairy chest bare when Yaya came, shaken and yet hiding it.

"Hello, mister wanderer," Sidi teased, the moment he stepped in.

"Oh! Hi, Sidi," he panted with a smile and a fresh feeling of security.

"How was your day?"

"Okay," Yaya said, sitting across from Sidi on the loveseat. His panting was subsiding. He glanced at the TV where Sidi had diverted his attention, watching Barbara Walters and Hugh Down on the ABC weekly *20/20* program on Friday evenings. Sidi was all absorbed in an exposé of a white-collar criminal who was using phony money orders to buy expensive real estate all over the country.

"No leads again today, Sidi." Yaya tried to get his attention. "But..., I'll just have to keep trying and hoping."

Sidi looked at him sideways, and smiled. "That's the spirit, man. It's going to only get better. Your chance will come, soon."

"I pray so."

Sidi turned towards him. "Yaya, a guy I work with was supposed to drop a video tape here for me, did he bring it?"

"No, nobody brought anything while I was here, and I was out for no more than thirty minutes."

"That's okay. Maybe, he will bring it on his way back. He goes to school in the evenings."

Still tensed, Yaya stood up and sat down. "But wow, Sidi, just now when I went for a stroll, I thought I was dreaming."

"Why?"

"Some strange experience out there."

"Where?"

"In this neighborhood. I went out for a walk around and all of a sudden I had eyes staring at me from the apartments, from the windows and at the doors, as if I had done something wrong. One woman that was getting out of her car actually fled to her apartment when she saw me, as if I was going to attack her."

Sidi was looking keenly at him. Even with the seriousness on Yaya's face he couldn't help but be amused. *Poor Yaya, another cultural shock for him. You ain't seen nothing yet, mister! A strange black man on the loose, wandering in such an affluent white middle-class neighborhood. Do you want to go unnoticed?*

To contain his amusement and in order not to laugh so as not to offend Yaya, Sidi was leaning forward, his elbows on his knees, with both hands propping his jaws.

"Were you close to their cars?" he mumbled.

"Well yes, I was on the sidewalk next to the parking lot."

"I thought so." Sidi sat up, permitting himself a little laugh. Then he got serious. "But you know that is close to the front doors and windows of most apartments."

"Yes."

"Yaya, don't forget that you are a black man and some people are very insecure about black men here. If anybody sees you walking by their cars, or their apartments, they are going to watch you. Some may even call the police on you. To put it bluntly, you carry the burden of a suspect the moment you step out of this door."

Yaya was rubbing his palms and flexing his fingers, feeling uneasy.

"But don't feel bad," Sidi said. *"C'est la vie*—that's life—for most black men. We are stereotyped in every negative sense. It does not matter whether you are African or African-American. We are all in the same boat as blacks, stigmatized and judged before the offense."

Yaya sighed in frustration. "But I thought they would have known me in this complex by now. I'm going on to my sixth month here."

"Yes," Sidi said and laughed inside. *They've known you alright, knowing that you don't work, from seeing you around all day, and thinking that you probably don't want to. All the more why you'd be watched.* He decided to spare Yaya's feelings of those cold facts.

"All I'm saying, mister, is that every time you step out just be on your guard. It is safest. And learn to stay as far away as possible from people's windows and properties."

"That I will do."

"And really, except you are unlucky, most times if you don't bother anybody, nobody bothers you."

"That's what I thought."

"Just never forget yourself."

Creeengn! Creeengn! The door bell rang. It rang again, and a deep masculine voice asked: "Anybody home?"

"That's Bill," Sidi said getting up. "Oh, hi Bill. Come right in."

Bill entered. After the greetings, Yaya absent-mindedly was gaping at the 6'7" tall, light-complexioned black man. From the accent, Yaya knew that Bill was African-American. He looked like some executive with a crew-cut on his head, trimmed mustache, and dressed in expensive looking shoes, slacks and tie. Bill had a briefcase in one hand and a videotape in the other.

"Here, man." He gave the videotape to Sidi. "I was rushing for a test this afternoon so I decided to drop it on my way back."

"That's okay, man. Bill, that's my cousin I told you about. Yaya, this is Bill, a coworker."

"Oh that's your cousin? Sidi has been telling me about you." Bill stepped towards Yaya and they shook hands. He sat down next to Yaya on the couch. "In fact, I was supposed to come to your welcome party, but man, it's been crazy for me."

"It seems you are a busy man," Yaya offered.

"Very. I'm taking this crazy course in electronics, trying to do a four-year program in three years or less."

"Oh, yeah? That sounds great," Yaya said.

"Yes, but it's tough. And with a job and a family too? I'm about wasted."

"Which university are you attending?" Yaya asked.

Bill crossed his legs and looked at Yaya. "I'm in a technical school man, it's called Silicon Institute."

"I envy you," Yaya said, not knowing what to say.

"Don't envy me yet, man. Wait till I finish and start making big bucks." Bill laughed big and clenched his fists in a hooray fashion. Yaya saw Bill's face shining with hope and wished he was also so hopeful.

"So how do you like the United States?" Bill asked, looking into Yaya's eyes.

"Oh marvelous! I love it here. This country is a wonderland!"

Sidi almost laughed. *My God, there goes again Yaya, the American fanatic!*

"Bill, can I offer you anything?"

"That's okay Sidi, I'll be out in a minute." Bill turned to Yaya. "Hey, man, I was in Mombassa, I loved it there."

"What?" Yaya almost stood up in surprise. "Were you?"

"Yes. Bill was in the Navy," Sidi said.

"I went to Mombassa twice, and I loved it every time. I went all over the country. And man, I was amazed at how nice and simple the people are over there." Yaya laughed.

"But times are getting hard all over Africa, these days," Sidi said.

"I know," Bill said. "I was talking to some youths at a Northwest community service seminar the other day, about feeling hopeless, getting self-destructive and losing their pride. I told them to draw on the survival instinct and strength of their African heritage; because if they think it's that bad here, let them go to Africa and see people surviving and taking poverty with dignity."

"Well, Bill, the difference is that the opportunities are here, while over there, people don't have much of a choice," Yaya said.

"I know," Bill acknowledged. "But brother, some white folks aren't going to simply share the opportunities equally with us here. To realize that is to become less bitter and focus on positive things which increase your options, rather than indulging in those that only limit you."

"You are right, Bill," Sidi said.

"Of course. Hey, man, I was bad as a teenager, and barely made the grades. And even if I wanted to go to college I had no money. And I knew they didn't cater to borderline kids like us. It was the smart ones and the athletes that got all the scholarships. So I went straight from high school to the Navy for five years, and today I'm happy because of the GI bill. That's what I'm using as my scholarship."

"What's this GI bill?" Yaya asked.

"It's a benefit towards higher education for serving in U.S. Military," Sidi answered.

"That was smart, Bill." Yaya said impressed. He raised both hands up. "You see, the opportunities are here, in America!"

"To me, Yaya, it's obvious that was a good choice. Because most of my best friends, a lot of those I grew up with, just fell in the system. Many were killed senselessly or are in prison. Some guys are in prison, they don't know what they're in for. They've been in so many times, it doesn't make any difference to them either. This—" Bill pointed to his skin, " —is what keeps you down in this country."

"Yes, Bill, tell that to homeboy here. He went out this evening almost rubbing on peoples' cars and came back shocked because they were watching him."

"Oh, man, you don't play that here. Remember that to be black in America is not the same as where you came from. Talk to your brother here, he's very knowledgeable. Hey Sidi, I've got to run. Bye, Yaya."

"Bye, Bill."

"I'll see you when you come back from vacation."

"It isn't but a week, just to catch up with classes. I'll holler at you later. And, Sidi, please keep me posted on the job."

"I will."

"Bill seems like a nice guy," Yaya said, immediately after Sidi locked the door.

"Yes, he is a wonderful dude, and very reliable."

"I'm happy I met an African-American that is positive about Africa."

"But of course, Yaya, there are plenty of them. People like Bill who have traveled and have been in the military, and most of those that have read about Africa, respect their origin. And more and more African-Americans are reading about the continent these days. There are still many, however, that don't even want the word Africa associated with them. They look down upon everything African."

Like Pat, your wife, Yaya thought.

"But generally, as a people, African-Americans have come a long way in appreciating their African heritage," said Sidi. "Did you read *ROOTS*, by Alex Haley?"

"Yes," Yaya responded.

"Think back about when Kunta Kinte went to *'massa Waller's plantation,'* after his foot had been cut, where he met Bell, the fiddler and the gardener. Do you recall that even Bell, whom Kunta later got married to, was previously offended when Kunta, trying to be nice, told her that she was as beautiful as a Mandinka woman?"

"Yes," Yaya laughed. "Bell didn't speak to him for long time after that. I was surprised they got married."

"And, Yaya, do you remember what both the fiddler and the gardener told Kunta about the master's attitude to things African, the moment he started coming around them? As to how white folks wanted niggers to forget about Africa and African stuff?"

"Yes." Yaya nodded. "I remember on one of Kunta's visits to the fiddler, he told Kunta to throw away the *saphie* charm on his arm, which Kunta had made for good luck as it was done back home, hoping to escape."

Sidi laughed. "The fiddler, of course, did not consider himself African, anyway. And neither did the old gardener, both of whom were born and had gotten old on slave row. The old gardener couldn't even sing one little song he had learned from his grandmother who was African, for fear of incurring the wrath of *'massa.'* That shows how far back their minds had been corrupted towards their origin. It became a prejudice which couldn't go away overnight, like all others that go deep down into ancestral roots—like racism!"

"You're right, Sidi. It takes a big mind to overcome such deep-seated indoctrination!"

"Yes, but, Yaya, let's be honest, the fact that blacks in America have decided to use the word 'AFRICAN' in identifying themselves shows they've made a giant progress. We as Africans should be proud of them."

"Of course," Yaya agreed. "But tell me, Sidi, what is the relationship generally between African-Americans and Africans in the U.S.?"

"Not quite what it should be. Not at all. But, Yaya, how did you feel about African-Americans when you were in Manika Kunda?"

"With great admiration and respect. We admire them so much that they become social magnates in the community. Like the Peace Corps and tourists? Man, it's up to them, if they want to be celebrities."

"Well, wait until you are here for a year or two." Sidi stood up. "The mainstream opinion about an average African-American here is negative, and you wouldn't know when you start changing opinions too along with the dominant vibes, which boils down to putting some fear in you."

"But that shouldn't affect how Africans relate to African-Americans."

"Yaya, if you go to a village, and a house is pointed to you, where they say some cannibals live. What would be your reaction to the house?"

"I'd keep away from it."

"Well, sooner or later, that's how the average African relates to African-Americans, because of the negative image that the mainstream generates daily about them. And that just balances their troubled feelings about us, as their minds had been poisoned against us long ago."

Yaya frowned. "But, Sidi, there is something missing, a forum or a channel that links us with them when we come here. That spirit of customary hospitality as we have back home. If we were to go by tradition, isn't it the responsibility of the host to bring the guest closer to gain his trust and respect or affection?"

"Yes, mister. But all I can say is that African-Americans are Westerners."

"It's all the more why they should initiate hospitality, Sidi. In Africa, you can invite yourself to a man's house but in America, you cannot. They will shoot you for an intruder. How can one go and say, 'Hey, man, I'm from the homeland and I want to know you, because deep down we are one and the same people?' Eh, Sidi?"

Sidi laughed. He thought, truly Yaya was just from Africa, so naive. He imagined Yaya going to stand before some embittered and broken dude in Northwest Philly and making that speech. 'And what's that going to do for me, man?' He might be asked, if not told, 'Get out of my face, you crazy African!'

"Remember, Yaya, the average African-American is under very challenging conditions. From the realities of most of them in this wealthy country, you'd think that they are either lazy or behind because they just don't want to do anything to better themselves."

"I have wondered so too, Sidi."

"Well, there is more to it. Just picture a mother with two children, hers and a stepchild, peers, both of whom look up to the guardian mother. In the house, the stepchild goes about always in shirts that are torn at the armpit and oversize pants that look like they were salvaged from some clothes demolition center. Yet every time the guardian mother comes from shopping, all the new clothes are for her child, which he tries on one after the other, while the stepchild stands by, watching and wishing. Now tell me, if the stepchild becomes sad and broken hearted, who is causing the havoc?"

"The guardian mother."

"You are right. It is the system." Sidi stood up, stretching himself, like he was getting ready to go to sleep. He turned and started walking towards the kitchen.

"Sidi, I needed to ask you a favor?"

"Yes?"

"I wanted to make a call, it's long distance, to a friend in Houston, Texas."

"Sure, whenever you are ready." He turned on the light that was over the dining table. There was a fruit basket sitting there; he got a banana from it. "But Yaya, remember it's cheaper in the evenings and on weekends. You can call now, since it's ten to ten. Or better still, wait till eleven, if those people wouldn't be sleeping, or if they don't mind. But try not to call daytime between eight to five on weekdays. That's business hours and very expensive."

"Sure, Sidi, thanks." Sidi disappeared into the kitchen.

"And oh, Sidi, you had a telephone call today from Mister Kakay, he said, he is having a naming ceremony for his son on Sunday, this weekend."

"Is that right?" Sidi asked over a running tap.

"Yes, he said he will call again. Is the ceremony done here like it is done back home?"

"Well, we try to do our best." He turned the light off in the kitchen and was peeling the banana. "Are you coming to this?"

"Of course, I'm looking forward to attending."

"You will enjoy it. Did you tell Pat about the call?"

"No, I forgot." Yaya got up, unwilling to tell Sidi about Pats's attack on him that evening, which had made him flee the apartment. "Good night, Sidi," he said, anxious to go into his bedroom to make the call to Houston that he just got permission for.

"Good night, Yaya, see you in the morning." Sidi turned and watched his cousin keenly as he left. The guy was all broken and down, and turning to be all bones. He promised himself afresh to intensify efforts to find Yaya something soon to keep him busy, so he wouldn't die in his hands out of frustration.

After eating the banana and wrapping its skin up in a tissue, Sidi reached for the remote control and turned off the TV which had been mumbling relentlessly in low tune. He then went into the kitchen and dumped the banana skin in the garbage can and left to join Pat in bed.

As soon as Yaya went into his bedroom, he quickly flipped the pages of his telephone and address book to the number he was going to call in Houston. He waited to hear the TV turned off and to hear Sidi's bedroom door close, as he debated the purpose of his call.

This is something I've got to do, but I know Sidi won't want to hear of it. Man! I'm giving up on Philadelphia, before going crazy!

Just imagine, I'll be starting my sixth month in America soon, and yet nothing. And worse, immigration will start looking for me any time now, and they have this address.

Nope, I can't take chances, not with one month and some days still remaining for Grandma Fatu to hand over her troublesome inheritance to somebody else. Besides, truly, I see no point in lying here idle only to be insulted at random and to worry everyday. Philadelphia may have nothing for me but deportation, if Sidi doesn't move from this apartment. And with Pat, I don't see that happening.

Well, a man has to fight for his head. It's time to start exploring chances—elsewhere!

Holding the headset of the telephone in his hand, Yaya vividly recalled what a colleague had told him on the night before his departure from home. Like everybody else, this colleague knew nothing about his situation with Grandma Fatu and the inheritance.

"As you leave for America, don't forget you're a seeker of success," he had said. "And remember no place is home until you are happy. If you can't make it in one place, search and move on, there is no telling where your luck is."

"Thanks, Joe," Yaya had said without giving it much thought.

But events have given that advice resonance. He was now casting his net. There was his childhood friend, Basi Ibrahim, in Houston. That was somebody to seek, for after Sidi, Basi was the next person in America that he knew best and could count on, like a brother. Besides growing up together, they were the same age and in the same class throughout high school. And they had lived in the same boarding home dormitory for five years.

When they graduated from high school, while Yaya and others were awaiting their General Certificate of Examination results to scramble for scholarship and a place at the only University in Manika Kunda, Basi was already gone. He did not have to wait for any results. His father sent him to America immediately, and got him into a college too.

Pa Ibrahim was a contractor and a successful business man with strong political connections, even before he got into the forefront of politics. In Parliament, he was quickly drawn into the Cabinet and made a high ranking Minister, adding to his already established financial clout.

Many people wondered about Pa Ibrahim's integrity as they always did with Manika Kunda politicians and the few rich people in the country. He was envied, of course, for having it all, from country estates with lighted tennis courts and swimming pools to office structures that harbored even the American Embassy. Basi was his only son.

Lucky boy. Basi has been in the U.S for almost six years. With all the wealth behind him, there is no telling what powers he now has in America. Well, maybe his needy brother should go lean on him for a way to stand on his own feet, for a man has to start somewhere.

"Hello, hello, is this Basi Ibrahim's residence?"

"Sure it is, who is calling, please?" a gentle female voice with an American accent asked at the other end of the telephone.

"This is Yaya LaTalé, calling from Philadelphia. May I talk to Basi, please?"

"Sure, hold on." *Whoever this is, you are in luck to get him home with his roving feet.*

After a brief moment, Yaya heard the phone picked up.

"Hello, this is Basi Ibrahim here."

"Hi, Basi, this is Yaya."

"Oh! Mister Yaya LaTalé? Hi, man, how are you?"

"I am fine, and you?"

"I'm doing great. So how have you been doing?"

"Nothing to brag about. Say Basi, I don't know about this your America, man. It's been rough for me."

"And why so, man?"

"Since I came, and I'm now completing my fifth month, all I have done is stay at home and languish. I've never worked. This paper problem, so no job and no hopes."

"No, that can't be. And what is your brother doing for you?"

"He said he is trying."

"For five months? Hey, let me ask you. Would you like to come to Houston?"

"Of course. I can't tell how Sidi would feel about that, but I would like to take the chance."

"Okay, you talk to him, and I will talk to my wife. I will call back in a few days and see what we can do about you coming here immediately."

Yaya was excited. "I will very much appreciate that, Basi. You may be saving my soul."

"Com'on, Yaya, that's no big deal. You are almost a brother to me. Don't forget, we lived in the same hall for five years, and we did about everything together."

"I know, man. Guess who just came to my mind. Pa Jusu, our principal. Do you remember your last major infraction with him? 'For being recalcitrant, and leaving the boarding home unauthorized to invade and disturb a sister school, Basi Ibrahim is hereby suspended indefinitely. He should vacate the school premises immediately.' Do you remember that speech?"

"Man, isn't that funny now? That old man wanted to keep us locked up like prisoners, and on weekends too, when those girls were over there longing for us. Is he still there?"

"He is, still strong, with a good grip on the school. But I heard the alumni association is planning to retire him."

"They should, man. It's about time that old man took a break."

"Yep, he has done well. And it's interesting that he has been principal of that school for as long as we've both lived. But after two decades and a half, the school definitely needs new blood."

"I agree with you. But hey, Yaya, thanks for the call. What's your number again?" Yaya gave him Sidi's telephone number. "Okay, man, I will call you back, right?"

"Please do. And say hi to your wife for me."

"I will. Meanwhile, take care. Bye-bye."

"Bye."

After talking with his friend, Yaya took out his diary and made his entries: Friday, May 21:—*I had a lengthy discussion with Basi in Houston today. It was positive and made me hopeful. I'm seriously thinking of joining him ASAP.*

CHAPTER SEVENTEEN

The weekend the Kakays were to have their naming ceremony arrived. It was a Sunday, the customary day for such occasions in Manika Kunda, and the same for her descendants abroad. By mid morning on that day, May 24, the sun had already emerged, and the Philadelphia climate seemed African, with an alluring warmth, and a sense of inner glow.

Sidi had risen early. Up to this morning, he still had to succeed at having Pat warm up to the occasion and come along, like a good wife. Also, Sidi hoped to have her motivated to step into the ceremony like other African women, tall and proud, and with a sense of belonging. Anything otherwise, Sidi held, would be disappointing and inexcusable—for his image and Pat's—to the Manika Kunda community. Thus he decided to coax her to endeavor.

The moment Pat stretched herself and yawned, blinking her eyes, he got started.

"Good morning, Mrs. Bérété," he said, and Pat drew in a long breath, opening her sleep-clouded eyes, suspiciously. "Wake up, Ms. pretty sleepy head." Sidi reached backwards and stroked her toes.

"I've been sitting here for over twenty minutes observing you as you sleep, and thinking what a beauty I have as a wife." Pat smiled and she closed her eyes.

Sidi moved upwards besides her, propping himself against the headboard of the bed, leaning over her. "Baby, you are definitely a black beauty. It shows at sleep and awake. Either way, you're beautiful."

"Thanks, Sidi, what time is it?"

"It's almost 7 o'clock; I've been up since 6:15."

"Really? This is Sunday, isn't it?"

"Sure it is."

"Then why are you up so early?"

"Getting us organized for the Kakay's naming ceremony."

"Oh, that?" Pat pulled her nightcap down her forehead.

Sidi sighed, realizing how nonchalant she sounded. "Yes, Pat, I've just finished pressing our gowns for the occasion, so we are all set."

Preferring not to say anything, Pat shrugged an arm he was holding. But Sidi was undeterred. "Girl, I can't wait to see you today in that beautiful lace gown, with it flowing on you like an African queen?"

Pat frowned. "Who said I'm going to wear it? Or, who said I'm going anywhere?"

"Me. Who else?" Sidi was serious faced. "Look, Pat, there is no reason for that attitude, and there is no reason why you shouldn't go. This has to be a family affair, everybody with a family goes with them. And since you are my wife, it's important that you go too."

"I ain't. No way. I don't even know what to expect there."

"That's precisely why you should go. To see and appreciate for yourself. It's a cultural event. In fact, as my wife, and according to our customs, you are not only expected to be there, but also, you are expected to prepare some food to take with you as an act of camaraderie with the hostess. That's the spirit among all the women, and I'm sure you know that by now."

"But they are Africans!"

"Of course, and so are you, by your roots and ancestry; besides, you are married to an African. And I think, Pat, it's about time for you to be positive about that. Believe me, there will be nothing in it but pride for you."

"I hear you." Pat turned to lay on her stomach.

"Good girl!" Sidi patted her curvy buttocks and pinched them, then slid his hand in the crack, and ran it up her back to her neck; there he started to work on her shoulder blades. Pat was lying still with her face buried in the pillow even as she was breathing heavily.

"Now, Pat, here is the plan. I went out last night and bought some chicken. I want you to fry that this morning, so that you can take it to the hostess of the ceremony as your own contribution."

"Boy! You're out of your mind!" Pat's reaction was like an electric shock just went through her, as she turned sharply to face Sidi. "Why should I do that? That woman don't even know me."

She sat up and folded her knees, and looked up at Sidi, who was rubbing his forehead feeling downcast. "I may come, but I ain't going to cook nothing," she said matter-of-factly.

"So be it," Sidi declared, indulgently. "Okay, I will do the cooking and you will come to the ceremony. Is that a deal?"

Yaya was melting with embarrassment in his room for Sidi. He had stepped out in the living room and met Pat sitting leisurely on the loveseat with her legs propped up on the center table, painting her fingernails. Careful not to make her flare up at him again this morning, he said good morning to her in a deep reconciliatory voice, to which Pat grunted something inaudible. He hesitantly glanced at her but seeing she didn't look up, he quickly skirted her and walked to the kitchen where he had spotted Sidi.

"Good morning, Sidi," he said, and his mouth fell open, upon seeing Sidi surrounded with plates on the kitchen counter full of fried and raw chicken. Sidi stood over a big pot on the stove simmering and bubbling with hot oil and chicken parts.

Sidi barely looked his way. "Hey, Mister Yaya LaTalé, good morning." Then he swiftly reached inside the pot with a fork and turned over some pieces of chicken from the yellow to brown sides. Some sharp cracking sounds suddenly came from the pot and hot oil splashed. Sidi quickly stepped back and stood on his toes, and gave Yaya a sidelong glance.

"Man, do you see me? I'm fixing some stuff for the Kakays. Do remember that they're having the occasion for their baby today?"

"Oh, yes, today is Sunday. This morning right?"

"Yep, before noon. Why else I'm busy here? Do you have any African clothes to wear?"

Yaya quickly looked at Pat and fretted. "Of course, man, I have a few new styles. I've even wanted you to check through them, to see if you'll find any that you like."

"Thanks, buddy, I have enough myself. Keep yours because you're going to need them."

"That was why I brought a lot. How often do you wear them here?"

"As often as one wants, but mostly at occasions thrown by Africans, like this today." Sidi then picked some nicely brown pieces from the pot and laid them on top of others on a plate that was nearly full.

"You are a chef, Sidi. I admire your confidence in the kitchen." Yaya was looking at some nicely brown and steaming pieces of chicken piled in juicy layers on the plates. The crispy sight and sweet flavor invading his nostrils made his mouth water. He looked up at his cousin. "Man, it's obvious that you really know what you are doing."

"Yep, Yaya, this's no big deal to me. From living for three years as a bachelor in this county, I had to learn how to cook, and presently I'm grateful for it."

"I can see that." Yaya shot a glance at Pat who was now busy painting her toenails. He cleared his throat. "Well, it seems you have things under control. I need to finish some letters that I want sent home by tomorrow. But call me if you need me."

"Sure, man, go write your letters. I can handle this," Sidi had said, unperturbed.

Relieved, Yaya had gotten a glass of orange juice from the refrigerator and withdrawn into his room. What he had seen and heard that Sunday morning shocked him beyond limit. In Yaya's traditional African mind, even granting for the expediency of the times, it was one thing for a man to cook for the house, but quite a different matter entirely, to have to cook for a function, and with his wife at arms length, occupied with looking pretty.

Yaya was not actually writing any letters, he had just made that excuse out of embarrassment, to escape a sight that he didn't feel like facing. As far as he was concerned, it was sad and unimaginable, almost some sacrilege for a woman to so demean her husband. If it were back home, Yaya thought, Sidi would have been a laughing stock, far and wide, even among the women who worked on rice farms.

Indeed, Yaya reflected that those women in their humble settings might often be tagged as 'primitive,' yet they stayed gratified and fulfilled with strong traditional values which would mock a modern woman like Pat. Should they hear a tale such as this about Pat and Sidi on this Sunday morning, they would flap their hands to their thighs and slap their heads, and scream in shock. Some might even utter a sudden cracking laugh, and it would have been all contemptuous. They would have felt sorry for Sidi and his mother. And they would have prayed that their sons never ran into a woman like Pat.

"I think with Pat, Sidi must have bitten off far more than he could chew," Yaya muttered as if conversationally confiding in somebody.

Baffled, he paced to his window and looked blankly outside. The rays of the morning sun harshly greeted his eyes. Yaya didn't even notice the onslaught, as he wondered how Sidi would be feeling inside. And for how long Sidi would take this? Pondering on such questions only vexed Yaya, because he had no answers. However, he swore that he would rather be single forever than wear Sidi's shoes.

"But if that's what the man wants, good for him;" he said, despondently swinging his arms, going into the closet to get out his favorite *buba*-gown for the ceremony.

Ironically, Sidi was resolved on looking good to the Manika Kunda community in Philadelphia. He was bent on showing that he was not losing traditional values by marrying an American woman, that he was still African in his thinking, and that his American wife too, could be as African as expected—when it came to it—even if it took quite an extraordinary effort!

By himself, Sidi prepared the 'pepper chicken,' enough to feed more than ten people, and meticulously laid the brown sizzling mouth-runners in a shining new aluminum pan which he covered with aluminum foil. That was for Pat to take to the ceremony, just like all the other women. He had already bought some drinks to go along with the food. This was all a gesture of good will from his household to the Kakays, and it made him feel good because he had done what most Manika Kunda families did on such occasion.

That Sunday morning, the Kakays were the common topic in most Manika Kunda households in Philadelphia. It was a day the community rejoiced with them for their baby. It was also the day the community rallied to welcome the addition in their midst. That was customary. It was the way it was done back home and how it should be done in Philadelphia.

On such occasions among Manika Kundans and other Africans abroad when honoring such ceremonies, the distance from home becomes immaterial, because home is revisited in spirit and in the rites, such that any place becomes home—wholly and traditionally!

On this day at the Kakays, in the crowded living room of their two bedroom apartment in Southwest Philadelphia, it was easy to reach out and hold the Africaness hanging—warm and proud—in the air. The local Manika Kunda community and others from afar graced the occasion in regalia: in their colorfully embroidered Guinea brocade gowns, down to their ankles, and in an assortment of trends in African fashion.

As the women conferred as per tradition to ensure preparedness, one could see a profile of their radiant ebony faces, their long shiny braided hair styles and their monstrous head-ties, all depicting the beauties of Mother Africa.

The Kakays were Mandinkas, a genealogical offshoot of the Mansarays, and descendants of Sundiata Keita of the ancient Songhai Empire. And thanks to the griots and Jaylebahs in Manika Kunda, most Kakays knew the glorious saga of their forebear, King Sundiata Keita as he led, conquered, expanded and protected the vast lands of Songhai against incursion by infidel tribes who threatened and envied the peace, harmony and civilization of his people. Legends like that, naturally gave the Kakays a sense of dignity and pride that could not be damaged even with the desecration of the Mandinka image through slavery by the West.

And of course, the Kakays were Muslims. In the nomadic exploration of their ancestors to cater and expand, they had met Arab scholars who had converted them to Islam as far back as the early seventeenth century. This became a tradition. A tradition that was revived in America by the birth of another Kakay, at whose naming ceremony that morning in Philadelphia, those same traditions became guiding principles.

"Ladies and gentleman, silence please. The ceremony is about to start," shouted a bearded middle-aged man dressed in a white flowing gown. He was standing over a piece of white cloth, about one yard long, spread in the center of the living room. On top of the cloth, at the upper end, sat a bowl of clear water with some coins lying at the bottom. Next to the bowl sat two white saucers. One of the saucers contained seven balls of *deh*—rice flour that had been mixed with water and sugar—which were white and shaped like extra large eggs.

Deh, like kolanuts among the Mandinkas, is a ceremonial regimen required at every important function. Each of the seven balls of *deh* in the saucer had a kolanut on top. They represented life and health, and were solicitations for God's blessings and goodwill to the living and the dead. The other saucer sitting near the one that had the *deh* contained something wrapped in a white handkerchief. That was supposed to be unwrapped as the ceremony proceeded.

"Will Mr. and Mrs. Kakay come now please, so we can start the ceremony," said the bearded man in officiating capacity.

The couple emerged from their room, with the baby cuddled in the arms of the jolly mother. They were beckoned by the man officiating to sit on the white cloth. Meanwhile, he took the baby from Mrs. Kakay. As the couple sat on the lower end of the cloth, he continued.

"Brothers and sisters, and all good people present, it is my pleasure to present to you baby Kakay." The baby was raised to his chestline—a sign of love—and was lying in outstretched arms for all the guests to see, as he slowly went in a circle around the crowded living room. "It's a boy, born seven days ago to Sheku Kakay and his wife, Mariama," he said.

The proud parents sat solemnly in humility, as parishioners would when kneeling before a priest for blessing. The boy was handed over to his mother by the man officiating, also called the Imam—one who leads in prayers—among Muslims.

"I am told," the Imam continued, "that the baby is going to be named after the husband's father. For those of you who have never witnessed this occasion, I want to tell you that in our culture, it is one of the three most important events that can occur in anybody's life. This ceremony marks the beginning of life, and it is a gift of a

240

heritage to the child. The next most important ceremony in his life would be at his prime, when he decides to marry his first wife. That would be another time for joy. And then, in the end, like all mankind, the final ceremony would be when death comes, which we pray should be at old age, when he goes to join his ancestors and give an account of his life.

"Meanwhile, today, we thank God that we have the honor and joy of participating and witnessing this most important phase of this child's life. As our people say, the sweetness of any corn naturally goes down to its cob. That is the luck this baby has. He was born to a worthy family, one that has not lost its values at a time when the style for our generation is to scorn tradition, and ridicule our heritage.

"Tomorrow, when this child grows up, he will know of this event in his life, and he will judge for himself if his parents did him justice. And then the mantle would be on him, like it was on his father, to revoke a proud past, or settle for the hollow winds that sway and stray like a withered stem that has no base. May God forbid us from that fate," the Imam prayed.

"*Amin,*" the *Jamaat* or dignified guests answered.

"May the Almighty God save us, and all our children from mistaking ourselves for what we are not, and may he grant us the wisdom to see the virtues in the ways of our ancestors."

"*Amin,*" chorused the *Jamaat.*

"Now, please, I want everybody to join me to recite the *Al-fatia*; we should all do so twice. If you are not a Muslim, or if you do not know the *Al-fatia*, please just say, *Amin.*"

The *Al-fatia* to Muslims is what the Lord's Prayer is to Christians. It is the first chapter, or *surat,* in the Koran. At every important function among Muslims, the reading of *Al-fatia* in prayers precedes the reading of all other verses from the Koran. Usually it is recited in Arabic as in the original version of the holy book. But when one cannot do the recitation, in most situations, as it was done now by the non-Muslims present, it is simply enough to say, '*Amin.*'

The Imam who was now kneeling by the baby and its parents had his hands raised up in prayers as he led the *Jamaat* through a chorus of recitations of *Al-fatia,* punctuated with cries of: "*Amin. Amin.*"

When they were through with the *Al-fatia*, the Imam placed his palms on the baby's head, and singularly started reciting verses from the Koran. The *Jamaat* responded intermittently with: "*Amin. Amin.*"

Next, the Imam reached for the saucer that held the wrapped

handkerchief. He unwrapped a pair of scissors and in a calculated stroke clipped some strands off the baby's hair. He wrapped the hair and the scissors in the handkerchief and laid them on the saucer. He then reached for the baby and stood up with it. Holding it by its arms in the air the Imam whispered the infant's name in its ears, for it was supposed to be the first person to know that. Then for the benefit of the crowd, he declared the name again towards the child's ears, this time audibly.

"*Ismu hu,* Dainday Kakay." This was repeated exactly four times, because it was a boy; if it had been a girl, it would have been said only three times. That was the actual naming of the child. The words, *Ismu hu,* being an Arabic derivation meaning 'your name is.'

After announcing the name, the Imam walked with the baby to the front door and took a step outside. He stood there for a minute silently praying over the child. When he returned, he gave the baby back to the mother. The act of stepping out with the new born was a ceremonial and symbolic gesture of welcoming and introducing it to life out of the womb.

With the baby in its mother's arms, the Imam knelt down and again started reciting verses from the Koran. The *Jamaat* responded with: '*Amin. Amin.*' When the Imam stopped, others that were versed in the Koran picked up in a chain of prayers, all in Arabic, amidst more cries of: "*Amin. Amin.*"

The last group to offer prayers was the non-Muslims, but countrymen of the Kakays and other guests, who felt the need, and were comfortable uttering their goodwill differently in that situation. They prayed as Christians, as native African religious worshippers, and as well-wishers of various persuasions. The *Jamaat* kept answering with, '*Amin. Amin.*' until all those who wished to pray had prayed.

"The Kakays, show us your hands," shouted a man in a green gown and a matching hat made of Guinea brocade. He had in his hand a bowl, big enough to hold food that would fully fill four grown men. He placed the bowl near Mariama and the baby. This was like a signal, as people began dipping in their gowns and putting money into the bowl. To a Christian it would have looked like offering time in a church; the only difference here, was that the bowl sat in one spot, and it was those who wished to give that came forth.

Traditionally, the paternal relatives of the child would set the pace by placing large bills in the bowl before others followed. That was why the Kakays were challenged by the man who placed the bowl. He was daring them to show their worth. The money was intended for both the Imam and the mother of the child. Usually the Imam would first take his share and leave the rest for the mother.

As the crowd calmed after the money flashing spree, the Imam said a brief prayer of thanks for the generosity shown. He then took the bowl of clear water and said some prayers over that. The water was for the ancestors who were believed to have in spirit witnessed the occasion. In their honor, the Imam gently poured the clear cold water from the bowl, outside the front door step for the blessings and gift of the heritage from the ancestors. That was the libation for this ceremony, as the celebrants were Muslims who in principle decried alcohol. Other Africans would have used potent alcohol, or spirit.

The coins that were at the bottom of the bowl which held the water were kept by the Imam on behalf of the ancestors—by virtue of his position as a link in prayers! Next, he took the bowl containing the *deh* and kolanuts and went round to the few elders present, inviting them to cut off pieces for themselves.

After serving the elders, the Imam chopped a piece off the *deh* and took half a kolanut for himself and then invited the *Jamaat* to the remaining *deh* and kolanuts. He also reminded them to take from the fresh lamb meat packaged in individual bags.

The giving out of raw meat at such occasions is customary but dependent on the financial might of the people involved. Some kill cows, others settle for a lamb; yet some simply maintain the thought, and wish they could do more. None the less, performing the ceremony consecrates the intention and serves the purpose.

If it were back home, with the naming of the baby and the prayers done, it would have been time for the *Jaylebahs* in their praise-singing glory to take over the ceremony. They would have been extolling and recanting the legacies of the Kakays from the days of Mansa Musa to King Sundiata Keita, and on to the magnificence and dignity of present day Kakays. They would also have been sweet-tonguing, amusing and captivating everybody with their vast historical knowledge and inspirational chants.

These *Jaylebahs* are known as walking archives who tell people valuable things about their heritage that they want to hear and may never have heard. Also, they are opportunists. They extol in order to be rewarded charitably. On such occasions, they would first exalt the people who threw the event, and eventually, they would visit the affluent people in the gathering and anybody whom they knew would grease their palms.

However, since the ongoing occasion was in America and

their were no *Jaylebahs,* a cassette tape recorded in Mandinka was playing on the stereo. When interpreted, the song went like this:

Jamarewooh! Glory to Allah! Jamarewooh! Glory to my people!
For who said, Allah didn't bless black skin people?
Nobody, nobody worthy will say so.
Or who said, Allah didn't bless the Mandinkas?
Nobody, nobody worthy will say so.
And who said, dignity doesn't run in black skin people?
Nobody, nobody with eyes will say so.
Or who said, dignity doesn't run in the Mandinkas?
Nobody, nobody with eyes will say so.
Who said, greatness doesn't run in black skin people?
Nobody, nobody in their senses will say so.
Who said, greatness doesn't run in the Mandinkas?
Nobody, nobody in their senses will say so.

Jamarewooh, you heard me! Jamarewooh that's the truth!
And now everybody say, like a I say,
We might be poor, or might be humble.
We might be hungry, or might be angry.
We might be labeled, or might be painted.
Yet, and yet. Yet, and yet. Yet, and yet.
Black skin people are great! The Mandinkas are great!
Black skin people are blessed! The Mandinkas are blessed!
Black skin people are good! The Mandinkas are good!
Black skin people are beautiful, and Mandinkas are beautiful!

With the *Jaylebahs* ranting and the drums beating, the melody of the sweet strings of the guitar interwinding with the praise song in a musical harmony—now coming across from two giant Sony speakers—the enchanted *Jamaat* began mixing. They were hugging, shaking hands and chatting.

At this time the long table upon which the food had been arranged was uncovered. And a few women were moving through the crowd bowing, telling people that food was ready, as if anybody needed to be reminded. The sight and smell of all that food was enough to cause havoc in many a yearning stomach.

There were *fufu and egusi* with *bitter leaf, fried plantain, jollof rice,* stewed beans, *cassava-leaf* cooked with palm oil to eat with rice, and an abundance of eateries. The numerous food went to show that the women had shown their solidarity. Now it was up to the guests to consume, and to take home some for their dear ones who could not attend. There were also different kinds of drinks. But in line with the Islamic tradition, the only drinks served were non-alcoholic beverages. Yet, that did not stop the spirit.

The ceremony touched Yaya. He was there from the start, with Pat and Sidi. He had on a light blue matching combination of cap, gown and pants. The gown was embroidered with white thread in delicate patterns around the neck, and the pants and cap were similarly embroidered around the hem. Yaya felt like he was home. He relished every moment of the ceremony, and felt exhilarated that the distance from home had not detracted from such an essential cultural practice.

Like many educated Africans, Yaya happened to arrogate to himself the prerogative of selecting what aspect of his culture he would embrace and what he would not. So even as he ran away from home because of a sacred inheritance, today, because of the ceremony, he was possessed in a manner similar to the triumphant spirit of the gladiators.

Now, as he moved among the crowd, Yaya kept beaming at Pat, full of pride, with a 'do-you-see-us' happy look on his face. In fact, he decided to take matters into his own hands, by declaring that day—in his heart—as an 'African day in Philadelphia.'

Pat sat quietly, uptight and with closed lips. She was not the type to give-in easy in an African setting. The problem was that Pat couldn't help battling with her ingrained estrangement with the culture and its people. She didn't even know what to make of the ceremony which she had just witnessed. Sitting there as she was, dressed in a pink embroidered gown directly from the homeland, one could mistake her for an African, or if one agreed with Sidi, she looked like an 'African Queen.'

Yet Pat felt no such sense of elation, and was ready to walk out of the place. Her concern now was that she was left out in this gathering. She knew that she was one of the few American women present. All the other women were Africans, and she did not trust them. There was that one with the big buttocks who kept grinning in Sidi's face. And she was not just starting it.

Every occasion they met, that *damn* African woman would brush her with 'Hi, Pat,' and she would go on to hug Sidi, and engage him in conversation in their native tongue. Usually, Sidi would apologize after she had left, explaining that they grew up together and went to the same school. But Pat had refused to buy that because the woman was single and the *bitch* was out to get Sidi.

Like now, having got Sidi in a corner, she was engaging him in a passionate talk. Pat could not see Sidi's face, with his back towards her, but she could see the lady's face. Her expressions and actions said it all. If she was not cracking with laughter, with her eyes all lit and pleading, she was touching Sidi and blushing seductively—like some hard up woman desperate for a date!

What a nerve she's got! Pat fumed, struggling to restrain herself from going over there and knocking both Sidi and her upside their heads.

That low down, two-timing Sidi, and his cheating home girl, that devil! Even with Pat's repugnance, she decided to restrain herself, not to put herself in the mouths of all the people present.

Then from nowhere, Yaya cheerfully went and joined Sidi and the lady. *What?* Now, Pat got furious. She wasn't going to wait any more for them to carry on with their dubious clannishness against her—just to get over her! No, not when she could help it!

Pat sprang up, caring less about interrupting the *dubious* group in their *cheating chat.* "Sidi, I'm ready to go home now!"

"Why so soon, Pat?" Yaya asked, forgetting himself.

"You shut up, boy. I'm talking to Sidi. Are you coming with me or not, Sidi?"

"But, Pat, I thought we were enjoying the occasion."

"You bet. Look, we either go now, or I leave with the car, immediately!"

"Okay, Pat, we will leave if that's what you want. Give me a minute so I can say good-bye to some folks."

"You better be quick!" Pat commanded.

Sidi abruptly left and got into the crowd, avoiding a scene.

Pat stood serious faced, arms akimbo like some overbearing school mistress who after shouting *silence* to a noisy class was waiting to see if some *tot* was going to disobey.

The lady Sidi was talking to drew Yaya to the side. "You see, that's what they get from marrying some of these American women. I'm happy that one is going to tame him well."

Yaya laughed.

"But didn't you see for yourself how he ran when she came just now?"

"I did." Yaya wanted to explain why it was best that Sidi ran, but he saw Pat staring at him, so he got mute.

That traitor, Yaya. Pat hissed. *But wait, I'll get him.*

246

CHAPTER EIGHTEEN

"And what were you talking about with that woman, Mr. Yajo."
Pat confronted Yaya as soon as they got home.

"Which woman?"

"That fat-butt African woman that you and Sidi were standing
with."

"Nothing, why?"

"You know why. Hey, let me tell you this, you ain't going to
stay in this house and team up with some damn woman against me.
She is your home girl, you like her for your brother? Move in with
her!"

"But, Pat, what are you talking about? What made you think
I want to connive with anybody against you?"

"You don't fool me, Yajo! And Sidi don't fool me either! All of
a sudden, you are chummy with that woman, as if I don't know
why. But you watch me!"

"For what, Pat? Sidi, please talk to your wife. She is just trying
to molest and torment me. I don't even know what she is talking
about."

"You'll know, kinky head, African nigger. You wait till I call
them immigration folks on your black ass."

"Pat! That is really uncalled for," Sidi injected. "You are being
unfair to Yaya."

"Hell, yes, that's what you'll say. You fool! But damn, I can't
stand that nigger one bit. And hey, Sidi, the sooner you get him out
of here, the better for us all."

"Yaya excuse us for one minute please, I want to talk to Pat."

Yaya went to his room, frantic. Things were changing from
push to shove. After insulting him over and over, Pat was now
threatening him with immigration. That had Yaya's whole mind on
fire. He took out his diary, sat on his bed, and started looking at the
calendar.

Geez! My God! Now wait.... Today is the 24th of May. Grandma

Fatu died on June 29 two years ago; for that to be two complete years, wait.... Oh, there remains at least 36 days, or better still two months more for my trouble back home to be over! But.., how am I going to make it in the U.S. till then, when Pat has started threatening me with Immigration?

Tormented, Yaya tossed the diary aside, bowed his head, and hooked his hands across his lap. He asked himself, what bad luck was this? And why was all this happening to him?

Yaya thought of Sobala, how he lived back then, and who he was, and what he had been through. Then this humiliation that he must now face. He lamented, but what was he to do?

"Pat, I don't like what you did at the party, and I don't like your attitude towards Yaya.

Pat just looked past Sidi, angry as he could be, as if he didn't exist. She had no intention of wasting her *precious* time, so she went and sat on her bar stool.

Sidi came to her. "Frankly, Pat, you shouldn't be doing all this, because that just takes away from us all. And we are family, you know?"

"Family, with who?" Pat crossed her legs. "He is your family not mine."

"That's ludicrous. But anyway, let me say this, that after you, in this country, I consider Yaya as my next of kin."

"You can consider him to be whatever you want. I don't care."

"But, Pat, you are both dear to me. I really wish you two could live together like responsible adults."

"I've done my best to deal with this situation, Sidi. But you can't just be forcing things on me."

"Have I said I'm forcing anything on you?"

"Are you asking me that question, Sidi? What do you think you're doing? You always do what you want. And yet, you want to tell me what to do, like your men do to their women in Africa. I ain't going to take it no more!"

"Pat, that's very interesting. I can see that you are a master of misjudgment. And I wonder when you will start thinking right."

"Soon as you stop telling me what to do, hell. There are different strokes for different folks!"

"I know, but just remember though that Yaya is my responsibility and I have to help him."

"Go right ahead then. And so from now on, Pat is going to look after Pat."

"Knock! Knock!"

"Come in," Yaya said knowing it was Sidi at his door. He mentally braced himself. He had to do this now, and it had to be with tact, he told himself.

"Oh, boy, Yaya, I don't know what to tell you."

"Don't worry, Sidi. It's none of your fault."

"But it makes me feel bad," Sidi screamed, then he lowered his voice and held his head. "I've just had a serious talk with Pat. I nearly gave her a good beating." He looked apologetically at Yaya.

"But man, in this country, these women can call the police on you if you touch them. And that's what the police want anyway, to take a black man to jail for anything, even a lie."

Yaya nodded, feeling hopeless.

"Really, sometimes, I don't know what to do about Pat. Besides her bad manners, she is terribly jealous. She doesn't trust anybody and when she is like that she acts anyhow. And I'm getting tired of it. But look, Yaya, don't let her acts get you down."

"No, Sidi, I think beyond such. I realize maybe, I might have overstayed."

"What do you mean by that? Com'on, Yaya, my place is yours. Besides, what am I expected to do? Send you to some motel to live because my wife doesn't like you? No. It is my duty to help you, until you can stand on your own in this country. If Pat doesn't like that she will just have to live with it."

"Thanks for everything, Sidi. I really know you mean well for me."

"Of course. I wish Pat would grow up mentally and stop this nonsense. But all I have to tell you is this; as you go through this experience, always know that it's just a stage."

"I know."

"And it's best to keep up hope, man. I have a feeling things will open up for you anytime now."

"I pray so. Come to think of that, Sidi, I wanted to talk to you about something."

"Go ahead."

"I've been thinking about this. I don't know how you will take it."

"What is it, man?"

"I hope it doesn't make you feel disappointed in me."

"Of course not."

"Really, Sidi, I've given this some serious thoughts."

"Well, that's what you're supposed to do. But, man, are you going to tell me?"

Yaya bit his lower lip thinking. "Remember, I told you I have a friend in Houston, Basi Ibrahim? We've been talking. He wants me join him there. He said I'll get a job the moment I get there."

"How can he be so sure?"

"That was what he told me. He said it won't be any problem for him."

"Is he the son of that tycoon and politician, Brima Ibrahim?"

"Yes, his only son."

"I've heard of Basi, yet we've never met. But Yaya, the riches and powers they've got in Africa don't mean anything here. Besides, how well do you know this guy?"

"We were together in high school, and were close friends until he left. He came here immediately after we graduated."

"That has been a long time, man. You may be surprised; he may not be the same person you knew. America has a strange way of changing people, Yaya. And as far as many of us here from home are concerned, don't be fooled by big talks, because frankly, most of us are in the same boat."

"I know, Sidi. But I want to try my luck in Houston."

Sidi got silent and felt sad. He looked at Yaya, wondering how to talk him out of the trip. "You said you've given this deep thoughts?"

"Yes, Basi has been very friendly and assuring every time we've talked. It's been just like old times. He told me he would happily welcome me, if you okay the trip. And I feel that I can trust him."

"Well, let me think about that."

"Okay, but remember, Sidi, I'll always be grateful to you. I may even come back to Philadelphia, after I'm a little established. And maybe then, I will get along better with Pat."

"Maybe," Sidi said going out of the room.

Yaya got his diary, and made his entries: Sunday, May 24:—I *witnessed my first naming ceremony in the US, by the Kakays. Thanks to Pat's utterances and behavior, I'm now decided to leave for Houston.*

On May 26, two days after their talk, Sidi came into Yaya's room and consented reluctantly to his trip.

"You may go to your friend in Houston," he said. "Because I don't want it to look like I'm standing in your way. After all this time here with no success, maybe things will open up for you there. But remember, I am here. You can always come back. And also, though I know that you are well-behaved, but one thing: Never forget that you are a stranger in America, which means, you must learn to put aside any foolish pride when it comes to surviving. Like they say, humble manners can only be the key to success."

"Thanks, Sidi, I will always remember that."

"Well, buddy, call your friend and tell him you are on your way."

"Sure, Sidi, I will. Thanks again."

When Sidi left, Yaya laid back flat on his bed, and took a deep breath, reflecting that he was now at a cross-road. As he thought of his trip to Houston, something was telling him to never leave the devil he knew for another he didn't. He wondered how Houston would turn out and prayed that it wouldn't get to be a replay of what he had gone through in Philadelphia.

He knew Basi was married to an American woman too, and she talked like an African-American. Was she going to be like Pat? He remembered Sidi saying that not all African-Americans thought or behaved like Pat; that it was Pat's background and bad experiences in life. But suppose Basi's wife had a similar history? Had Sidi not told him it was hardship in the system that alienated some African-Americans and made them like Pat?

The lady had sounded nice on the telephone the last time they spoke. She didn't speak with the usual repelling pitch that Pat used when people called asking for Sidi, like: 'Hello, who are you? What do you want? He's not here. Bye!'

Basi's wife was polite, and cordial. Yaya prayed to get along with her. He decided to call Basi and finalize his coming.

"Hello," a voice Yaya knew to be Basi's wife picked up the telephone at the other end.

"Hello, Madam, how are you?"

"Oh, I am fine, who is calling?"

"It is Yaya. Don't you remember me?"

"Not really. But maybe if I see your face I'll know you. Were you at TSU?"

"At TSU? No, but I'm a friend of Basi. I've just come to the U.S. and I live in Philadelphia. Didn't he tell you anything about me?"

"He sure did. You are the one that wants to move here, right?"

"Yes." Yaya's stomach tightened.

"Well, he is not here, but we are expecting you." *Great!* That was like sweet music in Yaya's ears. He felt happy.

"Thank you very much, Madam."

"Oh, you're welcome. When are you coming?"

"I don't know yet. That's why I wanted to talk to Basi."

"I will tell him to call you as soon as he comes."

"That will be fine, Madam, thank you."

"Sure. Bye, bye."

Yaya rested the phone, excited. He said to himself, "You see, she is nice. She even said that she's expecting me. Isn't that great?"

Basi called a couple of hours after Yaya's call. They confirmed plans for Yaya's travel. He told Yaya to expect a ticket in three days. Meanwhile, he said he would be making some calls immediately so that Yaya would start doing something as soon as he got to Houston.

After that talk, Yaya made his entries in his diary: Tuesday, May 26:—*Concluded talks with Sidi and Basi about my going to Houston. I should leave Philadelphia any time now.*

He closed the diary and holding it in his hand, he sat thinking. June 29, two years ago had become a statue in his mind. He reflected that it would be two complete years in about 34 days. But before that he would be in his sixth month soon. He sighed, thinking about immigration and how they picked people up in their sixth month.

Well, Yaya thought, by going to Houston, at least he would minimize his chances of being sent home before the coast was clear over there. Indeed, when the two years circled and the inheritance had been given to somebody else, he would be ready to go home. Because, from what he was seeing on American television about recession, layoffs and unemployment, what was the guarantee that he would get anything as decent and respectable as the job he had back home?

Yaya's last days in Philadelphia were emotional. It seemed like one arm had been plucked off Sidi. He found it hard to meet Yaya's eyes, and he acted like a broken quarterback of the defeated team in a Super Bowl. That was because he hated giving up. He wanted to stand by Yaya, and help him, and share in the good feeling of seeing life improve for him in America. That would have been something to write home about.

But abruptly, and regretfully, Yaya wanted to move, to go to Houston. And with a clear conscience, he could not stop him, as much as he wanted to. That might strain their relationship should things not work out for the better in Philadelphia. He thought, perhaps it was best to let the man go, since that was what he wanted, and to wish him the best.

The imminent parting subdued Yaya too. He thought Sidi was great, a true brother, and he knew he would always be grateful to Sidi. But, he rationalized that he was just a pawn in a game of fortune in America. That he was a seeker, and had to open himself up to chances; for there was no telling where a shiny sun awaited him in this sojourn. That was why he was going to Houston. To explore and to try. And as a bonus, he felt relieved that Pat would now be happy, with him gone, just as she had always said.

Indeed, Pat was already easing. Since she heard about Yaya's planned departure, she changed. Her hostilities towards him stopped. She started treating him in a companionable manner, like it was in Yaya's first few weeks. They would talk and eat, and watch television together with no reproachful glances or bitter words.

Sometimes, Yaya thought Pat acted like she would miss him. And he felt happy that things were going now between them like one happy family. In fact, the three of them in the household decided to treat Yaya's departure in secrecy. It was a conspiracy on the Manika Kunda community in Philadelphia. Nobody was to know, at least until after Yaya left. For whatever reason, Sidi thought it was best that way.

CHAPTER NINETEEN

Yaya arrived in Houston at 5:25 PM on a Friday, May 30th. He had been in transit for six hours, with a whole hour spent in Boston, Massachusetts—of the *Boston Tea Party* fame and home of the glorious Kennedys—which was the connecting point of his flight.

While in Boston, Yaya wished he could venture inland, into that historic city; to bathe himself in the memory of the Mayflower Immigrants and to rekindle within him the unbent spirit that was born thereby, in pursuit of liberty, freedom and justice. However, in view of the time constraint, he settled for the *Boston Globe,* and read the newspaper line by line until his plane landed in Houston.

Once out of the aircraft and into the airport, Yaya felt like a wandering Chinese in a remote African village. Yet he was at Houston's Intercontinental and in America, where blacks were in the minority, as was evident in that crowded airport.

Again Yaya's reality dawned on him; that he was a stranger in a white man's country, now farther into the South and its history of stubborn plantation owners, *Jim Crow* laws, and the black lot. Carefully, he followed his traveling mates to the baggage area. As he waited for his luggage, he searched in the few black faces in view for Basi.

Basi and his wife, Joy, were on their way to the airport when Yaya's flight landed. They were delayed. Just to come to the airport, Joy had left her car at home that morning and made Basi drop her at work. That way he would pick her up on his to way meet Yaya.

She had insisted on coming even when she got off work at 5 PM, while Yaya's flight arrived at 5:25. And it was a good thirty minutes drive from her job to the airport. In sensible traffic, Basi might have made in it time, permitting the additional five minutes for Yaya to disembark the plane and have his luggage come through.

Basi surmised that he could have been there just when Yaya would have started looking for him. But the rush hour traffic was bad and frustrating. Now, Basi felt like somebody caught in an 8 o'clock traffic which crawled, while several miles away from a critical job interview scheduled for that very moment. He took it out on Joy.

"I would have made it, if it weren't for you. Now look, we are caught in this dreadful traffic, while that boy is over there wondering as to what could be happening."

"I am sorry, Basi, I just wanted to come, okay?"

"But you could have waited at home. From the airport that's where we were coming anyway."

"Sure! But I wanted to be at the airport to welcome him, and I don't have anything to do right now. So okay, we are late. I'm sure a little wait won't hurt him," Joy said defensively, warding off guilt.

Basi decided it was irrelevant to pursue the argument. He knew Joy meant well. She was a caring person and he counted himself blessed to have a woman like her. Joy came from Norman, Mississippi. She was one of seven kids born to a large and very Christian family. She also was a country girl, he knew, for Norman was a small town of cotton farmers and peasants where rural values lingered, and where everybody either knew the other, or knew somebody that knew them.

Out there, by Joy's account, even a break and entry was still reported as headline news, and the police knew all the hoodlums by name. From Norman, Joy had come to Houston to attend Texas Southern University, a leading black university in the South. That was where she met Basi.

To Basi, Joy was like an African woman with an American touch. As far as her independence, her feminist ideas, and her free-spirited attitudes were concerned, in his eyes, those were uniquely American and Western. But she was humble, cooperative, loyal, and forgiving like the best from Africa.

And for an African-American woman, Basi saw Joy as a hopeful breed, educated, a professional, and confident with a positive sense of black awareness. From her interaction on campus at TSU, he saw that she did not look down on other blacks regardless of their origin, or he wouldn't have married her. Rather, she embraced her heritage and was no part of the ignorant degradation of Africans, like many others.

Equally, Joy was exceedingly proud of her husband and wanted to be in every part of his life, if he would let her. In fact, that was why she came to be going to the airport.

In the waiting lounge in Terminal B, people in all sorts of cowboy hats and thick boots, and big-buckle belts could be seen. They were reminiscent of Gary Cooper and John Wayne in some cowboy movies Yaya had seen years ago. Even so, they reminded him that he was now in Texas, home of the Wild West.

Wow, Yaya, watch it! Like in the movies, shooting and killing for these cowboys is like drinking coffee. They ride on horses and shoot at random, don't they? Texas? May God save you!

Alone and pacing around his luggage in a far-right corner of the lounge, his eyes were on the entrance of the terminal, not chancing to miss Basi. Sidi had given him a brown tweed sports coat a day before his departure, that was what he had on over an off-white shirt and black pants, with dark brown shoes.

He told himself his days of the African gown would wait for now, even if it were culture. For supposing he was in some big African gown presently, who knew how those cowboys might react to that?

Besides, Yaya thought, that considering his legal status in America, he feared the attention and the giveaway a floating cultural *buba* would be for him. As it was, he was thankful there were no Immigration checkpoints to go through on arrival at Houston since he came on a domestic flight.

But still he feared that he could run out of luck and stumble on an immigration officer. Already, people in different kinds of uniforms abounded around. Some looked at him, and he looked back at them, direct, like an American. With his hands in his pocket, he posed to say he was not lost, he was just waiting for his ride home. In fact, he acted like he was angry, like a man kept waiting by an absent-minded wife who probably had gone shopping.

When Yaya arrived in Houston at 5:25 p.m. it was moonshine in Manika Kunda. The moon was in its middle resting place in the center of the sky as it went from the east to the west. That meant half of the night was gone. Kondorfili Bunsor, the night owl, was sitting in his verandah looking to the heavens. He couldn't have been happier.

His old mud hut had been almost completely rebuilt with cement block; they had done all of the walls and the rooms, now it was the floors and the roof that were being finished. Yes, his roof—a bright silver zinc top! He had wanted his house completed before the raining season sets in and that was almost done. Now his big cemented house, which he would paint in red, would be standing proud in Korkordu, to show his prowess.

Yes, Kondorfili Bunsor was exhilarated. Because he, Kondorfili Bunsor, was like a king. No, in fact soon, he would be even more than any king. For a king's powers are limited within his kingdom.

Yet, he, Kondorfili Bunsor, would soon be the ultimate and sole bone healer as far away in the land as he knew. When the almost full moon in the sky dwindled to a silver streak, it would be less than three Fridays left. Then, that *black-white man,* who scorned his heritage and ran away to the white man's land, would know what he Kondorfili Bunsor knew...

At Intercontinental, Basi did not bother to park his car in the parking garage. He knew Yaya was coming on a Delta flight and would be at Terminal B, gate 20; so he pulled up a few yards to the entrance of the terminal and parked by a sign that read, 'NO PARKING. UNAUTHORIZED VEHICLES WILL BE TOWED AT OWNER'S EXPENSE.' In his haste, he decided to risk it, and was out in a flash.

Joy tailed.

Yaya immediately recognized his countryman. He could tell Basi's presence as he walked in with the confidence of a boy born lucky. Muscular with thick corded neck, Basi was short and chubby. He was dressed sharply in an off-white silk shirt with the sleeves rolled to his elbows, over burgundy pants. His black shoes were shining as if in competition with his dark oily hair.

As Yaya took in Basi, and felt relieved, he saw a slender lady in a pink dress, with a white scarf around her neck, coming behind him; they were like a cow and its tail, with Basi probably feeling her breath behind his neck. The lady was taller than Basi by at least a foot. She was brown-skinned, with big eyes that seemed loving and gentle even from the distance. And her face was as beautiful and pleasant, like a picture drawn by an artist after his own heart.

Yaya presumed that would be Basi's wife. He was in buoyant spirit.

"Basi, the boss!" he exclaimed joyously, stepping over his suitcase to meet them.

Joy felt slightly embarrassed at the loudness from Yaya. She sweepingly glanced through the lounge to see how other people were taking the distraction. Some lively guy, she thought, so excited! As the two men hugged, she wished Basi was as tall as Yaya, or at least in shape, with not that flatulent belly which he had protruding pompously. She smiled at Yaya, and shot Basi's protrusion a disapproving glance.

The two Africans were grinning, lost in their language, and locked in a handshake that seemed never to end. Absorbed as they were into themselves, Joy coughed, deliberately, to remind them she was there.

"Oh, I am sorry," Basi turned winking at her. "Yaya, this is my wife. Joy is her name."

"Hello, Ms. Joy. I'm pleased to meet you," Yaya said, deliberately using the prefix to Joy's name, to make an impression.

"Well, hello, Yaya. I'm glad you made it." Joy shook his hand. She was smiling generously and looking into his eyes as she said, "Welcome to Houston."

"Thanks, Ms. Joy." Evidently, Yaya had made up his mind about a pattern of addressing her that he would use henceforth. He turned to his countryman and decided to further push his luck. "Basi, I must compliment you. Like always, you went for the best. You couldn't have made a better choice for a wife. Ms. Joy is splendid, and she seems just the right woman for you."

Joy's eyes flashed gemlike, and her blue-shaded eyelids flipped closed to be opened widely. She seemed to have grown an inch taller as she smiled broadly.

"Oh thanks, Yaya," she gasped and then looked into Basi's eyes as if for collaboration.

Basi laid an arm on his wife's shoulder, "I know," he proudly stated. "Ms. Joy is a great woman. The best there is. But Mr. Yaya LaTalé, how was your trip?"

"It was okay. Everything was smooth."

"Great! Let's get your luggage and get out of here."

As they stepped outside, Basi sighed in relief that his Volvo 850 *GTAS* had not been towed. He apprehensively inspected it for a parking ticket but there was none. He felt glad, and took the wheel, steering in style.

Wow, Prince Wealthy!

In Philadelphia Sidi had a Cadillac, but Basi's convertible was a knockout. Indeed, Yaya thought, knowing how rich Pa Brima Ibrahim was in Manika Kunda, nothing ostentatious about Basi should be surprising.

As they drove off, Yaya reflected on how clean the terminal they just left was, even with all that crowd inside. Then, because of New York's world-fame, he told himself that Houston's Intercontinental wouldn't be as big as JFK. But that Intercontinental was beautiful, and bigger, and better than the *landing shack* in Sobala, Manika Kunda's main airport; which resembled some high school stadiums he had seen in Philadelphia, with one pavilion and a lot of flat ground—no wonder supersonic jets never went there!

Poor Manika Kunda, Yaya lamented, only tiny airplanes that fit on two lane bridges hopped in, impressively, at what they called an international airport. But indeed, this ultramodern airport, and JFK, were actual top-flight internationals.

At Continental there were aircraft coming, leaving, and hovering, all sorts. Buses and trail cats full of passengers, and luggage were going up and down the lanes that led to the terminals. And there were taxis and private cars by the terminals; they were parked, taking off, or being loaded. The activities were relentless. Basi swerved his way through the bustle.

"Hmm, America! Everywhere is developed," Yaya said with a sigh, fascinated by the grandeur of the airport as they left.

"Of course, to a large extent," Basi agreed. "This is a developed world where they know how important infrastructure is. When Manika Kunda starts doing such, the country will be on to business."

"Please, let's not talk about that," Yaya pleaded. "In progressive African countries like Kenya, Nigeria and Ghana, and a few others.., one hears about development everyday. Yet in Manika Kunda, even our ancestors are laughing at us. At least in their ancient times, they had smooth footpaths. But modern as we claim, even the main streets in our cities are full of pot holes..., waiting for ducks to duck in—as they wallow in neglect!

"As for electricity, we are communists. We get supplied communist style, by ration, this section today, and that section tomorrow. But you go tell our politicians about infrastructure; you will be lucky to breath freedom the next hour. They believe in infrastructure alright, all the way to their underground and foreign accounts."

"So that's still going on?" Basi asked. "So they're still stealing the country's money and shoving it away in their hidden private accounts?"

"Yes, many still do, hoping to escape to a safe haven abroad after their misdeeds in power. And the time they stop will be the time the word greedy ceases to be their creed."

"But don't they see that doesn't do either them or the country any good? Most times they die or get incarcerated and executed leaving those accounts frozen."

"Of course," Yaya said. "Take Haile Salassie, the famous last Emperor of Ethiopia, many Ethiopians alleged that he stole billions of dollars worth of his country's money, which was urgently needed by his people, and dumped it into his private Swiss account. And they say, the account was frozen by the Swiss government when he was dethroned and incarcerated."

"I heard about that," Basi said.

"Yes, for that and other alleged atrocities, some say, he was charged with treason and executed by a firing squad."

"Oh, no," Joy cried.

"But, Ms. Joy, can there be any worse case of treason than siphoning money out of your own country which you rule, and bankrupting it, while you make other nations richer?"

"There can't be any," Basi remarked. "I'm happy that some of those fools pay."

"Yes, indeed. But they won't learn. Very few of them turn around and invest in their country. That's why, Basi, I respect your father. He's one of the few that's really doing anything worthy privately, outside politics. He has investments all over the country, which provide employment for the people."

"But my father had already made it before he got into politics. And I think that was a mistake. He should have left that dirty game alone."

"But those are the people we need in African politics. Honest, dedicated, and financially stable or wealthy people who wouldn't steal. So far, the intellectuals, even those with lengthy credentials, have failed us, and so have the so-called common man. Many of the last two in power have proven otherwise, like giving the key for the wine cellar to an alcoholic."

Both Joy and Basi laughed.

"Yes," Yaya continued. "In fact, some of our prophetic Ph.D. holders have proved even worse. On the periphery of power, while in their university corridors, they are very radical. But it's been easy for many to put away their radicalism, and philosophies, and ethics, for ruthless power and stacks of cash."

Wow, Basi thought, Yaya could be a good African political analyst.

"As for a typical so-called common man, put him in power, and hope that he has a sack load of conscience; because for some, the tendency has been to grab it all, with the desperation of some unsuspecting paupers over whom a bunch of money is thrown in the air."

Joy laughed. "But what about patriotism, don't your politicians have any?" she asked, baffled by what sounded to her as nothing but criminality.

"Yes, they do in Manika Kunda," Yaya replied. "But it is claimed only at election time. Vote them in and it's suddenly replaced with self-aggrandizement, or self-preservation—take it or leave it!"

"Man, I've decided never to go back," Basi declared. "America is home for me. In fact, I've filed for my U.S. citizenship, because I foresee nothing in going back to Manika Kunda but to deteriorate."

Joy smiled. Yaya frowned, stunned and disappointed by Basi's statement.

To deteriorate in his homeland? And with all the opportunity and wealth at his disposal? When he should be going to help? To just give up on his country and folks like that?

"That is irresponsible and selfishness, just selfishness!" Yaya remarked.

What? What? Both Joy and Basi were startled. They looked at themselves. Yaya was realizing at the same time that he had blurted without thinking!

Joy had folded her arms and was looking at Basi who was looking ahead, biting his lower lip and frowning.

"Who's selfish, Yaya?" Basi asked between his clenched-teeth.

Yaya looked down at the mat of the car. "I'm sorry, man. I didn't mean to say it like that."

Of course you did! Joy and her husband seemed to imply by their shrugs. Then sudden silence fell in the car.

Yaya suddenly felt saddened in more ways than he could say. He realized he shouldn't have made that utterance. Yet, fresh from home—and having a strong sense of patriotism and nostalgia—he was hard hit by Basi's declaration. It got him wondering and baffled.

Eh, Basi, you too? But..., aha! It's one thing for one to come abroad, to seek education, or any other kind of fulfillment, but to be so carried away as to look low down on your fatherland? And to forever refuse to return home? That's sad. Really sad!

Now Yaya considered Basi lost, following suit of all those African intellectuals who got educated at the expense of their poor developing nations, only to bolt away to greener pastures abroad. Of course, Yaya told himself that he would never be like that.

Because his case was different. He had a timetable. In fact, if it were not for Grandma Fatu, he might never have come to America to go through what he was going through. But he had almost made up his mind. He now planned to be in America for only a short time till the cloud cleared at home, then he would go back. Already, he missed the relish of realizing himself as *a creme de la creme* and a productive member of society. And besides, if things were going to be better back home, some people would have to be selfless, and go, to play their part in the development and advancement seen abroad.

The traffic had gotten better than the hood-to-hood hubbub it was when Basi and Joy were coming to get Yaya. Like most American freeways, this pleasantry was what the designers of I-45 had in mind for Houston—a free-wheeling passage. The highway was well constructed, with eight lanes, four on each side.

Instead of taking I-45 North to Highway 6 as a short-cut to Cato, Basi decided on going south on I-45, to avoid the perpetual traffic jam that a construction work was causing on Highway 6. He was going to loop into I-610 and exit onto Westheimer. It was sheer joy to be flying on I-45.

No pot-holes and no broken bridges, Yaya thought; not even that ghastly dust which awaited to be inhaled on most roads in Manika Kunda. He wound down the glass on his side and inhaled the visibly clean air which rushed at him.

Basi took the Westheimer exit off I-610 at the Galleria—a majestic shopping mall with an ice-skating rink surrounded by several stores. It was 8:45 PM by the digital clock in Basi's Volvo 850.

Westheimer, the nocturnal nucleus of Houston, was beaming. Flashy party animals on two legs and in their automobiles could be seen everywhere along the street, ready for the Friday night action.

Yaya's eyes played omnipotence, scanning the street. Cars were loaded and the traffic was heavy, though of cruising speed. Dark-lighted and clustered high-rise office complexes, colorful neon lights and designer bulbs, burning brightly on single-level storefronts in that after-hour, now yielded a scenery as vibrant as the mood of its crowd.

Paved curbs and trimmed traffic islands, glossy-green, every so many yards, and at traffic lights, bragged a grand case of ingenuity in city planning. The motorists drove like they were automated with discipline. They stopped at red lights and obeyed the traffic rules. As Yaya watched those columns of cars and the order on the streets, he realized what a chaos the traffic was back home.

This is civilized driving.., just see! But discipline is our problem in Manika Kunda, even on the roads. Most of our semiliterate drivers can hardly drive here; not when they see traffic lights as decorations on the streets. Try making them conform! To obey a pole with a light that changes colors? They will ask you if you think you're in London or New York, or maybe Paris!

"You are pretty quiet, Yaya," Joy said, salvaging conversation.

She could feel Basi boiling over with resentment and knew it was at the unguarded babble from Yaya. She wouldn't know how

Yaya felt, or why he blundered so insultingly. And she didn't like it, but she found herself diffusing the situation.

"Are you okay, Yaya?"

"Sure, Ms. Joy. I'm okay. I was just admiring the scenery. Houston must be a beautiful city."

"Yes, it is. You'll love it here. According to Basi, the weather is just like what you find in Africa."

Basi stepped on the gas. They both looked at him. He didn't seem interested in conversation.

"Houston seems to be a big city, too," Yaya said.

"Yes, indeed," Joy said. She decided to jump-start Basi into conversation by teasing him, knowing he was a Houston lover and a Houston Oilers' fanatic. "But, Yaya, Houston is no match for where you came from. Philly is bigger and a far more beautiful city than Houston."

Basi grunted. Joy slyly smiled.

"And of course Yaya, in football you can't compare the Houston Oilers to Philadelphia Eagles, because the Oilers are dead meat."

American football made no sense to Yaya—in Manika Kunda the major game was soccer—so he didn't say anything. But Basi looked at Joy and shook his head.

"And usually, Yaya, the Oilers are knocked down completely at the start of every season, just when other teams are warming up to business. The only thing that they ever qualify for, is the championship for Super Losers' Bowl, and only people like Basi watch that."

Basi looked at Joy quizzically and seemed to slow down his speed.

"Joy, since when did you have interest in football or know anything about the Oilers for that matter? Don't you think you would be better off talking about your church and your church choir?"

Joy burst out laughing. "I know he can't stand for one to say anything about Houston or the Oilers. Yaya, Basi is in love with Houston. He calls it his hometown."

"Is that so?" Yaya asked, and he cautioned himself, not knowing what to say about that African now hoity toity! He looked at Basi seated behind the steering wheel with his long stiffened hair on his head, shiny and greasy like an oiled goat skin, and what he saw was an African detribalized.

They were off Westheimer, into a road that was not as crowded, or lit, then into another, even narrower, with houses on either side and cars packed along the street and on pavements before the houses.

The area was quiet, with thick branched trees lining the streets, and not a soul in sight, even in the verandahs.

The few cars that passed were driving slowly, carefully, and the occupants were all white people. Catching sharp eyes that seemed curious in those cars as they passed by, Yaya instinctively knew that they were being scrutinized, every time. He looked at Basi and Joy; they were comfortable.

A police car crawled along, and shot a torch-like blinding beam directly at them. Basi shifted, and blinked, but ignored the onslaught. Joy shaded her eyes, grunted something inaudible and looked ahead. Yaya stared at the police car, nervously, and on the car he read, *Cato Police*, as they passed.

Cato? Yaya wondered. He thought they were in Houston.

"This is our little suburb," Basi proudly stated, as if he was reading Yaya's mind.

"Suburb? That is where rich white people live in this country, right?" Yaya asked, showing off a knowledge he acquired from Sidi about the demography of American societies.

"Yes, Yaya. But actually suburbs are for anybody who can afford them," Basi retorted. "And of course, comparatively, their property values are much higher than most areas within the big cities. That was why I bought my home here."

"Yaya, maybe you will like it here, but I hate it," Joy said. "Even after three years in this neighborhood, I still feel like I'm from out of space, or walking on dynamite every time I step out."

Yaya thought of those eyes he had seen, like curious and angry cats in those passing cars, which even in that darkness had alerted him that all was not well, as if they were trespassing, and Basi and his wife didn't live in that area.

"Joy, you're just being too sensitive," Basi declared. "This is America. People can live anywhere they want as long as they can afford it."

"Indeed, but I like to live in a neighborhood where I feel free; where I am accepted as a part of the community, and not seen as a Rosa Parks whom they wish may drop dead sooner!"

Who is Rosa Parks? Yaya wondered. The name was familiar. Of course, he told himself. He had come across that name in his readings of civil rights struggles against Jim Crow or separatist laws in the Southern states of America.

Yes, Rosa Parks was the gallant black woman who, in 1955, refused to give up her seat on a bus to a white man in Montgomery, Alabama; whose scornful treatment sparked off the mass

bus boycott in Montgomery, which in turn contributed to the March
on Washington in 1963, where Dr. Martin Luther King Jr. delivered
his famous speech—'I Have A Dream.'

Joy was talking. "Do you imagine what it will be like when we
start having kids in such a hostile environment?"

"We'll teach them assimilation," Basi replied. "And really,
that's my least worry. Kids adapt fast."

"But adults don't, in many ways. I'm more concerned with the
adult attitudes, which flow over to the children anyway. If there
is racism in the church, you tell me where the kids are going to
escape it?"

"You worry too much, Ms. Joy," Basi remarked, pulling up the
drive way of a mighty house, which had a cathedral roof, double
French doors and an array of glass windows.

Yaya leaned back in his seat to eye-ball the massive outline of
the house. Even from outside, it had an aura of a castle. And
suddenly, in a bizarre manner, there was a motion inside the house.
The part of the house directly ahead of them, up the driveway, was
making way, folding upwards, automatically, it appeared to Yaya.

Who did that? He searched all over for hints, it was in vain. Yaya
only saw an open room ahead, like those used as merchant shops in
Manika Kunda. There was a small burgundy car parked on one side.
It said Porsche 944 Turbo in gold letters on the back.

Basi drove in, on the other side. As they came in, a green light
up the wall by a pack of switches was flashing the word, "ENTER."
It flashed "STOP" just when Basi hit the brakes.

With Joy and Basi fidgeting to get out, Yaya shook his head and
laughed silently: *The wonders of technology and automation.*
Indeed, the ultimate in convenience! You drive up to your house,
and it opens, and you get directed inside to park your car. Truly,
America is really a wonderland!

"This is home," Basi declared, flinging open a door that led into
the kitchen, and to the living room. "It's a four bedroom house," he
said.

For Yaya, the kitchen announced the house, its grandeur, and
expanse. It was the size of an adult room that could hold a king-size
bed and two night stands, with a standard chest and dresser. Almost
all the appliances were new. Everything from the stove to the
refrigerator, freezer, dishwasher, microwave, and even the ceiling
fan, matched, in a lemonade-yellow, blending with the paint and the
flowery wallpaper.

Yaya was taken aback at the massive cabinets which covered two-thirds of the kitchen, and more so at their doors, crafted like a human heart. *This place is all cabinets,* he thought; they were below the counters and above the appliances. And on the creamy tiled floor, tiny patterns like on a chess board sparkled, with not a spot smeared. He almost tip-toed.

Joy lingered in the kitchen, opening the refrigerator and bowing inside as Yaya followed Basi's lead into the living room. This was huge, with a raised ceiling, boasting of a marbled fireplace, a built-in bookcase and a walk-in wet bar. The place was furnished to the inch.

Yaya noticed that Basi had everything Sidi had, and more. His television alone was a gigantic tower, with a screen big enough for a cinema hall. Yaya estimated it to project up to at least 60 inches.

Wow, Basi, his chairs! Over ten sectional pieces, with fluffy opulent gray material. Hmm! This place is a palace. Look at the carpet, same color as the chairs, and so thick, you can hunt a rabbit in it.

But, even from his humble background, Yaya dismissed this luxury as not equivalent to not returning home. The place smacked of good living, of the highest standard he knew. But thinking of Basi's decision not to ever return to Manika Kunda shattered the excitement! Already, he was nostalgic for home, even as he just came.

To stay here forever? It is like a man who owns a motel, and because the motel is elegant, he abandons his home completely.

In Yaya's new room that night, before he went to bed, he got his diary and made his entries: Friday, May 30: —*I arrived in Houston. Basi and his wife met me at the airport. Oh! Basi is doing fine but seems changed and worse than I expected. The man said he will never go back home. I guess America is now his home. His wife, though, seems nicer than Pat. Overall, I'm hopeful here.*

Yaya laid his diary aside on his bed; and as he had started doing recently after his entries, he thought of Grandma Fatu and the two-year period that was rounding up. It was now exactly thirty days to June 29th when she died. He assessed his options after that date: whether he should go back home immediately if things didn't improve or whether he should stay and explore his chances in America. He concluded that that would be dependent on how he did in Houston.

That night, before Yaya slept he went into the bathroom and had a quick *ablution or wudu*—a mandatory cleansing that Muslims do before offering major prayers, which involves washing parts of the body that are usually exposed, like the face, both arms to the elbows, the feet up to the ankle, and with wet hands reaching inside of the nose and ears and brushing the head—as prescribed in the Koran, he washed all the required body parts, three times.

As Yaya came to his room, he thought of how if he were in Taényadu, his parents would have asked and insisted on him always offering the five daily prayers: *Salatul-Fajr*—the early morning prayer; *Salatuz-Zuhr*—the afternoon prayer; *Salatul-'Asr*—the late afternoon prayer; *Salatul-Maghrib*—the evening prayer; and *Salatul-'Isha*—the night prayer. And indeed, he knew that most fervent Muslims performed all those prayers on a daily basis.

But like many Westernized African Muslim youths when on his own, Yaya tried to occasionally perform mostly the late afternoon to the night prayers at their specified times. Or sometimes at night before going to bed, he would combine all the five prayers in one long prayer. However, in spite of his modern day excuses or youthful lethargy, as worried as he had been lately, he certainly prayed every night.

Now he was standing over an old gown spread in a corner. Facing what he thought was the east or Mecca, he recited the *Fatihah*-the opening chapter of the Koran and read some other verses. He did seven *rak'ats*, a total of praying while standing, bending and prostrating to touch his forehead to the floor fourteen times; at every *rak'at* or two times that he bowed, he took a short break in a sitting position with his legs folded under him. After the seventh *rak'at*, he sat down and read the *Fatihah* again and laid out his problems to Allah.

But eh, Almighty Allah, just see what happened to me. I didn't ask for it and was not even prepared for it in any way. My life was fine but now see, thanks to Grandma Fatu, I'm moving from one place to another. Yes, I've become a man of no fixed abode. But Almighty Allah, it's you that I'm asking to show me a way to overcome this setback in my life. All I want is to live a fulfilling life. And meantime, God, please give me a chance in this country; a break commensurate with my sacrifices and sufferings, if not my education. Yes, Almighty, so that I'll start singing aloud your praise.

He went to bed and started to sleep but thoughts about Basi lingered in his mind. The fact that he would forever never go back home. And yet the boy was born to money. He prayed for Basi so that God would cleanse his mind and make him proud of where he came from, and change his heart so that they could all go back someday and take part in the development of Manika Kunda. Or if he was not going to go, at least God should make him not to forget about the many needs of the people back home.

Yaya wasn't surprised to find Basi living such an impressive lifestyle. If anybody knew Pa Brima Ibrahim back home, you wouldn't be either. For if Basi's father had countless properties, office structures, four-story buildings and complexes that harbored shopping centers and people, why wouldn't his son live like a king anywhere?

Basi had it all from birth, as they say, with a silver spoon in his mouth. Unlike him, Yaya, who was born in a farm hut, with his pregnant mother visiting her father's farm. Such humbling start, which caused him constant mocking as a kid by everybody, who said he would be a good farmer. But school opened his appetite for Western education, which was no easy ride either. When other kids went to their parents for help with their homework, his parents couldn't even read his report card. Yet he got somewhere.

Yaya started to wonder about the trying times back home, how his family was coping, since he that made a difference for them was now depending on others for his basic needs. He prayed that God should sustain and protect his poor family and everybody at home. He asked for a chance soon, so that he would start helping as he did before coming abroad.

Struggling with his drowsy eyelids which burned, he prayed to never get corrupted in America such that he looks down on his people. Because Americans themselves don't teach that, not in such a progressive country of melting virtues. Of course, if given any chance in this great land, it would be an onward move henceforth for him. But in spite of all the success that might come his way, he would never forget who he was, and where he came from.

When Yaya woke up the following day, which was a Saturday, Joy was in the kitchen packing dishes in the dishwasher. She was just turning to pick up some dirty dishes from the sink when she saw Yaya's figure. She gasped, terrified, but suddenly calmed herself, realizing there was a stranger in the house. She thougt it was silly to be so scary, but attributed that to being usually alone at such times.

"Hi, dear," she panted, with a weary smile, dropping her hands limply at her sides.

"Good morning, Ms. Joy." Yaya smiled and, uneasy too for frightening her, he dropped his eyes to her hands, which up to her wrist were wet, foaming with burbles and particles of food. He looked up in her face. "So how are you this morning?"

"I'm fine, Yaya." She sighed. "Did you sleep well?"

"I did, Ms. Joy, thanks."

She continued packing her dishes in the dishwasher.

Yaya was now with her in the kitchen. Her bright eyes, smiling face and agility, all showed grace and beauty even as natural as she was.

"There is everything for breakfast, Yaya," she said, and seemed finished with the dishes as she was washing her hands. "I don't know what you want to eat, but there is bread, cereals, eggs, and sausages. If you drink coffee, there is hot water in the flask and you will find the coffee, cream, and sugar on the dinning room table. Fix yourself a cup, if you care."

"Thanks. Sure, I will take some coffee."

"Good. Would you like some scrambled eggs or sausages?"

"Anything, Ms. Joy. I eat anything."

"Great. Then, let me fix you something. It'll be ready in a few minutes. Please forgive me, we don't normally fuss about breakfast here. We are always running out first thing in the morning."

"I understand. I know that this is America. People are always busy."

"You're right about that," she said.

"Is Basi sleeping?" Yaya asked.

"Sleep? He doesn't ever sleep.... He's o-u-t!" she said. Yaya noticed a frown, the furrowed brows, and the way Joy said 'out' like she was spelling the word. He added that to her absent-mindedness, as hints of some bothersome concern. Or was it perhaps because she was tired? It was the weekend.

"Your home boy Basi stays on the street. And that's all the time. Sometimes I wonder why he got married." Now, the inflection in her voice showed protest edging on resignation, like one who has put her worries in perspective. Yaya didn't know what to say.

"Is that so?" he asked frowning, in line with Joy's seriousness.

"Yes, sir, he is like somebody who's got another house on the street."

"Another house like where he lives?"

"Yes, and perhaps another woman."

"For what, Ms. Joy? I doubt that very much. Basi won't do anything like that," said Yaya, even as he knew he could be covering up for Basi.

"But isn't that what you do in Africa? Don't men over there marry many wives?"

"Yes, and no," Yaya said. "Yes, because it used to happen in the past. Our fathers were the last generation to do so. Even then people were changing. At this point, for most young people, I say no. It is dying out."

"Oh yeah? Yaya, you tell me anything." Joy mockingly tilted up her chin at him, with disbelief in her eyes but yet smiling.

"For real, Ms. Joy, very few young men do that these days."

"Well, who knows, maybe Basi is one of those few," she wittingly retorted.

"You shouldn't think like that, Ms. Joy. You may be wrong about him as far as that's concerned. Take it from me, I'm an African, and I'm just coming from home; only the most illiterate do that these days." Yaya knew he could be lying, but he wanted to put the issue to rest.

Joy gave up on that topic and laid breakfast out for Yaya. As he ate, she got a glass of orange juice and sat with him. They talked generally, about Africa, about Philadelphia, and about the impressiveness of the house.

They enjoyed talking to each other and through that good communication, they struck a rapport before getting up from that table. In fact, like old friends, they were laughing their sides out at their jokes as if somebody was telling them the fable about the pastor at a pulpit who took out of his inside coat pocket a pink panty—thinking it was a handkerchief—to wipe his face.

With Basi gone most times, Joy saw Yaya as a companion, and she felt reassured by his talks. Maybe instinctively, that was why she had looked forward to his coming. That big house could be too much sometimes, all alone by herself.

CHAPTER TWENTY

Starting from Yaya's first couple of days in Houston, it became obvious to him that Basi was at the top of the world. An offspring of the rich, he grew up pampered, as expected of one born in opulence amidst a massive situation of destitution for most of the common folks. In Manika Kunda, the few rich were objects of adulation and envy. If they couldn't turn the night into day, they wouldn't fall too short of that; and the only reason they wouldn't breathe life into the dead was because the dead were destined to die.

That sense of power and privilege could not be lost on their offspring. Some kept a cool head about it, others didn't. Yaya knew that Basi never did. It showed all his life. In the boarding home of their high school, where it was natural to be friendly, Basi was aggravating, always making faces and condemning the food which the others ate happily.

Amidst a brotherly bond which reigned among the students in their happy little enclave, he snubbed and scowled others contemptuously. They excused him as being empty-headed and self-centered, wanting to be noticed without being able to compete or show any leadership ability. And as a friend, Yaya with humor, always accused him of being as egotistical as an actor in search of forlorn stardom.

In his invertebrate quest for attention and status in America, which came naturally back home because of his family's wealth, Basi was hard hit that America wasn't like Africa or Manika Kunda, to be precise. In America, rich people abounded. In fact, the average American seemed rich by African standards. He or she usually owned a car and lived in amenities that only the rich could enjoy in Africa. Also, in America, everybody seemed equal on the surface. That made it hard for Basi, for him to be known for who he was; a son of an African millionaire!

Basi did not see himself as common by any standard. If they only knew that he ran his father's accounts in America, and was in full control over scores of thousands of dollars in banks all over Houston, they would respect him; and know that he was not the average African or just any black man. He was rich, and could afford a Volvo 850 GTAS, convertible, and a Porsche 944 Turbo, which were all paid for and practically new. And he lived in the suburb of Cato, in a $250,000.00 home. Yes, the only black on the block!

Joy knew that Basi was immature, conceited and confused; and sometimes, she felt that he treated her like one of his possessions and as if she had no feelings. In the four years that they'd been married, she had been inclined to think that he was not ready for marriage; because it seemed like it was all part of a game to him, to conquer and to be, and to feed his ego to which he was addicted like a thumb in an infant's mouth. And she knew that he had long taken her for granted, doing whatever it was that he did on the street, where he spent more time than at home.

But Joy was no fool. She was a Christian and confident. She had married Basi for life. He was appealing, passionate, rich and generous and she was in love. She saw him as going through a phase of life and she was not going to wreck her marriage for that; when she knew they had their whole life ahead to make the best of.

She expected Basi to eventually flip out of his roving dog feet, and get tired of the street, as it had been with some of the best husbands of the day. She was convinced that if Basi did not change soon enough, by the time they started having kids he would change. She was sure of that and believed the Lord would see it happen.

Meantime, as long as she knew that he always came back to her and that he loved her, and provided for her, that was all that mattered.

Besides, she had long accepted that Basi wasn't quite American. She wasn't going to frustrate herself at trying to change him, because people changed only when they wanted to, and only fools became obsessed with changing other adults. Instead, now she focused her efforts on her personal growth. She was attending an evening class two days a week for her CPA exam and was a member of her church choir.

It did not matter to Yaya that Basi carried himself like he owned Houston. All he wanted was some of that power to rub on him so that he would stand on his own feet. Yet by the end of his first week with them, he realized that Basi's behavior towards him was condescending. Unlike the positive interaction he saw in Philadelphia among his countrymen, Basi wasn't even showing that common camaraderie born by attending the same schools or growing up together. Basi was his old snobbish self as always, except that, until now, he did it to other people, not to Yaya.

The two of them had gotten along fine; they had taken liberties with each other and had been comrades since elementary school. They had met in the fifth grade. Basi was from the capital city, Sobala. He told Yaya, his only friend, in their kiddy talk as they tossed a ball during a break period behind their fifth grade class, that he had no brothers or sisters, that after him his mother couldn't have any more babies all because of some surgery. He said he hated the school he went to in Sobala because their teacher, an old woman whom they called *Baddy Mama,* shouted and scared them with threats all day long, that she beat them too, sometimes, and said she would kill them if anybody told any lies about her to their parents, except to say she was a nice woman, which she wasn't.

Basi told Yaya that his parents went away all the time on business and left him in the care of a housekeeper. She liked to get drunk and bring men over, but that was only when his parents were away. They would throw her out if they found out. He promised not to tell, if she didn't make him go to school. Yet his parents found out. The headmaster, who always cried to his parents about money, came to see his father one day, and told on him. Next, his parents decided to send him to Taényadu.

Taényadu, Yaya's village, was where Basi's mother came from. They had a community of about a thousand people, many of whom knew only one way of life—the old way. They did without electricity, television and the telephone. Radio was the instant link to the outside world. The symbols of modernization were a courthouse, a few shops, an elementary school, a medical dispensary which they called a hospital, and a preparatory class for high school. Teachers and the dispensary staff in their white shorts or skirts and white shirts were the esteemed professionals, since most of the people farmed the land and raised livestock; over there, after school, teenage gangs knuckled it out on creative soccer fields and sang in the moonlight in camaraderie.

In that village of mud houses with thatched and zinc roofs, which were slowly but competitively making way for concrete buildings, Basi lived in the best house owned by his grandparents. Some said their rich son-in law built that mansion for them. Others said the grandparents built their estate themselves with their sudden wealth from wandering in the diamond mines. Yet such a mighty brick house with nine rooms was a mystery in the village.

And because Basi's grandparents failed to explain the puzzle about their *massive* wealth, amidst the potent suspicion between the rich and the poor in that rural community, there was a lingering awe in the minds of many. This led to several frustrated political bids by Basi's grandfather to represent the constituency in parliament.

In their disappointment, his grandparents recoiled and lived a changed lifestyle. They stopped going to even the town square for either communal ceremonies or the occasional meetings. Yet that did not change the trend of speculations about them. Some villagers kept whispering that his grandparents were cannibals who ate and sold people; if not any more, at least, some time in their younger days. And that there was some dark secret hiding in those nine rooms, where the only visitors that came were mostly from outside the area.

However, in the eyes of Yaya and the other little village kids, Basi stood out as opportuned. One of the few among them that had the luxury of having a ride waiting for him after school; because his grandparents had a white landrover, which dropped him and picked him up everyday. And his uniforms of khaki shorts and blue shirts were always starched and pressed pointed in all corners, with his tennis shoes immaculately white-washed.

But even then Basi was as saucy as he could be, and aloof. The other pupils didn't like him because he wouldn't speak to them. Some said they were afraid because of the *cannibal* stories about his grandparents. Yaya was Basi's only friend. In the high school preparatory class, they decided to select the same high school. It was a competitive high school in the country, and they succeeded. The school was on the outskirts of Sobala. It was all boys, and a public high school gone private, where the students were either very smart or had rich parents.

As expected of Basi, he hadn't made too many friends even in that close boarding school environment in which they lived for five years. The other students called Yaya his bodyguard, but he was more. Basi was always running back and forth home, missing classes and assignments. Yaya took notes for them in class and slipped in assignments on Basi's behalf when he was away. Basi valued and respected him throughout high school, up to when he left for America.

They had broken communication until Yaya got to the U.S. But now that he was living with Basi, who had the upper hand as always, it dawned on Yaya that he was getting to know the real Basi. It was nothing like the old days of mutual moral support and boyhood bond; or that rapport which Yaya mistakenly thought their reunion would bring. Rather he saw Basi as reserved, intransigent and full of himself. Perhaps Basi's stay in America had gotten to him, or perhaps his father's wealth which obviously was trickling considerably to him blurred his vision of the past and their boyhood solidarity.

Basi didn't see himself in the same class as Yaya. He felt embarrassed at the chumminess with which Yaya approached him, for he believed that they were worlds apart. Every time he looked at Yaya he couldn't help but mentally castigate him for what he saw as a crude appearance which he judged to be typically African, like the kinky hair, red eyes, and a perceived lack of coordination in manner of dress. To Basi, Yaya was traditional and hard-core, the type that would be in America for years and would never change.

Also, Basi couldn't help fuming over that incident in the car, on their way from the airport. It was an insult he would never forget. To insult him before his wife? Just because he brought him close? To Basi that was obviously a sign of that traditional African mentality which he was going to teach Yaya that he didn't share anymore.

He would have thrown Yaya out the very next day but for Joy. "You are all Africans," she pleaded, "and the same people too."

Basi was very upset at such silly talk from Joy, putting him in the same class with Yaya. "Look, Joy, I don't want to hear anything like that from you again," he fumed; because what she said took away from him so much! "So if I'm African, do you see us as the same?"

Joy simply closed that topic. Indeed she knew that Basi kept few African values. Sometimes she wondered whether it was because Basi came to the U.S. as a teenager who had nobody to look up to and so kept to himself. Strangely, even at TSU, he had no ties with other Africans, and seemed to have none whatsoever with the greater African communities anywhere in the U.S.

Joy was concerned about Basi's aloofness for a while, because before she met him, what impressed her about the African students on campus was their closeness, and she had been to many parties thrown by various African students' organizations which were so refreshing. Yet Basi acted so distant. She had asked him several times why he was like that, and why he refused to mix with his African folks? Basi's response had always been that she shouldn't bother him about that, because even as Africans they were as different as blacks and whites.

That didn't sound right to Joy. She thought Basi was losing touch with his culture, which she considered the greatest asset of an African. And it was a shame because she knew that some black folks in America were struggling so hard to regain their African heritage. Sometimes, in fact, even she who was an American, felt that Basi probably saw himself as more American than she, or a lot of Americans.

CHAPTER TWENTY-ONE

"Yaya! Yaya! Hey, Yaya?"

"Yes, Basi," Yaya screamed from his room.

"One minute!"

Yaya hastened. Of course, one minute or less, that was what he always got from him anyway, since his two week stay with them.

"Yes, Basi?"

"Here, man, press these pants and polish these shoes for me. Place them in the closet by the front door when you're through. I'm getting ready for an appointment, but thanks." And he walked off to his room.

"You're welcome," Yaya mouthed after him, and thought, or should I say thank you sir, for making me your house boy?

He got the iron, the brush and the polish and went into his room. He decided to do the ironing on his bed instead of using the ironing board.

Joy had gone for her evening class. Basi had come in barely an hour ago. After eating, he had been talking on the phone in his room ever since. It was only, "Hi, is Joy gone?" And next he was giving Yaya some task to perform. That got Yaya talking to himself.

Phew! Maybe that was why he asked me to come here, to be his house boy, and do his domestic chores. Interesting. I'll give him the benefit of the doubt by being his fool for some time, as I bide my time and find my way out. Our people say, if you have no legs and somebody is carrying you on their shoulders, it will be unwise to say that their breath stinks—no matter how bad the stench—for that may annoy your carrier and have him drop you promptly!

Yaya pressed the pants and polished the shoes, and continued with his reading of *An Autobiography of Malcolm X* by Alex Haley, which he got from Joy.

"Basi, can we talk, please."

It was on Tuesday, June 10. Yaya was in the middle of his second week in Houston. The time was ten past ten in the evening. Joy had gone to bed. Basi was sitting fully dressed, all flashy in a shiny pink shirt and a similarly glittering black pants, with gold rings on his fingers, thick gold bracelets on both wrists along with a Rolex watch on one of them, and three solid gold chains hanging down his necks. He was on the couch going through a pile of mail. Yaya was on the loveseat.

Yaya knew Basi would go out soon, but when he would come back, only God knew. He was an insurance agent and was always out on business, he claimed, with his portable cellular phone, which he carried everywhere. Yaya didn't even know the number to reach him on that phone, but Joy did. She told Yaya that Basi took no personal calls on it, except from her, and that she could reach him everywhere, whether it was at the office or at the residences of clients.

As for Yaya, catching Basi at home alone like this was a rare opportunity. Most times he had wanted to talk to Basi, Joy was around. But tonight, maybe they could talk like homeboys.

"Basi?"

"Yes?" He looked up from a letter he was reading, not meeting Yaya's eyes.

Yaya cleared his throat and sought his eyes. "But, my brother, is that how to treat a stranger, eeh, Basi? Since I've been here, we hardly talk. You're always busy and either resting or running out. Sometimes I try to talk to you, but it seems you don't either hear me or see me. And what can I do? I came here for you. If you desert me, where will I turn?"

Basi looked Yaya over thinking to himself: *Idiot, your mouth got you messed up. You think you can insult me before my wife and get away with it. You'll find out!*

"Hey, Yaya, this is America and not Manika Kunda. And just in case you don't know, everybody here have their problems. You see all these letters?" Yaya looked at the bunch of mail lying next to Basi on an end table.

"What do you think these are? They are all bills from creditors. Some are bank statements, credit card statements, and you name it, all of which I have to attend to now. They come first for me, before your problem, whatever it is!"

Yaya sighed. *Whatever it is? Now, my problem is whatever it is.* "Basi? We two go back a long way, you know? I hope you remember."

Basi frowned and wanted to say, 'Of course, Yaya, I know. You were always a leech.' Instead, he looked at Yaya with his face tightened.

"Hey, man, don't lay a guilt trip on me, right? If your brother cannot help you in Philadelphia all the time you were with him, how can I help you in less than two weeks?"

Basi's words and his dark glossy eyes which were half closed as he spoke, made Yaya groan silently with disappointment.

"But you said it yourself, Basi, that you were lining up something for me. Something I could do as soon as I got here. And now you say I'm making you feel guilty? Am I making you feel guilty?"

"Yes, man, that's what you're trying to do? It's clear where you're coming from."

"Well, Basi, I'm sorry. I've no intention of making you feel guilty. As it is, I appreciate everything you are doing for me. Though to be honest, at my age, I do not exactly feel proud to be dependent, which is my concern. You know I'm limited here, and with you already in the system, the most I can ask is for help to get me started somewhere?"

"That will be when I have time and when it's possible. And guess what? Don't push your luck!"

Oh, America, Yaya thought, everybody tells me, *"Don't push your luck!"* as if I've had any.

He thought of the chance that might, by now, have turned up in Philadelphia if he had stayed. And he thought of Sidi's words when he talked about coming to Basi. *"America has a strange way of changing people, Yaya; ...don't be fooled by big talks."* Yet he was.

"Good night, Basi." A downcast Yaya got up.

"Good night."

From his room, Yaya shortly heard Basi leaving. He reflected on how he was getting seasoned in his dilemma. This ordeal since Grandma Fatu died. Before that, about two years ago, life had been like roses, but now it seemed like some suffocating foul stench which hung over him, even threatening to engulf him. Yet he would survive it, he willed.

Now he wished he had stayed in Philadelphia with Sidi and the other Africans there to talk to, and who were willing to help. *Maybe I would have been on to something there by now. But regretfully, this guy raised my hopes, only for me to come and be treated like a nobody? Oh Basi, let him ride high, it's his day.*

The temptation to go back to Philadelphia hounded Yaya. He was ready to happily accommodate Pat, with whom relationships were on the positive side when he was leaving. He thought about Ahmed, Barbar, and all his the other countrymen over there who genuinely seemed to care.

But to run back to Philadelphia? Yaya dismissed that idea promptly. To return home when all the typhoon about the inheritance had cleared was one thing. But to go backwards in America from one worse situation to another, like the one he'd just been through with Pat, and on mere speculation? That made no sense. He considered such to be foolhardiness and a weakness of mind, which was unlike him. Or he would have yielded to the forces at home that sought to propel his life. He decided to tough it out in Houston and felt thankful that at least he had one consolation. Ms. Joy. She was solidly on his side; and she was a remarkable woman of substance. But with Basi, he still had to see.

It was 10:30 p.m. Yaya was sitting on his bed with his diary in his hand. He opened to the current date: Tuesday, June 10—*My second week in Houston. I talked with Basi today about my status. He sounded quite disappointing. Besides, I see a condescending attitude towards me. But I will cope.*

He closed his diary. It was June 10th now, he reflected. And from then to June 29th only nineteen days remained for his most consuming concern to be over. But the pace with which that date came was so slow for his excitement. He couldn't wait to know he had survived his nagging nightmare, as he knew he would soon. Yet he shuddered to think of the ominous date, June 29, two years ago when Grandma Fatu handed him the heritage and blew out on him, seeming by that to puncture his world, too.

Resisting all premonitions about the impending date, Yaya got up and went into the bathroom and had a quick ablution. He came to his room and stood in his usual corner over his old gown. He prayed his habitual seven *rak'ats* and two more. And after that he sat down and read the *fatihah* two times and then started beseeching God fervently like a penitent.

He declared that he was placing himself in Allah's hands, more now than ever; asking Allah to watch over him as that fateful day drew closer; so that he would sail free cleanly, and for the inheritance to be handed to someone more appropriate; because he was the wrong man and it served no useful purpose for his education to be wasted, when he knew he could do better for himself and his people if he was not limited by being tied to the profession of bone healing.

As for his luck in America, Yaya urged the Almighty to help him. He wanted to stand on his own feet like some of his happy contemporaries. Then he would not only write bright letters home but also share with his people whatever good that came his way.

He recited the *fatihah* again twice and went to bed. He felt so relieved after his long prayers that he slept off even without browsing through some reading material as he did usually.

It was 6 a.m. in Korkordu and Kondorfili Bunsor was getting up as Yaya went to bed at 11 p.m. in Houston. While Yaya was counting nineteen days to June 29, in his second week in Texas; finally, Kondorfili Bunsor yesterday saw the new moon. As usual, whenever a new moon was sighted, he marked his calendar the following morning, before sunrise.

Last night, he had looked at the sky when the moon was only a crescent. He had seen that over and over, and had watched many new moons grow from night to night, as they rose every night in the east and followed a set course to the west accompanied by the stars that usually surrounded them. In a moon's journey, Kondorfili Bunsor knew every stop that it made, the time of the night it was, and how old that moon was, as it grew to full moon and dwindled to the crescent that this one was last night.

To Kondorfili Bunsor, when a moon grew into half a *calabash*—a hollowed, round gourd cut in half—that meant it was five days old. When it grew into the size of a *calabash,* that moon was ten days old. And when it was full moon, that was fifteen days gone in that moon. And after that, the size of the moon would dwindle into a *calabash,* half a *calabash* and finally into the silver crescent that it was in the beginning.

With this moon rising immediately after sunset like it did yesterday, and coming shortly after the hunting moons, it would have some of their brightness. When it commenced shining until almost the first cockcrow, it would be seven days old; then it would keep shining longer as it matured, yet rising later and later until there was no more illumination from the tiny silver streak left up in the sky, which would be the twenty-seventh day and the last days of the waning moon. But before that, after full moon, when the moon turned into a *calabash* again, it would be like one Friday to the next for it to totally disappear. And then it would be twenty days old, that was when Yaya's Grandma died.

Kondorfili Bunsor had looked forward to the coming of this moon yesterday with growing excitement; so he was totally exhilarated this morning. Before any of his wives and children came from their huts and started knocking at his door, even without touching his *gbangba* stick that he used to brush his teeth or before putting any food in his mouth, he staggered to his calendar cloth in the corner and felt elated just by looking at it.

He couldn't help acknowledging that the misery of others had become his gain. In this four-rain period, from the dots under and over the X's, business had been booming, particularly since

Yaya's grandma died in the seventh moon after the harvest moon on the second rain of this calendar.

In fact, he Kondorfili Bunsor had prospered. His old mud hut was now a giant building of cement blocks. They'd done the roof—yes, his iron roof. They'd done the floors of all the rooms. Next it was the verandah. But for his parlor, he would wait until this calendar had been completed, which was only six moons more.

He got his *kala* and his *duba* and bowed down before the white cloth where he crossed the eighth line out of thirteen; it was the seventh moon after harvest moon in the fourth column—the last rain on this four-rain calendar.

Gleefully, Kondorfili Bunsor reflected that finally the two rains had rounded; that this was the twenty-sixth moon since Yaya's grandma died; and the very moon that completed the cycle. He stared at the dots up the X, next to the one he just made; those were two patients he just discharged, and he still had one on his premises.

Things would get even better, he mused; soon, when he became the sole custodian of this heritage. Yes, in a matter of days, and henceforth it would be only he, Kondorfili Bunsor. And counting from yesterday, he was sure there now remained only nineteen days to make him the incontestable bone healer in Manika Kunda.

"So, Yaya, how do you find the U.S., so far?" Joy asked.

It was 7 p.m. Wednesday, the day after Yaya's talk with Basi. He was gone. He had just touched home after work, to eat and change clothes. He had to go meet a couple for some policy, he said, rushing out. Joy and Yaya were sitting in the living room watching TV.

"Well, Ms. Joy, I don't know what to say."

"But why? How long have you been in the country?"

"About six months," Yaya said, rubbing his forehead like somebody massaging a pain away.

"Oh, Yaya," Joy waved her hands. "You're still pretty new in America then!"

Those words shocked Yaya. He thought he was not that pretty new. He came on the 29th of December last year, and it was now June 11, and by the end of the month he would be in his seventh month. *Seven months coming with a man dependent and unproductive? And she says with a wave of her hands, "You're still pretty new in America then!"*

"Maybe like you said, Ms. Joy, I'm pretty new here though it doesn't seem like that to me."

"But by now, you should know whether you're going to like it here or not." She winked.

"You are right, Ms. Joy. Indeed, I have to like America for me to come here in the first place. I'm afraid though... America has not liked me yet. When I start doing something instead of staying idle and sitting around the house, I will say yes..., America has smiled on me."

"Have hope, Yaya. Things will work themselves out soon. You should start paying attention to the employment section in the newspapers and start applying for positions. Somebody is bound to give you a chance."

"Yes, Ms. Joy, I hope so. But my problem is more complex than that. I don't have a work permit and my visa has expired. They say nobody would hire me in that situation. That was why I didn't get a job in Philadelphia all the time I was there."

"That's a shame. But aren't the immigration people the ones who are supposed to give you the work permit?"

"It's them. But as it is, I cannot even think of going to meet them. They would deport me for overstaying my visa."

"No, they won't. Don't believe that." Joy laughed it off.

"Yes, they will, Ms. Joy." Yaya was amused at her lack of awe for immigration. But of course, he thought, because she is an American citizen, how could she fear them?

"But Yaya, who said they would deport you when you came here with a visa? They've been bringing all those Russians and Cubans and Polish and giving them visas to live here. Ain't nobody going to deport you. Somebody is making you afraid."

"Not really, Ms. Joy. The cases of those people you mentioned are different. They are given political asylum because they are running from dictatorships in their countries. With me, I'm just somebody here that has come for a personal reason, which they won't understand; not especially when I'm from Africa. We are the least desirable by immigration."

"That's it then, because you are from Africa." Joy leaned back in her seat with the grim relief of somebody who has solved a jigsaw puzzle about a tormentor. "You are right," she said, in a flustered voice. "Some folks can't stand even us blacks that are born here; I know they aren't going to make it easy for you Africans."

"Evidently, Ms. Joy. But as our people say, when you fall into the sea, you must swim or you may drown. All I'm praying for is my first leap beyond the dark gloom; and then if I have to sit on the back of the shark to sail, I will."

"You sound intelligent, Yaya. What's your educational level?"

"B.A. Honors."

"Is that right? In what?" Joy shifted, crossing her legs.

"Greek and Roman History and Civilization."

Uh-huh! Joy thought. "That's quite a major, Yaya. Why did you decide on that?"

"Well, I did not really choose that major. It was forced on me. You see, in Manika Kunda, we have only one university that the British left us and those were the majors that the British were teaching. But since Independence, when the British left, our leaders have kept crying about no money and so can't expand even the university curriculum. Yet we see them living in luxury and getting richer and richer."

"That's like Basi's father, I guess."

"I would rather not talk about that, Ms. Joy."

"But aren't there other universities in Africa?"

"Yes, there are many. Nigeria alone has over twenty universities. But even then, that's not enough for their people, let alone foreign students. Africa has a massive need for institutions of higher education, Ms. Joy."

"If there are so few colleges over there what do most of the youths do after high school?"

"They waste very easily and our system perpetuates that. We have an exam which was a British legacy called the General Certificate of Examinations or GCE. That's our gateway to higher education, with no consideration for a student's aggregate performance through high school. Yet, all the exam does is fail two-thirds of high school graduates every year. In that case, they wouldn't be scrambling for the limited space at our lone university."

"That's a shame."

"Yes, Ms. Joy. That's how many brilliant students waste in Manika Kunda. I was lucky to scale through, but see where it landed me, with no practical skill in this technological age. As if all the country needs to develop is liberal arts."

"Maybe they want you all to be philosophers."

"I guess so. But can't they learn from the Greeks? Greece hasn't sent anybody to the moon yet, and even Korea now puts out more products than them."

Well, Yaya, you are now in America. I won't say it will be easy but if you have any dreams, this is the place."

"I hope so, Ms. Joy."

That evening after Joy's talk with Yaya, she was almost asleep when she heard Basi's movement in the room. She looked at the AM/FM alarm clock on the nightstand by her side; it was five past eleven. She decided to lie awake waiting.

"What are you going to do about Yaya?" she asked as Basi got into bed with her.

"Like what?" Basi snapped back.

"Since that man has been here, this is his second week rounding up, have you really sat down and talked with him? Can't you see he is looking up to you for help?"

"As if I don't know that. Why else is he here? I will get round to him when I can, but meantime he will just have to wait. In fact, he should count himself lucky to be living in a free house where everything is free."

"But is that what he said he wanted?" Joy sat up. "And is that supposed to take care of his plans or goals?"

"Who doesn't have goals? Everybody does," Basi said, covering himself to the neck. "Like I said, I will do what I can, but I just don't have the time now."

Joy sat up, and stood her pillow against the headboard, which she leaned against. "Basi, when will you have the time to do something for him?"

"I said, when I can," Basi looked up at Joy. "And don't pester me. Since when did you start being his advocate?" He covered his head completely.

"Basi, I was sitting right by your side when you were talking to him when he was in Philadelphia and I heard everything you said. Yaya seems like a gentleman, and that is what you, too, should prove you are to him.., by keeping to your words."

Basi sat up, frowning. "Look, Joy, don't compare me to that uncivilized, bush boy. Do you know where he comes from? They don't even have tap water in his village."

"That doesn't mean anything.., it is what the man wants to make of himself. I judge people by their seriousness and personality."

"But don't you see him? He doesn't even seem to comb his hair or pay much attention to his appearance. Just looking at him, one would think he has never been to school."

"You can groom him, Basi. That is what friends are for. I'm sure all that you know didn't just come to you like that. Somebody must have taught you. Since he has been here, have you offered to take him to a barber? Or have you taken him to a store so you can get him some decent clothing? You haven't."

"Sure, but I don't feel like that right now, and I don't have the time."

"But, Basi, oh yes, you could find time if you wanted to. And I think it is better to do that than to talk so low about him. You asked him to come here, remember?"

"Yes, so what? I can ask him to leave just the same!"

Basi's words that night shocked Joy beyond belief. She laid by his side thinking she was seeing Basi in a different light, sort of unpredictable and confused. Before Yaya came, Basi was all excited about him. But it seemed from the moment the man arrived, Basi recoiled. She saw no rapport between them like old school friends. Basi hardly even talked to Yaya, except to say, 'Yaya, do this or do that.' It seemed to her like a servant-master relationship.

Sometimes she had to tell Basi to use the word 'please' as it was proper when he asked Yaya to do something for him. Granted Yaya was not as sophisticated as him, but that could be understood. He was new in America and he had no money. But that was no reason for Basi to treat him like scum; besides they were all Africans.

Basi needed to change, Joy thought. He definitely needed to start going to church, because it was nothing but the devil in him that was doing him like that. As for Yaya, Joy felt overwhelmed with compassion for him. He seemed serious, ambitious and well-behaved. She didn't think he came from such a backward background as Basi claimed.

There were some things about Africans that Joy felt she could not understand. Like her puzzles about the relationship between these two men. In the past days, she had seen Yaya changing from his warm admiration for Basi, when they are together, to a cool but responsive indifference; while Basi, of course, outrightly snubbed him anyway. Joy believed that American men who attended the same school and sat in the same class wouldn't behave like that. Those two didn't seem to have even old jokes in common.

And as a Christian, Joy could not help blaming Basi for the changing countenance of the friendship between him and Yaya, because Yaya needed assistance and Basi asked him to come. Yet it seemed that if he came to Basi expecting a savior, then he had his hopes pinned on the wrong man. That much Joy knew.

CHAPTER TWENTY-TWO

It was Friday, June 13. As usual, Yaya had awoken early. In good faith, he had decided that performing the necessary domestic chores at least could be his contribution, since he was not working and had no money. So he felt no less about himself going down on his knees to scrub the tiles in the kitchen or to clean the bathrooms and leave them sparkling.

He had taken out the trash, and was straightening out the living room at 7 a.m. when Joy got up. Basi was still dozing. She stumbled upon Yaya in the living room, too busy to see her as he picked up after Basi, who always dragged in late at night and stuffed himself with what food there was, which he gobbled with beer, leaving both the plate and beer bottles exactly where he used them.

Basi's sloppiness was another of his habits that Joy had resigned herself to, believing that most men behaved like that. And like a dutiful wife, she had made it her chore to clean up after Basi, in addition to her other household duties every morning, even on days she had to go to work. But that was before Yaya came.

Now Joy was grateful that Yaya's help relieved her, and gave her those few moments it took on work days to get herself together and have a desired peace of mind, before going to work. That helped somehow in making her leave her domestic worries behind and prepared her to deal with all the pressure on her job.

Yaya turned and saw her standing as if she had been observing him.

"Hey, early bird!" Joy said sweetly. "Ain't you supposed to be turning in your bed by now? Isn't it too early for you to be doing all this?"

"Not really, Ms. Joy," Yaya stated, kind of shy at being caught unawares, doing all what he was doing. "I always get up early." He smiled at Joy.

"My mother used to say, when you get up early, your chances of getting sick becomes slim, because you get a head start with the fresh air of the day; while those that get up late get nothing but stale air, which makes them fall sick easily." He laughed inwardly at himself for repeating such a fable.

"Quite interesting," Joy said, smiling. "I can see that you were taught good by your parents."

"I do thank God for that, Ms. Joy." Yaya arranged some cushions and stood looking at Joy. "But if you think that I get up early, you should go to my village. Over there by 6 o'clock everybody is up, even the kids. That's when people start going to their farms, and by 8 o'clock, the whole village is empty except for old people and little kids."

"Everybody farms over there?"

"In my village, yes. Practically everybody."

"They must be some hardworking people," Joy said, going towards the kitchen.

"They have to be," Yaya said, following her with a damp rag in his hand. "They don't have any choice. That's life for them," he said, rinsing the rag in a sink and squeezing it dry.

Joy shook her head knowingly. She was from a rural background herself and could relate to what Yaya was saying. On this Friday, which was her pay day, with all the assistance Yaya was giving her, Joy felt the need to give him some hope so as to boost his morale.

"Yaya," she called after him as he left the kitchen. He retracted quickly. "Tomorrow, I'm off work for the weekend. I'll be taking you shopping and we'll be out the whole day because I have some other business to take care of. I'll talk to Basi about that. But do you think you'll be up to it?"

"Sure, Ms. Joy, I am ready whenever you are. I'm here for you people."

"Good, Yaya, you're a good man. I hope things work out for you."

"They will, by God's grace," Yaya said.

"I pray so, too. Well, let me try to get out of here." Joy said putting a kettle on the stove.

"Okay, Ms. Joy, and I'll finish my tasks." Yaya went on to replace the trash bag in the can under the sink.

"Are you ready, Yaya?" Joy asked as she did a quick check through her handbag which was sitting on her lap.

"Yes, Madam," Yaya said, coming out into the living room. He was still tucking his shirt from behind.

It was 10 a.m. on Saturday, June 14. Joy was making good on the promise she made to Yaya the previous day.

"Are all the lights off?" she asked leading the way out through the kitchen.

Yaya dashed back, doing a quick inspection around the house.

When he returned, Joy was already in the garage pressing a button on the wall, and the garage door was folding upwards creating access to the drive way.

"The door is open," she said, motioning to the car.

Yaya got into the passenger seat in the mint-condition Volvo with its convertible top and ivory leather interior. He deeply inhaled the sweet raspberry fragrance which danced at his nose. As if to feel the finesse of the upholstery, while waiting for Joy, one of his hands was roving at his side, over the smooth leather cover on the bucket seat in which he sat.

Joy joined him swiftly. She briefly warmed the engine and started to reverse. Yaya was watching attentively, ready to jump out to pull down the garage door. But Joy pressed a button on her key holder which closed the door. Yaya thanked God that he didn't make a fool of himself by asking to go do what the button did. 'Oh, Yaya, you bush boy; you still got a lot to learn,' he chided himself.

A tire skidded off the curb as Joy backed into the street. She straightened the wheel and glanced at their front yard. "Poor miserable lawn," she grunted. "It's a shame. I keep telling Basi he needs to do something about our lawn, or this house is going to be swallowed by a bush."

Yaya looked across the unmanicured lawn.

"It's an eye sore!" Joy exclaimed.

As they went down the street, even Yaya felt embarrassed to realize that they had the worst looking lawn in the area. All the other lawns had lush green grass and were well-trimmed.

"How do they call that thing?" he asked Joy as they passed a gray-haired man with a mower.

Joy turned and saw a few people mostly men and boys working on their lawns.

"The things that they are pushing." Yaya pointed.

"Oh, lawnmower," Joy smiled. "We have one, too, but I don't even know if it's working. It's been so long since it's been used. Basi, the boss, he always has to call a landscape company to come cut our grass. And he does that only when the city serves us a violation ticket."

Just typical of Basi, Yaya thought.

"Excuse me for asking this question, Yaya, but do you pray, or I mean, are you a Christian?" Joy asked as she took Bissonet Road off Westheimer, heading for Sharpstown Mall.

"The answer is, yes, to your first question, Ms. Joy; indeed I pray every night. But, no, to your last question, I'm not a Christian."

"Then what religion are you?" Joy was hoping Yaya was not some idol worshipper.

"I'm a Muslim," Yaya said and he looked at Joy's face to see her reaction.

Yaya knew that America was a Judeo-Christian society. He had learned that the majority of Muslims in America were black and that the Islamic religion had been a vehicle for political radicalism by civil right leaders like Malcolm X, Elijah Muhammad and Louis Farrakhan. He knew of the earlier separatist philosophies of these leaders, all of whom had been intolerant of white supremacy and uncompromising in their demands to stifle racism and improve the black plight. And because of that, he had known since he was in Africa that Muslims were looked upon in a negative light in America! He wouldn't have been eager to profess his religion, not knowing how he would be judged. But Joy had asked, and he did not feel like lying about that.

"Oh! So you have Muslims in Africa, too?" she asked in a subdued tone.

"Yes," Yaya said, warming up to the topic. "As a matter of fact, that is the dominant religion in Africa. We have more Muslims than Christians in most African countries."

"Oh, is that true?" Joy was shocked.

"Yes, very much true," Yaya said, leaning back in his seat. "Don't forget, Ms. Joy, Egypt is in Africa and Islam entered Egypt in AD. 640 in the crusades of the Holy Prophet Mohammed. It was from Egypt that Islam was spread all over sub-Saharan Africa. That was how my people got converted. To us it's become a tradition."

"Is that right? Well, Yaya, as you know I'm a Christian, born and raised. It's been a tradition to us too, as you would say."

"Nothing wrong with that, Ms. Joy. We are praying to the same God. And I've been to churches before, too."

"Really?" Joy smiled, amazed.

"Yes. As a matter of fact, I can pray with any group as long as they are praying to the Almighty God upstairs."

"Great, then maybe you will go to church with me sometime."

"Sure," Yaya responded. "But the only thing is that I cannot promise I will go every Sunday."

"I can understand that," Joy said as she made a left turn on Gessner off Bissonet, from where they could see the tall structures of Sharpstown mall, just a few blocks away.

At the mall, Joy opted for outdoor parking and swerved around several times looking for a spot. Like most Saturdays, Sharpstown was swamped with shoppers, which showed from the cars in the parking lot. After going for a while in rounds, and having other motorists hooting and springing before her at every turn, Joy was getting exasperated. Luckily, a van pulled out of a parking space just ahead; a desperate motorist from behind raced dangerously to beat Joy to the spot.

"What...? Hey, damn fool, get out of the way!" She maneuvered and got the nose of the Volvo into the space. "I'm sorry about that, Yaya. But wasn't that annoying?"

"Yes!" he nodded, because he had shared in the frustration too. As they got out of the car, they both had their hands over their faces, to shield their eyes from a hot Houston summer sun which scorched angrily, while the air was shedding some stickiness that stuck to their skins.

"It must be 120 degrees out here," Joy screamed.

"Yes, this is hotter than even in Africa," Yaya remarked.

"It's hotter than anywhere, I would imagine," Joy said, panting as she quickly paced to escape into the mall.

Joy and Yaya entered the mall through J.C. Penneys, a big merchandise store with numerous personal and household items. The store was so large that it took two floors and occupied a large wing of the shopping complex. To go from the ground floor to the second level which had the men's section, Joy led Yaya to a gliding escalator. In Manika Kunda, as a legacy from the British, lifts could be found in many tall buildings. But a gliding escalator was something one only heard about.

When Yaya saw Joy heading for the escalator, which seemed to wait for nobody, he thought, well, today is the day. He watched as she casually walked over and was going on the thing—just like that!

And even without looking back? Yaya was tapping his feet, reflecting on how dangerous and slippery such a sliding chain of metal could be. Yet he saw that Joy was going up farther and farther. Wanting to scream, 'Hey you thing, stop or wait!' he gathered himself and did a triple jump, and staggered, to be instantly swept in a moving whirl.

Joy could have laughed. What Yaya didn't know was that she was watching him from the corners of her eyes. Coming from the country herself, she had not ridden any such escalator until she came to Houston, and so seeing Yaya all stiff and jittery, she reflected with amusement on her first experience.

"Poor Yaya," she mused, "his eyes are all popping out. But he will get used to it."

At the J.C. Penneys men's shoe section, Joy presented Yaya to a salesman and asked that they select two pairs of Yaya's choice. He quietly asked the salesman to show him the least expensive ones and was directed to a rack that had a red 'sale' sign on every shoe. He ended with two pairs, each amounting to twenty dollars after the stated forty percent discounts on both.

From J. C. Penneys, Joy took Yaya to a black-owned clothing store in the mall. Like at the shoe store, she left him with a saleswoman.

"Let him pick two pants and two shirts," she said.

Yaya who was grateful but feeling so low within to be so provided for, modestly picked two dress pants and two shirts with each costing below $10. Joy checked his selections and went to the racks and shelves. She confidently selected another pant and shirt, the prices of which flabbergasted Yaya; they were $45 each—too much money for him to spend at that time on such items.

They browsed through the mall with Joy occasionally stopping and buying things for herself, Basi, and the house. On their way out, on the first floor at the other end of the store, Joy took Yaya to a Walmart store where she bought some shorts, T-shirts, tennis shoes and toiletries for him—this was as Yaya dipped his hands into his pocket, wishing he had some money to take care of those needs.

"I have an appointment at the beauty shop," Joy said as they came out of the mall. "It's around the corner."

"I'm ready to go anywhere you want, Ms. Joy."

Incidentally, Yaya found himself comparing this woman to Pat. He decided that Pat was no match for Ms. Joy; not because of the clothes she'd just bought for him..., he reasoned, but because of her pleasant and caring attitude—like a good African sister.

"Yaya, they have some barbers here too," Joy said as she pulled up in front of a long building with a cluster of small shops. Among the various signs up the roof was a 'Starlet Beauty Shop.'

As soon as Joy parked the car, she dipped into her bag and came out with a twenty dollar bill which she ducked into Yaya's hand. "Here, you hold on to this so that if you desire a hair cut, you can pay for it."

"Thanks, Ms. Joy," Yaya said, tightly squeezing the note, over-whelmed with embarrassment. He was not used to this; yet he knew he needed a hair cut badly. "Thanks again, Ms. Joy. But aren't you spending too much on me?"

"Oh, Yaya, just forget that," Joy said, flapping her hands as she came out of the car.

'Starlet' was an all-black beauty shop, Yaya noticed. As Joy had stated, there were some barbers there too, and he thought the place could as well be called a barber shop, for it was divided in two, with barbers on one side and hairdressers on the other. They had a common waiting room which was where Joy and Yaya sat after signing in two different registers that were labeled, 'barbers' and 'hairdressers.'

The common topic at the saloon was an upcoming Juneteenth celebration. Everybody was excited. There were talks of going to amusement parks, having parties and barbecuing. The hairdressers and barbers and some customers were exchanging information as to what was going to be happening and where. The sense of celebration was as thick in the air as if the event was happening right then. Even Yaya didn't miss it.

"What is Juneteenth?" he asked Joy who was seated next to him, still waiting to be called in the slowed pace caused by all the excitement.

"Oh, it's a celebration that marks the day Texas slaves were informed that they were free people," Joy informed him.

Yaya became interested. There was Black History Month in February when he was two months old in the country. He only heard of that on TV. But this Juneteenth sounded like a big cultural event for African-Americans, judging from the happy faces of the people in the salon. He felt good.

He imagined Juneteenth to be a festive rallying call for all African-Americans; to bring out the positives in their relationship with one another and to unify them as they reflect on what their forebears went through. Like the Jewish Passover, yes, the Jewish Passover. He'd written a paper about the Passover in a Sociology class, as an example of the principle of symbolic interaction in society. He recalled being fascinated at the rekindled spirit of a common heritage, cause, and values, held dear by most Jews as could be seen during the Passover.

Every year, Jewish families congregate for about one week to celebrate the Passover—*Haggadah,* as Orthodox Jews call it—which commemorates the sufferings of their ancestors and their exodus from bondage in Egypt to the promised land. The Passover period is marked by religious services, family reunions and communal kosher dinners—from food prepared in traditional Jewish recipes—which they eat as a history of the people is handed from the old to the young, thereby enriching and unifying them all.

This Juneteenth too, Yaya thought, must be of that sort, observed by all African-Americans as a commemoration of the struggles of their forebears. Yaya grinned. *Yes, obviously, a great event of communal interaction, to remind them of a common background, with pointers as to where they've been, where they are now, and where they should be going.*

As an African sitting in that crowd with such sentiments floating, he reflected on his historical knowledge of slavery, on the vulnerability and naiveté of Africans in days of slavery, and the exploitation and pains that the experience entailed. He judged that candidly, even more than the Holocaust, there had been no such indignity and torture of humans as blacks experienced in slavery.

Yet, Yaya now felt happier than he had ever been since he got to America, because of this Juneteenth and the spirit it invoked among the people in the salon. He linked himself instantly. *Indeed.., they are part of us Africans—our long lost people and even relatives.*

"When does this celebration come?" he asked Joy.

"It is next weekend. It's celebrated every year on June 19th."

"I bet that is a special day."

"Sure it is, at least for all blacks in Texas."

"But I thought all African-Americans celebrated that," Yaya pressed.

"Didn't you hear me?" Joy barked absent-mindedly. "I said it marks the day Texas slaves learned that they were free. Before that, other folks had been free, long time."

"Oh!" Yaya said in low voice, and started rubbing his forehead. He thought, *I guess my imagination ran wild; but still, if it serves as a day of black heritage in Texas that creates awareness and evokes pride in being black.*

Soon enough for Joy, she was beckoned to come over by her girlish and giggling hairdresser. After a few minutes, Yaya, too, was called to the barber's chair by a smiling, bearded man.

"Can you drive Yaya," Joy asked as they stepped out of the salon.

"Yes, Ms. Joy, I can try, but I don't have a license."

"But can you drive? Or, have you ever driven in America?"

"Yes, I drove a few times in Philadelphia when I was with Sidi and Pat. They taught me how to drive."

What Yaya was actually saying was that he drove when he was being taught. But he had never driven a car by himself as he made Joy think. And although he could start a car, move it and stop, his hands still weren't steady on the steering wheel, and he had problems with changing lanes. But Joy thought otherwise, and believing him, she decided to risk giving him the key to drive them home; even as he said he didn't have a driving license.

"This is the key that opens the door, and this one starts the ignition. Here, Yaya," she said giving him her key ring. "It's all yours. And now it's my turn to lay back and enjoy the ride."

Yaya licked his lips and felt worried without wanting to show it. Oh, boy! What has his mouth gotten him into now? Such empty bluff! Why didn't he tell Ms. Joy that he was not really a competent driver, but just somebody that was on his way to becoming one? Now, he must deliver. Or Ms. Joy would consider him a liar. And he couldn't afford to have her thinking of him like that.

In his predicament, Yaya silently walked with Joy to the car. He was holding separately the key that opened the doors. As they got to the glistening Volvo 850, he ran forward to open the passenger door for Joy. Then he got in the driver's seat and prayed silently to The Almighty Allah asking that nothing wrong happened. Next, he fumbled with the keys lost about which started the car.

Joy intervened. "It's that long one with the black bound," she said, pointing a finger at the dangling keys.

"Thanks," said Yaya, sheepishly.

Since the car had an automatic transmission, all he had to do was leave the gear in park, crank the engine while stepping with his right foot gently and gradually on the accelerator or gas pedal to get the motor going; after which he was to press the brake fully with the same foot, and engage the gear in reverse; because he needed to back out. Then he was to gradually release the brake whereupon the car would go backwards until he had room to go forward. And then he would step on the brake and put the gear in drive. Next he would switch his foot to the gas pedal, pressing gradually as he saw fit, to pick up a desired speed. While all such facts would come instinctively to an experienced driver, they were a novelty to Yaya, and they played hide-and-seek in his head.

With the key in the ignition, and Yaya ready to start the car, he cleared his throat with a forced cough. Meanwhile, Joy was preoccupied with receipts from the day's spendings, which she held with both hands over her open handbag on her lap.

Crekh-crekh-crekkh-ccrrekkh-crekhh. Yaya went with the ignition. *Crekh-crekh-crekkh-ccrrekkh-crekhh, creeekkkh.*

Joy looked up.

"Press some gas first, Yaya," she said.

Yaya embarrassingly repositioned himself on the steering wheel. He pedaled the accelerator, and cranked again. The engine ignited.

He kept pressing and pressing on the accelerator which hummed and hummed the motor. The car was ready to go, but Yaya was still humming it.

"Yaya, slow down on the gas, and get the car going," Joy said. She had suspected that he probably was not comfortable with what he was doing. Yet she decided to give him a chance anyway.

He released the gas and stepped on the brake as he engaged the gear in reverse. By now Joy had focused her full attention on him like a driving instructor. She guided him into the traffic, which on that Saturday afternoon was busier and crazier than a Texas expressway at rush hour. There were cars hooting from behind and aggressively overtaking them, while Yaya held tight onto the steering, going tortoise-like.

"Pick up speed, Yaya," Joy urged.

"I am," was Yaya's reply; yet the car wasn't going any faster. He was licking his lips rapidly and would complain to Joy when he was being overtaken. "Ms. Joy, you see these drivers? They are rough. I have to be very careful with them!"

Joy was laughing inside to the point of suffocation.

"Com'on Yaya, you can do it," she encouraged him when she got her breath.

"Thanks, Ms. Joy, thanks. I'm trying. Do you see me?"

"Yes," Joy said, and thought she was seeing alright, though she couldn't tell if he was doing, *you-know-what* in his pants.

"You're doing well, Yaya. You're doing very well. Just stay in your lane and look ahead of you, and don't worry about all these people behind you."

That encouragement did it for him as he smoothly chauffeured the car from then on, to Joy's total amazement. It seemed, all that he had learned in his previous driving practices, suddenly came to him. He even changed lanes a few times and drove the car without a single incident straight home.

Yaya, in his room, was elated that day. He had gotten some new clothes. He looked smart with his new American hair cut, and he had driven a car through Houston. Yet he wondered how was he going to pay for all those favors? Because he couldn't just be taking and taking, without giving something in return. But how was he going to square this deal?

He was sitting next to his new clothes spread on his bed and feeling grateful towards Ms. Joy, but sadly thinking of times he had the upper hand; when he would go on spending sprees before visiting Taényadu and Wuyadu, to put clothes on the backs of some naked children; something he had enjoyed doing, even as he was asked by some of the indigent parents whose children benefited if he ever got tired of giving.

Yet here he was, Yaya reflected grievously, now in such a shape that somebody had to see fit to clothe him. As he thought of Ms. Joy, all that she was doing for him, he cheered up. Quite fantastic! But was it not getting to be too much, especially as he had no means of paying back? And what could he do to make her happy in return?

Joy had thrown some potatoes in the oven, and had some broccoli, carrots and sweet beans boiling, while she fried some sirloin steaks. That was dinner for them. She didn't feel like doing any elaborate cooking. In fact, she wished they had eaten something while they were out. But as it was, they would have to make do with what she was cooking. Basi was gone anyway, and whenever he came back, Joy only hoped he didn't expect a wonder dish. As for Yaya, she knew he would eat anything. Poor soul, he never complained. But dinner was late. It was 5:35. She was hoping that by 6 o'clock, food would be ready.

While Joy was in the kitchen, busy, Yaya walked into the living room, very pleased. He had gotten a long and nice shower and had changed into his brand new shorts and T-shirt. He heard Joy in the kitchen and went over to her.

Joy was lifting some well-seasoned and brown steaks from the frying pan on the stove when Yaya came smiling generously. Standing there in his shorts and with his new hair cut and that happy face, Joy gaped, smiled, then laid the meat on the plate next to her and stepped back to look at him. She thought that if she had met Yaya down the street and hadn't spoken to him, she would've mistaken him for a *soul* brother from the south side of Houston.

She felt good to see Yaya so happy. She had spent close to $200 on him that day. But that was nothing compared to the satisfaction she was having to see him so pleased. Like a true giver at heart, she felt he deserved it. Joy rationalized that life had been nice enough for her to warrant such kindness.

To think of the humble home she came from, and the mighty house she was living in, or the luxurious car she was driving, all out of good fortune. Because fate had her to marry rich. And with all that luck, she thought, why wouldn't she do some little thing to brighten a flustered young man's life, particularly when she could do so without hurting? In fact, reflecting on her deeds of the day, she had such a natural high that a drug addict would envy, from seeing how she had affected Yaya's countenance and bearing.

What Joy did not know, however, was that Yaya had his own plan of making her happy. He said nothing about it. After dinner that evening, they watched television together in a state of mutual contentment. The movie playing involved cops, crime, drugs, and prostitution. Unlike the criminals who lived in plush penthouses, drove fanciful cars and glittered with heavy gold chains and rings, the poor police on the beat drove average cars and seemed like hardworking people.

Yaya noted the contrast. Since Sidi's discussion with him about how mainstream media subconsciously debased blacks, he had inadvertently started examining every situation on TV to see how black people were depicted.

"Tell me, Ms. Joy, in this movie, all the cops are white people, but most of the criminals and prostitutes are black. Why is that so?"

"Typecasting, Yaya. That's Hollywood for you. They reflect the general American mentality. When it is evil, it is black and when it is good, it is white."

"Indeed?" asked Yaya. "I didn't believe it could be so much. By showing these flashy criminals living gloriously and dealing in drugs, aren't they making them into role models or reinforcing negative stereotypes? "

"But they'll claim that doesn't stigmatize blacks," Joy said. "I don't pay them no mind."

Yaya thought of his college days, of an African-American professor back home who openly stated that he never intended to return to America, because he claimed he had dealt with enough racism while growing up to last him a life time. He was a professor at the English department who was greatly disturbed by the maligning of the black image in English language. His examples were words like: blackmail, black Monday, blackball, blacklist, black magic, black market, etc., with each of the words having a negative connotation. Yet, the professor would say, "There are words like: white Christmas, white lie, or even white collar crime, to cajole and go easy, or make acceptable what might otherwise be undesirable." He told Joy about the professor.

"Yes, I know. As if the word 'white' is supposed to make everything positive. But, Yaya, do you really have Americans over there who have decided to stay and never come back?"

"Of course, Ms. Joy, plenty of them, both whites and blacks. In fact, there are many white people from all over the world who have just decided to call it home over there. Some say they like the climate and the simple life, or have fallen in love with the place."

"Well.., well! My.., my! When Basi said he would never go back, it only made me happy. Because from what I've heard of Africa, and the pictures we see here on TV, I thought it would be a deathtrap to think of going to live there."

"No, Ms. Joy, it's not as bad as it's painted from here. True, we have a long way to go, and there is a lot of poverty and hardship among the people, as expected anywhere in the Third World; but also there's been some development and modernization everywhere in Africa. In fact, if you go to cities like Abidjan, Accra, Abuja, Lagos, and Nairobi, you would be proud of black Africa; because those cities can match many Western cities in most facets of sophistication. And as for the social life, one has the option to go traditional or modern, or half-and-half like I did."

"That sounds hopeful. You know, some of us don't know that. What we see here on TV about Africa, we don't like, and that's what most of us go by."

"But of course, Ms. Joy. That is so because when some Western journalists and tourists go to Africa, all they do is document the negative aspects of the societies. Some go to the suburbs and the most undeveloped areas precisely to take pictures of half-naked women, to show as proof of how backward and primitive Africans are; because nowhere else in the world would one see women going about in public with dissipated breasts hanging out."

Joy partly frowned and partly laughed.

"Truly, Ms. Joy, some even take pictures of people that they stumble on, in the suburbs, who know no better than easing themselves behind houses and on the road sides. And the illiterate and ignorant people seem to enjoy having such pictures of themselves taken too—especially when it's a white person doing it!"

"That's a shame, Yaya."

"I know..., but what can one do? Some people don't realize that it's only themselves that they degrade by carrying on like that. And Ms. Joy, they are so unsuspecting, and such ready prey for all sorts of exploitation."

"But can't your leaders do something about that?"

"You're kidding. In Manika Kunda, to stop tourism and exposure? They are part of the scheme. For them, exhibiting the ignorance and poverty of the people is a perfect case to get sympathy and foreign aid."

"What it sounds to me is that the people need help, or some kind of reorientation and a mass literacy campaign."

"Sure, Ms. Joy, if our leaders agree that that's a priority. Some would rather squander all the money to enrich themselves."

"Well, it will catch up with them," Joy said.

"Of course, they always pay for it eventually. But how does that help the poor people?"

"That sounds like a catch-22 and a no-winner game, Yaya. But wait till your people come around to demanding accountability, and see if things won't change. That's how we keep our leaders straight in America."

"Please, Ms. Joy, don't compare your American system to ours; you guys are very efficient, organized and productive. We know your political system is the ideal and we've tried to copy it. But we don't follow the rules and have no patience for it, as if we are going to wake up the next morning and have something as good."

"It didn't happen overnight here, either, Yaya. People were committed to seeing that it worked and they still are improving it." Joy stood up. "Yaya, I've got to go wash and set my hair, I should be going to church in the morning."

"Okay, Ms. Joy. I'm ready to call it a night too."

"Sleep tight then," Joy said, going towards her room.

"Sure, I will, good night, Ms. Joy." Yaya got up and arranged the cushions and turned off the lights. He passed through the bathroom and had an ablution and went to his room and prayed.

Then he got his diary to enter the events of the day: Saturday, June 14—*Joy really impressed me with her generosity today. She took me shopping and spent about $200 just on me. And thanks to her, I went to a barber shop and had a haircut today, my first in months.*

Yaya closed the diary and laid thinking about Ms. Joy, such a nice woman. He felt it was funny, the way things work. Because Sidi seemed like a better husband but had a *terrible* wife, while it was vice versa with Basi and Ms. Joy.

Yaya looked at his watch on the nightstand. It was ten to ten. Basi was still not in yet. But who said he was coming anyway? Wasn't it Saturday night? The boss, he would come in after 2 a.m. and leave by daybreak; only to sell insurance policies? Yaya couldn't answer that question, so he covered himself and slept.

CHAPTER TWENTY-THREE

Basi woke up at 6:30 a.m. realizing that it was Sunday, and that Joy would be up soon. Madam Holy, he thought, and decided to leave immediately, because he had an issue to resolve. He always did with Wendy. She was a 23-year-old, long-legged strawberry blonde with flashing sapphire eyes, a thin waist and a 5'9" athletic physique. Basi called Wendy 'Trouble,' because of how she bewitched him, like an obsession, and it was a war he had to win.

Three weeks ago, on a Saturday, Basi and Robert, a coworker, had gotten together on a night out. Robert was 27, white, solidly built with a professional appearance and about 5'11" tall. He was the accountant on their job. Like Basi, Robert was married, but unlike Basi who had more money than common sense, Robert was known for his precarious habits and peculiar fantasies.

He had seen the lust in Basi's eyes as he looked at the white girls on the job and felt sorry for him. The girls were of different interest and he knew Basi was not going to get any of them, short of making a nuisance of himself, as he had already succeeded. Because they were old-fashioned girls, and spoilsports, who laughed at Basi behind his back: *"That ignorant African with the hots for white girls who thinks he can just buy somebody with his money. He would have to bring his whole African wealth to America, and even then he won't get the time of day..."*

Sometimes, Robert had to laugh too. However, as was typical of him, he decided to lead Basi to a sleazy joint to fulfill his fantasy.

It was one of Robert's hangouts whenever his wife went away on her many conferences. The place was a striptease bar where the girls who went on stage seemed to shave their pubic hair so that their male patrons could take a good look.

Most men that came here like Robert were either bored out of their wits, or were voyeurs at heart who harbored unfilled sexual fantasies. So they came and got teased by feminine nudity as they fed their eyes, and shamefully sat with erections, and screamed for what they couldn't get; or if they did, they would pay a price that would bleed them cold, as Basi found out.

Wendy was in the middle of a *Triple-X* show and Basi was sitting in a crowd of drunks, most of whom were sexually aroused from watching nude female dancers on stage and around them; as the stark naked girls flaunted their nudity, and rubbed on the drunken heads to bilk them of their money.

Wendy was at her best, making easy money, with all eyes on her, crazy and yelping for her baby-doll body. She decided, 'I will give the perverts a run for their money, and pick a fool, too—to see me through my present difficulties!' Her mind was made up. She was going to pull a stunt that would say: 'Here comes Wendy to Texas!'

She was swaying sinfully to *You Are Not Going To Get This* by En Vogue. Then she ripped open her short dress with one stroke of the zipper from the top to the bottom. She held the dress open to show a scanty bra and g-string and her naked flesh, as she said silently, *'Feed your eyes weirdoes at Wendy, daughter of Eve.'*

She threw the dress off her shoulders, swaying seductively to the music. Wendy's act that she planned was on her mind. She went to where it was most bright on stage and turned and bowed so that her hands were touching her toes, with her butt in a g-string pointed at the audience and wriggling. She swayed sensuously in that position and yanked her g-string abruptly to one side, to reveal what was most hidden. Instantly, she was greeted with several catcalls. All the while, Wendy was looking at the audience between her legs seeking her target fool.

She got up like she was in the privacy of her bedroom and pulled off her bra, to more catcalls. Hear the perverts, she thought, as if they've never seen a pair of round tits before. Breaking her shoulders to the music, she swayed her chest bouncing her enormous milky-toned breasts with its rose-like pointed tips. Smiling, she came to the edge of the stage, over the jittery and longing crowd, as she poked her tongue out and went wild, cuddling and pulling on her breasts, like she was going to pluck them off and give them to the 'perverts.'

She went back to the center of the stage. The music had changed; it was now, *She Works Hard For Her Money* by Donna Summer. Dancing to that, she stepped out of the g-sting and stood with her legs open and started stroking herself between the thighs. Many in the audience applauded and stood up in riotous acclaim. Wendy decided now was the time for her plan.

Amid frantic catcalls, she walked across the stage to an ecstatic black man in a suit and tie, her target, among a multitude of white males in t-shirts and jeans—a type that had almost destroyed her life! She pulled Basi up there and gave him a bottle of oil which she asked him to pour and rub over her naked body. Then she laid flat on her back. As Basi dallied on her less urgent areas, she grabbed his hand and led it between her legs. "Rub it in!" she commanded.

Basi couldn't believe this. This was the most bizarre sex scene he had ever been in. Yet his ego was at full blast, to be picked from among that crowd especially being black among so many whites? He poured some more oil and got both hands working. While at it, he looked around and saw Robert grinning but red in the face, which Basi interpreted as envy. And he thought there was envy in the eyes of all the other men; all of whom wanted to be in his place. This was just like when he was in Manika Kunda, where everybody knew that his parents were rich, and highly respected and envied him. Basi's adrenaline was flooding from all the attention now on him and this devilishly beautiful girl. He was having erratic ecstasy. Hmmm! This was a special day. He looked into the woman's sparkling eyes which heightened his ecstasy.

"Yes, yes, Chief, you stud," Wendy was saying. "Be my prince. I will be your love slave, forever..."

Was Basi hearing right? Wendy had her eyes on him, bewitching him and evidently in need of him. He talked to her afterwards and learned that she was from New York. It was her first week in Houston and her first night on the job. Basi decided he had to have her. She made no bones about it. She was the type that would say, "You pour the wine; I will captain the ship."

In no time, Basi found her an apartment and furnished it. He believed the woman was in love with him and needed him as he needed her. He decided he would change her to be a better woman. For as beautiful as she was and being white, too, that was just what he needed for his prestige, like Dr. Dullah and his wife. In fact, Dr. Dullah's wife was neither a blonde nor beautiful as this doll-like angel here. Yes. And now, he will show all the other Africans in Houston and the whole of U.S. that they might all be in America, but they were not all equal.

But Wendy wouldn't leave her sleazy life, Basi lamented; thinking about their fight last night about her touching other men when he was bringing her home. So he decided he had to go see her early this morning before Joy woke up; since he now divided his time between the two of them and his job. As for Yaya—he could go to hell—Basi hissed contemplating. That was as far as he cared now!

When Joy got up that Sunday morning, June 15, she had nothing but church on her mind. Basi was gone, but she wasn't even thinking about him. For one, on such days when she prepared for service, he would be after her and pestering her with talks about how she acted on a Sunday morning like a party freak on a Saturday evening, getting ready to go clubbing.

She had styled her hair, immediately after bathing, and had picked a dress, and done a touch-up on her nails. She was now fixing some oatmeal to have with boiled eggs, just so she would have something in her stomach. Sunday services were a two-hour stretch, or longer with this new pastor, and then there was Bible school, and all the singing and praises to shout to the Lord. And for her, all that couldn't go well on an empty stomach.

Yaya had been up too. He had done the living room and thrown out the trash, after which it was the bathrooms; he was through with the one in his room and that for guests. He was now waiting for Joy to get dressed and leave, so he would do the one in the master bedroom. Meanwhile, he washed his hands and came into the living room. Joy was at the dining room table swallowing oatmeal.

"Slow down, Yaya. Is everything alright?"

"Sure, Ms. Joy, I was just thinking of cutting the grass in the yard this morning. Where can I find the lawnmower?"

"But, Yaya, I don't even know if that thing works."

"I'd like try it and see."

"It's in the den. But are you sure you want to do that this morning?"

"Sure, Ms. Joy."

"Okay, let me get you the key." Joy went into the bedroom and came out with her key ring. They went to a room in the back patio which was full of broken appliances, old boxes and various household junk.

"That's it," Joy pointed to a green dust-coated equipment, like a little generator on wheels with two long metal bars standing over it from the sides. "Yaya, I don't know how this thing works, or if it works at all. I wish Basi were here to try it with you."

"I will handle it," Yaya said matter-of-factly. He got the lawnmower out of the room and in the sunlight, he saw that it was fairly new, even though it was dirty with dust and mud, with patches of rust starting to sink in the paint. "Is there any literature on it?"

"I think so. It should be in that little box on the top shelf."

Yaya got the box, like a four-gallon milk carton, and found that it was full of manuals of various appliances and 'how-to' books on: 'How to fix minor plumbing problems. How to add a cabinet anywhere in your house;' etc. He fished out a book that had a picture of the lawnmower on the front cover.

"Well, Ms. Joy, this is all I need," he said, looking up at her, knowing that she had to go to church.

"I hope you can use it, Yaya."

"I will try. And please pray for me at church."

"Sure, I'll remember you in my prayers."

As soon as Joy left for Church, Yaya went and cleaned the bathroom in the master bedroom. Then he had oatmeal and made two sandwiches from four slices of wheat bread, boiled eggs and mayonnaise. He drank that down with a cup of coffee and a glass of orange juice, and felt he was ready for the grass and hoped the lawnmower worked.

He went to the backyard and sat at the edge of the tiled porch, pulling the lawnmower close to him. He browsed through the manual, dusted the mower, and tried it. It roared. He fiddled with it some more, and felt comfortable moving it as directed in the manual. He then went to the front yard.

In an old white T-shirt and blue shorts with tennis shoes on, Yaya's dark lean body glittered as that June morning sun rose and glared on him, while he restlessly put the lawnmower to task. For somebody who knew only the machete for cutting grass, using such a modern device was fun. He relished every minute of it.

There is nothing to this, he observed congruously—*because the white man has just about made everything easy! Really, to think that to cut grass in America, all it takes is to push something like a toy, and you are cutting grass?* —Yaya wished he'd known sooner about this lawnmower, and he would have been on this task long ago. For it was another way of killing time and taking care of his boredom.

The yard exhilarated Joy, even from the street as she came back from church. It was neat and trimmed as if it had had a professional face lift.

Quite a man, she grunted about Yaya. When she entered the living room, he was sitting in the recliner and rocking, with basketball on TV. "Thanks, Chief."

"You're welcome, Ms. Joy." He picked the remote control up and lowered the volume of the TV.

"Thanks for doing the lawn, Yaya."

"Oh, there was nothing to it. It was fun."

"That was a great job though, I appreciate it. And you did it so fast? Even the professionals take a whole day out there to do what you did. I nearly missed the house."

Yaya got up. "But there was nothing to it, Ms. Joy. That was just ordinary grass. You should go to Manika Kunda and visit my village, Taényadu, where huge and thick tree trunks are challenged and downed with just ordinary cutlass. Here you have the lawnmower for even grass. That makes everything easy."

"So you didn't have any problem with the mower?"

"Not at all. After I read the instructions in the manual, it was easy to use. I wish our people had things like that in Africa; there would be a lot of use for them."

"Well, with time they will. But, Yaya, thanks so much. You just don't know how pleased you've made me by mowing that lawn."

"It was fun, Ms. Joy. I even had company. One woman who was jogging stopped and talked with me. She gave me her telephone number. A white lady, she was nice."

"You better be careful with that."

"I will, Ms. Joy. I was reciprocating the friendship."

At six o'clock in the evening of the Sunday that Yaya mowed the lawn, Joy asked him if he cared to cruise through Houston. The sun was down and there was a mildness in the air from a quick rain that came with a suddenness not unusual in Houston. The rain had canceled the hot humid weather pleasantly for a kinder one which lured outside activities. Joy had the bug. She had talked Yaya into it and was awaiting him to join her so they could leave.

As soon as she came from church that afternoon, between twelve and one o'clock, she had quickly prepared a meal that turned out to be quite excellent. It comprised of beef stew, wild rice, sweet beans and fruit salad. As expected, Basi was not around for dinner. But Joy had a pleasant dinner with Yaya. After that she had left for her room to take a nap. She had just awakened with this urge to take a ride through Southwest Houston.

"I'm set," Yaya declared, hopping sportily in his new white tennis shoes, white shorts and white T-shirt.

"Let's go," Joy declared, standing and adjusting the tight legs of her shorts, which had crept up her hefty thighs when she was sitting. She had on a pair of sandals and a matching cotton blouse and shorts, of mostly yellow with multiple red flowery patterns.

As they went, from the way Joy was sitting or because of what she wore, her shorts had come far up her thighs, showing some smooth vibrant flesh. That sight made Yaya uncomfortable and embarrassed, because she was so exposed and so close, especially when she was not his woman.

Although educated and a *modern* man, yet stuck with relics of traditional African thinking, Yaya instinctively reflected on how he would have preferred Ms. Joy, in such situation, to be better dressed or not be so revealing—because the eye is mischievous. The eye has its own will and tends to feed itself. No wonder the Mandinkas insist that their women dress properly and be covered from their necks, if not their heads, right down to their ankles. But of course, Westerners thought different. And everybody knew that with the Western influence now in Manika Kunda, many girls and even a few rebellious women wore miniskirts and what they liked.

The leg and thigh exhibition among women in America was something though, Yaya noted. Even as they drove down Westheimer, there were women in shorts all over. And at one of the bus stops that they passed, he saw among the small crowd, a woman who was parading in flimsy shorts with the naked cheeks of her butt swaying and hanging as if they had no business being covered. And yet it seemed normal to the people around.

"Just the American way," he said to himself, wondering who was he to question the American way? So, if Ms. Joy wanted to indulge in that near-nakedness, it was okay. But he would ward his eyes off her smooth glowing thighs.

Joy had the top of the executive-style Volvo flung back. She was now cruising on South Gessner at 30 mph, going to West Belfort. Then she was going to make a left turn and come to Fondren, which she would take to Westheimer and back home. The car stereo was on FM 102, one of Houston's hottest rap and soul stations, to which she was humming and moving her body.

It was obvious to Yaya that Joy was immensely enjoying herself and almost oblivious of him. It pleased him to see her in such high spirits. She was like he had never seen before, girlish, and with a carefree expression on her face, as if she didn't have a thing to worry about. Looking at that silky smooth face and her big gentle eyes which laughed, with her perm hair resting in a curl on her shoulders and bouncing with the wind as they went, Yaya felt a fresh wave of warmness towards her, giving no thought to anything whatsoever.

Yet inexplicably, he started looking at Joy's bounteous breasts and their pointed ends which pressed so hard against her thin blouse, like they were going to burst through. And by no decision of his, the crotch of his pants, which had been flat, was now bloated, and acting erratic like a sack holding a wayward snake. He felt shocked and closed his legs, leaned forward like he suddenly got interested in watching how the wires on the electric poles connect.

He quickly castigated himself for his devious reaction—such unmanly thing—and thanked his stars that Ms. Joy, who was humming with a smile lurking at the corners of her mouth, was too preoccupied with the music on the radio to notice his lusty trance.

Nonetheless, he silently prayed that God should push away such thoughts as he just had, making him look at Ms. Joy as a sex object, when he had nothing like that on his mind.

In his sixth month now in America, sex and women had been nowhere on his priority list. They were non-existent. Of course, there had been one casual affair within his first month in Philadelphia. It started from the night of his welcome party in the glow of his success in making it to America.

But things changed as he went into his second month in the country; and as reality started blinking its ugly beam, with hurdles conceptualizing in the way of his dreams. That took his mind off any relationship he could develop, until he got a grip on life in America.

Thus he simply claimed to the lady he was seeing that he could not emotionally get involved with her because he had a woman back home whom he was expecting to join him. He knew it was not the best news to tell somebody who was looking at him as a prospect, but he could not see himself being comfortable in any relationship with all that he was facing. This was why he was surprised at himself, at his reaction to Ms. Joy's bare thighs, after she had been so kind to him. He prayed again that such thoughts should stay away from him, because they did nothing but brew stuff that could ruin a harmonious relationship.

When Yaya and Joy got home, Basi was already there. He was on the couch, wearing a light-blue pajamas with red trim. His chest and pot belly were bare, and he had a glass of what smelled like brandy and coke on ice cubes by his side. The stereo was letting out soft rock. He barely stared at them when they walked in.

"The Chief is in," Yaya saluted.

"Hi, Basi," Joy said.

"Hi."

Joy rolled her eyes, and wrenched her nose at the strong scent of the liquor. She was not pleased with the way Basi greeted her either.

"Did you see the lawn?" she asked.

"I sure did. Who was that?"

"Yaya, of course," Joy announced with her chin up as she rolled her eyes.

The way she answered his question sent Basi laughing. He raised his legs up on the couch and sipped his drink. He was amused that Joy was flaunting Yaya's prowess at him, to spite him for neglecting such mundane chore. Yet Yaya's effort impressed him. *But of course, Yaya is a bush boy, and that is what they are good for.* "Thanks a million, Yaya, for saving me from that task. You did an excellent job!"

"It was my pleasure, Basi. There was nothing to it."

Basi looked at Yaya. He seemed different and slightly groomed, with his hair even and his mustache trimmed. *The bush boy is getting civilized, thanks to Joy.*

Yaya sat on the loveseat and reached for the Sunday paper, still folded. He got the front page from the bundle and started scanning that. "Oh, Basi, before I forget, Sidi called this morning. He said I should thank you on his behalf for all that you guys are doing for me."

"So, how is he doing?"

"He said he was doing fine."

"What time did he call?"

"Around eleven this morning. Ms. Joy was out too; she had gone to church."

"I see. Your Ms. Joy and her church. Sometimes, I think she is holier than the Pope himself. I haven't seen anybody that is as church crazy as her."

"She is a good woman," Yaya said.

"I know," Basi replied getting up. "Man, I've got to go to bed now. I will be getting up early in the morning. We have an early meeting on the job tomorrow."

"Okay. Good night then, Basi. Please don't forget about keeping your ears open for me." Yaya picked up the voluminous newspaper and went inside too. He decided to meantime get his diary and do his entries. Sunday June15:—*I met Barbara, nice white woman. She said she was in the Navy and had been to Africa. I hope to let her know my situation. And oh, I knew today what makes Joy happy, mowing the lawn. I'll keep doing it every Sunday, so I'll stay in her good book.*

For Monday, June 16, Yaya had done all his morning tasks and was sitting in the living room. Since daybreak he had been debating about calling Barbara, the lady who stopped by while he was mowing the lawn yesterday.

Of course, Yaya believed that since Barbara was white, should she accept to help him, that would be his American problems solved. He tried to recall his impressions about her. A charming middle-aged woman, she seemed down to earth, caring and highly intelligent. He decided to approach her on an intellectual level. Because he considered himself educated, and an elite in Manika Kunda, so even though he might lower himself to be of service— and to survive—that was no reason for him to present himself any less than he really was.

What would he tell Barbara? The truth about his immigration status and his need for a job? Or should he rather not appear so desperate but still make her know his need for a job? He could say he only needed something temporary while visiting in the U.S., something to do for a month or two; which was his plan now, until this thing about Grandma Fatu resolved itself. After that he would go home to the safe feeling of being at home and not having to run from anybody.

He went to the nightstand in his bedroom and got the piece of paper that had Barbara's telephone number. He looked at his watch. It was 10 a.m. He dialed Barbara's number. The recorder came on: "You have reached ...."

"Hello, hi Madam, how are you doing this morning." Yaya thought it was the lady on the phone.

".....at the sound of the beep, please leave your name and telephone number. I will return your call as soon as I return."

"This is Yaya, the man you met yesterday, Do you remember—?"

"Paiiine...!" The beeping sound came on and the tape started rolling.

What? Yaya realized that he had been talking to a machine. He laid down the receiver and felt stupid, because he should have said something. But, he was not expecting to talk to a machine and didn't know what to say to create the impression he wanted to make by speaking in person. He decided he would call again and would be prepared.

Yaya called at noon but the recorder came on again. This time he said who he was, where they had met and left his telephone number. Then he went and stood at the window to see as far up the street as he could. A police car passed the house; there was always one going up and down the street.

Usually when he went for a stroll in the afternoons, he was the only person walking in that quiet neighborhood, and the police seemed to keep up with him every time he stepped out. He didn't feel like it today, so he went about his mundane activities in the house. He took everything out of the refrigerator and cleaned every corner of it. Next, he cleaned the oven until it sparkled. Feeling his hands sore from the mowing yesterday and the scrubbing today, he decided that was enough cleaning for the day.

For breakfast, he ate some corn flakes with milk and washed the bowl. Then he picked up a copy of *ESSENCE*, one of Joy's magazines. He read through it briefly and went to get his diary. *Monday, June 16:* There was nothing yet to enter. But he reflected that it was only *thirteen* days to June 29, which made Grandma Fatu's death two complete years. Already he knew that would be on a Sunday, less than two weeks more to come.

Joy came from work and went to her CPA class, like she did on Monday, Wednesday and Friday evenings. Basi had come and gone too, in a hurry as always.

At 6:30 p.m. the phone rang. Yaya ran to answer it.

"Hello!"

"This is Barbara Rogers. I'm trying to reach Yaya LaTalé."

"Yes, Madam, this is him. Is this Ms. Barbara Rogers? How are you doing today?"

"I'm fine. How can I help you?"

That quick? Not so quick, Yaya thought.

"I'm the guy you met yesterday mowing the lawn."

"I know. You've already told me that on the recorder."

"Yes, okay. Well, I'm from Africa and I'm new here. But..., I'm confined to the house, most times. Yes. And this can be challenging when you don't know the place; you are not mobile and have nothing to do worthwhile."

Barbara almost laughed and wondered what she had to do with that. "And how can I help you, Yaya?"

"Madam, I'm looking for something like a part-time job while I'm here. That is, so that I'll stop sitting in the house all day long. I can take any job or do any work except if it's technical. I have a degree from home in general studies but I don't mind taking even a menial job."

Foreigners! Barbara thought. "Yaya?"

"Yes, Madam."

"But you sound qualified above menial jobs. Look in the papers, there are a lot of good jobs around."

"I'm doing that, but no leads yet. And I have no car and don't know the place. I just need somewhere to start, even if something temporary." He left out his paper problems.

Barbara reflected. She was expected to be a magician on her job at the YMCA, due to the tightening of budget everyday and dependence on volunteers. And when there were no volunteers, she carried the burden. As athletic director, she had been coaching two little league soccer teams since spring. Yet she needed some free time this summer but didn't want the kids to lose out on the activity. They needed a soccer coach. If no volunteer came up, she had to hire somebody, even if at minimum wage.

"Yaya, do you know about soccer?"

"Yes, Madam!" Yaya got enthusiastic. "I've played soccer all my life, from primary school throughout, till college. And I've played all positions."

"Do you know the FIFA rules well?"

"Yes, Madam, we played by FIFA rules, and I know them very well."

"Good. But really, I cannot promise you anything. Let me find out about something on my job and I'll call you if we need you."

"Thank you very much, Madam. But how soon will I hear from you? I know soccer inside out, both as a player in all positions and as an officer, like a referee, a linesman, or—."

"Okay! Okay! You will hear from me by Friday."

"Thank you very much again, Madam."

"Bye."

Yaya was excited. That sounded like an opportunity. He decided that he wouldn't go anywhere away from the telephone until after Friday.

On Wednesday, June eighteen, at 9:30 a.m. the telephone rang only once and Yaya got it. It was Barbara. She said there was an opening for a part-time soccer coach at the Cato YMCA, would Yaya be interested?

"Yes, Madam," he said.

She asked him to come in at two o'clock to fill out an application. Could he make it?

"Yes," Yaya said, even without thinking about how he would get there. Barbara told him the YMCA was near City Hall in Cato, about six blocks and three streets away from where he lived. She gave him directions on how to get there.

Yaya immediately took a shower and put on a white long-sleeve shirt and black pants over his new black shoes that Joy had bought. He wrote a note to Basi and Joy about where he was going and placed it on the telephone on the center table. Then he watched the clock.

By 1 p.m. Yaya left the house. As he went up the street, he heard a car coming behind him and thought it was the police. He turned and was right; he flagged down the squad car and politely asked the officer for more directions to the YMCA. Although he didn't say it, yet with his head up, Yaya posed as he was given the direction, to let the man know that he was going to look for a job, so he would stop going up and down the street like an idler.

He got to the YMCA, a big white building like a school compound, at fifteen minutes past one o'clock. The lobby was narrower than an average room but plush, with a wine-colored carpet and four shiny black upholstered chairs on the left side. On the right sat a slim, brown-eyed brunette behind a desk. She was on the telephone. Yaya stood a couple of feet away from her desk, while she talked, and as he reflected on how every office in America had a computer.

"Yes, can I help you?"

"Good afternoon, Madam. I'm here to see Ms. Barbara Rogers. But..., my appointment is at two o'clock. I'll wait if you don't mind?"

"She just arrived from lunch, I'll let her know you are here."

"Thank you very much." He went and sat down.

Barbara came five minutes later. She raised eyebrows at Yaya and offered her hand. "Pretty early, right? Come to my office." She led in quick strides.

They went four doors down the hallway and entered a room on the left. She showed him a chair and walked around the table and sat.

Every office Yaya had entered in America had a computer, but Barbara had two on her table, with a dot matrix printer on a little cart behind her, near a chest of metal cabinets.

"Did you find it hard to get here?"

"No, Madam, your directions were good."

"Great. About this position, as I said on the phone, what we need is a soccer coach, for little kids. It's a delicate job and it doesn't pay well. I thought of you, because you said you are bored, and I know the feeling. Otherwise, we've always had volunteers. But it pays $4.50 an hour for fifteen or more hours a week. Would you be interested?"

"Sure, Madam."

"Okay, here's the application. Do you have a pen?"

"Yes, Madam."

"Good, you do that. I'll be right back."

Yaya bowed down to fill out the form and in less than ten minutes had answered all questions except those pertaining to his citizenship status. But since Barbara had not returned, he sat scanning the several pictures of young boys in athletic uniforms pasted on the walls; with the numerous trophies which stood on a high table in a corner. That made him remember the office of his high school principal with many trophies, shields and—

Barbara walked in. "Are you through?"

"Yes, Madam." Yaya gave her the form as she sat.

Barbara wore her thin silver-rimmed glasses. Her eyes traveled down the form, and they lingered for a moment. She looked up at Yaya.

"Tell me about yourself."

Yaya inhaled a lung full of air and eased it out gently. He moved to the edge of his chair. "I need a job right now where I can work. I learn and adapt easily. Also, I love kids. I'm from a big family and one of the eldest. I'm supporting my siblings through school."

"You sound intelligent and responsible. Let me tell you what this job involves. If hired, you will be coaching two teams of little boys, ages six to eight and nine to twelve. The hours will be after school, 4 p.m. to 6:30 on Wednesdays, Thursdays and Fridays. And from 10 a.m. to 2 p.m. on Saturdays, that's when they play their games. They have a Little League going on presently. If you know soccer, what you need is a little patience and the right words to motivate them. And you will do just fine. There are certain rules of course that you have to follow, but we will get to that after you've been hired. When can you start?"

"Today, right now. I just need to go home and change."

Barbara laughed. "Well, I would like you to start today, but the earliest it will be is next week. There are other applications I've to look through. But you should hear from me by Friday."

"Thank you." Yaya nodded and sat.

Barbara got up. "Well, it was nice of you to come." She offered her hand. "You should be hearing from me soon."

As Yaya went out of the building, Barbara's words kept ringing in his ears. *You should be hearing from me soon. ...you should hear from me by Friday.* He decided, well, he would wait by the phone until Friday.

That evening he made his entries. Wednesday, June 18:—*I had a job interview today, good prospect, by next week I should be working.*

He closed the diary and thought about how wonderful God was, to just imagine that he found this job all by himself, even when he didn't know the system. But like our people say, he reflected, '*A cow with no tail has only God to keep flies away from it.*'

313

CHAPTER TWENTY-FOUR

On Thursday, June 19, Basi's mother, Tidankay Ibrahim was hysterical in Manika Kunda. Her husband had been away for ten days on a government trip to Canada and was due back on the following Saturday. She had used his absence to visit her parents in Taényadu. But she had to cut short her visit and on her way back to Sobala, her heart was on fire, or so she felt, like she was going to die. And she preferred to die before anything happened to her son.

Since that morning, she had cried until she thought she would shed blood and her eyes were all red, because of how she felt. After she delivered Basi, they did a hysterectomy on her, which left her without a womb, and before Basi she had no kids; so he was her only child and son.

The week before she left for Taényadu, she had been having many strange dreams about Basi. In one dream, she saw him in a dark suit with a large crowd following him. She thought that was good, because Basi was supposed to be a leader like his father. But the day after that, it was like she was in America, waiting for Basi outside some house, but suddenly he came running past her and after him was somebody with a gun shooting at him. She didn't know if that person killed Basi, because she woke up screaming and frantic, all scared. And her husband was away, so she decided on a trip to her hometown to investigate the strange dreams and to see her parents.

In Taényadu, to believe in superstition was normal. And even though there were a few Christians, most of the people were Muslims or native African religious worshippers. And whereas Christianity was completely strange to the culture of the people, Islam seemed to sit well with their beliefs and lifestyles. They followed the five pillars of Islam by professing belief in Allah, praying five times a day, fasting in the month of Ramadan, giving away *Zakat* or alms, and those who afforded it went a on pilgrimage to Mecca. Yet their tendency to blame fortunes and misfortunes on superstition was high.

While many new breeds like Basi, Sidi and Yaya with their Western education would dismiss and scorn several of the superstitious tales that abounded, for many people in Taényadu that was living. When it was good, they said, the Almighty God or the gods did it with benevolent kindness. And in a case of misfortune, they maintained it must be the handiwork of agents of the devil.

Witchcraft and *juju*, a practice of purportedly casting evil spells on enemies, were the subject of notorious gossip in the mouths of the people. These were blamed for every catastrophe that befell individuals in the village. Although people seldom came forward to confess to practicing either witchcraft or *juju*—for fears of repercussions and the grinding wrath of the society—yet it was common knowledge that in secret hidings, and at night, under the cover of darkness, these associates of the devil went aloft in their deviousness, hunting and hurting unsuspecting people. Knowing so, people usually sought ways of protecting themselves, which was in addition to their prayers to God, or the gods.

To counteract the malicious forces in the society were the witch doctors, the medicine men, the Muslim spiritualists and other gifted people in the community. They used their powers to protect and help individuals and the community. These people who fought evil were accepted and respected regardless of the source of their powers, like Cherinor Tejani Jalloh, who Basi's mother went to see.

Everybody in Taényadu knew aged Cherinor Tejani Jalloh, a Fulani scholar of the Koran. His spirituality was what made him famous—him and his Jinni, an invincible spirit that appears and disappears at will in various forms with powers to influence human affairs. It was said that though Cherinor Jalloh recited and used verses of the Koran in some of his many services, yet his link and powers to invoke a Jinni and communicate with it had nothing to do with the Koran. That power was believed to be natural or handed down in his lineage.

Because although the Koran acknowledges three species of rational creatures—Angels, Jinns and Humans—and though it is maintained that God made Jinns out of roaring flame which had no smoke, while he created human beings and angels out of dust and light, yet no part of the Koran explains how to summon a Jinni and communicate with it.

Talking about Jinns in chapter LXXII of the Koran, the Holy Prophet Mohammed had professed that a company of Jinns heard him reading some verses of the Koran during his retreat at Al Tayef and decided to be Muslims, even as those converted acknowledged that there were some among them who decided to stay in their evil ways.

And many learned Muslims still believe that there are good Jinns and bad Jinns. So in Manika Kunda, with Islam engaging in a marriage of convenience with the native cultures, it was acceptable that Cherinor Jalloh would be seen as a pious Muslim, and be respected in society even with his special gifts which he used positively for people.

Arriving in Taényadu late in the night yesterday on Wednesday, Basi's mother couldn't wait for day break to go consult with Cherinor Jalloh. It was a trip she had made several times for her husband's protection, since he was in the public eye, which made him a good target for all sorts of malicious attacks—*this was like rumors of Nancy Reagan consulting an astrologer when her husband was President of U.S.A.!*

But now Madam Tidankay was concerned about her son—Basi, her only son! She was at the old man's door at the break of dawn, just when she knew he would be returning from offering *Salatul-Fajr* or the early morning prayers at the mosque.

Cherinor Jalloh came and found her sitting on a bench in his verandah and stood watching her, wondering whether she was brooding or nodding.

He cleared his throat. *"Assalamu 'alaikum."*

She jerked her head and looked up. *"Wa 'alaikum salaam. Wa rahmatulla,* Baba." She had gotten on her knees and was rubbing her eyes.

"How are you, Tidankay. When did you come?"

"I'm fine, Baba. I came last night. But I couldn't sleep all night because I was anxious to see you. I came this time purposely to Taényadu to see you."

"Then why didn't you come straight to me when you arrived?"

"Baba, I got here too late to disturb you."

"Is everything alright with your husband?"

"My husband is fine; he has traveled to somewhere overseas." She got up. "But Baba, I'm worried about my son in America. It's about him I've come to see you."

"Come inside." Cherinor Jalloh entered his six bedroom cemented house, and they walked through a large parlor, the floor of which was so smooth that you could see your reflection in the dried plastered cement. They got to a small parlor which had rattan mats. Before stepping on the mats, Cherinor Jalloh left his shoes behind, and Basi's mother did same. Then they walked across to the old man's bedroom. It was a large room with an Arabian rug covering the floor to a far corner where a wooden bed stood.

The old man gathered his big white gown and lowered himself with groans on the rug in a corner where he had, neatly stacked against the wall, copies of the Koran and other books with Arabic lettering. Next to him were his *walar*—the wooden board that he wrote on—and his *kala*—a grass quill pen—which stood in a little jar containing black *duba*-ink.

Madam Tidankay sat down too, and narrated the dreams.

Cherinor Jalloh's face got gloomy from what he understood the dreams to mean. But to be sure, he decided on divination; he wouldn't summon a Jinni for a case like this but would use his bowl of sand, from which he could see and foretell things like a psychic would from looking at a crystal ball. He got the bowl full of sand from under his bed and sat with it, and rubbed his palms together over it for a while. Then he drew lines of different shapes in the sand with a finger. He drew them and wiped them off, and drew some more.

"This person that you said was running after your son, was it a woman or a man?"

"Baba I'm not sure. I was shocked. But I know it was a white person, and I think it was a man, because he had on pants, although his hair was long."

"You are wrong. That was a woman. I see two women conniving, and one of them is your son's lover. Her name is Wanday." Cherinor Jalloh drew some more lines. "When you leave here offer a lamb for sacrifice immediately. And send a telegram to your son telling him to stop his affair with that woman, or she will cause his end soon without doubt. My advice is that you go and do as I've said now!"

Madam Tidankay's worst fear was now confirmed. Cherinor Jalloh had never been wrong. Her son was in danger. *A telegram? No!* She was going to Sobala immediately, to make a telephone call to Basi in America. Torn apart hopelessly, she was more furious than frightened.

"Was that what he went overseas for? To run after white women? The last time it was a black American, now it is a real white woman. What has that child seen wrong with his own people?"

The old man kept his eyes on the sand, but grunted.

"Baba, I just have to talk to him in person. I'm going to telephone him and stop him from ever seeing that woman called Wanday. And he dare not disobey me, because I'll curse him by my breast with which I fed him." She got up to leave.

"Wait, there is a boy with your son in America. Yaya. I see him in a big trouble too. Tell his mother to urgently come and see me, because for him we need to perform a special ceremony."

Madam Tidankay didn't have time to go see Yaya's mother; she barely had time to tell the first person that she saw whom she knew would deliver the message. Rushing back to Sobala, to make the call to Basi, she didn't even sacrifice the lamb. She had decided to wait until Basi's father came, which was any day now, so they could do it together. She got to Sobala at 5 p.m. but because of bad telephone lines in Manika Kunda, it was 9 p.m. before she got a call through to Houston.

"Hello, hello," Yaya was by the phone at 2 p.m. Houston time awaiting Barbara's call.

"Let me speak to Basi."

"He has gone to work, who is calling?"

"I'm his mother. Is this Yaya?"

"Yes, Ma." Yaya was shocked; how did she know that he was in Houston?

"Do you know Basi's work number?"

"No, Ma, I don't. But he will be back soon."

"Tell him to call me as soon as he comes. And Yaya, tell him that I've known everything about him and that white woman, Wanday. Tell him if he loves his life he should never go see her again. Just tell him that. And tell him that he should not defy me, and that he should call me immediately when he comes in."

"Okay, Ma, I will."

"And you, Yaya. Be very careful too. You came up in Basi's message. I don't know what, but your mother should be going to see Cherinor Jalloh. Tell Basi to call me when he comes without fail. Bye Bye."

Yaya couldn't believe it. His mother going to see Cherinor Jalloh? His mouth dropped. His bones chilled. His secret was out. With less than ten days remaining for this thing to be over, now it was an uproar.

Cherinor Jalloh? The man was rumored to be a spirit, because he evoked Jinns from the spirit world. And it was said there had never been a mystery that Cherinor Jalloh and his Jinns failed to reveal.

Of course, he didn't want his mother to know. Because the moment she knew, she would panic, and the whole world would know. Yaya held his head and sat despondently with his whole insides in turmoil. He felt worse, thinking that he couldn't even call home as Taényadu had no telephone.

Basi got in that Thursday evening at 7 p.m. and Yaya told him about the telephone call. "Call your mother," he said. "It is urgent."

"What did she say?"

"That you should call her immediately when you come in. But make sure Ms. Joy is not around when you call."

"Why? What's so urgent and secretive that they don't want Joy to know about? Did she say anything about my father?"

"No." Yaya went to confirm that Joy, who was in the kitchen, couldn't hear. "She said something about you and Wanday."

"Who? Who is Wanday?"

"I don't know. She said they've known everything between you and a white woman called Wanday, and that you should stop seeing her if you love your life."

Basi got angry as he wondered who had been writing letters about him to his parents?

"Yaya, has anybody ever called here with that name?"

"No, this was the first time I ever heard the name, Wanday."

Basi rushed to the kitchen. "Joy, have you been writing any letters home about my activities here?"

"What activities?"

"Anything about me, or what you might suspect."

"I don't spread speculations, Basi. But then I may help you if I know what you're talking about."

"Never mind!" Basi walked away and sat in his inclining chair, feeling baffled.

Yaya received the call from Barbara at 10 a.m. on Friday, June 20. He had the job and was to start on Wednesday, June 25. That news made him almost forget his worries since the day before when Basi's mother called. He rationalized that if his mother had known about the inheritance Grandma Fatu left with him, well, she had known; he couldn't help it. By now, of course, he realized, everybody knew why he ran away to America.

Yaya thanked God, though, that his luck was opening up. He thought of his new title, Yaya LaTalé, soccer coach, YMCA Cato, Texas, U.S.A.

Barbara had said there were practices on Wednesdays, Thursdays and Fridays from 4 p.m. to 6:30 p.m., and she was coaching the kids through the week. However, at 4 p.m. promptly, Yaya decided to go there and watch.

Basi got home at 6 p.m. The house was quiet. He knew Joy was gone to her CPA class. He checked in Yaya's room; he was not in. Where the idiot had gone, he didn't know. He ate his meal, then debated returning the telephone call from his mother yesterday. The fact was, up till now, he was still upset because he didn't feel like discussing Wendy with his parents.

Yet he wanted to know their source and he wished that they would quit worrying about what he did, because he was a grown man. How could they be in Africa and want to control his life in America? But how did they know about Wendy? Could she perhaps, have written to his parents out of some craziness? Maybe he had dropped something that had his father's name and address which she used. But why? He couldn't understand.

It's Friday, the weekend is here. Basi still debated about calling his mother. He decided that he would call the next day, Saturday, because that would be the best time to talk to his father too. But he would go see Wendy first, to know if his parent's knowledge about her was her act.

Basi had his shining red Porsche in overspeed as he flew from Cato through Southwest Houston to South Main street by the Astrodome. Normally it took fifteen minutes but today it was ten, driving at twenty miles above speed limit. He was upset. Besides, Basi assured himself that he knew too many nickel and dime lawyers who could arrange to throw out his speeding citations.

As he parked in the nearest vacant spot to Wendy's apartment, he looked at the clock on his dashboard, it was 6:45 p.m. Wendy worked from 8 p.m. to 4. a.m. She should be gone in less than two hours.

Funny, Basi thought, that even semi-hookers like Wendy worked eight hour shifts in America. He stuck his key in the lock and turned it.

Basi was transfixed at the door by what he saw. Wendy was in bed with a muscular man and they were stark naked, with the man on top of her. The man got off Wendy and Basi saw two big breasts hanging, bigger than even Wendy's. In a daze, Basi entered, now convinced that this person was indeed a woman, in spite of her thick manly body.

"Damn!" the strange woman cried and got up. She snatched her clothes and a thick bulging purse and ran into the bathroom.

"W-h-a-t are ya do-i-n-g here?" Wendy blurted, as she laid shamelessly with nothing on.

Basi moved and stood over her, near the headboard with his mouth open. Two women doing it like a man and a woman? This was only something he had heard about, and seen in X-rated movies on video. Obviously, this woman was much deeper than he thought.

He looked at Wendy who was now very red in the face and had swollen eyelids. Basi bit his lower lip. "So this is what you do, Wendy? I didn't know you are like that!"

Wendy didn't even look at him. She reached for a cigarette on the night stand. Basi grabbed her arm, intending to squeeze it so she would feel his anger, but he dropped it quickly, because his eyes caught something.

"What's this?" he picked up a pipe, which had some whitish stuff inside, from the night stand. Wendy snatched her cigarette pack and reached for a small plastic bag that was lying at the edge of the night-stand. Basi beat her to it. He held up a clear plastic bag that could fit into his palm, which contained more of the whitish stuff.

Basi's mind went to drug raids on TV with similar whitish stuff inside plastic bags, which drug addicts caught red-handed are said to have in pipes that they suck on, like sad cases of comatose patients on life-support.

This is cocaine. No, this is crack. Or is it morphine? Heroine? Forget the name, it's some drug. An amphetamine. What a hell!

Basi thought of the hopes he had pinned on Wendy; his plans for her, the risk it had been considering her rotten moral values from the filthy job she held—a nightclub stripper! He thought of all the money he was dumping on her, getting the apartment and fixing it up, paying her rent, and giving her money constantly so she wouldn't go whoring; not knowing that she was going to bed with another woman. Maybe that was why she always preferred doing her so-called private shows for him, teasing him, playing with him, and only sucking him off.

Wendy laid, licking her lips and blowing thick clouds of smoke in the air.

"So this is what you do, Wendy? So this is your life?"

"Well... you jus.... fig-u-r-e-d it out!"

Basi was trembling with rage. *She is high!* He hit her hard on the face. "You bitch!"

"Do-n't hit me, b-o-y." Wendy tried to rise up. Basi violently pushed her on her back, and slapped her several times.

Wendy struggled fistfully. "You're h-u-r-t-i-n-g me."

Basi grabbed her hair, jerked her head a few times and slapped her some more.

The strange woman who had disappeared was at the bathroom door with a gun in her hand. "Stop hitting her, you sonofabitch!"

"Shut up and go to hell, damn bitch!" Then instinctively, Basi looked up at the woman, and opened his mouth in shock.

Paw! Paw! Paw! She fired.

Wendy froze. Basi tried to run out but dropped at the door. The woman walked over and stood over him, and shot him once more.

"Damn it!" she hissed. "Hitting on my woman."

"Oh, Susan! I hope you didn't kill him, " Wendy cried.

Yaya had arrived at the YMCA at 4:30. Barbara and the kids were on the soccer field. Her face had a smiling frown as she walked outside the lines to meet him. The kids had gathered and were all looking as Barbara and Yaya greeted.

"I just wanted to come and see how you do it."

"I'm pleased you came." Barbara turned around. "Kids..., come over." As they came running, she stood next to Yaya. "Everybody, this is Mr. Yaya Lutor—"

"LaTalé."

"Yes, Yaya LaTalé. He is going to be your new soccer coach starting next week."

"Hello, coach!" "Hello, coach!" "He is black." "Hello, coach!" "He is black!" "Hello, coach!" "He is...."

Yaya waved his arms for silence. The kids all looked up at him. "Hello, everybody. Like Ms. Rogers said, I'm looking forward to being your coach. I hope we will all be friends. And you can call me Uncle Yaya. What's my name?"

"Uncle Yaya!!!"

"What's my name?"

"Uncle Yaya!!!!"

In his shorts and T-shirt, Yaya got the whistle from Barbara and asked the kids to form two straight lines. He then led them hopping around the field twice as he blew the whistle in rhythm with their footsteps. After that he got them to the center of the field where they did some gymnastics and calisthenics. At the end of the practices, he had learned a few names and struck a familiarity with the kids.

At twenty to eight, Barbara dropped Yaya home. Joy was not in yet from school. Yaya had his shower and turned on the TV.

"Knock! Knock! Knock! " Yaya ran to open the door. "Who?"

"The police!"

Wow, the police! What was he going to do? This could be immigration. He could go hide in the garage—

"Knock! knock! knock! "

"Okay, one minute, please." Why didn't he tell them nobody was home? Yaya prayed silently: *Bismillah-i-Rahman-ir-Raheem*—in the name of Allah, the Beneficent, the Merciful. He opened the door.

"We thought you weren't going to open up;" said a slim but firm looking white woman in a blue police uniform, as she walked in with a short stout man, similarly dressed. He was Caucasian too.

This was not the uniform Yaya saw on the police in Cato.

Which police are these?

The officers sized him up and their eyes got busy looking as far into the house as possible. "Is this Basi Ibrahim's residence?"

"Yes, sir..., Madam."

"Does he have a wife?" the male officer asked.

"Yes. She went to school."

"When is she coming back?" asked the female officer.

"By nine-thirty."

The male officer looked at his watch. "It's ten past eight o'clock. Who are you to Basi?"

"I'm his cousin."

"We are Houston police," the female officer stated. "We've got sad news for you. Basi Ibrahim was shot early this evening and died at Ben Taub hospital."

Yaya held his head and like a Muslim, he uttered the following words in Arabic. "*La ilaha ill-Allah, Muhammad-ur-rasool ullah!*—there is no deity but Allah and Muhammad is the apostle of Allah—*La ilaha ill-Allah, Muhammad-ur-rasool ullah! La ilaha ill-Allah, Muhammad-ur-rasool ullah!*"

"What is he saying?" the female officer asked.

"I don't know!"

"Sir, we will give you a number to call for further information."

"Give it to his wife when she comes back," the male officer added.

This panic scene was as usual with the officers, like a doctor watching a dying patient. They gave Yaya a piece of paper and left, expressing condolences on their way out. He dropped the paper on the couch and awestricken, he fell on it.

CHAPTER TWENTY-FIVE

Basi's father called in the morning on Saturday June 21 and asked that his son's body be flown home immediately.

Joy was as devastated as Yaya. That Saturday, her friends swamped her. Her parents called and said they were coming. The Manika Kunda community all over U.S. were quickly informed about the tragedy.

Susan was already out of jail before noon on that same Saturday. *"No charges. Self defense!"*

The story was that Basi was a drug dealer and pimp, who always forced his way into Wendy's apartment, harassed her and beat her up to make her get high so she would go on the streets to work for him. This time when he came bursting in, Susan was there, and couldn't stand it. *She was the Good Samaritan!*

The red marks on Wendy's face and the pipe and bag of the whitish stuff, later identified as *crack-cocaine* were the exhibits and incontrovertible evidence.

On Monday, June 23, the President of Manika Kunda called his Ambassador in Washington D.C. with an order to issue a statement to the American government to the effect that: *"The government of Manika Kunda is grieving at the ruthless murder of Basi Ibrahim, a son of a Cabinet Minister and the only heir to his father. And as the nation mourns, the government is interested in the results of investigations, and the handling of such a heinous crime against one of its most beloved and promising citizens."*

Basi might have lapsed into rotten morals, or he could have gravely erred which led to his death. But according to Shakespeare, when beggars die, it goes unnoticed, yet when Princes die, the heavens themselves weep. Basi's death stirred ripples in the Manika Kunda community throughout the U.S.

Associations were meeting, telephone lines were busy and faxed messages were pouring in. It was one death too many for Manika Kundan's to fold their arms about. They hired a private investigator.

The first feed back was that Susan was just out of prison for her involvement in a bank robbery, with a criminal record stretching from her teenage days. Wendy had served time, too, for drug possession, armed possession, public intoxication, etc.

Manika Kundans were furious when they learned about Susan's release forty-eight hours after she murdered Basi. Associations and American citizens of Manika Kunda descent all over the country were asked to present the case in their churches and mosques. Also, they were to complain to public figures and elected officials in their cities, counties and states about the wanton killing of Basi and other Africans before him that usually went unnoticed and dismissed across America. The collected voice was that justice be served.

Meanwhile, in Korkordu, Kondorfili Bunsor was outside his compound, standing before his just completed big house of concrete blocks. The raining season had started, yet there was so much dryness in the land. Kondorfili Bunsor could still smell the raw scent of cement; but his nostrils had to get used to this little inconvenience. It made him sometimes miss his little old hut, with its coolness and freshness. This building was needed, though, to show his manhood and social stature here in Korkordu and beyond.

In the stillness of the night, with everybody gone to bed, Kondorfili Bunsor was pacing in his dusty front yard and thinking that now he was aloft of all Sovereign Kings or Chiefs in Manika Kunda. For beyond boundaries, after every so many miles, another Sovereign King or Chief reigned. But where would they need a bone healer in Manika Kunda that they wouldn't call his name, or run to him? They had to, because he was the one and only natural bone healer as far and wide as he knew, that was apart from the hospitals who knew no better than to cut and pad.

He looked up at the full moon which hovered and seemed to have been moving with him as he paced. The moon glowed gloomily because the sky was dark, and clouds had covered the stars that kept guard. After five days, the tiny silver streak which had looked like a thin slice of orange became half a *calabash*; and after ten days, it was the size of a *calabash*. And now that it was full moon, fifteen days must be gone in this moon.

With the clouds up, the potential for rain was exciting to Kondorfili Bunsor. For after so much dryness in the past dry season, now more rains were needed to moisten the land and refresh the air. Two days ago, when there remained a gap to close in the roundness of the moon, there was a little tilt downwards. Kondorfili Bunsor had seen it. So he had expected this cloud and the coming rain with the relief that it was to most people in Korkordu. They were already wondering why the rainy season was so slow this year.

Kondorfili Bunsor looked at his remodeled house of fine cement blocks and a shiny zinc roof. He raised his arms wide open, telling himself that his whole compound would soon be all cement buildings. Yes, every one of those five huts behind his front house. And his place would look like a king's palace. Thinking of the orange tree standing at the center of the compound, and the mango tree near the kitchen hut, he decided that they would all be cut down, for they only invited blackbirds and insects.

In fact, all the grass in his compound would soon be smoothly plastered with cement. Because the bushes behind the back houses were enough greenery. And since he was building a palace, it should look like a palace, with no bizarre animals crawling or hopping in at random.

Yet for all this, he could only be grateful to Yaya and that boy before him, Alpha—fools who got blinded by the ways of the white man and kicked their blessings.

One day last week, when Kondorfili Bunsor went to Junhdu, he had seen Alpha, who foolishly ran away to *Urssia* to escape his inheritance. If somebody were to give him the white man's coat today, he wouldn't know it, because he had to know himself first. And nobody who knew himself would be like the Alpha he saw, all dressed up in leaves, and rags and dirty cans dangling on ropes which hung from his head down to his legs, as he sent out blows vacantly in the air and shouted at the breeze.

He was told by the driver of the passenger van he was sitting in, that Alpha was sleeping on the street, too; even with so many empty huts on the farms and everywhere. Of course, Kondorfili Bunsor reflected with grim satisfaction that he knew Alpha was insane till eternity, though he escaped blindness and deformity, which might have been due to a mild anger of his ancestors—for a saboteur like him!

With the full moon up now, it would start reversing and become a *calabash* in five days; that would be the twentieth day of this moon, which was when Yaya's grandma died two years ago. And since Yaya went in the footsteps of Alpha, in five days they would have something in common. Kondorfili Bunsor hoped Yaya was enjoying himself in America.

The Ibrahim residence in Cato had been full since Saturday, June 21, which was the day following Basi's murder. Joy's parents came that evening, and—except for her brother in the Army who was stationed in Germany—almost all other members of her family came from all over the United States, shaken. And sympathizers were coming and going everyday of the week.

Yaya was so grief stricken that he didn't even go to start his new job. Yet, with Joy all broken by the tragedy, he had to pull through to take charge and do the little things that needed to be done in the house. He ran to every call by her, her parents and three sisters who stayed with them, which was in addition to meeting the needs of other guests that came and left. That was his routine until the day that was set for Basi's funeral, after which Joy was to leave with his body by noon for Manika Kunda.

That morning, on Saturday, June 28, the funeral home in Southwest Houston was packed with as many Manika Kundans as Americans of all races. The Ambassador of Manika Kunda in Washington D.C. and the representatives of the government of Manika Kunda at the United Nations were all present. They were introduced by the President-at-large of Manika Kunda Descendants Association (MKDA) who was a professor at Georgetown University. He said chapter presidents of MKDA from fifteen states were also present.

A Reverend Father conducted the services because Basi was Catholic. After the Priest prayed and some hymns were sung, Yaya looked at his childhood friend lying wasted in his prime and felt there was something he owed him. He went up the pulpit in his white shirt, black tie and black pants, and declared with a quivering voice his childhood bond with Basi; and said that as a Muslim, he was going to recite some prayers from the Koran to which he wanted the guests to answer with Amen. He read the *fatihah* and recited some *surats*. After that, he intensely prayed more in English.

Then there were the speeches. The President-at-large of Manika Kunda Descendant Association, Professor Conteh, who was now an American citizen, made an emotional speech about the senseless loss of young lives like Basi's everyday in America because of cheap handguns and their easy accessibility to every hoodlum. He reiterated the commitment of the Association to pursue Basi's case so that it would not get dismissed like the routine killings which happened everyday, and went uninvestigated.

He said the MKDA would not relent and that they would go as far as seeking a Congressional hearing if Basi's murderess and her accomplice were not prosecuted. Again he appealed to all present, to join hands against reckless violence by fighting this case. He particularly appealed to Houstonians in the crowd to start calling on their elected representatives to create an awareness of the case and the injustice in the handling of it so far as evident in the, no charge and instant release of the murderess.

The Ambassador of Manika Kunda lamented the alarming rate at which what happened to Basi was happening sporadically to Africans of various origins. He regretted the circumstance of Basi's murder, and advised that it should be a sad lesson to all other Manika Kundans and Africans in America.

The Ambassador said that people must choose who they keep company with, and that no circumstance should force anybody to compromise the standards, morals and values instilled in them back home in picking associates, especially if they were to suspect drug use or amoral and criminal traits. He promised to press for a Justice Department investigation in Basi's murder if the outcome of the case at state level was unsatisfactory.

After the funeral services, a crowd of about twenty people went to Houston's Intercontinental Airport to see Joy and the corpse off. Most of the out-of-town guests also departed from there. The last guest to leave was Joy's youngest sister, a school teacher in Dallas. She brought Yaya home from the airport and stayed to straighten the house; after which she rested until in the evening when she left in her car for Dallas.

Up to today, when they saw Joy and Basi off, Yaya was debating about going with them; even as he knew he couldn't. First, he had his paper problem, going would have meant to never come back, and there was still June 29 to come, which was his most critical date.

That evening, alone in that big house, he got his dairy and made his entries: Saturday, June 28:— *Sad day today. Basi is finally gone. My childhood friend gone, killed like a fowl. May Allah be with him and render justice. And may God be with Ms. Joy too.*

Yaya closed his diary and suddenly realized that if it was June 28, then there was only one day left to make the death of Grandma Fatu two complete years. The speed with which the past week had flown completely overwhelmed him. *Wow! Only one day remaining?*

Yet, in spite of Yaya's immediate personal worries, there were memories of Basi which made him sink farther in despair. He couldn't stop brooding to think of Basi who was so alive but so dead suddenly. Yaya reflected on how Basi's mother tried to advise him. He recalled receiving the call and telling Basi everything that he was told to tell him.

But it seems, our Westernization and education is what is blinding us and alienating us from our roots.

Now Yaya was tutoring himself that it paid to listen to advice from home—*because the wisdom and wonders of our people are not something to toy with!*

He thought of his mother going to see Cherinor Tejani Jalloh and shuddered. Now he was grieving for Basi and afraid for himself.

CHAPTER TWENTY-SIX

In Taényadu, Yaya's mother had received the message from Basi's mother about seeing Cherinor Jalloh. That was on Friday of last week. Of course, like many mothers in that remote village in Manika Kunda, Yaya's mother had no Western education, like Basi's. And for them, Cherinor Jalloh was half spirit and half human—regarded with such reverence that would make them pack all their worldly belongings and give him, if he said their life depended on that. For they had seen his wonders again and again to swear by his words, which they knew failed only if dawn did not follow the night.

Cherinor Jalloh was an unexplained mystery, whom they believed that God sent with supernatural powers to help them fight the evil spirits in the land.

When Yaya's mother received the message that Friday evening, she took off as she was, from where she was sitting, as if a rope had been thrown on her neck which pulled her to the old man's house. In her haste she got there barefooted without even knowing.

"*Assalamu 'alaikum.*" Her breathing was heavy as she greeted Cherinor Jalloh's four wives and children sitting in the verandah of his front house.

"*Wa 'alaikum salaam. Wa rahmatulla!*" they answered in chorus.

"Is Baba in?" she panted.

"Yes," one of the women answered. "Musa, go tell your Grandpa that Madam Iye is here." A small boy got up and ran inside the house. Through the open front door, and the two wooden windows at either side of it that were ajar, the boy could be seen from the verandah knocking on Cherinor Jalloh's door.

Cherinor Jalloh appeared in his little parlor which led to his room like an office with a waiting room. He had his big white gown gathered behind him with one hand as he beckoned with the other. Yaya's mother took some hurried steps and as she got to him, she went down on her knees.

"*Assalamu 'alaikum,* Baba."

"*Wa 'alaikum salaam. Wa rahmatulla.* How are you this evening, Iye?"

"Baba, I'm fine, I think. But I heard you have a message for me."

"Yes, come inside." Cherinor Jalloh led her to his room and to the corner where he had his books and *walar,* etc. "Sit down over there."

She sat across from where he was standing. He sat down, too.

"Baba, what is it? Is it some bad news?" Madam Iye was still panting.

Cherinor Jalloh reached for his bowl of sand. And now it was like a psychic looking into a crystal ball to tell some desperate detective in a major Western metropolis the mystery surrounding a baffling crime.

"Baba, have you seen something bad that is coming to me?" She had her hands over her headgear and her eyes were standing out like a madman's.

"Calm down, Iye. I called you."

"Oh, Baba, thanks so much. You're a savior. May the Lord give you long life. May you live to be the oldest living person on earth, because you are a blessing to us, you and your many kind deeds. Where will some of us be today without you, when we have so many enemies everywhere—"

"Iye?" Cherinor Jalloh looked up from the sand. "This is a very serious matter. It is not what you think, and it is going to shock you. When your mother died, she appointed your son to continue with her work. He should have taken up after her, but he refused and ran away to America." Yaya's mother's mouth opened and stayed so wide that it seemed like her jaws got stiff.

Cherinor Jalloh looked into his bowl of sand. "Yes, that was why he ran away. There is a man called Kondorfili Bunsor, who advised him. He is an evil man."

Madam Iye had pulled her headgear off without meaning to, she was gaping at the spiritualist.

"Your ancestors are mad, because nobody kicks their blessing like your son did. It must be the white man's education. But on Sunday next week, your ancestors will act in their anger if your son doesn't get here before then and do as he is supposed to."

Yaya's mother shuddered and gaped, all bewildered. "Baba, what can I do? I didn't know anything about all this. He said he was going to study in America. I can't even call the name of the town he went to. How am I going to bring him?" She buried her face in her hands and looked up at the old man, shaking her head sadly.

"Oh, Baba, Yaya fooled us. What am I to do? We were wondering whom my mother left the inheritance with. We thought she was so sick and senile that she couldn't appoint a successor. But we knew she would come in a dream to somebody and so far we had been waiting. Some people were saying that she left it with Wusu, my brother, but that he was too lazy to bother. Nobody believed that.

"And nobody knew it was Yaya. But why didn't he tell me? I'm his mother. Baba, what can I do?"

"Ask your son to come immediately and do like he is supposed to, and that should be before sun down on Sunday next week, for you see this line here?" He pointed into the bowl of sand. "It is as short as the time left for your ancestors to wait."

"Baba, by Sunday next week? That is about eight days from now. How can I make him come before then? I don't have any money. Even if I had the money how can I bring him?"

"Bring him anyhow you can, Iye. But bring him. Or it will be bad. Have you heard of Alpha the lunatic who came in chains some years ago from overseas?"

"Yes, Baba. So it could be that bad, eeh? So he can be affected even when he is in the white man's land?"

"Iye, the boundaries of this world are human boundaries. For spirits, it's just one big universe; so yes, your son will still be affected, but I can't tell you how exactly, for that's up to your ancestors."

Madam Iye thought of the stories about this man—Cherinor Jalloh, the spiritualist—who could penetrate into the world of Jinns, those powerful spirits that could do anything. She got up and prostrated before him. "Baba, if it's one universe for spirits, with your blessing and powers, can't you help me to bring him?"

"Yes and no. I can bring his spirit but not his body, and I wonder if that will help."

"Baba, please call his spirit and talk to it, and make it promise that it will bring him home. He can't defy his own spirit, can he? And maybe the spirits of our ancestors will hear his promise and forgive him. I beg you, Baba, please do that for me before it's too late."

"To bring him at all, I will have to call Jinni Musa."

Jinni Musa? Madam Iye thanked God silently for there being some hope. Most people in Taényadu who knew Cherinor Jalloh also knew of the wonders he could perform with Jinni Musa. And Jinni Musa was no stranger to Madam Iye. From what she knew about the Jinns through a combination of listening to readings of the Koran, and testimonies, folklore and rumor, of all spirits, Jinni Musa was allegedly the most beneficent, famous and powerful.

They said that Jinni was a Muslim, with a kind heart. Madam Iye knew this old man could make Jinni Musa do anything. She held his foot in reverence.

"Baba, please, help me. Please call Jinni Musa. Can you do that for me, Baba?"

Cherinor Jalloh was touched. In his uprightness, because he considered himself a good servant of Allah, he wanted justice done. For like a computer printout of a data file, he had seen the misdeeds of Kondorfili Bunsor, like the havoc he caused to Alpha, the boy whom he ill-advised and who went overseas and came back cursed with insanity.

The spiritualist decided he would make Kondorfili Bunsor know that evil did not pay by bringing Yaya face to face with the dubious man, so his evil intention would be revealed. And in fact, since he needed both Yaya and Kondorfili Bunsor, he could as well call forth the spirit of Yaya's dead Grandma, so that they would have a court with Jinni Musa as the judge.

Cherinor Jalloh laid his hand on Yaya's mother who was at his feet. "Sit up, Iye, I will call Jinni Musa. And we will seek a way to resolve this. But we will have to deal with three worlds that you know: the spirit world of the ancestors, the white man's world and Manika Kunda.

"I'll ask Jinni Musa to bring the spirit of your dead mother, together with the spirits of Kondorfili Bunsor and your son together. It will be like in a court. Jinni Musa will be the judge."

Madam Iye was sitting up now and had her arms open to the spiritualist. "God bless you, Baba. And may you live long. For a problem like this, which thinking about alone is enough to kill one or make one go crazy, yet you have a solution. Please, Baba, call Jinni Musa."

"Go and keep your mouth quiet. And on Sunday next week, come here in the afternoon, immediately after *Salatuz-Zuhr*—the afternoon prayer—has been prayed. And bring a cock and an innocent virgin girl, one that has not slept with a man. Can you find one?"

"Yes, Baba, I know a few."

"Good, we will meet on Sunday, *Inshallahu*—God willing—and may the will of Allah be done."

CHAPTER TWENTY-SEVEN

It was Sunday, June 29th. Yaya knew this was the day that Grandma Fatu died two years ago. He remembered it was in the evening with the sun sinking when he got to Wuyadu that day. And she died in less than five minutes when he was with her. He estimated the time to be between 6 p.m. to 7 p.m. And by Houston time he knew that was around 11 a.m. to noon.

For this day, Yaya was fasting and early this morning, before doing anything, he prayed twenty *rak'ats* and placed himself in the hands of God. He asked God to judge him according to the contents of his heart. After his prayers, he decided to get busy to wear away his worries. He vacuumed a living room that did not need to be vacuumed, because that was done yesterday and except Joy's sister who left last, nobody had come into the house. Yet Yaya cleaned everywhere that he usually cleaned, the bathrooms, the kitchen floor, the back patio and even the garage.

Before the sun came up, he went and watered the lawn; all the while he was telling himself that he would survive this ordeal and be a free man so he could be what he dreamed to be. *Inshalluhu* (by God's grace).

The night before, which was Saturday in Korkordu, the moon was a *calabash*. So today made the twentieth day of the twenty-sixth moon since Yaya's grandma died. Now the sun was up, burning hard even when this was the rainy season. Farmers were busy planting their crops for the rains that were expected in earnest.

Kondorfili Bunsor was in a hammock, swaying in the verandah of his new concrete house. He rubbed his palms together and felt pleased that they were as smooth as any king's. Working in the farms under the burning sun and in the rain, day after day was not his lot.

He knew he was destined for glory and fame in this world, along with blessings from his ancestors. For he, Kondorfili Bunsor, had waged a war and won. He has resumed the glory that belonged

334

to the Bunsor family. For those impostors and usurpers who undermined and stole an inheritance that was originally only in his lineage have paid for it.

And on his deathbed, at the time for him to pass the inheritance to a successor, he would tell the story of how he, Kondorfili Bunsor, recaptured sole ownership of the sacred legacy of the Bunsor family.

He would become a legend and a martyr in the family. But meantime, his fame would spread henceforth uncontested. By sun down, Yaya, even if he were under the ocean, would become the golden seal of that blessing. Yes, and all the glory would be for him, Kondorfili Bunsor.

On Yaya's mother's last visit to Cherinor Jalloh, when he shocked her with the news, this critical Sunday was their concern. The spiritualist had asked her to come, so he would intervene on her son's behalf—before it's late by sundown—to avert the wrath of their ancestors!

But Cherinor Jalloh had no might of his own to resolve the problem that haunted Yaya. Besides Yaya was far away, and there were the angry spirits of his forebears to pacify urgently and in an extraordinary way.

When it was three days to this appointed day, Cherinor Jalloh began fasting and observing more solitude so that he would constantly pray and read the Koran. To him, this was necessary for inner purity because he was reaching to the outer world. And today, as he sat in his room, which was incensed and serene like a holy ground, he felt himself in a highly spiritual state enough to invoke Jinni Musa, whom he believed was the master in the Jinni world and a saint in his struggle against Satan and his evil ploys on mankind.

Jinni Musa and Cherinor Jalloh were friends. Their covenant was a mutual purity of heart and piousness in living according to the wishes of Allah, their creator. Cherinor Jalloh had summoned the chief Jinni several times before, and each time he came through a medium and did his wonders, by empowering Cherinor Jalloh with knowledge beyond human perceptions, for the good of individuals and the society.

Cherinor Jalloh did this work to the astonishment of all onlookers who saw him as superhuman; but he never claimed to be a prophet, an Imam or a leader; he was an indigenous Muslim scholar and spiritualist who lived simply and quietly, and served as a human link to the spirit world. What made him so miraculous was something that only he knew and perhaps the next person to know would be the one he would appoint to take up after him.

However, today, as an advocate for Yaya, Cherinor Jalloh would invite the chief Jinni and plead with his righteousness to arbitrate between Yaya, his dead Grandma and Kondorfili Bunsor about the inheritance Yaya absconded from.

Cherinor Jalloh was hoping that Jinni Musa—with his spiritual might and all seeing eye—would zoom through the human world and beyond, to fetch the spirits of Yaya, his dead grandma and Kondorfili Bunsor.

Yaya's mother had arrived by midday. She had been shaken since her last visit to Cherinor Jalloh. When she got home that day in their big and crowded compound, she thought it best to let everybody know that she felt sick. Because, she was worried and didn't want it to show. That made it easy for her to be quiet, as advised by the old man, about the plight of her son.

Coming today, she brought the cock, and as lucky as she was to have Umu, her youngest child—a fifteen-year-old virgin girl—she brought her along to be the maiden girl that Cherinor Jalloh had asked for.

The spiritualist, in his big white gown and white hat, was sitting on a white piece of cloth that was spread over the rug where he sat, by his books, *walar,* and a big bowl of water, which had by it a folded piece of white cloth. Iye and the little girl sat across from him, as he silently said his preparatory prayers with his *torsorbear*—rosary in his hand.

Immediately after Iye arrived with the maiden girl that afternoon for the ceremony, Cherinor Jalloh had inquired through his bowl of sand, if the girl would be an appropriate medium? It was an affirmative, and by Cherinor Jalloh's observation, the dark little thing seemed innocent and curious enough. He would make her bow over a bowl of water and cover her with white cloth from where she would be his eyes and mouth as she saw and talked with Jinni Musa, and transmitted messages back and forth, as if she was one president's emissary to another in a meeting with the host president, and simultaneously reporting home on the telephone.

And now with the sun cooling, Cherinor Jalloh decided on a head start with his horrendous task, before sundown when it would be too late.

"I'm ready," he declared smiling at Iye and the young girl, as he rolled his *torsorbear* in his palm. "Umu, are you ready?"

"She is ready," Yaya's mother responded with anxiety.

"Yes, grandpa, I'm ready," the young girl said, smiling at the gray haired-man.

Cherinor Jalloh knew this girl was the daughter of Iye, even though her mother had said nothing about it. "Iye, tell your daughter that she is safe, and that she should not be afraid of anything she sees while under the cloth."

"Umu, did you hear Baba?"

"Yes, mother."

Cherinor Jalloh looked at the young girl. "Your mother is here and I'll be sitting here, too, and talking to you. I will do the invocation and as you look through the silver ring under the water, you will see visions as clearly as you are seeing me and your mother now."

The little girl nodded.

"But remember this, regardless of what you see, do not be afraid of anything, because nothing is going to happen to you. And please, do not pull the cloth off your head until I say so. Did you hear that?"

"Yes, grandpa."

"You will not be afraid?"

"No, grandpa."

"Umu, I'm your mother, I would not permit you to do anything that will hurt you, so do not be afraid, right?"

"Okay, mother."

"Do like Baba says, right?"

"Yes, mother."

"Again Umu, do not be afraid right?"

"But I said I won't be afraid!"

Cherinor Jalloh got up and went to an open window on the plank of which he had placed a thin piece of board which was domed-shaped at the top and square at the bottom; it was like a meat cutting board on a kitchen counter, except that it was smooth on the surface like most *walars*. This had strings of Arabic lettering on it, written with a *kala* and a dark *duba*, which was why it was lying in the open window so the sun would dry the *duba* on it. What the writings meant was something only Cherinor Jalloh knew.

He brought the *walar* and bowed over the bowl of water and dipped it into the water. He washed the *walar* clean of all the writings. The water became dark from the darkness of the *duba*.

Cherinor Jalloh dropped a bright silver ring into the bowl. In spite of the cloudy nature of the water, the ring could be seen underneath. He got the cock which his clients brought, squatted with it by the bowl of water and beckoned to Iye and the girl. "Come, let's lay our hands on it."

As they sat around the cock, he started: " *Bismillah-i-Rahman-ir-Raheem*—I begin in the name of Allah, the Beneficent, the Merciful." He recited the *Fatihah* with the others saying: *Amin, Amin.*

"Jinni Musa, this white cock is for you. We are confused because we are only human and there are things that we can't know or do anything about. But, as our beloved spirit, you who were *named* after the Prophet Musa—*Moses*—who performed wonders in Egypt before Firon—*Pharaoh*—and divided the sea. Yes, you *namesake* of blessed Musa who led the children of Israel out of bondage and after that received the Taurat on a tablet to guide the morals of mankind.

"Today, now, Jinni Musa, you righteous saint and chief of spirits and the kindest, you who can take all forms and shapes and fly with the wind to work your wonders, great magician, we need you."

"Amin. Amin."

"We summon you here today, Jinni Musa, because we have a crisis. Please reveal yourself to us so that we may have understanding of the mystery in this matter, and to have a way of solving it, because an innocent man was deceived and is in danger. We now sacrifice..."

After the offering of the sacrifice, Cherinor Jalloh rubbed his *torsorbear* to his forehead saying, "*Inshalluhu!*" (by God's grace). He took the cock outside and came back. "Umu, come over here." He made the girl bow over the bowl of water and covered her with the white piece of cloth. "Do you see the ring?"

"Yes, grandpa. The water is dark but I can see the ring clearly."

"Good, look through the ring and let me know if you see anything. But remember, do not be afraid and do not get the cloth off your head by any means until I tell you so."

"Okay, grandpa," Umu had her eyes focused within the ring.

Cherinor Jalloh took his *torsorbear* and started saying things in undertone, obviously to invoke the Jinni. He knew that before the Chief Jinni comes, lesser ones would appear, sometimes some were messengers while others were the evil ones who came to sabotage the effort.

Cherinor Jalloh kept moving his *torsorbear* rapidly between his fingers as he moved his lips which let a breezy sound come from his mouth.

Suddenly, Madam Iye saw Cherinor Jalloh shiver, that was as the old man mildly jolted inside, and drew a long breath. At the same time, Umu's head slightly moved up with the cloth, and she let out a sigh, with the cloth shaking in waves. "Grandpa, I see a woman and a man coming. They have something like a horn on their head. The woman is pretty but she seems very mean."

Cherinor Jalloh could see everything that Umu was seeing, like he would hear all exchanges between her and whoever she talked to while she was under the cloth. But according to procedures, and for the benefit of Yaya's mother sitting there and to erode all doubts and skepticism, Umu would report everything that she saw and Cherinor Jalloh would instruct her as if he saw nothing.

"Tell those two that just came to go away! They are the evil ones; we don't need them."

"Woe and fury, Infidel! Woe and fury, Infidel! Woe, little Infidel, a word and a blow! What rages you? " the male Jinni asked.

"What beseeches you from us? What mischief you dare bid us do today? Speak, before we turn you into a fly!" the female Jinni screamed.

A confounded Umu shivered, and chilled, with dread and fear. Cherinor Jalloh vibrated some strength into her. He used their spiritual link, as half humans and half spirits, from the moment they both jolted when Umu sighted the Jinni.

"Please, please, I'm no infidel. Who are you?" Umu retorted.

"Toying, infidel? How dare you ask that!" the female Jinni yelled.

"You know us," said the male Jinni. "We are known by our deeds, which soar daily. We are the masters of destruction. Ask and your wish will be granted instantly!"

"But don't you ask us to do any good," the female Jinni cautioned, "because we triumph in wrecking, ruining, tragedies, havoc—"

"Hold!" Umu now believed what Cherinor Jalloh said about these Jinns, which was why she interrupted the mean female one who was speaking. "This mission is not for you, because our quest is to avert evil, for which we seek Jinni Musa, who is kind and believes in goodness. May you go now, please?"

Her mother was shocked at her confidence, hearing her speak like that. But Cherinor Jalloh smiled, knowing that Umu was speaking his mind to those Jinns.

The evil Jinns ran at the mention of Jinni Musa's name, like criminals running away from the police, because he made them feel rotten inside by chastising and scolding them in manners that belittled them even less than they imagined themselves.

"I see an old woman coming. She has a *torsorbear* in her hand. She is singing, it seems."

Cherinor Jalloh smiled. "Yes, she is singing a spiritual song. That's one of Jinni Musa's messengers who has taken the form of a woman. Greet her and give her our blessing but tell her we need her boss."

"We greet you, and may peace and blessings of Allah be

upon you, but we are awaiting Jinni Musa."

"May your wish be granted." The old woman bowed and left.

Umu heard some roaring from afar, like a storm coming; particles of rocks, soil, trees and branches of leaves were flying all over. It seemed the wind was paving the ground, leaving in its trail a garden of wilderness with beautiful flowers and plants. Then there was great brightness, brighter than daylight, to which Umu Blinked. As her eyes adjusted to the scene ahead, a princely-clad man, in a golden robe, on a white horse came galloping. Umu apprehensively looked into the man's face and his electrifying eyes gave her an instant charge.

"Grandpa, Grandpa, everything has changed. There is a man here on a white horse. I feel his eyes, his eyes..., oh, Grandpa!"

"Calm down, Umu." Cherinor Jalloh smiled and folded his *torsorbear*. "That is Jinni Musa. He is a friend. Tell him, we welcome and thank him for honoring us with his presence."

"I heard my name called, pretty little. Did you summon me?"

"Yes, mysterious Jinni Musa, we greet you and thank you for heeding our call."

Jinni Musa came down from his horse and leaned on it. "Deliver these messages of warning to your people: "Chief Brima should refuse a stunningly beautiful woman that he will be offered on his trip this coming Wednesday. She is sent in an evil ploy to destroy him."

"Thank you, Jinni Musa, we will tell the chief."

"A pregnant woman called Barlu has been bewitched so that she dies at delivery. She should offer a cock and seven kolanuts for sacrifice immediately. The cock should be given to an aged woman while the kolanuts should be given to people in her house."

"Thank you, Jinni Musa, we will tell her."

"And tell Iye, your mother sitting there that her gold earrings that she thought she dropped were stolen at the waterside where she does her laundry, by a young girl called Bintu."

When Umu reported that message. It stunned her mother, whose mouth was now ajar. So Bintu, a daughter of a mate, whom she often took with her to the waterside, stole her gold earrings? Well, she would let her mother know about that when all this is over.

"Tell Jinni Musa I say many, many thanks."

"My mother says, thanks, and may God bless you," said Umu, adding her bit to her mother's.

"May God bless you, too." Jinni Musa leaned away from the horse. He was rubbing his palms and looking at Umu. "Let me tell you why you summoned me. It is about a man who is haunted, because he disobeyed his ancestors."

"Yes, Jinni Musa."

"That is a grave matter with horrible consequences. Even now as I speak, the spirits of his ancestors are debating his punishment, which should be at sundown today."

"Grandpa! Grandpa! Jinni Musa said...." Umu, now uneasy, reported that information to Cherinor Jalloh with a voice cracking with anxiety and fear.

From his usual sitting posture on the floor, Cherinor Jalloh sat upright, with his legs crossed and his toes lying flat against the ground under his thighs.

"Tell Jinni Musa that we summoned him because we know that he stands against evil and he is a great pillar of justice. That is why we want him to stop what's haunting Yaya and to avert the calamity hanging over him. We are advocating on Yaya's behalf, because he is a victim of a corrupted mind, our values against the new ways. And worse, about the heritage he deserted, he was set astray by one of us that is evil and greedy. And as he, Jinni Musa, stands against evil, we implore him to champion this case and save Yaya."

Jinni Musa heard everything Cherinor Jalloh said, yet he waited patiently for Umu to repeat the solicitation.

"A society that disintegrates is a society where the elders have become callous and cold. A child does not pass over a heritage. It is the elders that pass it to their youths. Tell your people that they must look back into the ways of their ancestors and see where they went wrong."

Umu repeated the message to Cherinor Jalloh.

"Tell Jinni Musa that we thank him. It is true that we blame our children for deserting our values, but we are deserting them too. I shall pass this message to the chief and the Imam of this town so that it is announced as an observation from Jinni Musa. And they shall be left to make their judgments."

Umu told Jinni Musa. He looked vacantly over Umu in the direction of Cherinor Jalloh, like they were talking person to person.

"You have asked me to save Yaya. I shall prove my point."

As Cherinor Jalloh had expected, Jinni Musa's solution laid in bringing together the spirits of Yaya's Grandma, Kondorfili Bunsor and Yaya. But what Cherinor Jalloh didn't know was that Jinni Musa would summon some of their ancestors as well. He disappeared.

Next Umu saw Jinni Musa in a finely landscaped courtyard. It was a big room with an open view and one entrance which had purple, pink and yellow flowers by it. Inside the courtyard were several finely crafted high-back chairs with armrests. And there was a small crowd of people sitting in a line of chairs with their backs toward her, facing a bright platform, which was in line with the door. Umu counted the backs of the seated people. They were in two groups, five on each side, with a passage between them leading to the door, and the platform.

Looking through the door, Umu saw that the floor inside was sculptured with pink granite too pretty to walk on. She wondered what the platform was for. It had a big white shiny chair up there. And below it, before getting to the people that were sitting in line with their backs to her, there was a little space. In the middle of the space a vacant chair sat, and on either side of that chair, closer to the walls, two other chairs stood opposite.

When Jinni Musa moved from where he was standing and Umu recognized a figure which had been covered by Jinni Musa's back, she was excited.

"*Weeiii,* Mother," she screamed. "Jinni Musa has brought Grandma Fatu. She is sitting in a room with ten people. She is far from me but I know that's her. I don't know the other people, but maybe because I can't see their faces.
"Umu, do you really see my mother?"

"Yes! Grandma Fatu is glowing and her eyes are sparkling. She has on a blue gown and blue headtie. There are five men sitting on her side. They have on blue gowns and caps. But there's another group different from Grandma Fatu's; five people sitting on her left, wearing brown gowns. I see four caps and one headtie, so there is a woman among them, too. Opposite where Grandma Fatu sits—"

Jinni Musa disappeared.

"Shshsh!" Cherinor Jalloh hushed.

Jinni Musa reappeared.

"Grandpa, he has come with an old man that has a bent back, he is wearing a brown gown and hat and has something big on his back under his gown."

Summoned by Jinni Musa, Kondorfili Bunsor—or his spirit—seemed all confused as he was pulled by his gown and pushed back into a seat on the far left opposite Yaya's Grandma's spirit. How he had that brown gown on him, he didn't know!

At 10 a.m. that Sunday in Houston, Yaya called Sidi in Philadelphia and told him to call him at night because there was something important he wanted to tell him which he couldn't tell him now because he was going out. He resisted the urge to tell Sidi that there was something about this day that worried him. Twenty minutes later, he called Barbara. She was not in. He left a message on her recorder: *"Hello, Barbara, this is Yaya. I'm calling at 10:20 Sunday morning. There is something I wanted to ask you, but I'm going out now. Please call me anytime after 8 p.m. Thanks."*

Those calls were for security purposes, because he didn't know how the day would turn out—come noon—even as he believed, it would all end well for him. *Inshalluhu* (by God's grace).

At 10:30 a.m., Yaya knew it was approaching sundown in Manika Kunda. By Houston time, he surmised, his most critical period would be between 11 o'clock to noon. And with nothing else to do, he laid on the couch hoping to sleep the time off and wake up to a happy ending. Yet he couldn't sleep because his heart was pounding like one running with breathless speed from a lunatic attacker. Then his mind gravitated to Wuyadu, the source....

He was recalling how he had arrived in that wooded village two years ago and had rushed to Grandma Fatu's house; to be directed to her room where she was lying weak and gasping but able to wave everybody out. Again, he was recasting how she had handed him the inheritance as she said: *"My time has come, my child. I am glad you made it."*

He vividly remembered how she had strenuously moved her hand to get something from under her pillow—which was the *sacred* leaf, crumbled and withered. *"I want you to rub that leaf into liquid in your palms and put your palms into mine."*

Yaya could now see how the brown of her eyes had enlarged and were burning red. He was doing as she said, all confused, putting his palms into hers and looking into her flaming eyes—

Yaya laid quiet. It seemed a strange feeling was creeping over him. He shuddered and breathed deeply. But his mind had gone blank and he was feeling weak and drowsy, like somebody that had been doped with anesthetic. A shrill voice from afar was saying: *"Come, Yaya LaTalé! Come, Yaya LaTalé! Come, Yaya LaTalé!"*

Yaya wanted to ask who it was, but his mouth was now heavy like all other parts of his body.

"Come, Yaya LaTalé! Come, Yaya LaTalé! Come! Now! Yes come, Yes come, follow me, follow me, follow me...."

Yaya had never ridden a horse, yet he now found himself on a velvety white horse, which followed another like it, flying with the flowing gown of the person riding it. They were going through a rich wilderness, which got livelier and brighter as they went.

"Follow me, follow me, Yaya LaTalé. Come, Yaya LaTalé. Now, now, yes, yes..."

In a trance, from the couch on which he was lying in Joy's house, to a whirlwind ride on the speedy white horse, Yaya was led to the entrance of a stunningly beautiful courtyard sitting alone in an area colorful like a picture of the Garden of Eden. As the mysterious horses wandered off, he felt the luminous aura of the place, incensed and solemn, like a scared ground.

"I'm Jinni Musa. You may enter, Yaya."

Was he Yaya? Jinni Musa? The legendary mysterious spirit? The reflections from Jinni Musa were like an emperor's. Yaya entered but froze in awe as he saw a vibrant Grandma Fatu sitting at the far right, with Kondorfili Bunsor sitting opposite her.

He noticed two distinct groups sitting apart, graceful and regal with silver hair and beards, like a council of the elders in a peace conference from warring towns. On Grandma Fatu's side, it was five men in bright blue gowns holding *torsorbears* that sparkled like their eyes. On Kondorfili Bunsor's side, an aged woman sat with four men, all of whom radiated in their glittering brown clothes.

Jinni Musa pointed to the chair in the center of the space before the platform. Yaya sat down. He was still in shock. He knew he was awake but actually dreaming, because he had no logical explanation for this scenario. And though he was at a loss as to what was happening to him, he found it shocking that his mind was working, and was as clear as that of a judge sitting on a landmark case.

Jinni Musa went up the platform and sat.

"Stand up, Yaya!" Jinni Musa ordered. Yaya stood up facing him and felt strangely invigorated as their eyes met. "Turn to the men in the Blue and tell them who you are."

Yaya looked at the aged men, none of whom he knew. "I'm Yaya LaTalé from Taényadu, son of Backari LaTalé and Iye Béreté."

"That's enough," Jinni Musa said, and nodded to the people in the blue gowns. "Yes, please?"

A man on the far right spoke. "I'm Kefinba Béreté, forefather of your grandfathers."

The one next to Kefinba spoke. "I'm Sorie Béreté, great grandfather of your grandfathers."

"I'm Backari Béreté, grandfather of your grandfather."

The last one spoke. "I'm Brima Béreté, grandfather of your grandmother."

Grandma Fatu spoke. "Yaya, as you know I'm Fatu Béreté, your grandmother."

344

"Sit down, Yaya," Jinni Musa ordered.

Yaya blew out a long breath, and sat down.

Jinni Musa turned to the people in brown.

"Kondorfili Bunsor, get up and and introduce yourself."

"I'm Kondorfili Bunsor of Korkordu, son of Aligaly Bunsor and Memuna Sesay."

Jinni Musa nodded, showing his open palms to the elders on Kondorfili Bunsor's side.

The elder on the far left spoke. "I'm Karimu Bunsor, forefather of your grandfathers."

The one next to Karimu spoke. "I'm Ahmed Bunsor, great grandfather of your grandfathers."

"I'm Jaka Bunsor, great grandmother of your grandfathers," said the old lady next to Karimu.

The man sitting after her spoke. "I'm Lansana Bunsor, grandfather of your grandfather."

The last one spoke. "Kondorfili Bunsor, as you know, I'm M'ba Bunsor, your grandfather."

"Thank you, everybody," Jinni Musa said. "Sit down, Kondorfili Bunsor."

There was staring and nodding, and some smiles. Kondorfili Bunsor like many of his people in brown clothes, had questioning looks in their eyes. Those in Grandma Fatu's group sat with a gloomy and somber countenance.

The glittering eeriness and charged atmosphere made Yaya shiver, with every pore on his skin opening and the hairs in them feeling like whiskers on a cat. He could recall the whirlwind ride like a dream. But he was awake even if he couldn't tell where he was and why the gathering.

"You are all summoned here today because of a critical matter," Jinni Musa spoke. Serenity like a spell vibrated in the room.

"The matter is between Yaya LaTalé and Fatu Bérété on the one hand, and Yaya LaTalé and Kondorfili Bunsor on the other hand. Yaya's grandmother, Fatu Bérété, handed him an inheritance that is sacred in his lineage which he deserted. He left the land for the white man's land. Certainly, without any questions, he deserves severe punishment as prescribed.

"Yet I, Jinni Musa, was summoned, and in examining the case, I was disturbed and concerned about the oversight and the viciousness I saw in it, which made me decide to intervene and see that justice is done. Before I go on, does anybody have any questions?"

Kefinba Bérété raised his hand. "Jinni Musa, you are a blessed spirit, and we respect you for your righteousness and good deeds. Yet, what Yaya did was the undone. Never has anybody in our lineage defied his inheritance." Grandma Fatu and all the people in blue were nodding at what Kefinba Béreté just said.

"And as you know, Jinni Musa, we're all God's creations, meant for different purposes and those that know those responsibilities must do as Allah wishes them. Yaya was handed his, and he rejected it. We respect you, Jinni Musa, but please leave this matter in our hands." Old man Kefinba pleaded, visibly angry.

"I cherish what you cherish, Kefinba. The matter will be left in your hands soon. But remember, we as servants of Allah must do what is right. Therefore, I think we should hear Yaya's story."

"Let us hear it," Kefinba said, and the others nodded.

"Stand up, Yaya, and give your reasons for abandoning your heritage, if any."

"Jinni Musa, before you and all the elders here, I hereby apologize for defying Grandma Fatu and my call to undertake the inheritance. My dilemma is a war inside me. The new culture and knowledge that I have acquired, which is seen as the future, taught me to go one way, while the inheritance propelled me on another. From my teenage days, I was trained to think that I was a savior of my people because of my Western education. I was called a white man out of admiration for the ways of the white man, and I was treated differently, with a difference that made me think I was on the right track, by getting my education; and dreaming of a better life, like the white man's, to help my people. That was my dream.

"I love my culture, my people and my home, but I was not taught to belong there. In fact, it was not expected that I should go to live there. I was to learn about the city as a prospective home but not forget my responsibilities to the family. I accepted that. My goal was a good job, from where I could help, and live happily as I was. Then Grandma Fatu died. I could not take the inheritance after Grandma Fatu because as Grandpa Kefinba said, 'We're all God's creations meant for different purposes and those that know those responsibilities must do as Allah wishes.' I knew mine, which I was made to believe in all my life and which I enjoyed doing.

"To have gone back to Wuyadu and do the work Grandma Fatu wanted me to do, would have deprived the family of all that it had tried to make me, and I would have been seen by many as a failure and disappointment. Also, I wouldn't have been at peace with myself. And peace with Allah begins with peace with one's self."

Jinni Musa was nodding, like many on Kondorfili Bunsor's side.

Yaya looked around the quasi court room and felt thankful for having his mental faculties. He decided that if it had come to this, he might as well make a clean breast of the issue.

"Grandma Fatu shocked me with the inheritance, and left with me a hard choice. So I consulted Kondorfili Bunsor, the only person I could confide in because of the secrecy. He advised me to leave the land for a while and I would be free, which I did. I thought that was my best choice, if I had any choice at all."

Jinni Musa's sharp eyes, like those of many others, were now on Kondorfili Bunsor who had suddenly dropped his head. Those in Grandma Fatu's party had folded their *torsorbear* in their palms and were muttering, opening and closing their hands, obviously asking silent questions in puzzlement.

"Any questions from the Béreté Family?" All eyes were on their forefather. He raised his hand up. "Yes, Kefinba Béreté?" Jinni Musa prompted.

"Yaya, I'll ask you two questions. Did Fatu Béreté shock you with the inheritance without training you? And did Kondorfili Bunsor tell you to leave the land and you would be free?"

"The answer is yes to both questions."

"That's all." Kefinba folded his arms.

"Any more questions?" Jinni Musa asked. "Yes, Fatu Béreté?"

"Yaya, didn't I train you in your dreams and make you know how to do the work?"

"Yes, Grandma Fatu, you did in my sleep. But a dream is like an illusion, or seeing something in darkness, as opposed to reality, or what is seen in daylight. I didn't know whether to believe or not."

"Any more questions?" The forefather of the Bunsor family raised his hand. "Yes, Karimu Bunsor."

"Yaya, is this the same Kondorfili Bunsor that gave you that advice?"

"Yes, he is the same."

Both the Bunsor and Béreté families were shaking their heads. Some had unfolded their *torsorbear* and were now furiously rolling the beads.

"Any more questions?" There was no response.

Jinni Musa looked keenly at Yaya's Grandma. "Fatu Béreté, all your predecessors that were entrusted with the inheritance were Bérétés, why did you give it to Yaya, who is of the LaTalé lineage?"

"Jinni Musa, it was because we are from the same family root. We are the same. And Yaya is a son of my daughter. Also, he was born just when Grandpa Brima died and left the inheritance with me.

That was a spirit leaving and spirit coming to replace it."

"Fatu Béreté, did you bring Yaya up believing that he was your successor?"

"Yes, by showing the leaf to only him. As he grew up he was away from me most of the time, pursuing the white man's knowledge."

"How did he get on the white man's course?"

"His father. It was now the way of things, and Yaya had tremendous ability for that. Everybody was amazed at how well he was doing."

"Did that affect how you saw him?"

"Yes, it affected everybody. We saw him as a white man, because he was now different and knowledgeable about the ways of the white man."

"Did you ever call him a white man?"

"Yes, many times. He was behaving and dressing like them, keeping his hair long like them, and he spoke their language."

"Would you have handed the heritage to a white man with a white skin?"

"No."

"Fatu Béreté, who is a man without his mind?"

"A nobody, an insane person."

"And how different is a man from how he thinks?"

"No difference."

"Then if you saw Yaya as a white man, and called him a white man, who could you have been dealing with?"

"A white man maybe, but also one of us."

"Thank you. Any questions for Fatu Béreté?"

Kefinba Béreté raised up his hand. "Fatu, was it that there was no non-corrupted offspring in our family deserving to carry on with the work?"

"There were plenty of them, grandpa. I made Yaya my successor because of a dream I had in which I saw Grandpa Brima laying his hand on Yaya's new born head."

Brima Béreté raised his hand up and spoke. "I visited Yaya as an infant, I was blessing and strengthening the spirit in him as I was supposed to do." Everybody nodded to that.

"Any more questions?"

"No..? Alright. Kondorfili Bunsor, stand up."

Kondorfili Bunsor gathered himself and stood up, feeling worthless and broken like some cursed child molester coming to terms with his guilt and shame in a crowded court room.

Jinni Musa had a stern look on his face. "I'll let you all know that before Yaya, Kondorfili Bunsor had similarly advised another young man like Yaya. The boy, Alpha Kondeh, was cursed with insanity by his enraged ancestors. Kondorfili Bunsor, what were your reasons?"

"Jinni Musa, the youths of today are not like the youths of my days. They've all taken the ways of the infidels, and live like pagans. They even question what God made them to be. Many men among them are becoming women and the women are becoming men. I was disturbed and so decided to pluck some bad seeds."

Jinni Musa uttered a gushing sound and frowned in shock. "Kondorfili Bunsor, you were created by Allah, and he created those that you sought to destroy. They may have erred, but who made you a judge, and who gave you the sword to slay?"

Kondorfili Bunsor scratched his hunchback. "Umm..., Jinni Musa, I decided on my own. I was preserving the sacredness of my heritage, and reclaiming what originally belonged solely to my ancestors."

"Kondorfili Bunsor, who said the gift of bone healing, given to the Kondeh family, the Bérété family and many others in places you don't know, had at anytime belonged only to the Bunsor family?"

"That was my belief."

"But how did you get to believe so? M'ba Bunsor, you who handed the inheritance to Kondorfili Bunsor, did you ever tell him that?"

"No, Jinni Musa. I never even thought that. My duty was to serve all who came needing my help."

"Does anybody have any questions for Kondorfili Bunsor?"

"Yes," said Kefinba, the forefather and primary spokesperson for the Bérétés. "So your intention, Kondorfili Bunsor, was that we the ancestors of Yaya would be angry at him and punish him like the Kondeh family did to Alpha, after which the continuity of the inheritance would stop in our lineage, which would leave you alone with all the power, right?"

Kondorfili Bunsor only bowed his head.

"We don't have anything more to ask him," Kefinba said. All the Bérétés nodded.

"Now the Bunsor family, give me your opinion," Jinni Musa asked.

The forefather of the Bunsors folded his *torsorbear* and held his palms closed over it.

"We are ashamed of what Kondorfili Bunsor did. He is a disgrace to the Bunsor family. Therefore, for his malice, greed, and viciousness, we now henceforth curse and disown him. May his spirit be

349

tormented by the evils of his heart. May he go back and live for only thirty days. In those last days, may Kondorfili Bunsor lay in his feces, and ask that people come to hear him tell of his evil deeds. Jinni Musa, we don't have anything else to say," Karimu Bunsor said.

"Kondorfili Bunsor, your ancestors have spoken. Iniquities breed damnation. Those that plant evil harvest evil. May it be that as you lay purging your burdened soul that you tell all those that come, that the eyes of Allah are upon them, and he shall bless the good and curse the evil minded like you.

"Let it be said, that I, Jinni Musa, am indignant at your people because they've become their own enemies, such that violence, greed, malice, envy and jealousy all have become their tools as they scheme and plot, to impede and destroy each another in willful villainy. Tell them, Kondorfili Bunsor, that Allah made them rational, like us Jinns and Angels. But as Satan fell, and as the evil among us further damns themselves, so will those among you be doomed like you.

"For you, Kondorfili Bunsor, wanted to strip your society of what should have been shared. You wanted it alone, and like many others before you, you would have died and let it die with you, which only makes your people be in dire need of everything that God originally gave in abundance.

"Say, Kondorfili Bunsor, to those like you, that I speak with the voice of Allah, as I say, that their cups are full; and like you, their days will come; for Allah is all seeing and all hearing. And I, Jinni Musa, who manifests myself unto mankind, will convince them of the wonders of Allah. As in this case, I shall come whenever summoned, and I'll stand for justice and fight evil doers like you on earth, even to eternity. You may go now."

Kondorfili Bunsor's hunch back must have been much heavier than usual as he stood bent like he was folded. He tried to sit down but missed his chair and fell flat on the floor with his legs up. Like a notorious nuisance, he was ignored.

"Yaya, stand up." Jinni Musa ordered. "The case is now yours, the Béretés."

Everybody looked up towards Kefinba Bérété.

"Yaya, I, Kefinba Bérété, forefather of your grandfathers who passed down the heritage to Sorie, who passed it on to his grandson Backari, who in turn passed it to his Grandson Brima, who passed it to his granddaughter Fatu that passed it on to you, now today hereby forgive you.

"Poor wretched you. It is our rule that weak points in the chain be cut before they become some catalyst. You were a disappointment and would have paid for it today, but you were hoodwinked into thinking that there was an escape for you. There was none, for in the spirit world there are no boundaries, nothing hides. Those that wrong us only wrong themselves, for we only have to reach out to avenge.

"Yet you have been made innocent. Kondorfili Bunsor will pay enough for us, because he was a far worse link than you are. For no society thrives when the elders, for whatever reason, set astray the youths like Kondorfili Bunsor did to you, and before you, another.

"He got away with it then but paid for it this time. That saved you. Still Yaya, you cannot be off the hook completely. For you will learn that without your heritage you are nothing, even in the white man's land. Pursue it by cherishing what you have and respecting what they have, and you will find the missing key to your needs. I should not tell you how or where to look, for you know more about the ways of the white man than I do.

"Nevertheless, as you sojourn in his land, it is your responsibility to correct his ignorance about us, for the white man came to us and wrote his story, while we have our stories to tell. Now you go free with my blessing and God's to take in stride your new leash. May you live a rich and full life as we did. And may you hold your grandchildren and great grandchildren and tell them our story. You may go."

"But wait, Yaya!" Jinni Musa stood up. "Let me say again, that Allah is kind to all mankind, but as rational beings, those who dwell in evil shall be cursed, while the innocent and righteous shall be blessed. And a divine eye sees not only what's on the outside of a person but also what's in their inside. Now about you, for your inner purity, may you be the sun and let your rays gladden the souls of all allies and yet be like fire unto those who scheme and plot against you.

"But you must stay away from evil too. For to realize happiness and be fulfilled even on earth can only be an illusive hope for those who dwell in viciousness. Because it is their conscience that they torment as they damn their souls by becoming disciples of Satan.

"As you go back to the white man's land tell all mankind that Allah's message is peace. And that even I, Jinni Musa, feels behooved as I look upon them with their strategies and weapons of mass destruction. Let them know that they are only building toys for Satan which will burst into an inferno to swallow not only its creators, but poor innocent people. Sadly, many that are gifted have scorned a choice of helping humanity and chosen instead to destroy it. But they that slay shall be slain and shall pay more with tormented souls! Same for others engaged in wanton warfare, senselessly shedding innocent bloods; such must start cleansing themselves now!

"And tell all that Allah made no man or race superior than the other, but they that think and believe in peace and uplift their kinsmen and humanity shall rise! For again, it is a rational choice to be positively spirited and to serve, share, and soar, or to become crabs and crawl into ponds only to claw each other lower.

"Go now, Yaya, with my blessing and offer your gratitude, not to me, Jinni Musa, but to Allah, The Beneficent, The Merciful."

Creeegn. Creeegn. Creeegn. Yaya heard a distant sound like a phone ringing. Waking up was like sliding from a high slope to a gentle thud. Like someone regaining their senses after a stunning blow, it seemed hell had broken loose from the noises around.

Creeegn. Creeegn. He rolled on the floor and picked up the phone.

"Yaya, are you there? I almost hung up. That was the fifth time the phone rang. I thought you were out."

"Actually, Sidi, I was sleeping. What is the time now?"

"It's eight p.m., but that's Philly time. It's seven p.m. your time in Houston."

"Man, I must have slept for seven hours straight."

"I thought you said you were going out."

"Oh, yes, I did. Actually, I went out but it's a long story."

"Guess what? I finally can take some vacation days off. I know it's too late to come for Basi.., but I will spend a few days with you in Houston."

"Oh, Sidi, I will appreciate that very much. This house sometimes seems haunted with all the memories."

"Well, tomorrow is Monday, I will be in Houston by Wednesday, certainly. I will call you to give you the exact time."

"Okay, man, I'll be waiting for your call."

Yaya hung up the phone and fell flat on the floor, knowing that he was free. Everything he had seen was in his head. Maybe now that he was free, he would tell Sidi the whole story when he arrived.

And when Sidi comes, Yaya thought, maybe he should ask to go back to Philadelphia; or rather, simply go back home, now that he was free! But Ms. Joy, how was she doing in Africa? Yaya prayed for her safe return, and decided to keep thinking about his plans until she made it back.